BURY
OUR
BONES
IN THE
MIDNIGHT
SOIL

BURY OUR BONES IN THE MIDNIGHT SOIL

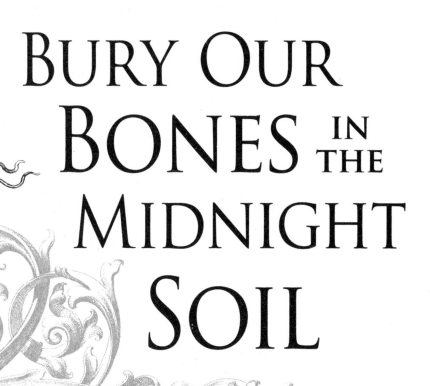

V. E. SCHWAB

TOR PUBLISHING GROUP NEW YORK

This is a work of fiction. All of the characters, organizations, and events portrayed in this novel are either products of the author's imagination or are used fictitiously.

BURY OUR BONES IN THE MIDNIGHT SOIL

Copyright © 2025 by Victoria Schwab

A Tor Book
Published by Tom Doherty Associates / Tor Publishing Group
120 Broadway
New York, NY 10271

Tor® is a registered trademark of Macmillan Publishing Group, LLC.

ISBN 978-1-250-32052-0

Printed in the United States of America

To the ones who hunger—
for love, for time, or simply to be free

BURY
OUR
BONES
IN THE
MIDNIGHT
SOIL

Bury my bones in the midnight soil,
plant them shallow and water them deep,
and in my place will grow a feral rose,
soft red petals hiding sharp white teeth.

MARÍA

(D. 1532)

I

The widow arrives on a Wednesday.

María remembers, because Wednesdays are for bathing, and her hair takes an age to dry after it's been washed and combed. She remembers, because it is warm for the end of April, and she is sitting in a patch of sun at the edge of the yard, sucking on a cherry pit (one of the first of the season) and holding a lock up to the light to see if the hair is turning darker, or if it is simply still damp.

María's mother says she is becoming too vain, but then, her mother is the one who makes her go to bed each week with clay in her hair, hoping it will mute the glaring strands. As far as María can tell, it isn't working. If anything, the hair looks even brighter.

She would not mind so much, María's mother, if the hair were honey-colored, or earthy, even auburn, but such an angry shade of red, she says, is a bad omen. Not a warm color, but the hot orange of an open flame. One she cannot seem to douse.

Something tickles María's shin. A thread has come loose on the hem of her dress, and she will have to ask her mother to fix it. Her mother is a seamstress, small fingers making perfect lines. The trick to sewing, she is always telling her, is patient hands and patient hearts, but María came into this world with neither. She is always pricking herself with the needle, losing her temper and flinging the work aside, half-done. Born restless, her father used to say. Which was fine for a son, but bad for a daughter.

María rolls the cherry pit along the inside of her teeth as she pulls at the thread, unraveling her mother's patient heart a little more, when the church bells begin to ring.

And just like that, the day is suddenly more interesting.

She springs up and takes off barefoot down the road, skirts tangling around her legs until she hoists them up out of the way. Heads for her favorite watching spot, the top of Ines's stable, only to find that Felipe is already there.

"Go back home," he calls as she hoists herself up into a cart and then onto the slanted tiles of the roof. "It's not safe."

Only three years between them, his thirteen to her ten, but he's taken to acting like it's an uncrossable distance, as if he's full grown and she is still a child, even though he still cries when he gets sad or hurt, and she has not cried since before their father died.

"I mean it, María," he scolds, but she ignores him, squinting into the late-afternoon light as the caravan rolls into town.

María cannot read or write, but she can count. And so she counts the horses as they come—six, seven, eight, nine—has started numbering the riders too, when a voice barks up at them.

"Madre de Dios. Get down, before you break your necks."

Felipe turns, almost slipping on the slick tiles as he does, but María doesn't bother. It is just Rafa, and she doesn't have to look down to picture him perfectly, hands on his hips and head thrown back, frowning the way their father did. The way her oldest brother has for the last year, since taking his place. As if that's all their father was: a set of shoulders, a stoic jaw, a hardened voice. A space he can so easily fill.

"Now!" he barks.

Felipe's bravado dissolves under Rafa's glare, and he climbs down, shuffling carefully across the tiles. María holds her ground, just to prove she can, but there is nothing to see now, the caravan has rounded the bend on its way into town, so she finally complies, and jumps, landing in a puddle that splashes her skirts. Felipe is just as dirty, but Rafa directs the full force of his glare at her, and her alone.

Before María can dance out of reach, he grabs her by the shoulder.

"You could have fallen."

"Nonsense," she says. "I would fly."

"I do not see your wings."

"I need no wings," she says with a smirk. "I am a *witch*."

It was only a joke. He called her one last week, when he came in and saw her sitting by the hearth, her red hair wild and loose, her attention lost inside the flame.

But now, as the word leaves her lips, his hand lashes out, striking her across the cheek.

The pain is sudden, hot, but the tears that brim are those of shock, and rage, and for an instant she imagines lunging at her brother, raking her short, sharp nails across his cheek, the look on his face, marred by bloody crescents.

But it is a feral kind of an anger, and María knows that it would only get her whipped, so instead she decides she'll fill his good boots with manure. She grins at the thought and the sight of her smile seems to unnerve her brother even more.

Rafa shakes his head. "Go home to Mother," he says, flicking his hand as if she's a stray cat, something to be shooed. He sets off down the path, and Felipe trails silently behind, a shadow in his wake, the two boys heading into town to greet the caravan.

María rubs her cheek and watches them go. Counts to ten, then shifts the cherry pit between her teeth and bites down so hard it splits.

She spits the broken shards into the dirt, and follows.

Santo Domingo is a blessed town.

It sits on the Camino de Santiago, the pilgrims' road. María has always been fascinated by the people who come down it. Her father told her that they made the trip to cleanse themselves of sins, and when she was small, she thought of those sins as boulders, heavy burdens like theft and murder and abuse, each enough to weigh a body down, bend a spirit low. María would marvel at the constant train of criminals, advertising their guilt even as they attempted to atone.

Only later did her mother say that not all sins were boulders, that most in fact were more like pebbles. An unkind thought. A hungry heart. Small weights like greed and envy and want (things that didn't seem to her like sins at all, but apparently they added up). More disappointing still was when María discovered that some who walk the pilgrims' road are not guilty of a sin at all. That they make the trip not to atone for their past, but to secure their future. To ask for miracles, or intercessions, or simply pave the way into God's grace.

That struck María as horribly dull, so to amuse herself, she's taken to concocting sins to assign to each and every traveler.

As the caravan unloads in the town square, she decides that the man at the front stole a cow from a family who then could not survive the winter.

The woman behind him drowned an unwanted baby in the bath, and then could not get with child herself.

The man with the red cross emblazoned on his cloak is a knight of the Order, there to shepherd the flock, but María decides that he has wives dotted like seeds along the road, a breadcrumb trail of sins.

The old man behind him prayed for his wife's death, and then it came to pass.

The young one slayed a man in a duel.

And the woman in gray . . .

The woman in gray . . .

María falters.

It's not that her imagination fails her, but it is hard to come up with a story when she cannot make out the woman's features. She is draped in fabric, all one shade, like a pillar cut from a block of stone, or a drawing made in mud. A ghost wrapped in a dark gray frock, a gray hat with a gray veil pinned around its rim, hands gloved in matching cloth despite the heat of the cloud-strewn day. She is a statue, cold and colorless, among the bright brigade.

María skirts the square till she finds Felipe. His gaze flicks toward her, and he gives a world-weary sigh. "Rafa will cane you."

"I'll bite him if he tries," she counters, flashing teeth.

Felipe rolls his eyes, seems intent on ignoring her, but she elbows him in the side.

"What?" he hisses.

She points to the woman, asking why she looks so strange, and he replies under his breath that she looks to be a widow, and that it must be a kind of mourning dress. María frowns. She has seen widows on the road before. They have never looked like this.

But Felipe simply shrugs and says that maybe she is French.

María's frown deepens, unsatisfied. She wants a closer look.

The bells have stopped ringing, and now the town is moving through its motions.

The baker's son appears with loaves of bread, the innkeeper with salted fish and ale. María's mother arrives, offering to mend any holes from travel wear, which gives her an idea. María slips forward, weaving toward the widow's horse as a man holds out a hand and helps her down. There is no pack, only a small wooden crate that he frees for her.

When it shakes, the contents sound like bells. María wonders what it holds.

She is almost to the widow's side, about to ask if anything needs mending, when the widow turns her way. She can't make out the woman's face, reduced to smudges by the heavy veil, but she has felt the heat of Rafa's glare enough times to know the widow's gaze is leveled straight at her. And María, who thinks herself afraid of nothing—not the dark corners of the yard at night, or the height of the stable roof, or the spiders that hide in the wood stack—stops in her tracks, the words turned to rocks in her throat.

She stares back at the strange woman, perplexed by the feeling that rolls over her. No doubt, she would have flung it off, continued forward, but before she can, Rafa's hand lands on her shoulder, and then it is too late. The widow is turning away and the party is dispersing, the horses for the stable, the humans for the inn, and María finds herself herded roughly back home.

The next day is hot and bright and cloudless.

By late morning, the caravan has moved on, but the widow hasn't. Her pale horse stays stabled by the inn, where she remains inside her room, the curtains drawn. The hours pass, and as they do, the widow requests no water or wine, accepts no offered food, till some wonder if she means to become a saint. If it *is* piety, it is surely the strongest kind. If it is sickness, they want no part.

The hours pass, and as they do, the gossip spreads like shadow, and here is what it says:

Perhaps she is old.

Perhaps she is weak.

Perhaps she needs rest.

Perhaps she is sick.

Perhaps the journey is too much.

Perhaps the heat—

Perhaps the sun—

There is no consensus, save that the men do not like her. They treat her like a nuisance, a parcel dislodged off another pilgrim's horse.

"What kind of woman travels by herself?" they gripe.

"What kind of woman stays behind alone?"

The answer is, of course, *a widow*.

But there is another word that trails behind it, in a whisper.

(*Witch*.)

But then, a witch would never go on pilgrimage.

Whatever the reason, the men lean away, but the *women*—they have always had a taste for gossip. They arrive at the widow's door throughout the day, pass an hour in her room, perhaps for company, or charity, or simply talk, a chance to hear where she has been, where she is going.

María thinks of the wooden crate, and wonders if the widow is selling something. It happens often enough—pilgrims act like ants, carrying things along the road, tracking other places in like mud on the bottom of their feet.

Her mother clucks her tongue, and hands her a basket of freshly mended things.

She does not like the widow, and has been out of sorts since she arrived. But when María asks why, she will not say, only crosses herself, a gesture that piques María's interest as she takes the basket and sets off for the families Baltierra and Muñoz and Cordona.

She passes Rafa at the edge of the yard, shoring up the fence, which always seems one strong breeze away from falling down. He glares at her as she goes by, and she knows he is looking to find something wrong. *Stand straighter, María. Be tidy, María. Have some modesty, María.* She smiles and curtsies as she passes, a gesture with all the flair of a curse.

The day started hot, but soon a swell of clouds rolls in, and by the time she's delivered her mother's work, a storm is churning.

She quickens her pace, the now-empty basket swinging from her fingers, the taste of rain on her tongue. She cuts through the copse that runs like a road along the edge of town, is startled when one of the trees steps sideways, and María sees it's not a tree at all, but the widow.

María stops, breath caught between her teeth.

The widow's face is uncovered, the veil tucked up into her hat brim. María stares at the curls of blond hair now visible against her neck. Stares at her smooth cheeks, her pointed chin, the smooth pink bow of her lips. She doesn't look sick, or old, or weak. If anything, she is younger than María would have guessed. And twice as pretty.

The wooden crate sits beside her in the grass, its lid thrown back, contents winking in the light. She's disappointed to see it holds only small, stoppered bottles and none of them look to have blood or feathers or bones.

The widow sinks to her knees at the base of a tree, gloved fingers sliding through the roots, and—

"What are you doing?" María asks.

The widow doesn't jump at the sound, doesn't even look up from her work.

When she speaks, her voice is smooth, and surprisingly low, and she speaks Castilian so well María doubts Felipe's guess that she is French.

"I'm gathering herbs."

"For a spell?" she asks, the words out before she thinks to stop them.

The widow looks up, then, revealing eyes that are a startling shade of blue, the edges crinkled in amusement. "For a tonic."

María frowns. "Is a tonic the same thing as a spell?"

"Only to a fool," says the widow. "Are you a fool, little girl?"

María shakes her head, but cannot help herself. "So you are *not* a witch?"

The widow straightens, and for a moment, the full force of her attention lands on María again, solid as a stone, before it slides past her, toward the town. "So much superstition, from a place that believes a roasted hen really sprang up off a dinner plate and began to sing."

She is speaking of the tale that made Santo Domingo famous.

"That," declares María, "was a miracle."

The widow seems to consider. "And how is a miracle different from a spell? Who is to say the saint was not a witch?" She says it blithely, as if the words have no weight. And María finds herself grinning at the sheer scale of the blasphemy. The way it would make Rafa scowl, and her mother cross herself.

"So you *are* a witch, then?" she asks brightly.

The widow laughs. It is not a witch's laugh, which María has always imagined would sound like the splitting of wood, or the guffaw of crows. No, the widow's laugh is soft, and heady, thick as sleep.

"No," she says, the humor clinging to her voice. "And this is not magic. It's medicine." She holds out a small red weed, pinching it between gloved fingers as if it were a rose. "Nature gives us what we need," she says, and for the first time, María thinks she catches it, the faintest trace of somewhere else, the edges of another accent, one she cannot place. "There are teas and tonics for many things," continues the widow. "To shed a fever, or ease a cough. To help a woman get with child, or get rid of it. To make a man sleep . . ."

María's gaze drops to the ground between them. She spots another crimson stem, is already reaching down to pull it out when the widow catches her hand.

Even though they were several strides apart.

Even though she never saw the widow move.

She is there now, a head taller than María, one gloved hand circling her wrist.

"Careful. In nature, beauty is a warning. The pretty ones are often poisonous."

But María has already forgotten about the plant. Her world has narrowed to the widow.

The sun is gone now, lost behind low clouds, and up close, she smells like candied figs and winter spice. Up close, her gray clothes are not so dull, but finely sewn, and trimmed in glinting silver thread. Up close, her blue eyes are fever bright, and there are faint shadows in the hollows of her cheeks, and María wonders if she was wrong, and the widow has indeed been sick.

The woman's mouth twitches, one corner tilting into a rueful smile. Her pink lips part, and the world goes small and tight as a held breath. María feels herself falling forward, even though she hasn't moved an inch.

Then thunder snaps like a branch over their heads, and the widow's hand withdraws.

"Run home," she says as the first drops of rain break through the canopy. And for once in her short, stubborn life, María obeys. She turns, sprinting out of the copse of trees and down the road, as if she can outrun the rain. She can't, ends up soaked through by the time she drops the empty basket inside the door.

Her mother mutters about wet clothes and catching cold as she peels her out of her dress and puts her by the fire, afraid she will take ill.

She doesn't, but that night, señor Baltierra dies in his sleep.

By dawn, the widow is gone.

It will be ten years before María sees her again.

II

1529

It is a late-October day, and María is sitting on the stable roof, her bare feet swinging off the edge. She knows that Rafa is searching for her, has been for the better part of an hour now. His fault, she thinks, for always looking down instead of up.

She hums, and twists a fiery strand around her finger.

Somehow, she is nearly eighteen.

María knows it did not happen overnight, that she did not go to bed a girl and wake a woman, though some days it feels that way. The seasons have worked their change in halting strides, stretching her slowly into a stranger, her body too narrow, no hips or breasts to speak of, and her features too sharp—a long jaw, a narrow face, a high forehead interrupted by fair brows. Felipe likes to say that she looks like bread dough that's been stretched too much and failed to rise.

But her *hair*.

In the end, all her mother's efforts were in vain. It has not been cowed, darkened by mud or time to a more ordinary shade. Instead, it has grown brighter, defiantly so, year over year until it now seems imbued with molten light, a liquid copper spilling in loose waves down her back. In sun, it shines. At night, it burns, like a lantern in the dark.

And if she is too long and lean, too wild to be considered comely, the strangeness of her hair has made her something even better. *Striking.* There may be nothing of Castilian beauty in María, but there is something *undeniable* about her looks. A primal grace that makes men turn their heads and their horses in the direction of the hunt.

She made note of this new power as the seasons turned and the men in her own village—some little more than boys, others old enough to be her father—began to stare.

She made note, and knew something must be done.

Someone whistles now, a short, sharp sound, and she looks down over the edge to see Felipe craning his head, cheeks still dusted from his work in the shadow of the blacksmith.

"Rafa's been looking for you," he calls, one hand up against the glare.

María lies back against the sun-warmed tiles, studies a passing cloud. "I know."

Below, Felipe lets out an exasperated sound.

"María, *please*," he says plaintively, and she sighs, and sits back up.

"Fine, fine," she says, flinging herself over the edge. The drop is high enough to make her brother suck in a nervous breath, but she lands like a cat, bare feet sinking in the hay.

Felipe conducts her like a jailer, one hand against her back as he ushers her to the house. Inside, their mother sits by the fire, sewing in her lap. Rafa paces a groove into the floor.

But María's gaze goes to the stranger sitting at their table.

The man is handsome enough, broad-shouldered and dark-haired, his beard trimmed short and his eyes a light brown at odds with the rest of his complexion. And though he is of average size, he seems too big for the narrow house, too tall for the low beamed roof, too fine for the threadbare rug beneath his boots.

"María," says Rafa, in the scolding tone that always accompanies her name. "This is Andrés de Guzmán, Viscount of Olivares, and esteemed knight of the Order of Santiago."

She wonders absently how long it took Rafa to memorize that string of words. But her attention hangs on the viscount. The cloak draped over his shoulders, lined with black fur. His vest, made from a fine brocade and fastened with jeweled clasps. The medallion of the Order on a gold chain around his neck. All of him flashing like a gem among the river stones.

"Sorry to keep you waiting," she says, adding a breathless edge to her voice, as if she's run all the way across town, instead of strolling up the lane.

Andrés de Guzmán rises from the chair, gives a flourish and a bow. "Encantado, mi señora."

"A pleasure to meet you, vizconde," she says, dropping into a low bow. A moment later, she feels the grip of his glove on her elbow as the viscount returns her to her feet.

"Now, now," he says, "a woman need not bow so low to her betrothed."

The air in the room tenses around the word.

But not María.

She is many things—stubborn, cunning, selfish—but she has never been a fool. She knows that she was born into this body. She knows it comes with certain rules. The question has never been whether she would wed, but *whom.*

So last year, when the heads began to turn, and Rafa started to worry the topic of marriage as if it were a wound, she looked around at the options in Santo Domingo, and found them lacking. She looked at her life and found it small. Saw the road that lay ahead, and there were no curves, no bends; it ran straight and narrow all the way to its end. She saw it in her mother's hands, gone stiff with age, as they now struggled with fine stitches that had once come easily, only a matter of time before María herself was expected to take up the tedious work. She saw it in Rafa's wife, Elana, round with a child that had already begun to waste her beauty and drain her youth. In Felipe's bride, Lessandra, promised to him so long that she had never thought to stray. Both women walked into their marriage beds without so much as looking round to see if there were other paths.

But María has known, all her life, that she is not meant for common paths, for humble houses and modest men. If she must walk a woman's road, then it will take her somewhere new.

She stares at the viscount now, seated at her table, as if they have not met before.

As if she did not see him riding at the helm of the caravan a month ago.

As if he did not see her standing at the edge of the crowd, and follow her across the square and into the shadow of the church.

As if she did not lure him there, feigning innocence as he cornered her, spilled praise at her feet and pressed to see what she might give. What he could take.

As if he did not reach out and coil a lock of copper hair around his glove.

As if she did not see the hunger in his eyes and know that she could use it.

By then she had spent nearly a year honing her gaze on the pilgrims passing through, balancing on that knife's edge between too brazen and too shy. She had learned when to hold a look, and when to drop it. When to let a smile flicker like light on her lips, and when to bow her head.

When to be the predator, and when to play the part of prey.

And that day, in the shadow of the church, she'd played it perfectly, bold enough to catch his eyes, chaste enough to stay his hand. Andrés de Guzmán had retreated, understanding that if he wanted to touch more than María's hair, it would be as her husband.

And so he went.

And here he is again, and the silence must be stretching on too long, because Rafa clears his throat.

"The viscount has come to ask for your hand," he explains, as if she is too thick to understand the meaning of the word *betrothed*.

They are expecting a performance, and so she gives them one.

"In marriage?" she asks, twisting her face into an imitation of surprise, eyebrows arching at this wholly unexpected ambush. She even looks to her mother, as if for aid, finds only relief and resignation on the woman's face. As if this is a burden lifted, when the truth is, it was never hers to carry. With their father gone, Rafa is the master of the house, and so the task of marrying María off falls to him. As he reminds her. *Often.*

"It is a happy day," says her mother.

"Indeed," says Rafa, looking as smug as Andrés, each convinced that *they* are the mind behind this meeting. As if she did not set the game and arrange the pins so all they had to do was knock them down.

"What if I refuse?" she asks, just to savor the surprise on Andrés's face, the shock on Felipe's, the horror on Rafa's. She lets the question hang only a moment before laughing. Her brother sags, relief and embarrassment flooding his cheeks.

"Apologies, mi señor," he says to the viscount, clearing his throat. "María has an odd sense of humor."

The viscount doesn't laugh, but he does not seem insulted either. He answers Rafa, but his attention is pinned to her. "María has only ever been a sister and a daughter. But she will soon learn to be a wife."

The slightest emphasis on the word *learn*, like a switch grazing a horse's flank.

But it will take more than that to make her flinch.

"Well, María?" says Rafa, urging her with a pointed look to accept the offer.

And for once, she does as she's told.

She nods, holding out her hand, and Andrés de Guzmán's mouth splits into a haughty grin, like he's the one who played the game, and won. And as he bends his head to kiss the bare skin of her knuckle, where the wedding ring will go, María imagines the road curving away beneath her feet, and smiles, too.

The viscount returns a fortnight later, a new kind of caravan in tow.

Cart after cart fills the road behind his horse, each one steered by a well-dressed servant and each brimming with gifts—fine tapestries and casks of wine, candied fruit and cured meats. One cart rattles with chargers and cups, enough for every mouth in town, another arrives with hens packed so tight their feathers jut between the slats and fly away like dandelion fluff. An homage to the miracle that made Santo Domingo famous, though hopefully none of these will rise up off their dinner plates.

In hours, the town's plaza is transformed.

Tables dragged from the houses and hauled into the square, every oven commandeered to prepare the wedding feast.

The night before, María's mother brushed her hair a hundred times, until it shone as bright as the fire in the hearth. And as she did, she told her daughter what it meant to be a wife.

Gentle. Loving. Obedient.

Words that made María tense. And, as if her mother could feel her stiffening, she leaned close and said, "You will learn, it is better to bend than to break."

María stared into the hearth. "Why should I be the one who bends?"

Air hissed through her mother's teeth. "I know you, daughter. I know you have always wanted more. And you have chosen a grand life. But it will not be an easy one. Men like the viscount, they take what they want."

So do I, thought María as the comb hissed through her hair like water on hot coals.

They marry on the steps of the cathedral, Andrés in his finery and María in a brand-new dress, the edges trimmed with gold. It is the finest thing she's ever worn, and during the Mass that follows, while the priest drones on, she runs her fingertips along the stitching, counting the pattern as if it were coins as she tells herself this is what she deserves.

This is what she is worth.

At last, the congregation spills out into the square, and the wine flows, and music tangles with the laughter and the toasts. To the viscount's health, and to hers, and to their happiness.

Her new husband covers her hand with his, and every time he speaks to her, or of her, he does not use her name. Instead he calls her mi esposa—*my wife*—the words chafing like rough wool. But María only smiles, and reminds herself they are a key, unlocking the doors to a better life.

His parents are not in attendance, though he assures her that they have sent their happy wishes, and that she will meet them soon enough. Meanwhile, Rafa is smug, and Felipe is drunk, and their mother is wistful, and María wonders if she will miss them when she's gone. She tries to conjure the image of it, expects to feel something, a happy sadness, a parting grief, but she can't.

And then it is time.

They do not linger at the feast. Andrés is eager to depart for his estate. María's mother cries, stiff hands clasped and tears running silent down her face, and her brothers embrace her, first Felipe, smelling of wood chips and soot, and then Rafa, who places a kiss on each cheek, and bids her *Be a good wife.*

Gentle. Loving. Obedient.

Felipe's wife, Lessandra, smiles and dabs at her cheeks, but Elana catches María's hand, hunger glinting in her eyes. "Do not forget us, sister."

María can feel the woman's greedy fingers inching toward the gold trim of the bridal sleeve. Knows she is trying to exact a promise.

"Of course, sister," she says, a smile in her voice. "I will carry you in my heart."

And then she pulls free, and takes her husband's outstretched arm, and lets him lead her away, not knowing, of course—

She will never see her family again.

ALICE

(D. 2019)

I

Boston, Massachusetts
2019

The house has a heart and it is pounding.

The bass shudders through the wall, and Alice leans back into it—that wall, as out of place as she is, a shock of freshly painted green, fairy lights running up and down like little neon flowers—and lets the beat knock against her own ribs, imagines herself in the belly of some great beast instead of the crowded blue co-op, one hand clutching her phone and the other holding a cup of something that smells like turpentine.

Everyone *else* looks like they're having fun, so Alice does her best impression of a mirror, and wonders for the third or fourth time what she's doing there. She vaguely remembers someone knocking on the suite door earlier that night, saying "Party at the Co-op," and an hour later being swept along with her suitemates, Jana and Rachel and Lizbeth, the mass of them not yet friends, no longer strangers, Velcroed to each other by their newness and the first few weeks of uni.

Lizbeth, who's from Kent (the university put them together, probably thought they were doing them a service, not realizing how different English and Scottish are), and has the kind of accent people call *crisp, clean* (which Alice cannot stand because it makes hers *wrinkled, dirty*, by comparison) and who actually called her *pastoral* the day they met, as if Alice were a painting and not a girl from the other side of the same island.

As for Rachel and Jana, one's from New Jersey and the other from New York (and the day they all met it took Alice half a conversation to realize they were speaking English, too, because they both talk so fast that it's like someone went in and took all the spaces out), and when Alice finally got a word in, Rachel let out a gleeful squee and said, "Oh my god, you sound like *Outlander!*" even though her accent has never been that thick. The only thing that made it better was the fact they made the same fuss over Lizbeth's clipped consonants, saying she sounded like the queen, and at least Alice got to keep her name, while the two of them only ever refer to Lizbeth as Queenie now.

(And Her Highness, but only when she isn't there.)

They're the ones who dragged her here. Alice doesn't even like parties, but she's trying, fresh start and all that, so she let them doll her up, and the four of them set out for the Co-op like a pack, and she was just starting to think that maybe it wouldn't be so bad, but then they hit the front door and just kind of broke apart, and now Alice is alone and hugging the green wall like it's an anchor, a finish line instead of a starting point. If her sister Catty were here, she'd nag Alice for being a barnacle, pry her off and fling her back into the social tide, but Catty's an ocean away, so Alice escapes into her phone instead, and opens the photo app.

Sometimes she takes pictures, but mostly she just watches. It's easier to look at the world this way, to take it in. (Four inches of metal and glass is as good as a shield, since no one notices a phone, and if they do, they just assume you're looking at yourself instead of them.)

On her screen, the party is reduced to a picture in a frame. Someone has thrown colored kerchiefs over all the lamps, and the crowded room becomes a medley of colored blooms. The music erased, transmuted into movement, a blur of bodies.

Alice stares through the screen, combing the sea of half-learned faces, searching for her suitemates. She doesn't find them but she does spot three familiar heads bent together in the open kitchen, pouring drinks. Not Jana or Lizbeth or Rachel, but more girls from floor three: Sam and Hannah and Elle.

(Though, in truth, Alice isn't sure which is Sam and which is Elle—not because they look alike, just because they always seem to come as a pair, and when Hannah first introduced them as "Sam and Elle," she didn't point out which was which, and now it feels too late to ask.)

Alice starts heading toward them, against the current, elbows and shoulders and hips bumping hers, but somehow she's the one who says, "Sorry," "Sorry," "Sorry." Hannah sees her coming but doesn't look happy, doesn't wave, and Alice suspects it's because Hannah tried to bond with her week one over the most fuckable guys on their floor (and Alice should have told her there and then that she was gay, but the last thing she needs is the drama or the pointed looks, like she'd try it on with any of them just because they had the right parts) so she'd shrugged and said they all looked nice enough and

Hannah had snorted and said she must have low standards because the pickings were so slim back in Scotland.

And now that Alice is remembering that conversation, her legs don't want to move, the current is too strong, and the other girls suddenly feel very far away, and she's about to return to her spot on the green wall when someone clips her elbow, sloshing the turpentine in her cup, and the drink didn't even spill, not really, just a few wayward drops on black jeans, but it's the excuse she needs to escape.

She ducks into the hall, and there's the front door, and past it, the mile walk back to the Yard, and it would be so easy to just leave, leave, go back to Matthews, which is probably a graveyard of abandoned rooms because it's Saturday night and everyone is here, and Alice *knows* she shouldn't go, because she decided, the day she left home, that everything back in Scotland was *then*, and this is *now*.

The moment when her whole life starts.

Only she's been here three weeks, and the *nows* keep piling up, keep passing her by. There was the now after she waved goodbye at the airport, and the one after the plane took off, and after she landed in Boston, and after the cab spit her out outside the nearest gate, and after she hauled her bags into her new room, and after classes started, and after she stepped into this house. And it turns out there's no magic threshold, no fresh start, and Alice is still Alice, and maybe it's the too-loud music ringing through her teeth or the fact a storm's been building all day and the air outside the Co-op is just as heavy as the air within, but she feels a little dizzy, a little sick, a little drunk.

She only had two shots back at Matthews, courtesy of Rachel, just enough to shave the sharp edges off her thoughts, and it clearly wasn't enough, because she can feel the panic ticking like a bomb behind her ribs, and—

(Sometimes, when her head used to take her body hostage, Catty would cup Alice's face and say, "Hey, hey now, you're just confused. You think this is panic but you're wrong. It's excitement. You're having fun! This is what fun feels like!")

This is what fun feels like, she tells herself now, turning away from the front door and looking for a bathroom instead.

A moment, that's all she needs, a moment alone, a chance to collect herself. There is a toilet halfway down the hall, but the line is four deep, so she keeps going, until she finds a bedroom at the end with an en suite. Alice crosses the room, lit only by a single bedside lamp, its light veiled purple by the scarf cast over the shade, and disappears into the bathroom, closing the door, a single wooden slab of armor against the world. For a second, she's cocooned in darkness, a solid, all-surrounding black, but then she flicks the wall switch on and flinches in the sudden, too-white light.

And there she is, reflected in the dingy mirror over the sink.

Alice Moore, eighteen and caught between.

Neither particularly short nor tall, hair more ash than blond, fringe growing out after she hacked it short over the summer, so now it falls right into her eyes, which aren't exactly blue, or green, or gray, but an uncertain mix, like every part of her is undecided, stuck midstride.

The kind of looks their gran always said she'd *grow into*, as if her skin is just an outfit that needs to be tailored, styled, worn right—she feels like there should be a manual for that. After all, she's seen those girls who can wear anything, and make it look natural, effortless, chic—and then there's Alice, who always feels like she's playing dress-up in someone else's closet, and looks that way, too. Nothing fits, even if it's fitted, because it's not really about the size of the body or how it fills the clothes, but how much space it takes up in the world.

Alice shrinks, is swallowed, disappears. No—disappearing would be better, because maybe in the absence of *Alice* she could become someone else. One of the feral girls, who have been planted and watered in their bodies, who have pruned their looks, or let them grow wild, the same girls who turn their full brows into a wolfish power, their painted lips into a weapon.

Now Alice leans in close, until her hips cut into the sink and her breath fogs on the glass, blurs the image of the girl on the other side.

You're having fun, she tells her heart, and her heart thuds back in all its stupid anxious glory *no no no no* and Alice wants to cut it out, wants to be a different version of herself, one that isn't so goddamn insecure.

The fog on the mirror melts away, revealing her face.

She'd done the makeup back at the suite, mascara and winged liner and a smoky lid, and she doesn't remember rubbing her face but she must have because one eye is already smudged, shadows streaking her cheekbone like a bruise, and instead of trying to fix it—Alice didn't bring the makeup, didn't even bring a purse—she smudges the other one, too, trying to make the imperfections even, wincing when the liner gets in her eyes and makes them water, burn, but the result is a stripe of darkness, like a mask. A disguise, and for a second, just a second, it feels like someone else is staring back. A different version of herself, snap a photo now and you wouldn't know about the cluttered head and anxious heart, all you'd see is those blue-green eyes made brighter by the surrounding dark, the pale blond hair made wild by the humid night.

She wishes she could trade herself for the girl in the glass. This other Alice, who doesn't care, who takes up space, who has no growing left to do.

If not for forever, then at least for tonight.

And maybe it's the bass thudding through the walls, or maybe she's just tired of being herself, or maybe it's all that *waiting waiting waiting* for her life to start, but she decides to take a chance. If Catty were here she would make it a game (not that Catty actually needed an excuse to be reckless, but Alice likes games, because games come with rules, and it's easier to be bold when there are boundaries, edges, and ends).

So here it is.

The game. The rules.

When Alice steps out of the bathroom, she will turn right to the party, not left toward the door, and she will be the girl in the mirror, the backward reflection of herself.

Not Old Alice, but New.

New Alice, who leans in instead of out.

New Alice, who doesn't say sorry every time she so much as skims the air around another person's space, as if none of it belongs to her.

New Alice, who knows that the knocking of her heart is just her body telling her brain that she is having fun—

(And besides, it's not for forever, time spooling away like a street, but just for a night, hell just for an *hour,* and then she can turn back into a pumpkin when it's done.)

She checks her phone and sees it is eleven, on the dot.

An hour, she thinks, and then she leans in and kisses the mirror, leaving a pale pink ghost on the glass. She flicks off the light and throws the door open, suddenly bold, ready to embrace the ticking clock—

And then she sees the girl on the bed.

II

Alice lurches back into her body, the entire pep talk erased by the sudden appearance of another person, the intimacy of it, not the crush of faceless strangers partying beyond, but a single girl sitting alone in the dark.

She's lounging on the edge of the bed in a silver baby-doll dress, leaning back on her hands, fingers sinking into someone else's pillowed comforter. Her legs are crossed and her head's tipped back, exposing the warm column of her throat. Her hair is a mane of curls that are probably brown, but look violet from the scarf thrown over the bedside lamp, and Alice's first thought is that she wishes she could take a picture. Maybe it's the way the light carves the other girl up, tracing hollows and points, grazing her thigh where it meets the short silver hem.

And then Alice realizes that the girl's no longer looking at the ceiling, but at her.

("You're staring," snapped the first girl Alice ever had a crush on, the words sharp enough to sear her cheeks, to make her duck her head even though she hadn't been, not then, was just daydreaming in the wrong direction.)

Alice *is* staring now, but she can't seem to tear her eyes away.

She knows if someone looked at her the way she's looking at this girl, she'd flinch, but the girl doesn't, only smiles, revealing a dimple in one cheek. She rises to her feet, and as she does, the fingers of light seem to bend and follow, like they want to keep touching her. And Alice doesn't blame them.

The girl walks right toward her, doesn't stop until she's close enough for Alice to see that it's not a trick of the light—her curls are truly violet—close enough to see the freckles dusting the girl's tan cheeks, close enough to trace the curve of her pomegranate lips, and Alice has the sudden urge to kiss her, and what a consecration that would be, of her new self. But then the girl's eyes drift past her and Alice realizes she's blocking the door to the bathroom.

"Sorry," she stammers, already forgetting the rules, but the girl only cocks her head as if amused, eyes trailing like fingers up Alice's front as her voice brushes her cheek.

"For what?"

And Alice is even more flustered now, doesn't know what to say to that, afraid she'll somehow make it ten times worse, apologize for the way she was staring, the longing behind it, the almost kiss as well as blocking the door, and then she might as well give up the whole silly game and go back to floor three and hide under the covers reliving every failed second of this night until the end of time.

Instead she steps aside, out of the doorway, and says, "All yours," and the smile that twitches at the corner of the girl's mouth makes Alice think it *is*—that this is in fact her house, her bed, her room Alice is standing in, but the girl just drifts past her into the bathroom, and closes the door without ever turning on the light.

Alice ejects herself from the room.

Decides as she does that what just happened was a minor hiccup, a false start to the game, but by the time she's halfway down the hall, New Alice is back on track. The music is loud enough to drown out most of her doubts, and her skin is buzzing from that brief meeting with the violet girl, cheeks warm from the memory of that raking glance, and she probably hadn't been flirting but even still, the weight of that look was like a shot of vodka, bold and burning in her chest, and that is the problem, she decides—New Alice is too sober.

She sees a boy from her building—floor two or four, she doesn't know— holding a half-smoked joint, and plucks it from his fingers, takes a drag, and for a moment she is three thousand miles away, sitting on a low stone wall, heels knocking pebbles and mortar loose from the rock while a song loops on her phone and then she exhales, sighing the smoke out into the space between them with her thanks.

The boy leans in, flirtation in his glassy eyes, but New Alice isn't inter- ested, doesn't linger, doesn't hand the joint back, either. She has laid claim to it, pink lip stains on the tip of the paper, and she turns and takes another draw, smoke trailing behind her as she moves down the crowded hall, and the bodies don't exactly part but she winds between them, no longer against the flow but with it as she passes through the kitchen, where bottles are lined up like stained-glass panels under the lights.

She reaches for the nicest-looking one and pours herself a shot of amber-colored scotch, throws it back, refills the glass, and when Old Alice whines that she has never had a head for liquor, that she has a paper to finish, that it isn't smart to drink from open bottles, New Alice downs the second shot, and drops the last of the joint in the dregs of the glass, dousing both the butt and the protest.

One night, she thinks, and the thud in her chest is the steady beating of a clock. *Tick tock. Tick tock. Tick tock.* And as the liquor hits, so does the weed, and warmth finally blooms inside her chest, and her head feels light, and this is the secret, isn't it, she thinks, this is the easiest way to become someone else.

She is out of the kitchen now, the music running its fingers through her hair, the bass like a rope around each bone, and she moves toward it, hand skimming the wall for balance, until she is back to the vivid green paint with its fairy blooms. She leans in, and lets her forehead rest against the wall.

Her wall.

She closes her eyes, cocooned in the noise, until she feels herself sinking into the green paint, the surface going spongy beneath her palms, turning to mallow, swallowing her hands up to the wrist.

Alice jerks back, expecting the wall to hold on to her, but the paint is just paint and she stumbles, shoulders colliding with another body. A hand steadies her, and she knows, somehow she *knows* before she ever turns, that it's her.

The violet girl.

And it is.

The *sorry* is halfway out when the girl smiles, one brow arched as if she's in on the game, and Alice bites down on the word, turning it into a *so*, her lips pouting around the shape. The girl's hand is still on her shoulder. It seems quite comfortable there, and the music is too loud to hear anything that's not a shout, but Alice can read the words on her pomegranate lips.

Dance with me.

If Alice looked around, she'd see it's not a strange request—everyone is dancing now, this section of the house a bobbing tide of limbs—but Alice doesn't look at them, because that would mean looking *away* from the violet girl, with her tinted curls, and high cheekbones, and wide brown eyes. Brown, the most common color in the world, but there is nothing common about them. They're gold at the edges, like some internal light is trying to peek out, but dark at the center, so dark she'd think the pupils were blown wide if she couldn't see them too, pinpricks despite the party's muted light.

And Old Alice might have stumbled, might have fumbled this flirtation, but the sheer volume of the music eliminates the need for coy replies or witty comebacks. All she has to do is nod, and then the girl's hand is sliding from her shoulder to her shirtfront, fingers tangling in the cotton of her shirt as she pulls Alice closer.

The music is a current, the bass a rolling tide, and they are rising and falling together, and up close the girl doesn't smell like vanilla, or coconut shampoo, or any of the heavy floral scents that hung in the air earlier that night when the girls in the suite were getting ready.

No, she smells like wet earth and wrought iron and raw sugar.

They don't so much tangle up as fold together, arm on arm, ribs on ribs, a girl and her shadow, or a shadow and its light, and she's heard a hundred songs and sayings about how the right person can make the whole world disappear, but the world is still there, raging around them, only it's background noise, it's set dressing, and for once in her life she is standing center stage, performing for an audience of one, this violet girl.

"I'm Alice," she shouts over the music, realizes as the words come out how useless it is; she can't hear her own voice. But the other girl seems to. She answers, her own name lost in the swell, and Alice frowns, and shakes her head, and the girl presses in, leans her cheek against Alice's, and says it again, and the name should be nothing but an exhale tickling her ear, but the music chooses right then to dip, and so she hears it.

Lottie.

And then the girl is ducking her head, curls tickling Alice's neck, and she feels the kiss as it lands on the bare skin at the open collar of her shirt. Alice is shivering, hungry for the touch, is about to pull the girl's face up and kiss her when her ears hum, filling with a noise too loud, too bright, and at first she thinks it's some kind of frozen note, a song's protracted beat, but the atonal chord rises above the music and then the music cuts off, and the note remains and she realizes what it is: a smoke alarm.

And everything unravels.

The lights come on, and suddenly the Co-op is just a house, too crowded and too bright, and Alice looks around, but the violet girl is gone, and the bodies she's been fighting through all night are moving in the same direction now, a tide carrying Alice away, down the hall and out the door and down the steps onto the street.

The night is a hand on the back of her neck, heavy, unwelcome, and she feels dizzy, unmoored, the world gone soft under her feet, her senses knocked off-kilter—like taking a nap in the afternoon and waking to find it's dark outside, or stepping off one of those moving sidewalks, or lying for too long under the stars on a clear night as they slide around so slow you don't notice until you stand up again.

Alice forces air into her lungs as a handful of students break off down the road, but the rest are too drunk and too high to make any quick decisions, so they pool on the curb in the humid night, dozens blinking away a trance, and Alice scans their heads in search of Lottie and her purple curls, but of course she doesn't see her.

Alice sighs, and lets her head fall back, and feels the first drop of rain like a kiss on her cheek.

She sucks in a breath, because she knows what's coming, and sure enough, by the time she exhales the humidity gives way, the night splitting open like a seam as it starts to rain. Not the steady drizzle Northeasterners seem so used to, but a sudden, crushing downpour, the water thick enough to blur the light posts.

The night around her fills with shrieks, students turned to birds by the sudden storm. They screech, and flock for the cover of the porch, desperate to stay dry, but Alice's body moves before her mind, away from the house and into the street.

In seconds she is wet, the rain so loud in her ears that the other sounds
All disappear—
The lines of the block washed away—
And just like that—

Alice is back home in Hoxburn, standing in the yard, arms outstretched and heels sinking into the sodden grass as the rain comes down so hard and so cold that the shock of it catches behind her ribs, and the air gets stuck in her lungs, the way it does when you jump straight into a freezing loch or wade into the North Sea. Catty taught her that the fastest way to shake the breath loose was to scream, but

Alice can never bring herself to do it, so instead she holds her breath and stands there, shivering beneath the storm, knows her teeth will chatter for hours after, her fingertips too cold, and she'll have to sit and thaw before the open fire. And the truth is, Alice loves that part, the drying off, the warming up, the coziness of coming back to life.

But that's not why she stands out in the rain.

It's because there's a moment, pressed beneath the weighted blanket of the storm, when her body stops fighting, when all the voices inside her finally go quiet, and her shoulders loosen and her lungs unclench and her skin goes numb and the line between girl and world gets smudged, and she is washed away.

Made new.

Someone shrieks and—

Alice opens her eyes and—

—her front yard is gone, and she's standing in the middle of the Harvard street, soaked to the bone, and the night is full of lights racing toward her, and it takes her a moment too long to realize they are headlamps on helmets, a tide of bicycles on some kind of night ride, a herd of rushing metal and voices shouting at her to get out of the way and then a hand catches her wrist and yanks her back onto the curb.

And it's Lottie, of course it's Lottie, her silver dress melting as the rain soaks the fabric, plasters it against her skin, the hair dye running from her storm-soaked curls, the violet rinsing out and rolling down her face like tears. Alice lifts her hand to the girl's cheek, as if to brush away the stain, but her fingers get lost along the way when Lottie leans into the touch and speaks.

But the rain is a sheet of white noise, so Alice doesn't hear what she says.

And then the girl is pulling her down the street, and then they are *all* moving now, the kids from the party, some sprinting toward the Yard, ducking under trees and awnings trying to stay dry, and others resigned to the rain, and Alice soaking it up like a sponge, Lottie's hand still around her wrist, both of them caught in the storm.

Somewhere around here the edges of the night begin to blur, moments dropping like stitches, the waterlogged minutes collapsing in so that the next thing she knows, they are tumbling through the nearest open gate, and then up the steps of Matthews, ducking under the cover of the awning, rain falling in a sheet to one side, the building rising to the other, both of them sopping wet and breathing hard from the run through the storm.

Their hands have come undone, and Alice wishes she'd held on, because now it would be weird, wouldn't it, to reach for the other girl again, when there's no reason to—or so she thinks, until Lottie reaches out and takes her hand, like she doesn't need a reason more than wanting to, and now there is a rope between their bodies, their fingers like a knot, and Lottie comes forward and Alice moves back, only it doesn't feel like she's retreating, more like being led, step-by-step, that rope drawn taut and slack and taut again, until her back meets the building door and she shivers as cold metal hits wet shirt, the sensation forgotten a second later when the girl's body presses against hers. And Lottie is a fraction shorter, with the curls now tamped against her skin, but there is something about her that makes Alice feel like she is looking up, and—

(why is she taking measurements when there are hip bones buzzing against hers, when her heart is slamming against her ribs so hard the other girl must be able to feel it knocking, their wet bodies plastered together against the door)

—and it is not enough, there is still too much space, and maybe Lottie feels it too because she lets her head fall forward until their lashes tickle and their noses brush and their lips almost almost *almost* touch, and right there the other girl hesitates and meets her hungry gaze and whispers—

"May I?"

—as if *this* is the moment for discretion, and Alice nearly bleats out the word *yes*, and the other girl must see the letters taking shape before the sound is fully out because her mouth is already there, catching the *s* with her kiss.

That kiss—the one Alice has been waiting for since their bodies tangled in the house's throbbing beat, since she recoiled from the wall and felt that cool hand on her shoulder, since she saw the girl sitting on the bed in the dark, since the cab first spit her out in Harvard Square three weeks ago with her whole life stretched ahead.

That kiss.

Rose-petal soft and deep as a well, and then teeth skim her lower lip and her knees threaten to go, and she's thankful for the door at her back and the girl who now tastes like rain, and honey, and hunger.

Then the kiss is gone, her mouth, gone, as Lottie draws back, and Alice tries to move with her, but the girl's hand is splayed across her ribs, holding her gently, but firmly, against the door.

"Shall we stay out here," she asks, "or are you planning to invite me in?"

And for the first time Alice hears the faint edges of an English accent, like dead leaves cracking underfoot, expects to feel herself put off, but something about those sounds coming from that mouth—the mouth that has opened a door inside Alice, a want, a hunger, a heat pooling in the bowl of her hips—suits her perfectly.

"Well?" asks Lottie, lips twitching in a teasing way, as if the question is mere courtesy, as if she already knows how this will go. And Alice, Alice, under a spell, manages to free one hand long enough to swipe the key card, pulling the girl into the entryway and up the stairs, wringing raindrops with every touch, the water leaving a trail like a crime scene in their wake as they make their way up to floor three.

Two feral, hungry girls.

The suite is still empty, and dark, and Alice doesn't even stop to feel self-conscious about the narrow room she shares with Lizbeth, or her unmade bed, the pile of clothes in the corner, the books littering the desk. The night has taken on a soft focus, narrowed itself to only them, and Alice is trembling, but Lottie is steady. Sure-footed. Sure-fingered as she tugs Alice toward the bed.

They don't turn on the light.

She casts her phone aside without looking at the time.

(If she *had*, she would have seen that it's well past midnight now, the game long over by her rules, New Alice returned to Old. If she had looked, she might have lurched back into her body, her cluttered head and anxious heart, might have realized that the magic potion of the shots had in fact evaporated, the buzz of the joint worn off, leaving only *Alice*, eighteen and alive and high on the heady pleasure of being touched, wanted, spelled by the power of the other girl. If she had looked, she might have stopped. If she had looked. But she doesn't.)

Lottie pulls her close again, and something changes. Up until now she's felt like the other girl is humoring her, like this whole thing was just another kind of game, but this time, as their bodies meet, Alice hears the other girl's breath catching, a hitch of desire that makes her blush, makes her flush, makes her *ache*.

(She is used to wanting plenty, but it is another thing to be *wanted*.)

Teeth graze her collar, light as a feather drawn over bare skin, and then a hand slips between Alice's legs, fingers curling, palm pressing hard to the front of her wet jeans. Alice arches into the touch, the touch that cannot get close enough because there are—

"Too many clothes," she gasps.

Lottie chuckles softly, a soundless, heavy thing like distant thunder as she pulls back, watching as Alice tries to peel out of the sodden layers, and quickly discovers how hard it is to make the gesture sexy. It is awkward, but Lottie seems to delight in that awkwardness, eyes laughing as Alice fights with the fabric. The shirt's okay, but the jeans are stuck fast, and she's left wriggling and prying them away, something between a sausage casing and a durable layer of plastic wrap until she's finally winded but free.

And even though Lottie must have gotten just as wet, somehow there is no struggle, just fabric falling, revealing warm bare skin, and Alice takes her in, trading mental pictures for the real ones she never took—ones she'll wish she had.

A silver dress pooling like a mirror at her feet, streetlight streaming through the window, painting lines across skin, the utter confidence of an eighteen-year-old girl standing stark naked and rain-damp in the center of her room, curls plastered to her face and neck, violet ribbons running like ivy between her breasts, over hourglass hips—

(Tomorrow morning Alice will find purple stains on the cheap rug, like drops of blood.)

—and she waits like a canvas, waits for Alice to make her first move, leave her first mark, but it takes a steady hand and a solid will and she's never had either so of course she falters, skimming the girl's waist, the skin so soft and smooth and tan, trailing her fingers through the purple-tinted stream as it follows the curves of the girl's hip, but she feels less like a seductress and more like a child fingerpainting, and the thought has her wanting to curl inside herself, makes her draw her hand away.

It might have ended there, but Lottie catches her wrist, guides her to the bed, eases her down, down among the tangled sheets.

Alice looks up, and in the lightless room the other girl is nothing but a shadow, lithe and looming, edges lit and center dark, and Alice realizes Lottie is still waiting. Waiting to be invited in, just like Alice has been waiting all her life. Waiting to get out of her small town, waiting for her life to start, and here it is, right here at the edge of an unmade single in a college dorm, and the freedom is dizzying, and it scares the shit out of her as well—but fear and fun could be neighbors, right?

(Like the time Catty's boyfriend, Derrick, gave Alice a ride on the back of his motorbike and when he tipped to make a turn, she could have reached down and skimmed her fingers on the asphalt—the world was suddenly so close—and then the bike righted and the world balanced and Alice's heart kept pounding, but it wasn't fear, at least not fear alone. It was the *thrill*. And afterward, every time she was in her dad's car, with its walls and its roof, she rolled the window down and held her arm out and felt the wind whip against her skin, and relived that tip, that turn.)

And here she is, no car, no walls, just open air, and all Alice has to do is lean in, lean in, lean in.

So she does.

Leans in so hard that she feels like she's falling, even though it's the other girl being pulled down into the bed, on top of her, skin so velvet, petal soft, and warm where it fits against hers, and her whole body hums because still they are not close enough, Alice fumbling as if it's her first time—

(It's not, no, that honor went to Rebecca Pierce when they were both fifteen and that really was full of fumbling, nervous laughter punching holes in the seduction, a tangle of limbs, and unsteady touches—*Like this? Like this? Like this?*—a leg pressed hapless between knees, grinding in search of rhythm before they gave up, collapsed into a pile on the blankets, unfinished but spent.)

—and she doesn't remember saying any of this out loud but the girl above her smiles as if she did, as if Lottie can see the whole thing written in Alice's breathless want, her blushing face, and the violet-tinted girl is catching her mouth, kissing her down into the sheets, and then the lips are changing course, leaving a trail of kisses down Alice's jaw, her throat, one leg pressed between her two, the pressure of it so delicious it makes her thighs clench, and the world could stop right there, but the girl is rising off her and Alice wants to say *wait, wait*, is bereft, reaches out, grasping, greedy, to pull her back but the other girl catches her fingers and kisses them and then presses them into the pillow, and gives her a look that says *Stay*, and Alice does, even as the girl kisses her way down the pale slope of skin between Alice's breasts, down her stomach, wet curls painting the skin in her wake.

And Alice—Alice is a square of chocolate melting in the sun, edges soft enough to smudge, and this is what she dreamed of when she dreamed of college, of freedom, of life, and now that it's happening to her she's torn between the urge to hold the moment on her tongue, and the urge to spit it out before it can dissolve, and even now she is still thinking too much, still stuck somewhere inside her head, until Lottie nips the soft skin inside her thigh and it is enough to bring her back, to send her pulse skipping and her limbs stiff, to put her firmly in her body as the other girl's mouth settles in the dark between her legs and she stifles a gasp, blood rushing to the surface, and then Lottie does something with her tongue and the night unravels, and Alice—

Alice finally stops thinking, and simply comes apart.

LOTTIE

(D. ???)

I

The girl sleeps like she is dead.

Face turned into the pillow, pale hair drying on her cheek, limbs flung out like roots, no longer shrinking like she did against the wall, but stretching, sprawling to fill the space. Her lips are parted slightly, her shoulders rising, falling, rising with the bellows in her chest.

Lottie lies there on her side and studies the girl.

Alice—a name like a whisper, like a sigh, sound slipping between her teeth.

Lottie stares, unblinking, as if she were a piece of photo paper, a slow exposure, soaking in the angle of Alice's limbs, the shade of her hair—dry sand—the kisses Lottie left like breadcrumbs on her fair skin.

She reaches out a cool and cautious hand, careful not to wake the girl, and twines a blond lock around her finger, thumbs the edge like a painter testing their brush, catching the scent of rain, and want.

It would be easier, she knows, to let go of these details, instead of clinging to them.

It would be easier, but it would be lonelier, too. And she wants to pretend. Pretend that when she gets up, the spell won't break. Pretend that when she leaves, she might come back.

Pretend that this is a beginning, and not an end.

Lottie stays as long as she can, which is never long enough.

She imagines dozing off, waking with her arms looped around Alice, the morning spilling through the window. But despite the time, she isn't tired. Her skin buzzes with a restless energy, a longing for fresh air, and she knows, she knows, she has to go. Has learned to rip the Band-Aid off. The danger's in the dwelling, and so before the voice in the back of her mind can start to whisper *What if, what if, what if,* Lottie is up. Slipping from the bed, and picking her way, barefoot, through the cluttered room, reclaiming her outfit piece by piece and dressing in the dark.

She is Orpheus, she tells herself. She won't look back.

And this time, she almost makes it. Her back is to the bed, her hand is on the doorknob, but then she hears the girl sigh, and turn over in her sleep. Lottie looks over her shoulder and falters at the sight of Alice, pale limbs tangled in the sheets, one arm out, palm up and fingers curled as if to say *Come back.*

Lottie chews her lip, then drifts over to the desk, cluttered with textbooks and Post-its. She scribbles a note and presses it like a kiss against the bedside lamp before she goes.

Lottie steps out into the night and sighs, the hours sloughing off like clothes.

She pads, barefoot, across the rain-damp quad, heels hanging from hooked fingers as she drifts, unhurried, savoring the hour when everyone's asleep except for her. The storm has passed, the weight replaced by something light and cool as she makes her way through Cambridge. The second one she's known.

She twirls across an intersection, empty at this hour, carried by a song so faint she can't tell where it's coming from, or if it's simply in her head. She makes her way across the bridge and back into the city proper, where the night feels empty, but it's not.

A car slows as it passes.

A man comes toward her down the block. Shoulders hunched, eyes hanging on her body. Her curls are drying wild, her minidress still damp and clinging to her hips, and she knows *exactly* what he's thinking.

A girl like you, alone at night.

Dressed like that, you're asking for it.

His hands twitch in his pockets, and then he's close enough to meet her gaze, close enough for her to feel the menace rolling off him, the *If I wanted to, I could,* but she doesn't shy back, doesn't make herself small. She looks right into his eyes, and smiles, and whatever he sees, it's enough to make him flinch and shuffle sideways off the curb, just to get away.

And Lottie ambles on, thinking *If I wanted to, I could.*

The bell chimes over the door as Lottie ducks into the mini-mart, the one that's open day and night, trading the softness of the lampposts for the harsh blue-white of the overhead lights. She wanders the aisles, the snacks and cereal boxes, the bottles behind fridge doors, before ordering a black coffee and a Danish.

The coffee smells burnt.

The Danish, a little stale.

But then again, they're not for her.

She pays and covers the last two blocks to the hotel, where a sleepy man behind the front desk says, "Welcome back, Miss Hastings."

"Hello, George."

"Awfully late," he muses, no judgment, just an air of fatherly concern.

"Awfully early," she counters, depositing the paper cup and sack on the counter.

"Come now," he says, "you didn't have to do that."

But he smiles, and she knows the exhaustion on his face has less to do with the graveyard shift he's pulling, which pays double, and more to do with the med school books he's got stashed behind the counter.

Lottie says good night, and drifts up the stairs, fingers skimming the blue wallpaper as she heads to her room, the tiredness just beginning to catch up as the darkness thins beyond the windows and the first gray light of dawn creeps in.

She shrugs out of the silver minidress and into a plush robe, sinking onto the sofa at the foot of the bed. She unzips her bag and reaches in, drawing out a battered paperback, cradling it lightly, the edges foxed, the cover fraying after so many years. She thumbs past the novel's end, to the three blank sheets in the very back, a printer's excess paper—only they're not blank anymore. Lines of small, dark writing run down the inside seam.

Heather. Green eyes like bottle glass.
Isabelle. Tattooed flowers down her throat.
Renee. Smelled like lavender and smoke.

Lottie fishes around in the bag until she finds a pen.

She runs her tongue thoughtfully along her teeth as the pen tip hovers just above the page, her gaze sliding down the list.

Maddie. The bluest eyes I've ever seen.
Jess. Freckles like stars across her cheeks.
Chloe. Rings on every knuckle.

On and on. Each encounter bound to a single line, a token, a snapshot, a memory.

She could fill whole journals with her thoughts on each and every one, brief as they were—but what would be the point, except to haunt herself?

Isn't that exactly what this is? whispers an unkind voice inside her head. A *gallery of ghosts.*

But that's not true.

After all, *these* girls are still alive.

Lottie bows her head over the book, and adds her latest entry.

As she writes, she lets herself look back, one final time, savors each and every moment of the night, reliving the warmth of the girl's skin beneath her fingers, the heady beat of her heart, the way their bodies tangled in the cheap dorm sheets as Alice gasped her name in the dark. Savoring it the way she would the last bite of a meal. A parting kiss.

And then it's over, and all she has is a line.

Six words at the bottom of the list.

Alice. Scottish. Gentle. Tastes like grief.

Lottie frowns, not at the words, but the punctuation on the end.

She must have lingered, let the pen rest a beat too long against the paper, because ink has begun to bloom outward from the period, throwing tiny black roots. She curses softly and sets the pen aside. Blows gently on the paper till it dries, studying the words one last time before she closes the book, and climbs into the lush hotel bed, and sleeps.

MARÍA

(D. 1532)

I

Andrés has gifted her a horse named Gloria.

A dappled gray mare, its coloring as strange and striking as her own. At first María thrills—at the beast's size, and the way she feels when set upon it. She has little experience with horses, but at once they seem to understand each other. She can feel the beast's potential coursing through its flanks, its longing to charge ahead, and her heart quickens at the thought of letting it, feeling its power on display. But Andrés insists on keeping his mount at her side, close enough to hold her reins as well as his.

The servants and their carts have all been sent ahead—or trail behind, she isn't sure, knows only that they travel alone save for a pair of men on horseback, trailing in their wake.

They move at a graceless trot, and as the day wears on, she grows tired and temperamental. Andrés has told her nothing of the journey, how far it is, how long it will take, so when they turn a bend and she sees the shape of buildings on a distant rise, red-tiled roofs clustered close as grapes, her spirits lift.

"What do you think?" he asks, and María marvels, gaze drawn to the castle looming on the hill.

"That is la casona?" she asks. "Your estate?"

Her husband laughs, a barking sound with all the softness of an ax. She will learn, in time, how well he wields it, how efficiently it cuts.

"That is Burgos," he says between chuckles, as if she is a fool. "No, my wife, this city and its castle belong to the king. We are only stopping for the night."

María musters a smile, as if she were only joking. But there's no need. Andrés has already turned away.

The sun sets as they approach, and all over Burgos, lanterns begin to glow with amber light, first a handful and then a hundred, until the city looks like a bed of embers spilling down the hill.

Up close, the first thing that strikes her is the smell. The smell of beasts and unwashed bodies, sweat and shit mixing on the trampled road. María scrunches up her nose. She is no stranger to the scent of farms, but this is different, stale and close and smothering.

They stop at an inn—the finest in town, according to Andrés—but María is too tired to appreciate the fuss the owners make over the viscount's arrival, or the quality of the house itself. There is little sense in savoring what isn't hers.

Andrés orders a meal to be sent up, then takes her hand and leads her to an upstairs room. There, a fire has been struck in the hearth, and a bed stands, proud and stalwart, four wooden pillars and a heavy quilt. It takes all María's will not to fling herself upon it, the way Andrés flings himself into a chair, shrugging off his coat and undoing the laces of his mud-caked boots.

How strange, she thinks. She has never been alone with a man who isn't kin. Knows that she should blush, demure, but only stares, as if bemused by his presence. This stranger, who is not a stranger now.

Husband.

Wife.

Words that hardly fit, especially here, in this odd state of in-between, one game ended and another not yet started.

María goes to the basin in the corner, a pitcher of scented water at its side. She pours, and dips a cloth, begins removing the hours on horseback, the dust and sweat of the ride. She hears Andrés rise, his weight crossing toward her, and for the first time she feels her boldness slip, tells herself it's just the strange nature of the day, which began in one place and is ending in another.

She is not afraid, she tells herself, and yet, her body tenses when she feels him at her back, half expects him to start pawing at the laces on her dress. Instead, his hand closes over hers as he takes the dampened cloth and sets upon the task himself, polishing her stroke by stroke, as if she is a piece of silver.

Her head aches, her hair bound up too long in braided copper ropes, and as if he knows, Andrés begins to pluck out the pins, dropping them one by one into the bowl until her hair comes free, bringing with it a sound, like a growl, in the back of his throat.

"For you," he says, and she turns to face him, finds something glinting in his hand. A ruby the size of her thumbnail, on a glinting rope of gold.

"A wedding gift," he says, sliding the chain around her throat. The ruby comes to rest like a kiss between her collarbones. She fondles it, and smiles, looks up to thank her husband, only to find his eyes lidded, dark. "Esposa mía . . ." he begins, taking her chin between his fingers.

A knock sounds at the door.

Their meal arrives. A heavy tray covered with a metal cloche.

"Leave it," he orders gruffly. The servant nods and sets the tray on the low table by the hearth, is gone again, the door whispering shut in their wake.

The scent of fresh-baked bread and roasted meat drifts toward her, and hunger blooms, sudden and bright, but when she moves toward the table, Andrés catches her wrist.

"Leave it," he says again, and María knows, by the tone of his voice, the weight of his touch, that his hunger has a different shape.

When he peels her out of the dress, and takes her to bed, he is not gentle. *Men like that, they take what they want.*

And sure enough, as he presses her down into the bed, María feels like a pair of doors forced open. A house invaded. She wants to fight back, to fling him off. Instead, she digs her nails into the bedding, and bites her lip until it bleeds. Her gaze escapes to the ceiling, and she searches for faces in the wooden beams.

Andrés winds her hair around his fingers as he thrusts, grunting until, at last, he spasms and collapses, spent, one hand splayed across her stomach, and the last thing he says before he falls asleep is not "I love you," or "Thank you," or even "My wife," but "Let it be a son."

II

That night, María doesn't sleep.

She lies in bed beside her husband, body aching as it cools, fingers drifting not to the pain between her legs, but the ruby at her throat.

She lies there, trapped beneath the weight of Andrés's hand, and stares up at the ceiling beams, trying to find faces in the whorls of wood.

She lies there, and for the first time in years, she thinks of the widow who came to town.

There are teas and tonics for many things, she said. *To shed a fever, or ease a cough. To help a woman get with child, or get rid of it.*

María lies there, and listens to the fire die, one crackling ember at a time, until the room is as dark as the night beyond, and Andrés finally, mercifully, rolls over. Then she rises, footsteps silent on the floor as she crosses the room, past the untouched meal. Steps back into her dress, eases the door open, and slips out.

Not yet dawn, but she finds her way to the kitchens using a lamp stolen from the stairs, begins studying the herbs stopped and bottled on the shelf. They clatter softly as she turns them, studying their labels. She cannot read, and even if she could, she doesn't know what she is looking for, but she can still feel her husband's hand on her stomach, the ghostly weight of it turning rancid in her guts, and—

A gasp. She turns in time to see a short woman in the doorway, one arm clutching a bowl of dough, the other crossing herself. The light lands on María's face, her hair, and she exhales.

"Mi señora," gasps the startled cook. "I thought you were a ghost." She starts forward, setting the bowl down on the counter. "Is something wrong? Are you unwell?"

María weighs the words in her mouth. "Not yet," she says after a moment, "and I do not wish to be."

A knowing look enters the cook's eye, displeasure on its heels.

"This is a kitchen," she scolds, "not an apothecary."

But María has never been easily cowed, not by a tone, or a look. Not as a child, not as a woman, and certainly not as a viscountess. Hers is a problem as old as time, and she expects there is more than one cure.

"Kitchens have some of the same herbs," she says, holding the cook's gaze, "and more discretion."

As she says it, she draws a coin from her pocket and sets it on the counter. Even in the low light, the metal shines. The cook flashes it a hungry look, then swipes the coin into her apron, and shoos María from the shelf.

The cook moves quickly, fetching the right bottles with a surety that makes María think this isn't the first time. She watches as the cook adds small spoonfuls of each herb into a cup, then stokes the embers in the fire, swings the kettle over the flame to heat just until tendrils of steam begin to rise, then pulls it off and pours the water over the herbs to steep.

To this, she adds a drop of honey.

"For the taste," says the cook, handing over the concoction. She looks like she wants to say something else, but a look from María is enough to change her mind. The cook purses her lips while she lifts the cup and drinks.

It is bitter, and earthy, and the first sip sends a cramp through her empty stomach, but she doesn't stop. She swallows every drop and then exhales, her muscles loosening in relief.

She hands the cup back, but when the cook reaches to take it, María catches the other woman's hand and pulls her close. The cook is short, much shorter than the new viscountess, and María looms over her, thin fingers digging into old wrists.

"If you tell a soul," she whispers, her voice low, almost gentle, "I will come back and cut out your tongue."

The cook looks up at her in horror. María smiles down, and then lets go, returning to her room, where she climbs back into bed beside her new husband and sleeps soundly until dawn.

III

María's spirits soar at the sight of her new home.

The Olivares estate may not be a whole city, like Burgos, but it is still a magnificent domain. A village sits in the crook of the slope, and smaller houses dot the surrounding hills like sheep, but the casona rises above them, a massive building with tall stone sides and a crimson-tiled roof, all of it surrounded by a high rock wall. The gates stand open, and their horses pass within, into a courtyard trimmed with trees, half a dozen servants waiting to welcome the viscount and his bride.

The servants shuffle into motion, stewards unloading the carts. María's trunk is carried off, and Andrés helps her from her horse and takes her arm.

"Come, my wife," he says, leading her inside. "Let me show you everything."

María smiles, and today there is no need to feign excitement. Their house is grander than anything she has ever seen, and her husband preens, one arm swinging wide to gesture at this detail in the archway, this pattern in the floor, this painting on the wall. His voice echoes through the hallways, that is how large they are.

"It is yours," he says as they pass a room with a table longer than her family home.

"It is yours," he says as they cross another, inner courtyard, dotted with olive trees, and climb a set of stairs.

"It is yours," he says as he unveils the room that will be hers, the bed heaped with blankets that spill over the sides.

"It is yours," he says as he draws her to the open windows, and gestures to the rolling land beyond, its stables, and orchards, and fields. María drinks it in with hungry eyes, one triumphant word ringing through her mind.

Mine.

They dine together in the great hall, flanked by doting servants and paintings of her husband's family. His parents stare down, stern-faced, from their respective frames—a small shrewd woman and a large-bellied man. His younger brothers, each on horseback, swords raised, despite the fact they're dressed not for crusade, but court. A sister, round-faced, reclining in a chair beside a hound. And then, of course, there is Andrés himself, standing proud, the Order's red cross emblazoned on his breast.

The painter has been generous.

Her husband is a handsome man, but an artist's tools have further chiseled out his jaw, lengthened his limbs, graced him with a godly stature.

The real Andrés sits below and drinks with a mortal mouth. He slouches in his mortal frame, and talks with his mortal voice, and she pretends to listen. The food, when it arrives, is sumptuous, and soon her senses are subsumed by the jeweled pears and honeyed carrots, the roasted pheasant and ruby wine. For the most part, her husband seems content with the sound of his own voice. Only once does he stop and notice the object of her attention.

"You have a healthy appetite," he says, and she knows he means despite her shape. María may be lean, but it is not for lack of appetite. No, she has always been hungry. Even when the crops were good, the winter kind, and there was no shortage of food in Santo Domingo, and she could eat as much as she pleased, she never felt *full*.

Her mother always wondered where it went.

Her father, when he was alive, liked to joke that she had an extra stomach.

María would chew stems of grass in the field, suck on cherry pits until they were pebbles, lacking any taste, and at night, the plates would be empty, her brothers leaning back in their chairs, content, and she would long for more, wish the satisfaction lingered past the time it took to taste it.

And that was mean fare compared to this.

Her mother warned her against rich foods, how they would turn her stomach if she ate too much. But perhaps that was the problem all those years.

Perhaps *rich* is what her body hungered for, she thinks, as she spears another candied carrot with her fork.

⁓

Her husband comes again that night.

His room, she will soon learn, belongs to him alone, while hers must be ready to hold them both. A small enough price, María tells herself, for what she's won.

He climbs into her bed. Into her. His breath hot, his voice wine-loose, his body pressing hers down into the linens—she will later find their folds like patterns on her skin, unwelcome echoes of his weight.

His face contorts in pleasure.

Her own draws tight with pain. She clutches at his back, nails digging into flesh, hoping it will hurt, but it only seems to spur him harder. Again, her gaze escapes to the ceiling, but the wooden beams are lost behind the canopy.

Again, her husband's hand drives into her hair, his fist tightening with every thrust.

Again, when he is done, he puts his palm against her stomach, as if she is nothing but a vessel. An attractive pot, waiting to be filled.

She resists the urge to recoil.

At least this time he does not stay. Eventually he rouses from his stupor, rises, and returns to his own room.

The bed is hers again.

María touches the place between her legs and finds it sore, a warmth and wetness in his wake. She wishes she had paid more attention to the cook's hands at the inn, the jars she pulled, the tonic brewed—hopes what she took will last another night. She doesn't dare go to the viscount's own kitchens and ask his cook for remedies. And so, even though she has never put much faith in God, or asked him to intercede, María now closes her eyes and says a prayer.

Then she rises, cleans herself as best she can, and considers the twisted linens, the indent of her body like a ghost. The bed smells of his sweat, so María pulls the linens free and dumps them on the floor, before climbing back beneath the blanket.

~

A hand throws open the curtains, letting in a vicious streak of morning light.

A voice she doesn't know speaks up. "Mi señora."

María groans and drapes an arm across her eyes, cursing the sun, and Andrés, and whoever designed a room with windows facing *east*.

"Mi señora," comes the voice again, and this time she sits up, one hand holding the blanket to her chest. There is a girl in her room.

She reminds María of a deer, fawn-colored hair and doeish eyes, a narrow body balanced on fragile limbs. When she speaks again, her voice is soft, and low, and coaxing. As if María were the one about to spook.

"I'm sorry to wake you, but the viscount . . ."

The girl trails off, as if the mere existence of the title renders any other words unnecessary. But María is still taking her in.

"Who are you?" she asks.

"Ysabel," says the girl, as if the name means something. Then, when it clearly doesn't, she adds, "Your maid."

"Ah." María has never had a maid before, but she's determined not to let it show. She slides out from beneath the covers and stands, clothed in nothing but ropes of red hair, the light running fingers down her skin.

Ysabel casts her gaze down, but María catches the blush that spreads over her cheeks as she takes up a heap of fabric and comes toward her. María lets herself be guided, limb by limb, into a dress she's never seen before, smiles at the fine stitching and the weight of the cloth.

New clothes for this new life. A gown the color of rich wine, trimmed with creamy lace. Bronze buttons that catch the light and flash like sparks.

Ysabel's touch is gentle, and steady.

"The viscount is waiting in the dining hall," she says as she fastens the clasps.

"Already?" asks María, glancing at the window.

From the corner of her eye, she catches Ysabel's face, the mouth twitching up.

"Sí, mi señora," she says gently. "It is almost noon."

The maid shifts her hair out of the way, to reach a button there, and when the girl's fingers graze the skin at the nape of her neck, María *shivers*.

Ysabel apologizes quickly, asks if her fingers are too cold.

María lies and says, "Yes."

Andrés is not in the dining hall.

She is greeted only by the remains of his meal, the dregs left in his cup. A servant informs her that the viscount has come and gone.

To where, she asks, and learns that her husband is meeting with his vassals.

The table is still laid, a bounty waiting in the center, and so María eats alone, picking at the spread of meat and cheese and fruit and savoring the quiet.

Silence is a kind of wealth, she thinks, taking up a pear. The house in Santo Domingo was so cramped with life that it was always loud. Here, she can hear the crisp skin of the pear splitting beneath her teeth.

A bowl of black cherries sits in the center of the table, the dark fruit nestled in a cloth. María pops one in her mouth as she looks up and finds yet another painting of her new in-laws, the Count and Countess Olivares, staring sternly back.

She rises, taking the cherries with her. Wanders the halls, as she did with Andrés on her arm the day before, but this time she lets her mind run up ahead. Lets it smooth its hands against the walls and change these tapestries, those chairs, this rug, draping her taste like gossamer. Paintings come down, and curtains go up, sculptures move and furniture's replaced until piece by piece, the house begins to suit her taste.

She steps onto the patio and surveys the rest of the estate, feasting on the bowl of cherries, and despite the tightness of her dress, the stiffness of her shoes, María feels herself expanding with the scale of her new home.

One by one she spits the cherry pits into her palm, until the small stones look like bloody teeth. It should repulse her, but it doesn't. They have always been her favorite fruit. In fact—she scans the fields beyond the walls and decides that she will have one tilled, and turned into a cherry orchard. And then, because she does not want to wait, she passes through the gates, and spends the next hour pressing pits into the soil in the nearest olive grove, burying them like secrets just beneath her feet.

It will take time, she knows, but it will be worth it, to see the cherries growing up like weeds between the olive trees, to imagine Andrés's surprise, his annoyance, even, as her black fruit invades his green.

When her palms are stained and the bowl is empty, she sprawls in a shady corner of the estate and lets the warmth lure her to sleep.

⁓

She wakes to the sound of Andrés's horse coming up the road.

María blinks, and rises dreamily, brushes the dirt from her dress, and goes to meet her husband on the path.

"Esposa mía," he says, but this time there is no kindness in it. Only a tight contempt. He dismounts and takes her arm, fingers digging roughly through the sleeve.

"What are you doing out here?" he demands, as if he'd come upon her in the middle of some foreign city, and not the fields surrounding their estate. He does not wait for her to answer, is already turning her back toward the walls. "You must stay within the gates."

Must is a word that has always made María bristle.

"Why?" she asks. "These are your lands." And she is quite proud of herself for saying *your*, not *our*, or *my*, but the words do nothing to appease him. A groom hurries up to relieve Andrés of his horse, and he turns her toward him, surveying her as if for damage.

"Because," he says, one hand drifting up to cup her cheek, "you are a jewel. Others might see you and grow greedy."

María wants to laugh. There are nothing but field hands and workers, and if she wanted one of those she could have stayed in Santo Domingo.

"Do you think so little of me?"

"I think the world of you," he answers blithely as he leads her back into the house. "And that is why I want you to myself."

That night, in bed, when Andrés runs his fingers through her hair, his grip is tighter. He wraps the strands around his fist as if they are a set of reins, doesn't let go until he's come.

When he is gone, María dumps the soiled sheets onto the floor and parts the heavy curtains, throwing the windows wide to let the night air in.

And the sun.

In the morning, the first light spills in, unobstructed, waking her early.

She doesn't call for the maid, even though the dresses in the cupboard all seem to require more than two hands, and she is surprised to find her own trunk empty, the garments from her old life gone. She selects one of the simpler gowns and does her best to draw the ribbons and fasten the stays.

Then she stands at the open window, brushing her hair as she waits for Andrés to ride out. She has just finished combing out the knots, is about to braid it when she hears the gate groan open, and sees her husband set off on his horse.

As soon as the dust has settled in his wake, she goes straight to the stables, finds a groom, and asks to have Gloria saddled.

The groom stares at her, aghast—perhaps by the sight of the viscountess's loose hair, or the undone ribbons at her back—then blushes deeply and says it won't be possible. And yet, the dappled gray mare is right there, black eyes blinking in the stall behind him.

María runs her hand along its neck. "Is something wrong?"

The groom shakes his head. "No, mi señora. The mare is fine. But you are not to ride her."

Her temper flares. "She is *my* horse."

The groom only grows more flustered. "I'm sorry, mi señora, but it is not safe. You do not know these hills, and the mare is young. You might come to harm, or fall . . ."

It quickly becomes clear he is nothing but a puppet, Andrés's orders fed between his teeth.

"So the *viscount* forbids it, then?"

The groom bows lower. "Please understand," he says, and those are the first words that do not have the echo of her husband's voice.

María scowls at the wooden gate that separates her from her horse.

"What did the viscount tell you to do, if I try and ride her?"

The groom gives her a miserable look. "I am to hobble the horse."

It has been a warm morning, but now, the air goes cold. Anger rises in her throat, and she can almost feel the rough fingers knotting in her hair.

María swallows hard. Touches the ruby pendant at her collar. Forces the breath out of her lungs and bends her mouth into a patient smile.

"There will be no need for that," she says, looking up at the stable roof, the slices of sky beyond. The beginnings of a cloudless day. "The weather isn't suited anyway."

The groom sags in relief. "Very well, mi señora," he says as María turns and strides back into the house, as if it is her choice.

IV

The tapestries, the chairs, the rugs.

María paces the house, reciting to herself the many changes she will make, but soon grows bored. She goes upstairs and lets herself into her husband's rooms, surprised to find them a cluttered version of her own.

A suit of armor poses on a wooden model, the metal polished to a shine.

Another portrait of the viscount himself looms over the hearth, this artist's hand flattering to the point of jest. Andrés's hair rendered a glossy black, his chin as hard and sharp as stone.

A desk sits before the window, a trio of books perched along the back. María takes one up and turns the pages. As a child she had learned to count using lines drawn in the dirt, and to write her own name, common as it is—even that was less a knowing of letters and more a memorized design—but beyond that, there seemed no point.

Now, as she weighs the book in her hand, she wishes she'd had cause to learn. She can tell that it's valuable—leather-bound, the pages full of painted shapes, the edges filigreed with gold—but the lines of ink striped across the paper are nothing but a pretty pattern.

She returns the book to the table and turns to survey the bed.

A carved four-poster frame surrounds the pallet, pillows full of down and blankets hemmed with gold. She climbs up and flings her body across the massive bed, but when she turns her face into the pillows she's met with her husband's smell, sudden and sharp enough to turn her stomach.

María recoils, abandoning the bed as well as the room.

And goes to find her maid.

The servants startle at the sight of the viscountess, bowing and veering out of her way, no doubt wondering if she is lost.

Their quarters are simple compared to the casona's main rooms. The same stone walls, minus the adornments. The rugs worn bare by rushing feet.

María finds Ysabel in the kitchen, elbows resting on the counter, a fistful of cards in one hand and a cup of wine in the other. Across from her, a man—so old that his face is more wrinkle than skin—lays down his own cards as the cook elbows him aside to turn out a loaf of bread.

There is a moment before they see María.

A moment when Ysabel's eyes are not cast down, and the sun catches the strands of light in her braided brown hair and turns it gold. A moment when her expression is unguarded, open, and she looks both tired and amused, one brow arched, and a wry smile tugging at the corner of her mouth.

And then her gaze drifts to the doorway and—

"Mi señora!" Ysabel yelps, nearly spilling her cup. She throws the cards down as if they've burned her, and ducks her head, eyes going to the floor at María's feet. The old man shuffles backward and bows, and the cook stops waving a towel over the bread and looks around as if searching for escape. Finding none, she too goes still.

Eventually, Ysabel chances a look up.

"I'm sorry, mi señora. I thought you would still be sleeping." Her gaze flicks over the half-fastened dress, the ribbons María tried and failed to reach. "You should have called for me."

María thinks of her horse, locked in its stable, and smothers the flare of rage before it spreads. She shakes her head dismissively. "What's this?" she asks, flicking her fingers toward the cards on the counter.

"Nothing," answers the maid quickly. Then, "Only a game."

María grabs hold of this, as if it were a rope.

"Teach me."

"It's called Chinchón."

They have traded the servant quarters for the inner courtyard, two chairs drawn up to a low table. It took several polite invitations, followed by one firmly worded command, to get Ysabel to sit across from María, but now that the maid is seated, her shoulders have begun to loosen.

She lays the cards face up. "There are four *suits*—that's what they're called.

Cups, coins, swords, and clubs. Each card holds a certain number of these things." Ysabel's finger taps the cards as she points this out. "Three cups. Four coins. Five swords. Six clubs."

María's gaze flicks over the many cards, trying to keep up.

"They're beautiful," she says, fingering a delicate illustration. "How did you come by them?"

Color rises in Ysabel's cheeks. "They were a gift. From the count."

Count Olivares. Andrés's father. María lifts a brow. "How generous."

"Yes," says the maid, adding under her breath, "he can be." She sets down a new kind of card. This one has a king holding out his cup. "The highest cards have men on them."

María can see that. There are men holding clubs. Men holding swords. Men holding coins. Men holding cups. "Where are the women?" she asks, and Ysabel only laughs, as if it were a joke.

"We shuffle the cards," explains the maid, gathering them into a pile. "And then, we deal."

She begins to place cards on the table, alternating between María and herself, as she explains the rules. It is a matching game. The goal is to create a series in the same suit. Or a set of the same cards in different suits.

They each take up their hands.

María studies her own set, one finger silently tapping on her skirts as she adds the numbers on her cards while her maid rearranges her own hand.

"Where did you learn to play?" she asks.

Ysabel's gaze flicks up, then down again. She throws away two cards. Draws two more, says at last, "By watching my father."

María studies her maid instead of her hand. She may only just be learning to read cards, but she has always been good at reading other people. There are two parts to every answer. The part that's said, and the part that isn't. Which is how she knows that Ysabel is holding back more than just her cards.

She lays her hand out on the table. So does María. It takes her a moment to count, and realize she has won. She is used to winning, but Ysabel beams, praising her for being such a quick study, and María feels sun-warmed by the words.

"Another?" she asks, and María nods.

Ysabel shuffles and deals again, and as she does, María finds herself studying the girl's hands. The length of her eyelashes. The way she bites her bottom lip when she is thinking, turning the pink flesh red beneath her teeth.

This time, María loses.

For once, she doesn't mind.

She only wants to play again.

V

A fortnight passes in this pleasant way.

By night, María subjects herself to the viscount's attention, but by day, she's left largely to her own devices. Andrés is always busy, though she is never sure with what. Something to do with his lands, and the direction coin is meant to flow, upstream. Honestly, whenever he speaks of work, her mind begins to wander, already planning how she will spend her day once he has gone.

She *does*, technically, obey her husband. She resists the urge to venture out unchaperoned, instead finding ways to amuse herself within the walls.

She takes her meals in different rooms each day, and learns the details of the house by how the light moves across the walls. Has the furniture rearranged in odd ways to suit her whims, the pieces all returned again by the time Andrés gets home.

And restless as María is, at least she is not alone.

She claims Ysabel for company.

At first, she finds excuses to commandeer her maid's time, but soon that proves unnecessary. Ysabel is more than happy to pass the day however her mistress sees fit. And so they do.

Sometimes they walk the whole house, arm in arm, as if preening for suitors instead of statues. Other times, they sprawl across sofas and play cards, or dance barefoot on stone floors, taking turns who leads and who follows. The other servants look on, their mouths set in disapproving lines, but María does not care.

One day she dresses Ysabel in her clothes, ignoring the maid's protests as she fastens the clasp at the collar and binds up her brown hair, pausing only to study the strands that curl along her nape.

When she is done, Ysabel stands, stiff as a doll, in the ornate dress. And then, at last, she gives a careful twirl. "How do I look?"

María stares, because she can, taking in the crimson fabric cinched around the other girl, revealing the curve of her bosom, the divot of her narrow waist. She is not striking, like María. Her looks are much softer, the edges filed smooth. When María grabs her arm she can feel the skin dimple beneath her fingers, as if the girl is made of down.

Ysabel looks lovely, she looks gentle, but above all, she looks like what she is.

The illegitimate daughter of a count.

They have not spoken of it—they do not need to. It is clear enough, in the shape of Ysabel's face, the slope of her cheek, the roundness of her eye. After all, María is confronted by these features every day; their like stares back from every painting, and even if she weren't surrounded by members of the Olivares clan, she has looked into Andrés's face enough times to see the resemblance. To understand that not every one of the count's children earns a portrait on the family walls.

"Well?" presses Ysabel, her voice a nervous flutter.

"You look lovely," says María, "and uncomfortable." And Ysabel smiles and admits that it is far too hot for all these layers, holds out her buttoned wrists, and waits to be set free.

Andrés sags on top of her when he is done.

He rolls over, but makes no move to rise, and María clutches the ruby pendant and waits, thinking, with dread, that he means to spend the night there, in her bed. His body is a quickly cooling thing, plunging toward sleep, while María lies, wide awake, beside him, a sore pulse between her legs, and decides that if she must be kept awake, then he will too. So she rolls toward him.

"What does it feel like?" she wonders aloud.

Andrés mutters something into the pillow, but it hardly constitutes an answer.

"What does it feel like?" she asks again. "When you reach your peak?"

Andrés twists his head on the pillow, brow furrowing at the question. "Why do you ask such things?" And perhaps the scolding in his voice is meant to cow her. But it doesn't.

María props herself on an elbow. "I am by nature curious. Besides," she adds, "I want to know my husband better."

He sighs, looks around the room as if for refuge. Finding none, at last he says, "It is a building pressure. And then, a release."

María hums in thought. "And it seems to bring you pleasure. Yes?"

"Of course."

"Well then," she says, sitting up. "What of mine?"

Andrés looks at her as if she's grown a second head. "Your *pleasure?*" he asks, dismayed.

"Perhaps, if you touched me in other ways," she ventures, fingers drifting almost absently to the nape of her neck.

The viscount's dismay hardens then into something like contempt. "This is a sacred act," he says. "*Your pleasure* is of no consequence."

He rises as he speaks, putting distance between them, as if the very conversation is indecent. As if he did not spend the last half hour buried inside her.

"My body was made to expel," he says. "Yours to receive. And God willing, to grow heirs."

God willing, thinks María when Andrés is gone, and she is straddling a basin, doing her best to wash away his work.

The next day, María declares that they will have a picnic.

They creep into the kitchen stores, like thieves, Ysabel filling a basket with food and María liberating a tankard of wine from the cellar. Together they flee to the far reaches of the western hall—the days are quickly growing hotter, and the stones there are the last to warm, holding fast to the coolness of the night before.

They take refuge in an alcove, lay a blanket on the floor, and gorge themselves on bread and wine and candied figs. When the bowls are empty and the bounty gone, María lies with her head in the other girl's lap, loose hair pooling like a molten pillow in the maid's plain skirts.

A drowsiness rolls over her, her limbs as loose as honey in the heat, as Ysabel runs her fingertips along María's brow and tells her stories of miracles and saints, the stones around them warming as the sun gets high.

Ysabel has a soft and breathy way of speaking, which gives the impression that she is always on the verge of sharing a secret. It is . . . intimate. She smiles easily but never quite laughs, never exhales anything above an airy chuckle, and María decides to make it her mission.

To coax a real sound from Ysabel.

At some point, the maid runs out of words.

At some point, a silence settles over them.

At some point, María looks up into Ysabel's face, studying the freckles in her eyes, the bow of her lips, her gaze lingering so long the maid asks what she is thinking.

And María wants to say that Andrés's hands have never stirred such heat in her.

Wants to say she is still hungry, though her stomach is full.

That she could stay here for a hundred years. So long as Ysabel stayed, too.

"It is so quiet in the house, during the day." Her gaze grazes Ysabel's throat, traces the lines of her collar, the swell of her breasts. "It feels as if the world is empty, except for us."

She reaches up, as if to cup Ysabel's face, draw her closer. The maid catches her hand, folds her own fingers over it, and a brief, beautiful heat flares through María, until Ysabel smiles.

"Just wait," she says, "until you are with child."

The words are cold water.

The heat inside María dies.

Ysabel continues, unaware. "It will not feel so lonely then," she says, but all María can feel is the ghostly weight of her husband's hand on her belly.

Let it be a son.

She swallows hard. She knows, of course, what is expected. She watched Elana's belly began to round, month over month, her body swelling as her face grew thin.

But María has no wish to be a mother. Not yet.

She has just become a wife.

Surely, she should be allowed to enjoy one station before she's forced to occupy another.

Ysabel's fingers are still clasped over hers, but the moment has turned, the alcove too warm, and María tugs free, her hand dropping like a piece of ripened fruit back into her lap.

⌒⌒

And then, one day, María wakes to find the house in tumult.

Andrés stands in the courtyard, giving orders as horses clamber through the gates, pulling carts piled high with furniture and finery.

That is how she learns there is to be a feast.

"In your honor, esposa mía," he says, and María wonders why, if that is true, this is the first she's hearing of it. But he kisses her hand when he says it, good humor bathing him like sunlight, and as she surveys the mountain of deliveries, her mood improves.

It is to be a grand affair—he has invited nobles, yes, but also subjects, vassals from across his lands, a celebration meant to introduce each and every one to his new wife. María asks what *she* can do, to help prepare the house, but he insists it is all being handled. She has only to be ready, to welcome their guests. And of course, to receive his parents, when they come from León. He says this last as if it's no great feat. She will soon discover otherwise.

The Count and Countess Olivares arrive just after noon.

Andrés leads them in, his father at his sleeve and his mother on his arm, the former flushed and the latter looking faint from heat.

María stands at the doors, ready to greet her new in-laws with a practiced smile, if not modest then at least beneficent, but they brush past her as if she is a ghost, take no notice until Andrés steers them back in her direction.

"Mother, Father, allow me to present . . . my wife."

María hates them instantly.

They speak of her as if she isn't there, or worse, as if she is, and her presence doesn't matter.

"Let's see this commoner you *had* to have," declares the count as he takes her in, his gaze like a hand pawing at her dress. She is reminded of the men who passed through Santo Domingo over the years, the way their heads turned as she grew into her looks, but the count's is brazen, in a way that makes her chafe. "I will admit," he says, wetting his bottom lip, "there is something to her."

"Looks fade," says the countess, who was clearly no great beauty. Her vision is failing now, giving her a permanent squint. "And that *hair*."

María looks to her husband, but he does not come to her defense.

"You must be weary, from the ride," he says, guiding his parents to the stairs. "You should rest before the feast."

By dusk, the house is full to bursting.

The whole estate has come alive, the rooms all lit by torches, a constant procession of horses pouring through the open gate.

Upstairs, Ysabel brushes María's hair until it shines, spends the better part of an hour piling and pinning the copper mass above her head, before trapping it beneath a net of pearls. More than once, María tries to make idle chat, but it is clear her maid's mind is somewhere else. Between the way her fingers tremble as she sets the pins, and the way she hardly answers, María might as well be talking to a pane of glass.

Not even the dress can lift her sinking mood. It is extravagant, expensive, even laid out on the bed, a heap of lush green velvet beside a dozen lengths of white silk ribbon and a variety of jewels. She is bound into it, layer by layer, weighed down with cloth and gem, despite the stifling summer heat.

Ysabel steadies her as she steps into her slippers, studies her from every angle and declares that she looks beautiful in a breathy tone that makes María flush.

And yet, when her husband meets her on the stairs, and says the same, the words stir nothing in her.

Andrés himself is dressed in the crest of his Order, the crimson cross trimmed in white fur, and she is reminded of the day she first saw him, mounted with the caravan, and thought, *Yes*, thought, *That will do.*

He takes María's arm and guides her down, into the crowded hall, and as he leads her through the house, the heads all turn. They stare, outright, the many guests, expressions ranging from the curious to the appraising, the approving to the greedy.

And yet, she thinks darkly, *I could not ride my horse.*

But of course, she knows, this is different—*he* is there, her husband, his arm linked with hers as if they are two lengths of chain. She is beautiful, and bound to him, an object on display.

Andrés introduces her, but every time María tries to say hello, or thank you, or simply to make pleasant conversation, his grip tightens on her arm or waist, his meaning clear. She is not there to speak. Only to be seen. He does not even name her in the introductions, calls her only *the viscountess*, or *my wife*.

And María quickly comes to understand—the feast has not been thrown in her honor, but in his.

A tour of victory. A celebration of his conquest.

After that, she lets the names and faces roll over her like water. There is no point in catching hold.

Andrés leads her into the great hall, where tables have been set edge to edge to edge, so that they run like rivers down the length of the room, heaped with serving trays and carafes of wine. At their head a single table waits, raised upon a makeshift step.

There María takes her seat, and Andrés stands, his voice booming through the hall as he welcomes friends and subjects both into his home, invites them all to share this marriage feast.

The chairs scrape back, the guests all sit, and somewhere, musicians begin to play, the cheerful tune tangling with the sound of so many people in one place.

María finds her husband on one side, and his mother on the other.

Andrés takes her hand and lifts his glass, and she thinks he means to toast her, but he is only pausing to admire the color of the wine before he drinks. The countess, meanwhile, picks at her food, and finds nothing to her liking. She declares the pheasant overcooked, the sauce too rich. She complains about the music, which is by turns too soft and then too loud, insists the instruments are out of tune.

María spears a piece of meat, and scans the hall.

The servants of the house have been given leave to stay and celebrate, so long as they sit with the vassals, not the lords. It takes her a moment to spot Ysabel, at the far end of the hall. She has changed into a finer dress, and María wonders who helped her close the clasps she couldn't reach.

They share a look.

And then a bony hand clutches at María's sleeve.

The countess has run out of other things to hate, and now those beady eyes narrow to slits as she squints not at María's face, but at the copper hair piled so carefully atop her head, beneath its net of pearls.

"There was a cat that lived in the stable," says the countess, "when Andrés was young." She leans in close, too close, till María can see the flecks of food between the woman's teeth. "It was a decent-looking creature, white and brown, and my youngest son has always had a fondness for such things. So we left it be. Until one day, when it had ginger kittens. Such an awful shade."

The countess pauses, and María thinks of leaning in, of lowering her voice, of telling the countess how her son cannot take his eyes off her hair, how he likes to wrap whole lengths around his hand every time he fucks her.

Instead she asks, "What did you do?"

"What must be done with wretched things. I put them in a sack, and drowned them."

María knows the words are meant to make her feel small, knows that she should go ahead, pretend to shrink beneath them. But she doesn't.

"Well then," she says brightly, "good thing I am not with child yet." She reaches for her wine. "And when I'm blessed with heirs, I'll not ask you to bathe them."

The countess recoils a little, and for the first time all night, María smiles down into her cup.

The next day, she rises late.

The room is dark, the curtains still drawn. How strange, that Ysabel has not come to fling them back and drag her mistress out of bed.

María rubs away the veil of sleep, and dresses in a simple shift and robe, her body sore from hours bound within the heavy dress.

Outside, the only sound is the tread of horses, the rattle of departing carts, and she marvels, as she moves through the house, that all evidence of the feast has been so quickly swept away. The floors have been washed, the windows and doors thrown wide, the house returned to its usual state.

She finds Andrés dining alone, last night's good humor replaced by a hung-over scowl, a tonic at his elbow and a parchment in his hand.

María takes her seat and looks around, relieved that the count and countess are not there. She asks after them, adding, "I do hope they have not fallen ill."

"Not at all," he assures her. His father has gone for a walk. His mother prefers to take meals in her room. But he has mistaken her question for concern.

"Rest assured," he says, "you will see plenty more of them."

María's hand tightens on her cup. "Really?"

Andrés sets aside the paper. On it, she sees the red wax seal, the indented cross. "I have been called to action."

"How long will you be gone?" she asks, her mood instantly improving.

Andrés tells her that he is not sure, and María nods, already dreaming of her independence, how she will command the house in his absence, how she will pass the days when there is no one to obey.

"Well, do not worry," she assures him. "I will look after the estate."

A sound tears through the room, as bright and vicious as a slap. It takes María a moment to understand that it is coming from Andrés himself.

He is *laughing*.

"You? Stay here?" His amusement bounces off the walls, even once he's stopped. "Impossible." He laces his hands in his lap. "You are a woman. A wife. You cannot live *alone*."

María feels her hopes go leaden. Her visions turn to stone.

"Where am I to go?" she asks.

He waves his hand, as if the question is a gnat. "To León, of course."

To León. With the count and countess.

"If I must stay with your parents," she says, annoyance spreading like cracks, "why can they not stay *here*?"

Here, where there is space to breathe. Where there are quiet corners to be found. Where there are cherries growing hidden in the grove.

Andrés only shakes his head. "My mother has always enjoyed the city more."

Having met the countess, it's hard to imagine her enjoying *anything*. María's mind is still fighting to catch up as he rattles off the details, and it's obvious he's had time to think this through, though it's the first *she's* hearing of it.

She is to leave with his parents the next day.

She is to *live* with them.

To provide them company when he's away, and be his prize again when he returns.

They will share her, he says happily, as if she is a cup to be passed around.

"Do not make that face, querida. It is the best outcome for everyone."

Everyone? she thinks, fighting the sudden urge to break something.

She takes a long, slow breath. All is not lost.

"At least I will have Ysabel."

But her husband shakes his head. "That would be . . . inappropriate."

María's stomach lurches.

"The countess doesn't care for her," he adds, but there's more beneath the words. Andrés knows, she is sure, about his father and her maid, the matter of her lineage. "Besides," he brushes on, "there is no need. My parents have servants of their own. You will have one of them."

"I don't want *one of them*," she snaps. "I want my own."

He shrugs and says, "She is already gone."

María stills, remembering her darkened room. The curtains never drawn.

"One of my vassals took an interest in her at the feast," he continues absently. "He asked for her hand, and I gave it to him."

Gave. As if she were a pretty vase. A well-upholstered chair.

"It will be an improvement in her station."

The room feels like it's tipping. María presses her hands into the table to steady herself. There is a serving fork balanced on a nearby tray. She wonders how much force it would take to drive the tines into his head.

Instead, she forces her hand to her throat, grasps the ruby pendant there.

"Don't worry," he says, as the edges of the jewel cut into her palm, "this will be our home again, once you have given me an heir."

A bead of blood runs down María's wrist.

Her husband does not even notice.

ALICE

(D. 2019)

I

When Alice wakes the day after the party, her first and only thought is this:

The world is far too fucking bright.

Sunlight splinters through the dorm's cheap curtains, attacking the room with daggers of white. Alice sits up, and immediately wishes she hadn't. She groans, a feral, miserable sound, and slumps back down, shivering as her cheek hits the damp pillow. Her wet hair must have soaked in overnight and even though the hair dried, the down-filled cushion didn't, and is now a damp and lumpy block under her head.

Her skull is throbbing and her mouth is dry and she is unbearably hungover.

(The first time she ever got drunk, it was on a bottle of sherry Catty swiped from the pub, shared on the picnic bench out back, and it had gone down sweet and come up sour, a headache so fierce Alice could feel it behind her eyes, and this is ten times worse.)

It takes her a moment to remember where she is, another to remember where she was last night, a third to remember that she wasn't alone. She rolls over, half hoping and half dreading that she'll find the violet-haired girl curled up beside her in the bed, but it's empty.

There's no sign of Lizbeth, either, her bed still made, as if she hasn't been back.

Alice presses her palms into her eye sockets and tries to think. There's something there, a memory just out of reach, something between collapsing into bed and now, something just beyond the ache inside her skull, but she's still grasping in the dark when she hears the sound.

A soft drumming, like fingers on a desk.

"*When I was a child / I got lost in the woods,*" sings an eerie voice, and it takes her a second to realize it's just her phone's alarm, the song she programmed coming from the shelf beside her bed. Alice slams her hand down on the screen, killing the alarm, and that's when she notices the purple Post-it Note tacked to the lampshade above.

Three words, written in a slanted cursive.

Goodbye, Alice.
xo Lottie

And even with the sickness rolling through her skin, she feels a wave of disappointment at the sorry little note. There's no *call me,* no number, not even a *see you round.* Just *Goodbye.* So formal. So finite.

Alice squeezes her eyes shut again and the night before comes blinking back, like a lightbulb on the fritz before it steadies; fragments of music and rain and tangled hands, and heat, and if Alice didn't feel like death, she'd probably play the whole thing over in her head, not to relive the good, but to assess the damage. Trace over everything she said and did, trying to decide if she'd made a fool of herself, what her classmates would think. Play out the scene with the girl in her bed—*Lottie*—until the pleasure of it soured, replaced by shame over the sounds she made, the sheer, mortifying abandon of being that other, reckless Alice.

But embarrassment requires energy and she has none, and it doesn't matter if she made an idiot of herself because Lottie is gone.

And Alice can't stop shivering.

At some point in her sleep she must have kicked the comforter off, because the bulk is now piled down around her feet, and she's naked except for the scratchy sheet tangled around her legs and torso. The once-white cotton is dappled with pale purple splashes (the last dregs of hair dye, a watery ghost).

There's another stain on the sheets.

The unmistakable red-brown of dry blood.

Alice frowns, touches the place between her legs, wondering if that's what this is—not a hangover, just the world's worst PMS—but her fingers come away clean. And anyway, the stain isn't a smudge, or a smear. It's three perfect drops, like someone dripped paint, and looking at it gives her the weirdest sense, a kind of mental vertigo, like she's leaning over the place where a memory should be.

But it's not there.

Nothing to grasp. Nothing to hold on to.

She peels off the sheet, still searching for the source of the blood, and yelps at the sight of half a dozen bruises blotting her pale skin, before she touches one and realizes it's not a welt or a wound, but the remnant of a kiss. Pomegranate lipstick dotting her thigh, her stomach, the inside of one wrist.

Alice shivers, less at the memory than the fact she's naked and cold, and feels like total shit.

She looks around, searches for something in reach because the thought of getting up is just too much right now. The old oversized T-shirt she normally wears to bed is draped on the desk chair and she tugs it on, shaking from that smallest effort as she hauls the comforter up, and curls beneath the blessed dark and tries to sleep—

Her head pounding—

Like a fist against a door—

Bang bang bang—

Until it slams shut—

So hard it bounces in its frame and—

Alice takes off, nine years old, all elbows and knees, bare feet slipping in the marshy grass as she tries to catch up with her sister.

Because Catty is running away.

Not *away* away (because if Catty were serious, she'd have headed for the train station instead of the hilly slope at the edge of their yard), but away from the house, and the dinner, and Eloise Martin.

Eloise, who walked into their lives a year ago, and upended everything.

Eloise, who hails from Edinburgh and has an accent so soft it might as well be English, who never raises her voice, and who once made the fatal error of telling Catty to "call me whatever you like."

An offer that Catty put to rude use until Dad intervened.

Eloise, who was apparently Dad's childhood sweetheart, way back before he went to uni and met Mum. A fact they just learned about that night at dinner, because Eloise has friends visiting from Leith, and while dessert was cooling on the counter, she took Dad's hand and said that maybe they were meant to be, which Catty took as Eloise saying their mum *wasn't*, and did that mean that Mum was *meant* to die, and no, of course that wasn't what Eloise was saying, but it was too late, the chair was scraping back, and the door was slamming, and Catty was off.

It's the second time she's run—the first was after Dad came home from that first date, looking almost happy, like the lights were finally coming on again inside his house, and it was such a relief—or so Alice thought—but Catty saw only a betrayal. As if there was an unspoken agreement that when they buried Mum, the grave would follow them home, a six-foot hollow in the bed, a hole at the table, a plot of land left fallow for their entire lives, and then Dad broke his word by planting something there.

The first time Catty ran, Alice didn't go after her, but only because it was dark, and her sister was gone before Alice could see which way she went. She had cried herself sick, and when Catty finally showed back up the next morning, Alice made her promise—not to *stay*, but at least, next time, to wait, to take her with her.

But she's twelve now to Alice's nine, and *fast*—so fast that Alice can't catch up, the distance between widening a little more with every stride.

"Catty!" she calls out.

(Catty, not Catherine, or Cathy—Alice couldn't make the *th* sound when she was small, so it came out Catty, and then one day their neighbor Mary Galford tutted at the name, said it wasn't nice, so of course her sister went and looked up the meaning—*mean, nasty, spiteful*—after which she gleefully declared she'd answer to that and nothing else.)

"Slow down!" shouts Alice now as Catty lopes up the hill, but of course, she doesn't slow down, doesn't look back, just tells her to "Catch up!"

Catch up, as if that's easy, as if she doesn't have three years on Alice.

Three years that don't feel like much, not unless she's running. Or the subject of Mum comes up, which it doesn't—not directly, but it's always *there*, like a hazard, a pothole they have to skirt, and every time they hit it, the years between them open up.

The difference between missing and memory.

Because Catty remembers their mum.

And Alice doesn't.

It's not her fault—she was only five when Sarah Moore died, and the few memories she has are mostly smudges, like old dreams.

Here is what she *does* remember: the sadness that hung over the house like a shroud, the sound of her dad weeping into a dishcloth when she was supposed to be in bed, the way his shoulders bowed beneath a weight no one could see but everyone felt.

The way the air in the house got lighter after he met Eloise.

But still, Catty is too fast.

She crests the hill, and vanishes, and a strange terror grips Alice, that she's crossed some invisible threshold, one long stride carrying her forward, out of Hoxburn, out of the world, and by the time Alice scrambles, breathless, to the top, she's convinced Catty will be gone.

But she isn't.

Alice sees her, a dozen strides down the hill's far side, fetched up against the low stone wall like it's a finish line, one that holds instead of breaking.

(The hills around Hoxburn are dotted with sheep and crisscrossed with dozens of low stone walls that always look as if they're about to crumble but never do, and for a long time Alice assumed it was some kind of magic, or imagined that the walls went deep, deep beneath the ground and that's why they never fell, but now she knows that there's a mason who walks the walls once a season and patches them up.)

Alice slows, gasping for breath.

Catty's back is turned, but even from here she can see how hard her sister's gripping the wall, her knuckles going white, and Alice is sure one of them will break—the rock or her fingers, she doesn't know which—so she starts forward, ready to pry her sister's hand away. But Catty hears her coming, and lets go, scrubbing a palm across her cheeks.

"Hey, Bones," she says.

It's a nickname, going back to the time when they shared a room, a bed, when Alice liked to sleep with her knees curled into her chest, so some sharp edge was always poking Catty in the side, the back, and she would shove a pillow between them, muttering that Alice was all bones.

"Needed some fresh air."

Catty slumps forward, resting her elbows on the wall, and Alice pads forward like her sister's not a girl at all, but one of those nervy dogs that is always on the verge of startling.

"It's nicer out here anyway," she adds, even though it's not, it's cold, and windy, and wet, and there was cake inside, chocolate with vanilla icing.

But Alice only nods, and says, "Yeah," running her palm along the top of the wall.

(This one isn't on their property, but that didn't stop Catty from declaring it hers—"See, right there, a C stamped into one of the stones"—and Eloise once explained to Alice that it's because the stones came from the old church before the town built a new one, and that letter was just a maker's mark, but she didn't tell Catty because it doesn't hurt anyone, to let her have it.)

Her sister swings her legs over the wall, and Alice climbs up beside her, shivering as the cold soaks like damp into her jeans. The sun's going down, shadows growing dense around them, but up here they can see most of Hoxburn—which admittedly isn't much, but it looks even smaller now, and kind of quaint, like it could fit inside a snow globe, or an open hand, and Catty must be having one of her psychic moments because she lifts her hand and squints, and Alice can picture her cupping the whole town in her palm.

Catty closes her fist. Lets it fall.

She sighs, and then stretches out along the wall like it's a bed, and it's too narrow for them to lie side by side, so Alice twists round and lies so they're head to head. Cheek to cheek.

Sisters, staring up at the darkening sky.

On paper, they look the same.

Fair skin, blond hair, blue eyes.

But Alice's skin is too pale, burns in summer, where Catty's is dusted with freckles. Alice's hair is a lifeless shade, Catty's the color of melted butter. Alice's blue eyes are tinged with gray and green, Catty's the cold, clear shade of winter mornings.

They don't talk about the dinner, or the fact that when Catty bolted, it was Eloise who stood up first, meaning to go after her, but Dad caught her hand and told her not to bother, to let the daft girl go.

They don't talk at all.

Alice sucks a breath, wishes she knew what to say to make Catty happy, or at least to make her hurt less. But she knows that the *wrong* words will make things even worse, and she's still searching for the right ones when Catty pulls out her phone and shoves an earbud in one ear. She offers the other one to Alice and taps the screen and the music comes spilling out, and Alice exhales.

She knows the song, recognizes it just by that opening beat, which isn't a drum, exactly, but the primal thud of a palm striking wood, a summons. It's always made Alice think of the Pied Piper, it has the same strange effect of pulling you along in its wake. Sure enough Catty starts rapping her knuckles on the wall in time with the beat, and Alice feels her own pulse work to match the rhythm.

It is stripped bare, this song, a simple, hypnotizing thing. The beat never rises, but after eight counts, a girl's voice kicks in, haunting and high, carrying the air of incantation.

"When I was a child / I got lost in the woods
The trees parted for me / made such a clear trail
Then closed up behind me / now I'm turned around
Been trying so long now / to find a way out."

They don't sing along, it's not that kind of song, would never show up on someone's karaoke list. Instead, they simply lie there, and let it wash over them.

"The woods want to keep me / the ground wants to eat me
The trees want to hold me / can't find my way home.
The night's getting dark now / the air's getting cold
So tired of walking / can't find my way home."

The music unfurls over them like a tent, and it isn't comfortable, bits of loose rock dig into Alice's back, but this is an enchanted moment, and she knows better than to ruin it by moving. It's almost over now, anyway, the drumbeat slowing like a tired heart as the voice becomes higher and softer.

"I live in these woods now / the trees hold me close

The voice is a whisper as it gets to the last line.

"No longer lost now / I found my way—"

But before the last word, Catty taps the screen and the song starts over. Alice fidgets. By now, the sun's gone down, the shadows growing dense, and she's cold, and Eloise and her friends are probably gone, and they really should go back, go home, but when Alice brings it up, Catty says *Yeah.*

Says *Sure.*

Says *We will, we will, as soon as the song is done.*

And Alice wants to believe her, so she stays there, sprawled on the cooling rock beside her sister as the music unravels again. Holds her breath and waits, sure that if the voice can just get out that final word, the spell will break, the world will come unstuck, and Catty will agree to get up with her, to come home.

But the end comes around again, and Alice knows what's going to happen, and sure enough, when the voice hits the last line, Catty taps the screen and starts the song over. And over. And over.

"No longer lost now / I found my way—"

"No longer lost now / I found my way—"

"No longer lost now / I found my way—"

Alice hits the phone, silencing the alarm a second before the singer says the word *home.*

"Bloody hell," says Lizbeth from the doorway. "I thought you were dead."

Alice groans. The sun is gone, but her skull is still pounding, and her jaw aches as if she's been clenching her teeth in her sleep.

"That alarm's been going off for ages," adds her roommate curtly. "I had to study in the common room."

Alice frowns, head spinning. She's always been a light sleeper, usually wakes up somewhere around the second verse, but she was buried somewhere deep, had to climb up through layer after layer of sleep, the panic rising as some distant part of her heard the lyrics passing by, carrying her close to the end.

She stares at the screen now, trying to understand how it's somehow still nine o'clock, until she realizes that it's now nine *at night* (she must have nudged the AM/PM button when she turned it off before) which means she's gone and slept through all her classes and now she has a whole new reason to feel sick.

(Catty used to ditch class all the time, but Alice never missed a day of school unless she was well and truly ill, and even then, she made sure she could borrow someone's notes so she wouldn't fall behind, and now, three weeks into her first year of four, the professors will have it out for her, and and and—)

Alice is well along the panic spiral when she remembers that it's still Sunday.

She heaves a strangled breath and slumps back into bed.

"No offense," adds Lizbeth, hooking her backpack on the edge of her chair, which is never a good way to start, "but you look wretched."

Alice tries to answer, but her throat is full of cobwebs and her skull is full of rocks and her tongue is a useless mass inside her mouth, so it takes two tries to manage a bone-dry "Thanks."

"Are you ill?" she asks, but there's no real caring in the question, only a prodding worry and a measure of distrust. She might as well be poking Alice with a stick.

"I'm dying," answers Alice, because hangovers require a measure of hyperbole, and because she has truly never felt so awful. The words come scraping out, leaving a horrible taste in her mouth, and Lizbeth starts packing a bag and explaining that she really can't afford to be getting sick, with her course-load being what it is, and it's no problem, really, she will stay with Jeremy.

(Jeremy, who was assigned to show Lizbeth around campus when she came to visit that spring, after she'd been let in, and "he must have been smitten" because they kept in touch all summer, and now that they're in the same place they're attached at the hip—"making up for lost time" she likes to add, as if he's been in a war and not studying biology).

The phone slides between Alice's fingers as she starts to shiver again, and she wishes there were a kettle in the room, but she hasn't got around to buying one and Lizbeth is one of those rare English monsters who for some reason favors coffee over tea, and insists on getting it made fresh by someone else.

Lizbeth scurries out, and Alice thinks of folding herself back into the nest of her duvet, but her whole body aches from lying down so long, and what Alice really wants in that moment is El. (She resists the urge to call her *Mum*, even now, even just in her head, Catty's glare pinging like a pebble against the side of her skull.) Dad was never any good when his daughters were sick, all awkward head pats and *there, theres*, but El always knew exactly what was needed, a hot water bottle or a ginger tea, a day in bed or a bit of fresh air.

Fresh air.

The thought suddenly feels better than lying in this sweat-soaked bed in this too-small room, the air around her close and stale. Alice flings the covers off, gets to her feet, instantly regretting the sudden rise as her limbs tremble and the whole room dips like a cheap ride. She squeezes her eyes shut and waits for space to steady before she attempts the daunting task of getting dressed.

Her jeans are sitting in a pile on the floor, still rain damp, which is just as well because the thought of anything tight against her skin makes her nauseous. Alice fumbles in the drawers for a pair of sweats and an oversized jumper. Catches her face in the mirror on the closet door and pauses long enough to see the remains of last night's makeup streaked black around her eyes, making them look sunken, hollow, the irises fever bright, the only time they look pure blue. Her hair has dried wild, a gorse-like tangle, her fringe askew, but she doesn't have the energy to scrape it back—her arms feel too heavy when she tries—so she settles for scrubbing at her face with the cuff of the jumper, and leaving it at that.

Alice stumbles out into the suite common room, and she must truly look as shit as she feels, because Rachel physically startles at the sight of her, and Jana looks up from the sofa and says, "Uh-oh, do you need a burrito or a bucket?"

Her stomach twists, the way it does when part of you is hungry and the other part is sick, and your insides can't agree on what should go down and what should come up, so Alice keeps her mouth clamped shut as she shakes her head, and soldiers out into the hall.

Students pass, their voices echoing, too loud, inside her battered skull, and twice on the stairs she has to stop and brace herself against the banister. Each time she looks down and half expects to see the trail she and Lottie made the night before.

But it was water, only water, and has dried to nothing now, leaving only Alice, who sighs and shoves open the door, hoping a bit of fresh air will set her straight.

MARÍA

(D. 1532)

I

León, Spain
1531

The roof is full of odd angles.

Stretches of harsh light, and crevices of shade in which to hide—if one is reckless enough to climb through the open window and brave the slanted pitch.

María has always been reckless.

It is late morning, and she is lounging in the shadowed crux, the tiles warm beneath her bare feet. If she were to lean forward and peer over the side, she would see the street, two floors below.

Sometimes, when she is bored, she lets her bare toes skim the roof's edge, simply to feel the thrill of it, the chance, however small, of falling.

"María!" calls the countess shrilly. A sound so high and flat it could be mistaken for a bird's, and so she pretends it is, and makes no move to answer. Instead, she pulls at a loose thread on her sleeve, winding it slowly around her finger as she imagines the old hag sitting in the rooms below her own, head flung back as she caws upward at the ceiling, her impatience turning more to ire with every moment no one answers.

María has learned to find joy where she can.

It has been nearly two years since she was forced to leave her estate for the crowded quarters of León, and entombed inside her in-laws' house. Two years, in which Andrés has come and gone a dozen times. Two years in which María has only grown more striking, her looks sharpening like a blade against a whetstone, while every time Andrés leaves, he seems to come back rounder, softer, cheeks ruddier with drink. And where once she was . . . if not truly attracted to her husband, then at least ambivalent—now she finds herself *repelled*.

By his breath, stale and hot against her neck.

By the clumsy pawing of his hands, and the scrape of his beard.

By the way he still insists on wrapping her hair around his fist as if it is a rope, a rein. More and more she thinks of cutting it off. Her hair. His hand. Depending on the day.

But what disgusts her most of all is the way his gaze goes first and last and *always* to her stomach.

So far, she has been lucky.

So far—but then, luck has a way of running out. Her breath still catches with relief every time she feels that telltale ache inside her, every time she starts to bleed. The household mourns, and privately, she celebrates.

"María!" shrieks the countess, and this time the sound is closer, accompanied by the tapping of a cane on stone. The countess has clearly left the comfort of her chair and is making her way upstairs.

María sighs, abandoning her hiding place. She climbs back into her rooms, and takes up a bit of sewing right before the countess enters.

"María," snaps the woman in the doorway. "Did you not hear me calling?"

She looks up from the patch of cloth (she has made ten stitches in as many months, not that the countess knows it). "When? Just now?" She sets the ruse aside and rises. "Apologies, señora mía," she coos as she goes to the wretched woman. "You must call louder next time."

The countess scowls. Her vision has continued to grow worse, her eyes reduced to small dark pits from constant squinting. But just when she thinks the countess truly in the dark, the old woman's head will swivel, and she'll comment on the cut or color of María's dress, her shawl, her posture, her hair.

This last is her obsession.

She finds the color by turns offensive, ugly, and unchaste.

María supposes she'll know when the woman is truly blind when she fails to comment on it. In the meantime, the countess sucks her teeth whenever María leaves the copper mass uncovered.

"*Modesty*," she warns, gripping the word as if it were a riding crop.

And so, despite the scorching heat, María reaches for a veil. She takes her time to wrap it round, while the countess shifts impatiently, tapping her cane against the rug.

"You could have sent a maid," María says, as if she did not hear the pad of footsteps searching every room.

"I did," answers the countess curtly. "They could not find you."

"How strange," she muses, recalling the footsteps, the servants' frantic searching, as she offers the woman her arm. The brittle fingers wrap like a manacle around her wrist. Andrés may be away for weeks, but his parents have gladly taken up the role of jailers. They keep her shut up in the house.

María is angry. She is annoyed. But most of all, she is *achingly* bored.

None of the servants know how to play cards, and they are kept too busy to be taught, rushing about as they do to serve the count and countess. She is visited, now and then, by friends—if one can call them that—young wives and daughters of good standing, chosen for her by her husband's family. They come, and circle round her in the courtyard, these dull girls who talk and talk and talk of nothing, or worse, talk only of children, half of them rubbing their rounded bellies as they prattle on. María suspects the countess chose them for their fertility, as if the condition might prove catching.

The only time she is allowed to venture *out* is in the company of the countess, escorting the old crone to the only place she truly loves: the weekly market.

"Pick up your feet," snaps the countess as they reach the stairs. "At this rate, we'll be left with scraps."

María thinks, briefly, of letting go, perhaps giving the hag a push, but it is a short flight, only eight steps. Hardly enough to break a neck.

Outside, the city is full and foul, too many people in too little space.

The street beneath her feet is slick with muck and grime, and the air smells of shit and bricks. It makes her long for the swept stone halls of the casona, the olive groves and spacious courtyards.

There are surely nice corners somewhere, tucked like secrets in the massive sprawl, but María has never been given leave to find them. And so, she's left with this—the crowded, cart-filled road, and the gnarled fingers clutching birdlike at her sleeve, talons leaving dents on her fair skin.

At first, she could not fathom her mother-in-law's love for such a place, but she soon learned: the Countess Olivares trades in two things, misery and gossip, and the market brings her both. There is so much she can complain about—the smell, the people, the weather, to name a few—and she attends the market less for the vendors and more for the stories they collect for her.

Have you heard? Did you know? Yes, a second boy. No, a stable hand!

The countess is a crow, collecting shiny bits of talk, and the other birds in town flock to her like magpies with their offerings.

They reach the market, and María leads her husband's mother between the stalls, describing details the woman can no longer see. It is a servant's job, but apparently *the servants never do it right*, and María craves the air, fetid though it is, so she submits to the role of well-dressed walking stick. Hardly the life she dreamed of for herself when she scanned the men on horses and tried to choose which one would carry her away.

She slows before a stand of candied fruit, mouth watering at the sight of plums dusted with sugar, but the countess drags her on, insisting that such indulgence will pollute her humors. And, invariably, the subject turns to her lack of children, and why she is not trying hard enough to please her husband.

"Our seed is strong," insists the brutal bitch, and so the fault must be with *her,* and not with Andrés, who is often too drunk to know when he is between María's legs and not inside her. Three pumps, maybe four, before he spills his seed, strong as it may be, into the sheets.

And she feels nothing but relief.

María feels no maternal urge, no envy when she sees a babe swept up into a mother's arms. Everyone insists it is her *purpose,* and it drives her mad, the idea that the shape of her body determines the shape her life must take.

That her beauty is something she is expected to pass on instead of keep.

That anything she makes will thrive while she is left to wither.

And while she cannot stop her husband from coming to her bed, it is one thing to be stormed, and another to be conquered—the difference between a brief invasion and a long-term siege.

"I told you not to marry her."

The words draw her back. Sometimes the countess, trapped in her fog, mistakes María for her son, and the rantings take on a bolder note.

"A woman like that is the kind you bed, not wed, Andrés. She's not good stock, and here is your proof. Two years, and her womb is bare. I did warn you, didn't I? There is something rotten . . ."

María lets the countess ramble on, does nothing to remind the hag that it's not Andrés's arm she clings to. No, instead, she imagines sharing her *own* thoughts.

"Did you know," she would say brightly, "that sometimes I think of the cemetery plot where you will lie, beneath all that dirt and stone, and it brings me joy. And if by some unlucky spot I ever get with child, I will take them there, and let them frolic on your bones."

She smiles to herself and leads her mother-in-law down another row.

And that is when María sees the widow.

It is not the same one she met ten years before. It cannot be.

And yet.

María feels her balance tipping forward. A graceless step. She tries to counter it; her body halts so suddenly that the countess hisses at her side. "What has gotten into you?"

María says nothing, only stares.

The widow stands out like a spot of ink before the stall, bundled as she is in the same heavy shades of gray, covered head to toe despite the heat, her face shrouded by a gauzy veil, her hands hidden beneath gloves.

María has not thought of the widow much over the years, and yet, the sight of this uncanny echo here, in the markets of León, leaves her with a strange light-headedness. For an instant, she is ten again, standing in the copse of trees, the widow's blue eyes blazing, a gloved hand curled around her wrist. *Run home.*

Ahead of them, the widow buys nothing. Only passes a parcel to the merchant and withdraws, slipping back into the crowd.

María wants to go after her, but the countess is a weighted chain. She scans the rows.

"Oh," she says, feigning interest, "these are lovely." She leads the countess to a table across from the stall, explaining that she'd like to find another scarf. "Something more *modest,*" she adds, leaving the woman to pick over the fabric as she turns to face the merchant, bidding him good day.

"There was a woman here just now," she ventures, once the niceties are done. "Dressed all in gray."

For a fleeting second, she fears that the figure was not a woman at all, but a ghost, that he will shake his head, and she will be left haunted by the sight.

But thankfully the merchant nods. "The widow, yes."

"You know her, then?" María brightens, something flaring hot in her for the first time in years. Hope. "I saw her drop a glove and would like to give it back. Do you know where she lives?"

The merchant shakes his head, and the fragile flame gutters, until he adds, "But I know where you can find her." He points to a narrow road just off the square, explains that the widow owns an apothecary down the lane.

"María?" calls the countess.

"How sad," the merchant muses, "to be widowed so young, and so devout, to be shrouded still, with her husband gone more than a year." There is a hungry gleam in his eye. "Surely God is satisfied by now . . ."

"María," snaps the countess, flapping her hand like a pennant in the wind. She excuses herself, returning to the woman's side.

"I'm right here," she hisses, forgetting herself a moment as the talons sink into her sleeve. Her heart races as she scans the market for an alley. An escape. The countess begins to talk of going home when María spies a familiar neck of pearls.

"Oh look," she says, turning the old woman round. "It is Baroness Artiz!"

She steers the countess toward the noblewoman, who has sought refuge in the shade, fanning herself while her maid shops.

"Countess!" says the baroness, rallying. "It has been too long."

They are just pleasantries. Artiz is a frequent visitor at the Olivares house, and her taste for gossip rivals the countess's own.

Sure enough, the next words out her mouth are: "Have you heard about señor Riva's son?"

María lets the baroness take the countess from her, as if she is a parcel.

"No, not his eldest, the middle son. He was to be wed this month, to the Perezes's first, Sofia—yes, the lovely one, and sweet as well—but he absconded with her sister!"

The countess gasps, and María chooses that moment to interrupt.

"Señora mía," she says gently. "If you don't mind, there is a shop nearby I'd like to visit."

The countess bristles at the interruption. "A shop?"

"An apothecary."

"Oh dear, are you unwell?" asks the Baroness Artiz, nose twitching as she tries to sniff out news.

"Not at all," says María quickly. "Only, I have not yet been *blessed*." She touches her stomach when she says it, hopes the countess wants a grandson more than she wants to spite her. The countess purses her lips, and María can see her weighing the two, but it's Baroness Artiz who tips the scale.

"Come," she says, hooking the countess's arm through hers. "I haven't gotten to the best part. Walk with me, and I will tell you *everything*."

As they stroll away, María feels lighter than she has in years.

Then the countess twists her head and calls out, "Don't be long!"

The words echo and die without reaching their target.

María is already gone.

II

Something in María loosens as she steps into the widow's shop.

It is cooler than she expected, a welcome reprieve from the glaring day outside.

"Close the door behind you," comes a soft, melodic voice. "The herbs prefer it cold and dark."

María obeys, and is plunged into a disorienting wall of black, a shadow so thick it leaves her briefly blind. She blinks, and as her eyes adjust she can make out the bundled sprigs that hang from the ceiling, the variety of jars and pots shelved along the walls, a pale mortar and pestle sitting on a low table.

The place smells damp and dry at once. Sweet and citrus, spiced and earthy.

It smells like the stone floor of the western alcove, like the tincture brewed by the cook at the inn, like a palm full of cherry pits.

"Can I help you?"

María turns, and there she is.

Not a stranger, but the woman she met all those years ago. Her veil tucked up, revealing the smooth, pale slopes of her face, the sharp point of her chin, fair hair falling in a plait, and eyes a shocking blue.

Ten years, and María begins to doubt herself, to wonder if her memory is flawed.

Because the widow has not aged.

Of course, some wear the time better than others, but they wear it still. Not her. She looks the same. *Exactly* the same. As if the years have made no mark at all.

"What brings you here?" asks the widow, and it takes María a moment to realize she means to the shop, and not to *her*.

She considers, trying to gauge whether the other woman can be trusted. After all, she has witnessed the city's taste for gossip.

"A tonic," she says, touching her stomach.

"Ah," says the widow. "Are you hoping to get with child, or get rid of one?"

María cannot hide her surprise. She has never heard anyone speak so boldly.

But the other woman only shrugs. "Children can be a blessing, in the right bed. And a kind of sickness in the wrong one. Don't worry, I am known for my discretion."

María cocks a brow. "If you are known for it," she says, "are you really so discreet?"

That earns a smile. And perhaps it is the knowing twitch of the widow's lips, or the steadiness of her blue eyes, or simply the dimness of the shop that draws out the truth.

"I am not with child," says María. "And I want to stay that way."

The widow shows neither judgment nor surprise, simply says, "Very well," and rounds the counter, taking the mortar and pestle with her. She collects a variety of herbs and oils from the shelves on the wall, and María realizes that her gloves are gone, her hands long and thin and lovely, and so pale they seem to shine in the low light as she fixes the tonic. She seems content to work in silence, but María cannot hold her tongue.

"You know," she says, "we've met before."

The widow's hands keep moving, but she glances up, a small groove between blond brows. "Are you sure?" she asks. She holds María's gaze, and her lips twitch again, as if toying with a smile. "I think I would remember you."

María is surprised by the heat that rushes to her cheeks. "I was much younger then."

"Ah," says the widow. The pestle grinds against the mortar walls. The widow tips the contents into a small, dark bottle, closes it with a cork.

"But *you* have not changed."

Again, that almost smile. Those blue eyes trail across her face. "What is your name?"

And she knows she should claim her husband's mantle, announce herself as the *Viscountess Olivares*, but the only name that rises to her lips is the one she would have given all those years ago.

"María."

"María," echoes the widow thoughtfully. She rounds the counter, stopping only when they are close enough to touch, then holds out a hand, and María is already reaching for it when the widow turns her palm up and says, "the price is three reals."

María blinks, recovering her senses. She is not permitted to carry her own money—there is no point, insist her husband's parents—but she has taken to skimming coins from the countess's purse whenever she finds it unattended. Now she draws the reals from her dress pocket and sets them in the widow's waiting hand, startled to find the skin so cold.

Like a compress on a fevered cheek, and yet, María feels herself flushing.

Just then, the door swings open, sending jagged light into the darkened shop, followed by the countess's rasping caw.

"María."

She turns, and the widow withdraws a step, into the deeper shadow of the counter. The countess does not bother coming in, simply stands there on the threshold, clutching at the baroness, who looks ready to divest her burden.

"Come, María. I am tired."

The widow slips the small dark bottle into María's hand. "It does not keep well," she says, lifting her voice so the countess will hear. "You'll need a fresh batch every fortnight."

As María clutches the tonic, she hears the words for what they are. An invitation. She turns toward the door. Sunlight burns at the threshold, the day beyond still hot. She wants to linger in the dark.

The countess waits, impatient, but María glances back. "My thanks . . ." she says, trailing off because she never learned the other woman's name.

The widow has begun sweeping the dregs back into the mortar on her table. She pauses and looks up from her work, those blue eyes like chips of sky.

"They call me Madame Boucher." The smile breaks free at last, revealing a wolfish point to her longest teeth as she adds, "But you may call me Sabine."

III

María cannot wait a fortnight.

The countess sucked her teeth at the request, muttered about spending time on tonics that would only go to waste while Andrés is still away. But then her husband sent word that he would be back in León soon, and thus the old hag gave her leave to come again.

And so María steps into the welcome dark a second time.

The widow, Sabine, does not look surprised to see her, but she does look glad, rising from the table where she was bent over her work.

"María," she says, the name easy as an exhale. It is the first time in her life she has enjoyed the sound.

Sabine glides toward her, hand reaching not for the empty bottle María was about to offer, but past it, toward her shoulder, her throat, her cheek, cool bare fingers resting on warm skin.

"I remember now," says the widow, meeting María's gaze, and she doesn't realize a strand of copper has escaped her scarf until Sabine twists the lock around her finger. "The child in the woods, blithely plucking poisoned blooms." Her hand lingers, the curl twisted like a ring. "How long ago was that?"

"Ten years," answers María.

"So many?" asks Sabine.

"And yet," says María, who has thought this week of little else, "you were a new widow then as well."

Sabine's palm dips, the hair abandoned as she plucks the empty bottle from María's hand and turns away. María wonders if she's angered her, but when Sabine glances back, there is amusement flashing in her eyes.

"Two kinds of women have leave to wander through this world alone and unmolested. Nuns, and widows. And I am not close enough with God to be a nun."

"So it is a lie, then."

Sabine taps the empty bottle thoughtfully against the table. "No. I did have a husband. Once." There it is again, that flash of teeth. A smile so slight and yet so dazzling that when María sees it, the ground seems to pitch downhill. She finds herself leaning forward, the urge to follow, or to fall.

"How did he die?" she asks.

The widow's smile widens. "Slowly."

Sabine. Sabine. Sabine.

María finds herself holding the name, like a cube of sugar, on her tongue, in the days between their meetings. Dwelling on how strange and sweet it tastes.

Sabine Boucher.

It is French, she tells María on her next visit—to think, her brother Felipe was right, all those years ago—and yet, there is hardly any accent to the widow's speech, her Spanish crisp and clean.

"All things wear smooth in time," she says by way of explanation, though she does not look old enough to have such wear.

Sabine. *Sabine.* María finds cause to say the name aloud as often as she can. On the third or fourth visit, she finally admits how much she likes the sound.

"María is a lovely name," counters the widow.

To which the younger woman only snorts. A short, derisive sound. "My mother told me once that it means *bitter.*"

Sabine plucks a stem of lavender from its bundle, twists the sprig between her fingers. "It also means *beloved.*"

María wrinkles up her nose. Perhaps, she says, but she has never liked it. It is so commonplace, so plain, like starched linen when she dreams of silk. She hates the way it sounds in her mother-in-law's mouth, like a sharp tug on a short chain.

Sabine looks at her kindly. "A name is like a dress. It might be by nature pretty or plain, but it is the person wearing it who matters most."

María considers, looking through a jar of herbs. Studying the face beyond. "If names are dresses, mine simply does not fit."

"So take it off," says Sabine blithely, handing her the lavender as if it is a torch. "Who would you be? What name would better suit you?"

María brings the dried flower to her nose. To that, she has no answer ready.

But she will think on it.

The summer drags itself over coals.

The day is blistering, the city baking in the August heat, and for once, María has not had to orchestrate her escape. The countess declares she cannot endure the sun and has skipped the market, preferring instead to soak her feet and hear the gossip in the comfort of her home. María would surely have been forced to stay and keep her company if not for the widow's gifts. Last time, she returned with a tonic to ease the countess's headaches, another to help the ever-restless count sleep through the night, and so they've deemed these visits a suitable pursuit.

Of course, María is not allowed to go *alone*. She is sent in the company of a maid, a makeshift jailer, but it's shockingly easy to buy an hour's peace with coin and threats, and she came armed with both.

The dark shop welcomes her when she arrives, and so does Sabine.

"Come," says the widow when María produces the empty tonic bottle. "I will show you how to make this batch yourself."

María recoils slightly at the prospect, not because she doesn't want to know, but because it feels like a door threatening to close.

"Surely that is not good business," she says, trying to make her voice light, playful even. "After all, if you teach me, I'll have no need to visit your shop."

No need, she says, when what she means is no reason, no excuse. When what she *wants* to say is that these stolen hours have been some days a saving grace, and others the only thing that keeps her from stepping off her in-laws' slanted roof.

Sabine purses her mouth in disapproval. "Knowledge is power, María. Never turn it down. Besides," she adds, cupping the stone bowl, "no one *else* needs to know what *you* do. It can be a secret, shared. Now, fetch me the jar of nettle from the shelf behind you."

María turns to the wooden ledge, and frowns. There are a dozen jars of herbs, their names written in a quick, sloped hand. She studies them, as if the curved lines will arrange themselves to sense. They don't.

"You cannot read?" ventures Sabine, appearing at her elbow.

María's jaw clenches. "No." A simple word, when the truth is messier. She'd broached the subject with her in-laws over supper, more than a year before, when the boredom reached its peak. She had been eyeing the books in the count's study for some time, in hope of a diversion, had even anticipated the shadow that crossed the countess's face, and quickly said she wished to learn so she could teach her children. Even touched her stomach for good measure.

To María's surprise, the count himself agreed to teach her.

But every time she went to meet him in his study, his hands began to venture from the page and purpose to her arm, her back, her waist. He'd lick his lips as he sounded out the letters. Sniff her hair as he leaned close.

When the man's wrinkled hands began to wander farther south, she'd abandoned the pursuit.

"I wanted to learn," María says now, glaring at the apothecary shelf, the labels nothing more than mocking curls and crosses. "But I lacked a proper teacher."

"Well then," says Sabine, reaching past her to pluck the nettle from the shelf. For a moment they are as close as cloth, draped together in the dark. The widow's breath a cool whisper on the back of María's neck. Her mouth, inches from her skin.

"Let's see if I can help."

⁓

María is not a patient pupil.

Her temper is quick to burn, and hard to quench.

Sabine makes her draw letters in a layer of fine sand, again and again, until she knows their shapes, before slowly stringing them together.

"What a cursed venture," she hisses more than once, slashing her hand through the sand with such force that it goes everywhere. A cloud, raining silent on the wooden floor. But the widow only produces more.

Week after week, the lessons little more than snatches, her annoyance clashing with Sabine's persistent calm, until slowly, somehow, the tangled letters become sounds and the sounds take shape.

"Ro . . ."

She sounds out the letters on a label.

". . . me . . ."

Wills it smooth.

". . . ro."

María blinks, as the sounds become a word.

"Romero."

Rosemary.

She thrills in recognition. It is like finding the keys to a locked door in your house, discovering a whole new room beyond.

Sabine cups her pupil's face, delighted. "You have such a quick mind."

María blushes, brief and hot, then scoffs, and slumps, frustrated, back into her chair. "At this rate, it will take a lifetime."

"There are worse ways to spend a life," says Sabine, still looming over her.

María lets her head fall back, looks up into the widow's peculiar eyes.

This close, they are not an even blue, but shot through with silver light, somehow bright despite the darkened shop. Only a foot of space between their faces, and it has never felt so far, so close. For a moment, María thinks of Ysabel, head bent over hers in the western alcove. But she suspects that if she reached up now, to touch the widow's cheek, the other woman would not pull away. Not even if her fingers drifted, if her thumb slipped across the widow's lips, soft and petal pink.

But the moment passes, and María does not reach.

Her fingers twitch, but stay against her dress. Sabine withdraws, and María is left feeling strangely winded.

The hour is almost up, and she knows that she should rise and go, and leave the widow to her work. But the fact is, she does not want to. So she lingers, lets her eyes drift closed, savoring the fact the summer heat has broken, the shop stones cooling in its wake.

Soon, the room fills with a strange new scent, warm and woody.

María glances toward Sabine, finds the woman stirring a mixture in a small bowl balanced atop a flame, the heat contained within a metal dish. Watches as she pours the contents, which are dark and thick as pitch, into a little cup.

Sabine returns to the table and places the cup before María.

"What is this?" she asks.

"A reward," says the widow, "for your resilient study."

María considers the mixture. It is the color of polished wood, the thickness of tallow, and according to Sabine, it is called *chocolate*.

"It was a gift," she explains, "from a grateful patron."

María nods at the single cup. "Surely we should share."

But Sabine only shakes her head. "It is too rich for me," she says, a little sadly. "But it would be a crime for such a gift to go to waste. Go on," she adds, and then, a little softer, "I want you to enjoy it for me."

María lifts the cup to her lips and takes a sip.

The liquid rolls over her tongue, at once bitter and sweet, thicker than wine and thinner than fruit, and her eyes slide shut as she holds it in her mouth, savoring the taste.

It is unlike anything María's ever tried. It coats her tongue, and the flavor lingers in her throat. And yet, as soon as she has swallowed, she wishes she hadn't. It is gone, and she is left not satisfied, but wanting.

When she finally opens her eyes, she finds Sabine watching her with rapt attention. Her teeth prick at her lower lip.

"Well?" she asks, eyes blazing in the shop's thin light.

And what can María say? In that one sip, she has drained the little cup. She would gladly have another. She would have it with every meal. Every day for the rest of her life. And it would still not be enough.

"If I had this," María says, "I would drink nothing else."

Sabine's mouth splits into a shallow smile.

"Strange, isn't it?" she says. "The more you taste, the more you want."

IV

"Are you ever lonely?"

It is late autumn now, and they are sitting together at the wooden table in the shop, María straining long-steeped herbs under Sabine's unblinking gaze. She has grown used to the widow's company these past few months, to her startling beauty and her cool touch, to the heat it stirs beneath María's skin, even to the strange way the world tips when she is near. To her own freedom, the loosening of her restraints, when she is in the woman's company.

But the widow's stillness is unnerving.

María herself has always been restless, some piece of her perpetually in motion. A bobbing thigh, a rolling wrist, her hands, her head. But when the widow is not crossing the shop, or making a tonic, she is a statue, only her blue eyes marked by life. And even those sometimes seem fixed on something far away, miles beyond the darkened shop.

But when María asks if she is lonely, Sabine blinks, and returns to herself.

"What a strange question."

"Is it?" she asks. "You are a widow. You are alone."

Sabine sits forward, elbows on the table. She laces her fingers and rests her chin on top, a small gesture that transforms her entire face, makes her seem suddenly girlish, young.

"One can be alone without feeling lonely," she muses. "One can feel lonely without being alone."

María twists a cloth bundle over a bowl, watches the tinted oil drip.

"Have you never thought of remarrying?" she asks. "Or taking a companion?"

Sabine cocks her head, a coy smile tugging at the corner of her mouth. "Who says I have not?"

Jealousy runs like gooseflesh over María's skin. She forces out a brittle laugh and says, "I envy your freedom."

Sabine doesn't laugh, only holds María's gaze. "There's no need for envy, when you could have it, too."

"I doubt my *husband* would agree."

Husband. A word bitten like a loose thread between her teeth. As the days have grown shorter, Andrés has returned, and this time it seems he means to stay the winter, in her room. In her bed. But something has shifted.

Her beauty has begun to make him angry, her figure now an insult. Where before he looked at María with hope, now he eyes her with impatience, as if she's nothing but an empty vessel he has not yet managed to fill.

And he is nothing if not determined.

His efforts have taken on a painful frequency. María occupies herself by silently reciting the ingredients in her tonic, spells them in her mind, letter by letter, until he's done.

"You could give him a child," Sabine suggested thoughtfully, several weeks before, "one, to put his mind at ease."

But María's stomach clenched at the suggestion. She fought the urge to scream, and simply shook her head. "It would not be enough," she said, and she knew it was the truth. "They are hungry people. They will breed me until I die. In the childbed or otherwise wrung dry."

Now she shifts in her chair, wincing at the steady ache between her legs, and across the narrow table the widow's girlish demeanor drops away, replaced suddenly by something older, ancient. It is uncanny, how little Sabine changes, and how much.

"Have you heard?" she says, a hollow in her voice. "There is a sickness sweeping through, a few days north. A plague, they say. Perhaps it will make its way to León."

María has often glimpsed the morbid streak buried in the other woman's humor. Still, it takes her by surprise. Talking of plagues as if they are poor weather.

"Who knows?" adds Sabine with an airy shrug. "Tragedy could yet befall your husband."

"As it did yours?" counters María.

Months spent in each other's company, and yet Sabine has told her nothing of her life *before*. María is hungry to know more, but sure enough, the question is met only by that enigmatic smile.

Sabine sits up a little straighter. "Of course," she says, scanning her shop.

"There are *other* ways to make one's self a widow. Not *all* of them rely on chance."

Her blue eyes burn when she says it, and María thinks of the day the widow left Santo Domingo, all those years ago. The day after señor Baltierra died in his sleep.

It would be a lie to say she's never dreamed of killing Andrés.

At night, when he sleeps and she cannot, she has taken to letting her mind wander, her imagination conjuring the ways in lurid detail. Knives buried in soft skin, bodies thudding down the eight short steps, fire catching on the curtains, spreading room by room.

No, it is not a question of whether she is *capable*; María has never doubted that.

But what would it gain her? What would she be left?

Humor dances like light again across Sabine's face, and María realizes—she is joking. Of course she is joking. And why not? There is no harm in jest.

"I *would* make an attractive widow," she muses.

"Without a doubt," says Sabine.

"But gray has never been my color. An emerald green, perhaps, or plum."

"The shade of mourning doesn't matter," says Sabine, rising from her chair. "What matters is that you would be free."

"Free," echoes María, the word heavy on her tongue. "To do what?"

Sabine strolls to the wall, runs her fingertips along the jars. "Free to live as you please. Be who you please. Take what you please."

Her hand stops at a vase filled with dried flowers, petals the soft white of eggshells.

"That is the best thing," Sabine says softly, lifting a flower from the bunch. "There is no one to stay your hand. No one to tell you no. If you see a thing you want . . ."

Her fingers vise shut, crushing the fragile bloom.

"It is yours."

She dusts off her palms, and when she turns back to face the table, María sees the look on her face and understands. This is not a game. The widow is not joking. A shadow has crossed her cloudless eyes, drawn hollows in her cheeks.

"I am growing tired of León," she says. "I do not think I'll stay much longer."

María feels the ground beneath her tremble.

No, she wants to say. *I won't allow it. You cannot leave me here, with him.*

She catches the words before they spill out, but Sabine seems to hear them all the same.

"You could come with me, when I go."

Something lurches inside María. The way Sabine says those words, as if it's all so very simple, only a matter of saying yes, makes anger rise like bile in her throat, bitter and hot.

"That isn't funny," she snaps.

Sabine eyes her levelly. "It isn't meant to be."

María grits her teeth. It is all well and good to play, to dream, but she has let it carry her too far. What was the point, of her imprisonment, her suffering, if only to shed it, run away, with nothing?

"Tell me," she seethes, "is this before or after we murder my husband?"

Sabine gives her a pitying look, and María cannot stand it anymore. She rises to her feet, decides that she has stayed too long. Andrés will be waiting.

She heads toward the door, but for once, Sabine follows in her wake. "You are too young to be so discontent."

Just as María reaches for the handle, she feels the other woman's touch, one cold hand coming to rest on her shoulder, the other sliding around her waist. Sabine's body, flush with hers, her smooth cheek against María's own. The two of them momentarily tangled, bound.

Her hand comes to her stomach, finds Sabine's fingers, splayed against her front, questing. Laying claim. So many nights, María has dreamed of this touch, hungered for it. Now, she fights the urge to lean back. To let the gray fabric swallow her.

If you see a thing you want . . .

"All you have to do is ask," whispers the widow.

And then her hand is gone, and María feels herself being nudged forward, over the threshold, and back into the street.

V

Andrés is waiting in the hall.

The floor is made of stone, and yet María imagines she can see the line he's trod with pacing.

"There you are, my wife," he says curtly.

His gaze goes straight to her hair, and María realizes that in her haste, she left the shop without her scarf. Or her tonic. She swears softly to herself, even as she paints a breezy smile on her face and says there must be a storm coming through. The wind came up so strong it tore the scarf away.

His eyes go past María then, to the maid who has appeared behind her, the one who was assigned to chaperone, and she resists the urge to turn and glare in silent warning at the girl. She resists—and so is left to guess at what Andrés sees there, before he takes María's arm and leads her into the house.

At supper, the loudest sound is the cutlery as it scrapes against the plates.

María picks at the charred corpse of a small quail. The food is to her in-laws' taste, which is to say it is both bland and overcooked, proof that money does not buy a palate.

The count and countess tend to eat in silence, but her husband usually prefers the sound of his own voice. María knows her contributions are not needed, and so her mind makes its way back to the apothecary. Because of that, she doesn't notice how little Andrés has been speaking until they are on their way upstairs, and his voice cuts through her thoughts.

"You spend too much time with her."

María blinks. "With whom?" she asks blandly.

He lets out an impatient huff. She has clearly not been listening. "With the woman in that shop." It's not the *first* time he's made mention of Sabine— there have been offhand remarks—but there is a stiffness to his shoulders, a shadow in his look.

María feigns indifference. "She is a *widow*, Andrés. A pious one at that," she says, though her husband turns his eye to godly things only when it suits him. "Besides," she adds, "I do not do it for myself. It is for *us*."

Us—a word that makes her wither, almost as much as the weight of his meaty hand on her too-flat stomach. His expression darkens, and she feels the stairs beneath her turn to glass. One step, the difference between shattering and safe. His hand is hot, and horrible, and María wonders when the road she chose veered so badly off its course.

Two kinds of women have leave to walk through this world alone and unmolested.

María's other hand goes up, and comes to rest upon his cheek, the coarse hair scratching at her palm as she turns his face to meet hers.

And I am not close enough with God to be a nun.

Andrés looks at her, *through* her, as if she is a common thing. As if he did not worship at her feet the day they met. As if she did not make him bow with want.

I was meant for more than this, she wants to say. Instead, she smooths her own features, tamps down her disgust, summons a wife's obedience.

"If you disapprove," she says, "then it is done. I won't see her anymore."

He nods, expression softening. Good. Let him think she is a horse that has finally been broken.

"Come," she says with a placid smile. "Let's go to bed."

He snores beside her like a beast.

María lies awake and marvels at how easily sleep takes him. How heavy. He has jokingly said, more than once, that he slumbers like the dead. Now she imagines tipping a vial of milky poison between his sleeping lips, listening to him quiet, the measure of his heart winding down, the steady knock slowing to a crawl and then at last, a stop.

Imagines the silence that would fill the room.

She rises up onto one elbow, fingers the ruby at her throat as she studies her husband's sleeping face, tries to conjure fondness.

And waits.

Waits, until she's sure he will not wake. Then rises in the dark, pulls a robe around her gown, and opens the window. She steps out in slippered feet, edging along the sloping roof the way she has a dozen times in daylight.

María eyes the drop, and perhaps it looks shorter in the dark, or perhaps she simply doesn't care.

She jumps.

Jumps, and falls, weightless for a single, exhilarating breath before the world catches up. Before the ground catches *her*. She lands in a crouch on the street below, bones shaking, but unbroken from the force of the fall.

María stands, and looks up at the roof again, in wonder.

It was not such a long way after all.

How strange it is to walk alone at night.

During the day, the streets are cluttered with bodies and carts, and she struggles to navigate the crowded market, cocooned within layers of dress and veil.

But now, by dark, the air is crisp and cool, the city emptied, and quiet, having long drawn in its limbs and gone to sleep. María savors the breeze as it slides through her loose hair, finds the seams of her robe, grazes the gown beneath, and wonders if this is what it tastes like—freedom.

When María reaches the apothecary, no candlelight seeps beneath the door or around the shuttered window's edge. She knocks, certain that the widow is asleep.

No answer comes.

María clenches her teeth as her mind turns over what to do. Now that she has made her choice, she cannot turn around, cannot climb back into her husband's bed, cannot stand another day inside that gilded cell. She knocks again, presses her ear against the wood, listens for sounds of life within, and hears nothing. Nothing. Until—

"María."

The widow's voice, not coming from within the shop, but on the street behind her.

She turns, and finds Sabine standing, fully dressed, an empty basket on one arm.

Her widow's veil is gone, and the moonlight glances off her pale hair, turning the blonde to silver. It is an ungodly hour for either woman to be out, and yet, while María's whole body is humming, tight as strings, Sabine looks perfectly at home in the dark.

The widow steps past her and opens the door.

The darkness is deeper in the shop. Thick as smoke without the help of moon or lantern. María waits for Sabine to light a candle, but the other woman moves around the space as if she can see every line and shape. María's own eyes refuse to adjust. She blinks, and blinks, but all she sees are shadows. Shadows—and Sabine.

"I've changed my mind," declares María.

Sabine comes close, reaches up and winds a lock of copper hair around her finger. "I guessed as much," she murmurs. Then, "What do you want?"

María frowns. "You already know."

"I want to hear you say it." There is a velvet lining to her voice that makes María flush. "Tell me."

And it is not so hard to shape the words, she has been thinking them all night.

"I want to be free," she says. "By any means."

It is like laces being loosened. At last, she feels like she can breathe.

Sabine leans in, then, so close María thinks she means to press her lips to hers. But at the last second the widow stops, their mouths a breath apart, her words a whisper in the space between. "Do you trust me?"

It turns out, it is an easy thing to tell the truth.

"Yes."

In the heady dark, the widow's smile shines. And then she's gone, stepping past as if to fetch a bottle from the shelf. By memory, María finds her way to the table, grasps at the back of the chair and waits, wishes there were light, so she could see how the poison's made.

But too soon, Sabine is back, and close enough to whisper in her ear.

"Do not be afraid."

María doesn't understand, not until she feels the bright and sudden stab of pain.

Her hand flies to her neck, thinking she's been cut. But instead of a blade, or ragged wound, her fingers find soft hair, the widow's head bent against her throat.

And yet, beneath that softness.

Something violent, sharp.

A searing heat spreads across María's skin, up like branches, down like roots, and her pulse starts thudding in her ears. She panics, and tries to free herself, driven by a sudden, primal need, a certainty, old and animal, that she's in danger. But before she can force Sabine away, the widow's arms have closed around her, soft but firm. A cage.

María struggles, but Sabine might as well be made of stone. Her teeth—that is what it is, her *teeth*—sink deeper still into María's throat, and she feels something crack inside her from the force. Her head begins to spin, the air around her filling with the metal scent of blood.

Now the pain subsides, becomes a heavy ache, and as it does, María feels the strength leech out of her. She fights against the spreading weakness, a losing battle as her head begins to spin, her heart a dying animal, kicking useless at her ribs. Her pulse falters, seems to lose its rhythm in her chest.

Do not be afraid, the widow said. But for the first time in her memory, María *is*.

Because she does not want to die.

She cannot die.

She—

Her heart skips, and stumbles, the world receding with its tripping steps. A flat black darkness is sweeping in, and in that dark, María sees her short life unspool.

She is a skinny girl on a stable roof, spitting cherry pits over the side.

She is watching caravan after caravan go by.

She is sitting by the hearth while her mother twists bridal knots into her hair.

She is stretched in an alcove, and sitting silent at a wedding feast.

She is a small flame, smothered before it has a chance to burn.

María sees it all unravel, and her anger rises at the meager sum of it, and at its sudden ending.

By now the pain is gone, and María can feel the moment Sabine's mouth finally lets go, when teeth slide free of skin.

It is like the last string of a puppet being cut. The last ounce of strength goes out of her. Her legs buckle. She would fall, but Sabine is there to hold her up. As if she weighs nothing.

Sabine, who turns María in her arms.

Sabine, whose lips are dark now, blood trailing in ribbons down her throat.

Sabine, who smiles, teeth stained red, as if she has not just killed María.

Sabine, who now touches her own neck, drags a nail over the skin, which parts, blackish blood welling as she holds María close, and tells her, "Drink."

Drink, she says, as if it is a cup of chocolate.

Drink, she says, and María does.

The widow's blood spills across her tongue, sweet, and strange, and slightly rotten, turned with loam, and leaf soil, honey, and ash. And as it rolls down her throat, her pulse recovers in her chest, reclaims a slow but steady beat. Her legs grow strong enough to hold her up. Her mind begins to clear.

"Enough," Sabine says gently, stroking María's hair.

But it is not enough. She bites into the widow's throat, and the blood, which had begun to slow, now courses faster. One cold hand presses against María's chest.

"Enough," says Sabine again, and this time there is an edge of warning. The word rolls through María with surprising force. But it does not hold a candle to her thirst. She feels hollowed out with hunger. And so she drinks, and the blood fills her mouth, blooms inside her as it spreads.

"*Stop,*" hisses the widow, but María doesn't *want to.*

Her teeth stay locked against the other woman's throat, and now Sabine is the one struggling against *her,* locked inside the cage of *her* embrace, and she is strong, much stronger than María *was,* but with every passing beat, María steals a little more, until she can taste it in the widow's blood, the *fear* she felt moments before.

María doesn't stop.

She drinks, until the widow weakens, sags.

Drinks, until the blood stops rising to her lips.

Drinks, until Sabine goes stiff, then still.

Drinks, and does not realize the body in her arms is dead until it breaks. Crumbles between her fingers, crashes soundless to the floor.

She startles, then, as if from sleep. Stares down at what's left of Sabine Boucher. The shop is not as dark as she first thought, and moonlight finds small fissures, glances off the ash that was the widow's skin, the silver strands that were her hair, the gray cloth of her dress, which has fallen in a formless heap, mingled with the rest.

She reaches up to touch the torn skin of her throat, ruined by the widow's teeth, only to find the gash is gone, the skin already closed. She marvels, does not understand what's happened, or what's happening. Only knows that death was close enough to touch, and then cast off.

And yet, she doesn't feel truly rid of it.

María sits on the floor beside the widow's remains, and feels a moment of—not of regret, but disappointment. At being left, even though she knows it was her doing.

She knows, as well, something is wrong. No, not wrong, just—strange. Out of place. As if a piece of her has been ripped away, but something new has grown up just as quickly in its wake, so that she doesn't feel the absence.

Something new, and yet *familiar*, some version of her that has been buried for a long, long time, and has at last been watered, tended, given leave to bloom.

She reaches out and runs her fingers through the ash.

Knows she should feel horrified.

But as she rises to her feet, all she feels is hungry.

VI

María looks up at the Olivares house.

The window she climbed out of, the pitched roof she crossed, the place she dropped, and feels no desire to go back the way she came.

Instead, she strolls up to the door and knocks.

Despite the ungodly hour, she swings the iron ring against the wood, shattering the quiet of the house. The servants are roused first, of course. She can hear them scurrying about like mice inside the walls. Then the door swings open, and what a sight she must be, their viscountess, standing on the wrong side of the threshold, dressed for sleep and stained with blood.

Their eyes go wide with panic—how strange, that she can almost *taste* their worry, like sugar on the air—as they usher her inside, asking her what happened, is she hurt, where has she been?

"It is nothing," she says, and it's the first time María has spoken, since the widow, since the bite, since the hunger and the ash. Her voice is hers, and not, loud, and not, strange, and not. Calm, and not—stitched with a giddy thread.

She brushes the servants away and climbs the stairs as if nothing is amiss. As if she has not been buried and born in the same night. In her room, she finds Andrés, already on his feet. Half-awake, confusion painted on his face.

It quickly turns to rage as he takes in the open window and his disheveled wife, standing in the doorway and not beside him in the bed.

"What have you done?" he demands. "Where have you been?"

She shrugs, and says it doesn't matter, delighting at the anger that sparks across his face. He grabs her arm, and yesterday his grip would have been hard enough to bruise, but now it feels like nothing, and María simply watches, curious to see what he'll do next.

He's spitting venom now, calling her a whore, saying he will teach her what happens to an unfaithful wife, but his pulse is louder than his voice, a drumbeat smothering the rest. It is all she can hear. He drags her, roughly, to the bed, pushes her down and climbs on top, and that is when the moment turns.

She turns.

Rolls, and is on top, her red hair loose and pooling like a curtain around them. Lovebirds locked within their nest.

"Esposo mío," she coos, the slender fingers of one hand curling round his wrists, pinning them over his head. Andrés stares up at her, furious, perplexed. He is twice her size, but it doesn't matter now. In the intervening night, he has grown soft, and she has turned to stone.

And now, in her hand, he is bruising.

"María," he gasps, calling her by her name—at last, little as she likes it.

She can feel the blood pumping in his veins, can see it at his temple, in the thicket at his throat. Her mouth begins to ache, and she grabs his hair, the way he did hers so many times, yanking his head back to expose the column of his neck. His life, right there, beneath thin skin, so close. Her teeth prick her bottom lip, and the air begins to taste like fear.

His, of course, not hers.

She has done away with that. Left it in the ashes of the widow's shop.

"María," he pleads again, and all she can think is that she's always hated that name. How it has never fit. And then she remembers what the other woman said, about being free to live as you please. To be who you please, take what you please.

If you see a thing you want . . .

And she has, hasn't she? Turned it in her mouth a hundred times, just to savor the sound. So as María's husband begs his wife to stop, she leans low and lays her face against his so they are cheek to cheek.

"María is no more," she whispers in his ear. "My name is Sabine."

Right before she sinks her teeth into his throat.

His skin breaks like ripened fruit, life spilling across her tongue, flooding her mouth, and if the widow's blood was bread, then this is wine. Bright and dizzying and sweet.

The viscount thrashes, bellowing in rage and pain—how strange that she can taste them both, right there in his blood—but she has heard enough of Andrés Olivares. She wraps her hand over his mouth, and drinks, and drinks, and as his heartbeat slows, her own begins to quicken, or so it seems.

She doesn't yet know that her own heart has ceased to beat. That what she feels now is nothing but an echo of a stolen pulse, a rhythm borrowed for the time it takes to drink. That as quickly as it ends, she will be raked by thirst again, not only for the taste of blood itself, but for the drum it beats inside her.

She doesn't know.

All she knows is that, at last, she feels alive.

Andrés has gone limp beneath her. She stares down at his corpse.

"Who is the empty vessel now?" she asks as she climbs off him, the pulse already dying in her chest.

She passes an iron lamp, candles burning in their posts, and tips it over, watches the fire meet the rugs and catch. Takes a lantern and trails the flame against a tapestry, sets it to the edge of a portrait.

The count appears, his hair askew, his face a mask of shock and fear. She knows she must be quite a sight, hair loose, and crimson spilling down her front.

"María—"

She presses the old man back into the wall, and smiles, showing her sharpened teeth. "Not anymore."

His blood tastes like arrogance, like greed, his pulse barely a flutter in her chest.

How disappointing.

The countess stumbles from her room, pawing down a wall, squawking for the servants who have already fled. Her son's wife, his murderer, his widow, stands and watches the countess reach the edge of the stairs, watches her trip, and fall, crashing down, only to shatter at the bottom.

Eight steps, it turns out, *is* enough to break a neck.

The fire spreads, licking the stone walls of the Olivares house.

And just like that, her old life burns.

By the time they put the fire out, she will be gone.

By the time the city guards search the ruined house for corpses, and find the young viscountess missing.

By the time the family's bodies are buried, and the servants who fled begin to talk.

There is no point in lingering.

No, she has had more than enough of León.

The stable door is locked, but one swift push and the wood splinters around the iron, a second and it gives. She takes her husband's horse, since he won't need it anymore.

The massive mount stands in the farthest stall, but when she reaches out to pet its neck the beast rears back, as if she's holding a hot poker. Its eyes go wide, a feral panic taking hold, and she withdraws her hand, marvels at the way it *knows,* when Andrés didn't. Knows what she now *is,* and isn't. Knows enough to fear. Perhaps the horse simply smells the blood, but she thinks it senses something *else*—violence, danger, death.

Either way, it stomps its hooves, warning her away, and so the woman who was once María—how easy, to cast the old name off with that old self—abandons the horse and the stable and the burning house.

And Sabine never once looks back.

ALICE

(D. 2019)

I

Alice spills into the darkened Yard.

She was right, the fresh air does feel mercifully good. The heaviness is gone, the wall of low clouds replaced by open night.

She walks, her body coming unstuck a little, stride by stride, as she heads across the lamp-lit quad. The sky overhead is more indigo than black, and the breeze runs its fingers through her hair, swipes a cool palm against her cheek, and when she drags in a few lungfuls of cold air she can taste the damp pavement from the storm the night before, and the decaying leaves, and at last she feels better.

Then her stomach cramps.

A sudden hollow twist, a reminder that Alice hasn't had anything to eat since well before last night's party. She thinks—hopes—the pangs might just be hunger, knows it's too late to grab a proper dinner at Berg, but she heads there anyway, hoping to find *something* she can stomach.

She steps inside the dark wood hall, with its vaulted ceilings and its chandeliers, and as she grabs a tray and joins the narrow queue, her appetite flares, sudden, and surprisingly deep. She waits her turn, tries to roll the stiffness from her spine, her attention drifting as she does to a pack of guys on their way out.

(She's always thought of it like that, a *pack*, whether it's the men who huddled, shoulders hunched, under the awning of her granddad's pub, or the boys who went racing through the streets of Hoxburn on bald-tired bikes, or the lads who stood outside the chippie swapping joints and bottles in paper sacks. It's something in the way they perch, heads swiveling together like dogs scenting trouble, or mischief, or prey. And every time Catty would see a group, she'd flash a feral grin, and snarl as they passed, and when Alice would ask what she was doing, and she'd shrug as if it was obvious, and say, "I'm showing them my teeth.")

Alice reaches the front of the line, and ladles oatmeal into a bowl, tops it with honey and dried fruit. At an empty table, she sinks onto the bench, her mouth watering as her body finally comes online and she realizes she isn't just hungry, she's famished, she's *starving*. She spoons a heaping bite, and it is the best thing she's ever tasted.

Right up until she swallows.

Somewhere between her tongue and her stomach, something goes wrong, some vital miscommunication, and that one bite begins to fight its way back up. Alice rises, and runs, makes it across the hall and out the doors to the nearest bush before her stomach empties, wrings itself out hard enough it leaves her doubled over, heaving and shaking and sick.

Her legs tremble, and her head spins, and she crouches, forehead against her knees, waiting for the shudder to run through her, waiting for her stomach to unclench and her world to settle. Her body is waging some kind of war against itself. She can't make sense of the signs. Her stomach rumbles, even as it revolts. She tries to swallow, and feels the drag of sand inside her throat, and if this is a hangover, it's officially the worst she's ever had.

Alice tries to make a tally of the shots she took the night before, even though she knows, deep down, this isn't that; has spent a good portion of her first month here being subjected to lectures by well-meaning adults, trying to ease the transition from dependent to independent life. Cautionary tales of sudden freedom, and the dangers that go with it.

(As if Alice didn't grow up in a place where kids drank well before they ever learned to drive.)

No, this is something else.

A stomach bug, maybe? Some kind of flu?

Alice is still sitting on the curb, feeling well and truly sorry for herself and trying to catalog the symptoms in case she has to find a clinic, when she senses movement—the twitch of a body drawing closer—and looks up to see a guy jogging toward her. She tenses, suddenly on guard, before the guy slows, steps into her pool of light, and she thinks, *I know him.*

(Well, not *know*, but he has one of those familiar faces, the kind stamped on half the underclassmen she's passed between the halls and the classrooms and the student mixers. Floppy brown hair and a crimson jumper, and a mon-eyed slant to his vowels that says he's not from Boston.)

The important thing, in that moment, is that he seems to know *her*.

"Hey," he says, "it's Alice, right?" She nods, trying to place him, and after an awkward moment, he says, "Colin," and sounds a little hurt, and she
mumbles that she's sorry, she isn't feeling well, says she's never been good with
names and faces. Which is true, even though she didn't have a problem back
in Hoxburn, where strangers were few and far between.

"Here," he says, holding out a water bottle. "You look like you could use it."

It is a small, kind gesture, and she takes the bottle, which is unopened, so
she breaks the seal and drinks. Her throat is desert dry, and she is thirsty, so
thirsty, but the water won't go down. She feels her throat snap shut so fast she
almost chokes, has no choice but to swirl the water in her mouth, and spit it
back onto the curb.

"Thanks," she says, handing the bottle back. Her nods for her to keep it.
But he doesn't leave.

"Bad night?" he asks, and Alice nods, getting to her feet. She wobbles, her
vision dipping in and out. He holds out a steady hand, and she is too tired
not to take it.

"Come on," he says. "Let's get you home."

II

It's only a few blocks.

That's what Alice thinks she says, along with, *I can make it,* but honestly, the words might have gotten stuck inside her head because he's still there, at her side, and they're going through one of the gates but when she turns to see which one, she stumbles, and he steadies her.

"Whoa there," he says, a laugh catching in his throat, but she doesn't know what's funny. Her stomach clenches, and she wants to lie down, clings to the thought of her room, her bed, and does he know she lives at Matthews? Did she tell him? Is that where they are going now?

He makes small talk, and she doesn't, jaw locked tight against the urge to hurl again.

He compliments her accent, and she mumbles that his is nice as well, and he crinkles his nose and says he doesn't have one and she doesn't know if she's supposed to laugh or not, and honestly, it is taking all her focus just to stay on her feet, to hear his voice past the dull throbbing in her head.

She should have stayed in bed, she thinks.

She stumbles again, and again he's there.

"I'm okay," she murmurs, even though she's not. Something is really wrong, and she tries to disentangle herself as she says it, gently, so he doesn't think she's being rude, but he pulls her closer, his arm now around her waist, and she thinks of telling him that she's gay, but this isn't the time or the place and after all, he's just helping her get home, so there's no reason to bring it up, to make things weird, not when he's just being nice.

But the closeness of him tickles something in Alice's throat, and the pounding in her head gets louder, and finally she stops, bracing herself against a cold brick wall, afraid that if she takes another step her legs will buckle, or she'll faint.

(She'd only fainted once in her whole life, when she was six, and Dad took her and Catty on holiday to southern Spain, and she didn't know the sun there was strong enough to make you sick, just from lying in it.)

Alice stumbles again, her body and her mind both lurching back as Colin's grip tightens on her, like he's the only thing holding her up.

"Hey," he says, "I've got you," and his tone is still steady, still undeniably *nice*, but the air tastes wrong, rancid, a sour odor that must be coming off the bins behind the dorm. When did they end up on the wrong side of the entrance? Alice twists, trying to see where she is, and the night tips with the motion.

"I don't feel well," she says, aloud, trying to pull free. "I need to go lie down."

"Sure thing," he says. "Of course," he says, but he is still standing between her and the world, and then she feels the scratch of a tree trunk at her back, and the weight of him against her, and for a second she thinks he's trying to hold her up instead of back, instead of down, but then his hands are groping at her shirt, and his mouth is mashing against hers, and she bites down, feels flesh break between her teeth.

He wrenches back, blood welling on his bottom lip, and on her tongue, and just like that—

The night tears open—

Splits right in two—

Like an old movie, the kind on film, a tear in the reel—

The image on the screen goes black—

And when it flickers back, the tree is gone, Colin is gone, and Alice is standing in a shower stall, fully dressed and soaking wet, cold water sluicing through her clothes and pink ribbons circling the drain around her shoes. Iron in her mouth, the taste of pennies on her tongue.

Blood, she thinks, and at the same time, she knows it isn't hers.

(How can she know that?)

Presses her palms against her eyes, trying to force the moments back like camera flashes. But all she sees is red. Another stretch of missing time.

Alice peels away the clothes, leaves them piled like a soggy shadow in the corner of the shower stall, salvages the last dregs of soap from an abandoned bottle and scrubs herself pink, then red, then raw.

And as she does, she notices how much better she is feeling. Her teeth still ache, in that dull sinus way, but her head no longer hurts, and she's stopped shivering, despite the water running cold.

She snaps the shower off, realizes she doesn't exactly have a change of clothes, but someone has left a towel to dry outside a nearby stall, so she swipes it, pulls it tight around her as she pads to the sinks, and studies her reflection in the glass above, expecting to see the violence—his, or hers?—written in the hollows of her face.

But Alice looks *fine*.

Which is wrong, isn't it?

Because she shouldn't, not after what's just happened.

She shouldn't look fine, shouldn't *feel* fine.

She should be freaking out, but she's not, and she knows it's probably shock, but shock eventually passes and she doesn't want this to—doesn't know if she can handle panic on top of everything else—and then, as if she's gone and cracked the seal, it all comes crashing over her.

Her throat tightens and her reflection blurs, tears welling up, and the weird thing is, for a moment, the whole bathroom looks like it's been tinted red, and then the tears slide down her face and Alice yelps, hands going to her mouth.

Because she's crying *blood*.

Two red lines running down her cheeks, like something out of a horror film. She swipes at her face with the hem of the stolen towel before realizing her mistake, the red leaching right into the pale cotton, the metal scent making her stomach twist again as a jagged memory comes rushing up, and—

—they're on the ground—

—the two of them—

—and he's the one begging her to stop—

—and then his throat is open—

—the crimson sweater matted dark and—

—and then it's just Alice, in the bathroom, wet hair sticking to her skin.

She scrapes it back, turns on the tap and splashes palmfuls of cold water on her face until the crying stops, watches the pink water swirl in the drain, then forces her gaze back up to her reflection.

It stares back, startled, but unhurt, so she leans closer, till the tip of her nose touches the mirror, close enough for her breath to fog the glass.

But it doesn't.

And that is how Alice learns she isn't breathing.

She reels back from the mirror, as if she's seen a ghost. Her hands go to her mouth, a preemptive gesture, in case there is a scream, but nothing comes out.

She takes in a massive gulp, sucking the air in and then out, as if to prove she can, but it feels forced, so instead she tries holding her breath, which she's never been good at. The panic always kicks in before the need for air, but she still tries, counts to thirty, then sixty, then ninety, even though she's never been able to hold her breath for more than forty-five. Alice waits for her lungs to twinge, her head to spin, her heart to start pounding in her ears, but the only sound she hears isn't a sound at all, but a kind of white noise in her skull, no pounding heart, no bodily reaction to the lack of air, or the panic now ringing through her bones, and she's lost count of how long it's been since she started holding her breath, and when she goes looking for her pulse, she can't find it.

There's a heavy *nothing* behind her ribs, a stillness so dense there's only one word for it.

Dead.

Dead weight, dead air, dead space.

Which is ridiculous, of course, right, because Alice isn't *dead*—she's standing right there in front of the mirror, but all that does is put an "un" before the word, which is somehow even worse, so she decides that this is something else, something making her sick, delirious, even. That's it.

Alice isn't *dead.*

She is just having a very bad night.

That is what she tells herself as she makes her way out of the bathroom, and down the hall, and back into the shared suite, where Rachel is still sitting cross-legged on the couch, laptop balanced on her knees.

If Rachel looked up right then, she'd see Alice, wide-eyed and terrified and wrapped in someone else's towel, the cotton spotted red, but she doesn't, just keeps typing, as she asks Alice if she's feeling better and Alice says *Sure*, or *Yeah*, or *Heading to bed*. It doesn't matter, so long as it's not the awful laugh that's clawing up her throat.

She escapes into her room, grateful Lizbeth fled to Jeremy's, and closes the door behind her. She locks it, then sheds the towel, and stands before the full-length mirror mounted to the closet, wearing nothing but the thin gold chain around her neck, the one she always wears, the pendant swinging at the end, her little piece of home.

Alice stands there, naked, and alone, fights the urge to hide behind her folded arms, because she's never been good with this kind of up-close scrutiny—look for any length of time and the picture unravels into problem areas, knobby elbows and awkward knees, a litany of imperfections—but now, she studies herself with the cold remove of a crime scene, searching for clues in place of memories.

A mark, a bite, some evidence of an infection.

Yes, that is a good word, *infection,* a logical, medical word. Like cause and effect—if *p* then *q*—one thing leading to another, because something led to this. She's on a road, and she just has to turn around and walk back the way she came until she finds the intersection, the moment that led here, to her, to this.

Alice thinks about last night, about waking up this morning. She remembers the lipstick stains, like bruises, grazing her wrist, her ribs, her throat, but she's scrubbed them away, and now there is nothing but cold, pale skin.

She has scars, of course, but they are all familiar, ordinary marks. A silver dash on her left knee, from racing Catty along the top of the stone wall. A pale hook on her forearm, from a tumble in the glass-strewn lot behind the pub.

Nothing else.

Which *should* be a relief, but it's not because the fact is, Alice still can't find her pulse, not at her wrist, or her throat, the veins too still beneath her skin. She goes to her toiletry kit and finds a razor, thumbs the edge and watches as the flesh parts neatly, a single too-dark bead of blood welling sluggishly up onto her skin.

It doesn't hurt, but she flinches at the sight, sticks her thumb into her mouth on instinct, and feels her stomach *vise,* her teeth clamp shut, so sudden and so sharp she gasps, wrenches her hand free, and sees a deep gouge in the meat of her thumb where she's bitten down.

Alice stares in fascinated horror at the depth of the puncture, and then, right before her eyes, the wound begins to close, like a movie in reverse, skin knitting neatly back together. She glances up at the mirror as if looking for a witness, locks eyes with herself just in time to see the tips of two white teeth retreating behind her upper lip.

Her reflection stares back at her, surprised.

"Oh," she says aloud to no one. "*Fuck.*"

She backs away from the mirror, almost laughs.

Because it's ridiculous.

First the thing with the breathing, and the pulse, and now this. Like some bad dream, only she's pretty sure she's awake.

But here's the thing. Alice is no fool. She was raised on good books and bad TV, and she knows what this looks like, but she also knows that it's not *real*. It's not real, and yet she *is*, and she's not sure how to square the two, and there is a word she will not use. Not because it doesn't fit, but because it feels absurd even to think it, just the shape of it in her mouth makes a nervous sound rise like trapped air in her chest—the place where her heart isn't beating—and as long as she doesn't use the word—doesn't even *think* it—then she can still be sane, and this can still be salvaged.

Alice Moore has always been smart, top marks in maths and physics, both, and this seems like a logic problem, right, so here is what she knows:

She went to a party.

She came home with a girl.

She went to bed well.

And woke up sick.

(Not dead.)

(Because that can't be fixed, and this can.)

This is a problem she just has to solve.

She went to a party.

She came home with a girl.

She turns and plucks the purple Post-it off her bedside lamp.

Goodbye, Alice.
xo Lottie

Alice drags her laptop into the bed. When it comes to life, she winces at the brightness, turns the screen as dark as it will go, then pulls up the school directory and begins to search.

SABINE

(D. 1532)

I

Somewhere outside León, Spain
1532

It is the darkest hour before dawn, and yet, Sabine sees *everything*.

The night, which had appeared so solid as she made her way to the widow's shop, now looks as thin as cobwebs, lace. As if she's carrying a taper, its soft light glancing off of every brick and beam, illuminating the world ahead, and the one she left behind.

Sabine walks on, putting León and Andrés and María firmly in her wake, and with every passing mile she expects the dream to shatter, the thrill of the night to give way to exhaustion. But it doesn't.

She has not slept, and yet, her body doesn't long for rest. In fact, she feels glaringly awake.

Until the sun begins to rise.

A strange feeling steals over her as daylight tints the sky, a deep fatigue, a dragging weight. A weariness that turns to sickness as the sun cracks and spills across the hills. Sabine begins to shiver, even though she isn't cold.

She has always been hearty, hale, never so much as a fever in her childhood, no illness—save those feigned to gain a respite from the marriage bed. But now, with every forward step, she feels drawn and dizzy and weak. By the time the sun is fully up, she is shaking, her body beating a warning drum, its tempo saying *wrong, wrong, wrong.*

And yet, she is somehow hungry too, having hardly eaten the night before, with Andrés in such a mood. So when she passes a thin grove of young apple trees, the fruit small and hard and months from being ripe, she plucks one anyway, and bites in, savoring the bright crunch of the fruit before the taste hits her tongue.

It is not just unripe, but *rancid*.

She tries to swallow, can't—her stomach twists, and the single morsel comes back up, the strange drum beating louder still: *wrong, wrong, wrong.*

After that, the fields roll on and on, providing neither shade nor shelter.

The day is growing hot, but the sun does nothing to banish her chill. In fact, the higher it gets, the worse she feels. The light chafes, makes her want to climb out of her skin. She understands, then, the veil the old Sabine was always wearing, the constant shadow of her shop. The herbs and flowers weren't the only things that needed cold and damp and dark.

By the time Sabine spots the wooded barn, shabby as it is, her vision is blurring. She feels half-mad with the urge to lie down, claw up the earth and bury herself there, beneath the wild grass and soil, just to escape the glaring sun, the pounding light.

Instead, she wades across the field, toward the shelter of the barn.

The moment she steps inside, her body shudders in relief. The sickness recedes like a tide, but still she feels the drum where her heart should be, telling her it is not dark enough, what with the sunlight streaming through weathered boards and gaps in the roof.

A rough blanket hangs on the wall, and Sabine crosses to it, startling a donkey in its stall. It begins to bray with the same animal panic as the horse back in León, and the sound is a rock against her skull. She wants to snap the creature's neck. Instead, she drags open the gate and lets it flee, moving into the deeper shade of its empty pen.

There Sabine collapses, folds herself into the welcome slice of dark between the hay and the stone, and drops, like a rock down a well, into a deep and dreamless sleep.

There is no gentle waking, no state of in-between. One moment Sabine is dead to the world, and the next she is back in the barn, alive. Awake.

But not alone.

She looks up and sees a man standing several feet away. In one hand he holds a rope, the donkey tethered to the end. In his other hand he holds a pitchfork, the wooden pole hovering over her side. She has the sense that he has prodded her with it.

"Get up," he says.

Sabine stands, and sways, still feeling weak, and ill, despite the many hours' sleep. The barn door is open at the farmer's back, late-afternoon light slanting in, and she winces at the sight of it. The glare still makes her dizzy.

"Are you hurt?" he asks, and in the daylight she can see the stains that paint her gown, the unmistakable shade of long-dry blood.

He sees it, too, and yet, he doesn't flinch. There is no trace of fear around him, and it rankles her. That despite the look of her, he is so certain of his safety, convinced she is the damsel, not the danger. Sabine watches as he takes in her unlaced collar, the ruby at her throat. For a moment, his attention wanders lower, drifting over the bare skin that pitches toward her breasts. A quick flick down to her bare feet, the slippers cast off somewhere amid the hay, before cutting back up to her face. Her hair. The jewel.

"Are you hurt?" he said, but there was no caring in the question, only a man trying to gauge the trouble in his barn, deciding whether her presence is an inconvenience or an opportunity.

Sabine supposes she could cry, or beg for help, spin some story about scoundrels, make herself small and play the part of helpless maiden.

She could, but she doesn't.

Instead she meets his gaze, and holds it, the way she used to when the caravans came through. Her attention is a fishing line, a hook flashing in the stream, and sure enough, he snags, and twitches, can't seem to tear away.

"Tell me, señor," she says, and there it is again, that new timbre in her voice. A low, almost feline purr. "Are you married?" She lets her own gaze roam over the man, measuring his body the way he just measured hers. He colors, and scowls.

"I am," he says, rough hand tightening around the rope.

Sabine takes a small step forward, and even though he is slighter than her husband was—*was*, what a lovely word that is, a perfect tense—the farmer makes no motion to retreat. Of course he doesn't. After all, she is just a woman, isn't she? Half-dressed. Alone.

Her fingers drift up, tugging at the laces on her gown, exposing another inch of skin. "Where is your wife?" she asks, and sure enough, she can feel his heartbeat quicken.

"Inside," he mutters, the air around him thick with want. Simple and animal and raw.

She takes another step, and then another, until she is right there, close enough to touch, to take, close enough he should notice the amount of blood on her clothes, the fact she isn't wounded.

"Are you a good husband?" she asks.

His expression sours. "What?"

"Does she love you?"

"She is my wife," he says bluntly. "She does what she is told."

Sabine's mouth turns down. Her teeth click together. "Is that so?"

He only nods. How strange, that he cannot taste her thoughts, the way she has tasted his. That as he grabs her arm, he is so sure that he's the predator, and she the prey.

By the time he realizes, of course, it is too late.

She slams him back against the gate, teeth sinking deep into his throat.

At some point, he drops the donkey's rope.

At some point, it flees through the open door.

At some point, he swings out with the pitchfork, drives the tines into her side, and what she feels then isn't *pain*, not as she once knew it. She is aware of the tearing flesh, the metal scraping against her hip, but it is nothing compared to the strength of the blood spilling in, filling her again.

Sabine drinks, hoping it will steady the ground beneath her feet, and the farmer tries to scream, but his throat is already open, his voice nothing but a drowning breath. His heart pounds inside her chest, a stolen beat, but it dies there shortly after he does.

His body slumps, lifeless, to the floor. Hers stays on its feet.

She looks down, then, at the metal prongs piercing her side, driven finger deep. She pulls, and they slide free, like teeth. The blood on the tines is dark and thick, and when she grazes it with her tongue, the taste reminds her of the widow.

Earth and ash, the tangle of salt and rotten sweet.

No longer living. Far from dead.

Sabine lets the pitchfork fall beside the farmer's body and feels the flesh across her stomach sew itself together, stitch by invisible stitch, with a skill María never had, leaving nothing but smooth skin. She runs her fingers over it, impressed by this newfound resilience. She takes a step toward the barn door, only to feel the ground tip, the world sway.

Still, she feels dizzy.

Still, she feels sick.

She looks accusingly at the open door, the light streaming in. It is thinner now, lower, too, the sky stained pink with the impending dusk, but the sight of it still hurts, more than the pitchfork did.

Sabine doesn't know for sure, but she *suspects* the sickness and the sun are somehow tethered, so she sinks onto the dead man's back to wait, plucking bits of straw from her loose hair to pass the time. An hour later, when the sun has safely disappeared behind the hills, there is a tidy pile on the floor, and her copper locks lie smooth and plaited down her back.

She rises to her feet and steps outside, and sure enough, as the day retreats, the illness recedes with it.

She has not taken a breath—no longer *needs* to breathe, it seems—and yet, her entire body sighs in relief. She marvels at the change.

Her head no longer aches. Her limbs no longer tremble.

Across the field, a window glows with light. The farmhouse.

She makes her way toward it, savoring the grass on her bare feet. The breeze whispering against her skin.

There is no sign of the farmer's wife, but the door stands open, and Sabine decides to let herself in.

But she cannot.

She makes it to the threshold, but there her body lurches to a stop. It makes no sense—the door is open wide, and she can see straight into the little house—but no amount of force will let her through. Suddenly *she* is the fish on the line, an invisible cord holding her back.

Sabine hisses at this new obstruction.

The widow only ever spoke of freedom, said nothing of these *rules*. She finds herself wishing she had some manner of instruction, wishing, perhaps, she had not drained the woman dry. But there is no purpose to regret. And Sabine is no lost lamb, in need of shepherding. She will decipher this herself.

She is still testing the doorway when, from somewhere in the house, she hears the wife calling for her husband. The footsteps drawing near, and she does at least consider leaving, slipping away into the settling dark.

But, despite the emptied body in the barn, she is still hungry.

The farmer's wife appears, a small, tired-eyed woman, who stops right before the door, nothing but the empty frame and half a stride between them. She startles at the sight of Sabine, surprise and suspicion rising off her like steam.

Sabine stares back, appraisingly. The woman's clothes are simple, boring, but they're clean, and a glance says they will fit.

"Where did you come from?" asks the farmer's wife, glancing past her at the yard, the barn. Perhaps looking for her husband.

"I need help," Sabine answers. "I was robbed."

The woman's gaze snaps back. Takes in the tattered dress. The bare feet. And then, the ruby glinting at her throat. Sabine curses herself softly, waits to see if the lie is ruined, but the woman only proceeds to ask if she is hurt, and unlike the farmer, there *is* at least an edge of worry in the words.

"No," she answers. "But if you give me shelter for the night, I'll see that you're rewarded." She reaches up as she says it, unhooks the necklace for the first time since Andrés clasped it there. The jewel sloughs into her palm.

The woman looks past her one more time, her thoughts so sharp Sabine can almost hear them. *Where is my husband, I should ask him, will he be mad?*

But then Sabine holds out the necklace, lets the ruby catch the light, makes her fingers tremble for good measure.

"Please," she says. A small word, with so much weight.

The farmer's wife swallows, veins flashing in her throat. "All right," she says. "Come in."

As soon as the words are out, Sabine feels the hook slip free, the hold give way. She takes a testing step, and this time, when her bare foot meets the threshold, there is no resistance. Nothing but an open door.

She smiles, and steps inside the house.

"Is that blood?" asks the farmer's wife as the lamplight catches on her dress.

"Don't worry," says Sabine as she reaches back to close the door. "Most of it's not mine."

II

Seville, Spain
1542

Beyond the city walls, ships bob, listless, on black water.

Just inside them, Sabine ambles down a narrow road. The Sailors' Row, they call it.

It is an indecent part of town and an indecent hour, and a woman walking alone must be indecent, too. A body in search of purchase. A body inviting trouble.

Sabine smiles at the thought, her shoes—black leather, almost new—clicking against the cobblestones, her body draped not in widow's weeds, but a lush green dress, a shawl around her shoulders warding off a chill she doesn't even feel.

What would her late mother-in-law say, if she could see her now? Wearing no scarf, no veil, her hair twisted up into a coil, the threads of copper catching fire every time she nears a lamp. She is a flame in the dark, and the night is full of moths.

Their eyes land on her as she walks, trail after in her wake, and she wonders if they can taste her hunger on the air, the way she can taste theirs. Some animal instinct warning them away. And yet, she knows it does not take much to tip the scale, a coy smile, a playful wink, a hand outstretched in invitation. But she has had more than enough of their attention.

Ten years she has been free of that old life.

Ten years she has had to make her way in this one, to carve a path, between the hours of dusk and dawn, to stretch, and grow, and bloom, and while it has not been *easy*, nor has it been arduous. The widow was right. She is free to do what she wants. Take what she wants.

And that is everything.

Sabine walks on, heading for the wooden steps on the western edge of the Row, five rotting stairs where women are known to gather every night.

Indecent women. Young and old, dark-skinned and pale, thin and wide, with painted mouths and weary eyes.

A pair sits at the base of the steps, passing a cup of wine back and forth and waiting for a caller. The air around them smells like need, and sadness, and just beneath, the barest thread of hope.

There are men, of course. So many, and so eager to follow a woman into the dark.

But Sabine has found she far prefers the taste of other women. Just as their skin is softer, she finds their life tastes sweeter, too. More earth than metal. Like burned caramel, perhaps? Hard to say.

After all, it's been ten years since she tasted anything but blood.

In ten more, she'll have been Sabine longer than she ever was María. And she does not miss much about that life, but the bitter tang of citrus? The sour bite of black cherries? The spiciness of coarse mustard? She misses those, has learned the hard way that she can consume a life's worth of blood, but not a bite of fruit. And while she now understands the hungry way the widow watched her hold that chocolate on her tongue, watched her savor, watched her swallow, Sabine does not see the point in dwelling on it. Food holds no appeal, except in memory, and as long as she can recall a taste, she will be haunted by it, the longing like a pebble in her shoe.

Far better to forget.

"Good evening," she says now, stopping beside the women on the step.

The younger one looks up, eyes a little glassy from the drink. But the older one scowls as her gaze rakes over this red-haired stranger in her fine-cut dress.

"Shove off," she snaps. "This is our plot."

Sabine's mouth twitches in amusement. "I'm not here to sell *my* company," she says, drawing the small purse from her dress, the silver rattling as she turns out three coins. "I'm here to purchase yours."

Good money, and yet, the older woman recoils, as if struck. Disgust stains the air around her, and Sabine feels her teeth go sharp inside her mouth. She has already taken a step toward the sitting woman when the younger one rises from her perch.

"I'll do it."

The girl steps into the light, revealing a purple dress washed out to gray. Her mousy hair is braided down her back, stray strands escaping round her

face. Her nose is small and pointed, her eyes wide, alert. She reminds Sabine
of a rabbit, or a fawn—

Or Ysabel.

It is not a true match, of course—the girl is shorter than María's maid,
plumper, too, but the tawny color of her hair, the shape of her face, the way
her lips part even when she is not speaking—it is enough to stir something
in Sabine.

A memory comes nipping at her heels—a picnic laid out on an alcove
floor, her head resting on pillowed skirts—but she pushes it away. Now and
then, that old life rises up to haunt her. But it dies a little more with every
passing night.

"Coin is coin," says the girl with a shrug. "Don't see how it matters which
way I come by it."

The older woman lets a word slide between her teeth, and Sabine pretends
not to hear. She will come back for her, when she is done. But first—

"Come," says the girl, taking her by the hand, and drawing her down the
dock. Away from prying eyes.

Sabine lets herself be led into a gap between the buildings where the lanterns do not reach. But there, the girl's bravado fails her. There, she lets go,
and her hand drops, and even as she turns to face Sabine, she begins to fidget
with a charm around her neck.

"I've never been with a woman," she admits, as if it isn't obvious. As if the
air isn't full of the girl's worry, and her want, her uncertainty, and hunger.
A different kind, of course—a lust for the coins in Sabine's pockets, not her
touch. But hunger all the same.

"I don't know what to do," she stammers, and Sabine smiles, knowing the
darkness will hide her teeth.

"Don't worry," she says. "I'll take care of you."

The girl blushes fiercely. She's younger than she seemed at first, her cheeks
still round with youth. Her hand goes again to the makeshift charm around
her neck. A simple penny, stamped flat and pressed with a V. A bauble, made
herself, or perhaps a lover's token, judging by the way her fingers keep drifting
to it, thumb skating nervously across its surface.

The next time she reaches for the charm, Sabine stops her hand. The girl
jumps a little, startled by the suddenness, the touch, but doesn't pull away.

Relaxes a little when Sabine's grip shifts, gloved fingers grazing the girl's bare skin as she lifts the hand to her mouth and sets a gentle kiss against the knuckles.

What follows is a kind of dance.

Sabine steps forward, and the girl steps back, once, then twice, tensing slightly when her shoulders come up against the wall.

In the dark, she didn't notice it.

Sabine did.

There is nowhere to go, and the girl lets out a shaky laugh, her fingers going to the laces of her dress. "Should I . . . I mean, or do you want me to . . ."

But she trails off as Sabine continues forward, snuffing out the little space left between their bodies. She is a head taller than the girl, and lifts her chin, guiding her face up until their eyes meet.

It is a cool night, and the girl's breath comes out in clouds.

Sabine's does not.

"It's all right," she murmurs, cupping the girl's cheek. She can feel the pulse quickening beneath her skin. Her lips look soft, and for an instant Sabine considers kissing her, the way she once longed to kiss her maid. But then the girl giggles, breath like stale wine, and the illusion breaks.

Sabine's hand slides past her cheek, and through her hair, settling at the nape of her neck.

"Don't be afraid," she says, and a question fills the girl's eyes, right before she pulls her in and bites down, hard, fangs sinking deep into her throat.

Fear spills into the night as the girl stiffens, gasps in pain, tries to push away, but Sabine snakes her other arm around her waist, holding their bodies flush, tight enough to feel the girl's heart hammering against her ribs. And then it is no longer hers.

The silence breaks inside Sabine as the pulse pours in, filling her mouth, her chest, and soon her own heart begins to beat. She comes to life again, teeth driving deeper as the blood floods in and the world goes bright.

A muffled cry escapes the girl, a sound that could pass for pleasure, if not for the terror on the air, the panicked clawing of her limbs. But this is the dark side of the dock at an indecent hour. No one comes.

And so, Sabine drinks, and drinks.

Too soon, the girl stops struggling.

Too soon, the brightness fades, and Sabine's teeth slide free, and the girl slumps lifeless in her arms and a few moments later her own heart begins to slow again, before dragging to a stop.

How brief it is, how fast it fades.

Sabine sighs and withdraws her arm from the girl's waist. She lets go of the body, but not before catching hold of the little charm around her neck. The hammered penny with its etched letter V. The girl collapses, the chain breaking with her weight.

Sabine slips the charm around her neck, settles the pendant in the ruby's place. The ruby, sold off years before, when she had nothing else. A crime, to get so little for the gem, but she was all too happy to be rid of it, to shed the last piece of Andrés, and María. A dozen other trinkets now hang around her neck, a dozen more adorn her hands and wrists.

The heartbeats fade. It's nice, to have something that lasts.

She looks down at the body on the ground, amazed she ever found any resemblance to Ysabel in the unwashed hair, the ruddy cheeks. She feels no guilt, no grief, for what she's done. Given the girl's poor lot, it might as well have been an act of mercy.

Death is a kind of freedom, after all.

Sabine returns to the five rotting steps, intending to bestow that freedom on the older woman, too, but she finds only the wine cup, empty now. She sighs, and tips it over with her shoe.

The night is young, and so she takes the long way home.

Home—a word that once meant something solid. Caravans arriving in a square. Cherry pits tucked like secrets in an olive grove. Bare feet at the edge of a peaked roof.

Now it changes almost nightly. Rooms taken like tokens from her kills, their doorways rendered powerless by death, their contents hers to take. Like this green dress, this purse of coins.

That night, home is a manse that belonged to a wealthy merchant with a long-dead wife, a soft bed, and heavy curtains. Sabine is halfway there, thinking of the well-stuffed mattress, the way she'll sprawl across it, when three men stumble out into the road.

Three men, linked together like old friends, a half-drunk bottle passing from hand to hand. And even though Sabine prefers the lives of women, can still taste the girl's blood on her tongue, she is not one to waste an opportunity. She falls in step behind them, hunger knocking in her chest.

That is the maddening thing about the hunger: it is *always* there.

It quiets, or grows loud, varies in scope, in scale, but never disappears. She drinks as though dying of thirst, but she might as well be a barrel shot through with holes. Incapable of being filled. The life leaks right out again. The hunger redoubles in its wake. It clings to her, even in sleep.

Her dreams are vivid, bloody things.

Sometimes she wakes with her teeth sunk into her forearm, mouth filling with the rotting iron tang, but her own blood seems to hold no nourishment. Nothing but a memory, a ghost of someone else's taste.

Ahead, the three men turn down a narrow road.

And so does she.

One begins a song, and the others take it up.

Their steps ricochet against the stones. Their voices echo on the alley walls. They make so much noise, and she makes none, and so they do not notice her. As she follows, she amuses herself by guessing how the next few minutes will unfold. Perhaps she will kill them all. Perhaps she won't. Perhaps she will get their attention, just to see what they will do. She could wait until they separate, and take them one by one, or simply trail behind them like a ghost, savoring the knowledge that their lives are hers to end.

Sabine is still deciding, when an odd thing happens.

One man slows and peels away, fumbling with the front of his trousers, overcome by the sudden need to piss. He half stumbles to the nearest wall and braces himself, groaning in relief as urine splashes on the stones.

But there is nothing odd in that.

No, it is the other two.

As Sabine watches, one of them sheds his inebriated swagger, easy as a body shedding layers in the heat, revealing a sober stride, a different breed of boldness. Between one step and the next, he is transformed. His companion doesn't notice, but she does. Watches, rapt, as the man runs a hand through his loose curls, then turns toward his drunk compatriot, and sinks his teeth into his throat.

She stiffens in disbelief. Delight.

Sabine, who has only once been the victim of such an act, and ever after the assailant, now finds herself spectator. Witness to the intimacy of the embrace, the head bent low, the mouth against the curve of skin, the arms that fold, viselike, around the man's body, the gasping absence of a scream.

In an instant, the singing dies, the smell of piss overtaken by the scent of blood. She cannot taste the life, but she can see it fleeing, the expression slipping with the color from his face. She feels a phantom pain, as if she's the one whose heart is failing. A phantom pleasure, too, her own mouth aching as the stranger drinks, and drinks, and drinks.

The third man remains oblivious, still humming as he puts himself away, fastens his trousers and turns back toward his companions. The melody dies on his lips. He is too drunk to understand the scene in front of him, but fear is a primal thing. It slicks the air around him as he stumbles back, twists round, movements made slow and sloppy by the night's festivities. He staggers, and she can hear his heart thudding with a single, urgent word.

Away. Away. Away. Away.

The man does not give chase, so *she* does, or means to, but she has hardly moved when another gets there first.

A woman.

She peels away from the alley wall, like a shadow freed from the surrounding night, her skin dark, her hair darker still. Sabine doesn't know how she didn't see her before, but now that she has, she cannot look away.

The woman is doll-like, small and curved, with jet-black eyes and hair that floats around her face, a halo of tight curls. She steps into the third man's path as he stumbles for a second time, goes down, and as he struggles to his feet she catches him, draws him up like a lover, her expression lovely, gentle, sweet.

"What's wrong?" she asks, the scent of violence heavy on the air as he clutches at her and stammers out, "Diablo."

Her face, contorting with concern as she looks past him. At the first man, still feasting on his friend. And then past him still, at *her*. Sabine. The woman's eyes are bright with mischief as she says, "But sir, there are no devils here."

Her tone is so earnest that for a second, his fear seems to fumble, gives way to confusion, even hope, as he turns to follow her gaze. Sees what the woman sees. Opens his mouth to scream. But it's too late. She has already torn open his throat. Blood courses in a bright, metallic stream.

Sabine watches the woman drink until the sound of a body falling, dead weight against the cobblestones, tears her gaze away. The man stands over the drunkard's corpse, wiping an arm across his face as his dark eyes land squarely on Sabine.

His mouth draws into a bloodstained smirk, and for the first time in ten years, Sabine feels herself *retreat*. A step—only a step—her limbs moving before her mind, instinct taking hold before she thinks to smother it. But in that step, he moves, blocking the alley's mouth as if she means to *flee*. As if the thing washing over her is *fear*, instead of fascination.

Sabine bristles at the thought.

She turns back in time to see the woman vanish, the body in her arms dropping lifeless to the street. By the time it hits the ground, the woman has reappeared, her face now inches from Sabine's, her black eyes glowing faintly, like windowpanes at night.

"Hello, little shadow." Her voice is soft, and strangely gentle, that same unnerving sweetness she directed at the man, so at odds with the manic gleam, the sharpness of her teeth.

"Where have you been?" she coos, her lips stained dark with blood—in that moment Sabine wants to kiss her, just to taste it. And even though she can hear the minds of others, when their thoughts are loud enough, she is still shocked when the woman leans close and whispers, "Go ahead."

Sabine stiffens, and the woman laughs, a bright and airy sound.

"Does she speak?" asks the man, his voice a low rumble, like far-off thunder, and yet it carries, reaches Sabine and rolls right over her.

Before the woman can say anything, she turns toward him and answers for herself. "She does."

"Oh, Hector." The woman's hand trails between her shoulders, a touch that makes her shiver. "Can I keep her?"

Sabine prickles. She was thrown by their appearance, but she will not let herself be tossed around. "I am not a pet."

"No," says the man. Hector. "You are not. Come, Renata."

The woman pouts a little. But she doesn't leave. Instead, she reaches out and touches Sabine's face, cool fingers cupping her cheek, and to Sabine's horror, her body betrays her once again, this time by leaning *in*. Those night-sky eyes, black and flecked with stars, fix on her, and hold.

"Not yet, perhaps," she says. "But I can taste your longing."

Sabine wants to knock her hand away, to tell her she's wrong, that the only *longing* she feels is that relentless hunger, a need for blood, and nothing else.

But it would be a lie. And Sabine knows that this stranger can feel the truth, messy as it is. That she is glad—glad her husband is dead. Glad he can no longer storm her bed, her body, glad she does not have to fear a seed, a growing womb, a child. Glad that she is free of Andrés, and his family, free of that old life, free of age, and illness.

But sometimes, when Sabine is sinking into sleep, or waking from it, she skirts a dream, a life where she did not leave León alone that night. And she fears she left something important in the darkened shop.

That sometimes, when she walks at night, Sabine imagines the widow at her side. And she feels a deep, simmering rage, because it does not seem fair that the only two choices she was given were to be alive and bound, or alone and dead. And no matter how much life she drinks, it does not seem to touch that other thirst, that want for company, and—

The woman brushes her lips against Sabine's.

A ghost of a kiss, carrying the taste of blood, the air of promise.

A ghost of a kiss, and yet, the first one she has ever welcomed—wanted— and if she had a pulse, it would be racing. Even still, something quickens in her, and she feels herself lean closer, hungry for—

"Renata," calls the man again, and just like that, the mouth is gone, she is gone, Sabine left standing there, alone again, licking the blood from her lips as Renata slides her arm through Hector's, lays her head against his shoulder. They stroll down the alley. Away from her.

Sabine feels the night tip. The ground no longer steady.

Wait, she thinks as they reach the mouth of the alley. Renata looks back over her shoulder, her smile crooking like a finger.

And Sabine follows.

III

The night splits around them, giving way like skin beneath a blade.

The other two walk several strides ahead, but now and then, Renata glances back, flashes Sabine the very corner of a smile, as if to say, *Good, you are still there.*

And she is.

For the first time in her life, she follows without protest, driven on by curiosity, and something else. There is an echo of the widow to them, not just in their languid motion, but the current in the air, the same aura that caught María's eye that day in Santo Domingo, the visceral pull she felt at the market in León.

She does not know where they are going, if they are friend or foe, if this is an enticement or a trap. She only knows that they are like her.

It is enough to hold Sabine in their wake, even when they turn away from the city instead of heading deeper in. Even when they pass through the outer gates and head toward the bay and the line of bobbing ships, boots sinking in the sand with every step.

Soon they reach a waiting boat, a wooden ramp, and there—for the first and only time—she hesitates.

It is an elegant vessel, the hull almost new, the sails crisp, hardly weather-worn. But she has never sailed, has always thought a ship a kind of house on water, the deck's edge a doorway. And yet, when the two reach the ramp's edge, they simply step aboard. As if it belongs to them. It must.

Sabine slows, waiting for an invitation, but the two strangers have already disappeared from sight, and so she follows, expecting any moment to feel that lurch, that backward pull she first discovered at the farmer's house, the space gone solid—but it doesn't come. The air is simply air. The place where ramp meets deck nothing but wood beneath her feet.

She steps aboard. Up ahead, Hector strolls over to the wheel, and Renata twists her fingers through the rigging and twirls, skirts rippling around her calves.

"Isn't it pretty?" she says, appearing suddenly beside Sabine. She moves like light, quick and silent.

Sabine looks around. Knows nothing of ships, but it strikes her as too large for only two people. Especially ones confined to night.

"Is there no one else here?" she asks.

"Not at the moment," says Hector, abandoning the wheel. He strides across the deck, toward a set of stairs that pitch into the belly of the ship.

Renata loops an arm through hers, the gesture so casual, so intimate, Sabine does not even think to fight it, only lets herself be led down into the dark.

A lantern swings from the low ceiling, though Sabine's eyes do not need the light to see that they have traded the world above for a narrow hall, one studded with alcoves, where hammocks stretch between posts, and belongings lie piled on the floor.

Sabine crinkles her nose at the closeness, the clutter, but Renata draws her on, to the end of the corridor, where a door gives way onto a larger cabin.

A proper room at the front of the ship, porthole windows facing out onto the open bay. A bed, piled high with blankets. A broad desk, and plush curtains, and a high-backed chair. A sofa, where Renata promptly sprawls like a cat.

Sabine's attention lingers on her, her body small and curved, skin dark and delicate as window glass at night. Hector wanders toward the desk, and Sabine turns to shut the door behind them, only to find her reflection staring back from a polished glass mounted to the wood.

Ten years, and she is as striking as she ever was, her hazel eyes now lit by their own internal light. Her skin has lost none of its smoothness, her hair none of its luster. She hasn't aged, not since the night María died, and she became—

"Sabine."

Her head snaps round, startled by her name on Hector's lips.

She is sure she never said it.

"Don't look so alarmed," he says, leaning back against the desk. "Some minds whisper. Others shout. Yours is loud. What amuses me, though, is that your name is louder still."

"*Sabine, Sabine,* it echoes through you like a bell," adds Renata cheerfully, and she bristles, not just at the truth of it, or their intrusion, but the fact that no matter how carefully she listens, all *she* hears is the slap of water on the hull, the groan of wood around them.

Sabine tries harder to catch the current of their minds, only to find it is no use.

They are twin patches of deep shadow, the first her heightened senses have not been keen enough to pierce.

"I can't hear you," she says, trying and failing to hide her annoyance.

"You are young," says Hector, lifting a decanter from the desk. "And we are not. But rest assured," he adds, "I won't go turning through your thoughts. That would be rude."

He reaches for a goblet, and pours, a ribbon of red unfurling from the spout, too thick to be anything but blood. The metal scent of it fills the room, the air, her head.

"But your maker should have taught you this," he says, frowning a little as he hands Sabine the cup.

Maker.

The widow.

Nothing but ash on an apothecary floor.

"She did not," says Sabine, staring down into the cup. She thinks briefly of that night, knows that it was wrong. Can taste the taboo in the roots of her teeth, and so, before she can dwell, or they can hear, she lifts the goblet to her lips and drinks, knowing the blood will clear her mind, wash away everything.

It does—and it doesn't.

It has never occurred to Sabine to drink from anything but the source, but now, as the liquid pools in her mouth, she knows why. It tastes of blood, yes, her body soaks it up the same, but it is . . . thinner. There is no moment of transfer, no point when the life goes from being someone else's to being *hers*. There is no stolen pulse, no borrowed heart inside her chest.

It feeds, but does not fill her.

Still, she drinks. Stops before the cup is empty, though she'd gladly drain the goblet and decanter both. Looks up to find Hector sitting on the sofa, arms stretched along the back. Renata melts into his side, and she wonders how long they have been together, to fit like that, wearing space into each other's bodies.

Envy twinges between her ribs. "You are lucky to have each other," she says, handing back the cup. "I have always been alone."

Hector clicks his tongue. "But you are wrong," he says, sitting forward, and she can see his eyes are not dark, as she first thought—the pupils have retreated, revealing a medley of gray and green, fringed with thick lashes. "Those grown in the midnight soil are never alone."

"The midnight soil?" she echoes. It is an odd choice of words.

"Ah, you do not know . . . ?" Hector stands, arms spread like a player on a stage.

"Oh, dear," murmurs Renata, resting her head on her hand. "He loves an audience."

Hector pretends not to hear her as he pushes the curls from his face and clears his throat.

"Bury my bones in the midnight soil," he begins, infusing the words with the air of theater. "Plant them shallow and water them deep. And in my place will grow a feral rose." He leans down to Renata and cups her face, running a thumb across her bottom lip. "Soft red petals hiding sharp white teeth."

He kisses her then, and Renata nips at his lip, drawing blood. He swipes his tongue across the cut, and smiles, before straightening, his attention sliding back toward Sabine.

"We are the roses that grew in the midnight soil," he says, eyes bright as candles now. "Our thorns are sharp enough to prick. We are watered by life, and with its bounty, our roots grow deep, our blooms unmarred by age. In fact, for us, time fortifies, renders us more noble. We are no monster, no mean thing. We are nature's finest flower."

Renata rolls her eyes, playful, but bored. This is a speech she has clearly heard a hundred times. But Sabine cannot hide the hold it has on her, the way she hangs on every word.

"There are other names for us, of course," continues Hector. "Night walker. Blood drinker. Abomination. Vampire. But those are words crafted by mortal tongues. They are imperfect, incomplete. They lack the poetry, the brutality, the grace. No," he says. "We are roses."

With that, Hector sags onto the sofa once more, as if spent.

"A feral rose," muses Sabine, rolling the words across her tongue. "You are a poet, Hector."

He chuckles. "Time makes poets of us all," he says, crossing his ankles, "but I am not so old as that. I did not write those words. I learned them from my maker, who learned them from his." He strokes Renata's cheek. "After all, it is a maker's job, to teach the ones they've made."

He tips his head to one side. "Tell me, Sabine. Did yours teach you *any-thing?*"

An image sparks behind her eyes. The widow, in her shop, plucking the soft white flower from its vase, speaking of freedom, of laying claim, satisfying any want as she crushed the blossom in her hand. The widow, crumbling beneath her teeth.

"No," she says. "She was already gone."

"How sad," murmurs Renata.

"Yes," says Hector, "that is unfortunate."

He kisses Renata's temple, but his eyes hang on Sabine. And though he said he would not go pawing through her thoughts, she feels exposed. Not un*dressed*, but un*raveled*, shot through as well as seen.

No, she thinks, imagining the doors slamming shut, not around her body, but her mind.

Can he feel the rebuff, her refusal to let him in? She doesn't know.

He doesn't flinch back, or frown, show any signs of registering the rebuke. But the pressure of his gaze falls off. He eases himself out of Renata's embrace and rises to his feet, turns his back on them both as he fills the goblet and drifts to the porthole.

"It's time to go," he says, and Sabine flinches at the dismissal, assuming he means her. Until he turns back, and flashes a rakish smile, showing teeth. "Seville is nice," he says. "But I think we have had our fill of it."

So they are the ones leaving, then.

But to Sabine's surprise, she does not want them to go. Or rather, she does not want to be left behind, not when there is so much she clearly does not know. And if that is not the only reason, if there is a small piece of her that longs for company—well, it is nothing but a sliver, compared to her curiosity, her hunger to learn what they are, and how they live, and what they know.

She lets her thoughts ring through her mind, as loud as she can make them, hoping they will hear. And sure enough, Hector nods and says, "You're welcome to join us."

Renata sits up, suddenly buoyant. "We can teach you."

Sabine smiles. There is no need to say yes. Renata is already on her feet, snaking her arms around Sabine's waist, finding the space and way that she will fit.

"When do we leave?" she asks.

We—a word that feels strange on her tongue. It has been so long since her life was tethered to another's. A wedding ring, a marriage bed, a ruby like a collar at her throat. But this is different. It does not feel like being bound so much as linked.

"Tonight," says Hector, leading them back up onto the deck.

Sabine runs a hand along the ropes. "I know nothing of ships," she admits.

Renata only laughs. "Neither do we."

"I sailed, for a time," says Hector. "But it's been a century at least."

Sabine frowns. "I thought this was your boat."

"It is," he says, unwinding a rope, "as of tonight."

"We killed the crew," adds Renata. Which would explain the size of the boat, the number of empty hammocks below. She leans over the rail. "We sunk the bodies with weights, but it's shallow, and the tide is going out."

"A good first lesson, dear Sabine," says Hector, unfurling a sail. "You should always be found ahead of your corpses, and never in their wake."

IV

How strange it is, after so many years alone, to find herself with constant company.

Strange, but not unwelcome.

That first month, they play at being sailors. Most days they drift, safe in the darkened belly of the ship. Most nights, they go ashore. They skim a dozen harbors, docking long enough to sate themselves, gone again before the bodies can be found or counted.

Now and then, they pretend they have been stranded, run up a white sail and wait for aid to come, and when it does, they feast and cast the corpses over the side, leaving empty vessels, like fruit peels, in their wake. And when they grow bored of sailing, which they do as summer nears, they find the nearest port, sell the ship, and set off in search of trouble.

Every night, it seems, they find it. In taverns and on travel roads, in plaza squares and busy inns. Hector and Renata fold Sabine into their games, as if each were made for three instead of two. How seamlessly they hunt, how carelessly they kill. How much fun they make it all.

And every night, Sabine's collection grows. When she walks, the charms and pendants at her wrists and throat knock against each other, chiming like bells. Now and then they break off, fall away, shed like bits of skin. She lets them go, knows there will be plenty more.

Hector and Renata tease her for the little tokens, but she doesn't care. She likes the weight of them, like armor, the way she can run her fingers over the bits of metal, glass, crystal, stone, and remember the bodies that they came from, recounting each and every kill.

The seasons change, and bit by bit, so does Sabine.

She didn't realize how stiff she'd grown in solitude, how tightly she was coiled, until her new companions begin to loosen her. They are so intimate, so physical, and they extend that tenderness to her. Liquid as they are, Hector and Renata massage her into movement, like coaxing winter into spring, until Sabine feels herself unfurl.

Welcoming Renata's fingers as they dance up and down her spine, or smooth the crease that forms sometimes between her brows. A touch that makes heat bloom beneath the surface of her skin.

Welcoming Hector's palm as it strokes her hair, or grazes her cheek. His touch so different from her husband's, firm but never laying claim. A touch both familiar and familial. And unlike Renata's, it holds no heat, only a pleasant, steady warmth.

Sabine heard once that happiness makes time move quick.

Perhaps that is why their first year passes in a blur.

And yet, she will always remember *this*:

The three of them, drawn into a square by the rise and fall of a guitar, the steady beating of a drum, the music like a pulse calling them forward. Her red hair flashing like a fishing lure alongside Renata's glowing skin and Hector's charm. The air around them heavy with curiosity and want. Their limbs tangled like roots.

And after: Renata's laughter skipping down stone walls, and Hector, plucking a pair of white roses from a bursting hedge, and gifting one to his love, and the other to her as he declares Renata his *petal*, and Sabine his *thorn*.

"Espina mía," he calls her, like a ghost of esposa mía—my wife—the sounds so similar, the weight so different. Ironic, that *wife* is meant to be a gentler word, and yet on her late husband's lips it always felt like a rebuke, a sharp tug on a short leash. And as for *espina*—

"It is a compliment," he says, tucking the rose behind Sabine's ear. "We grow in the same soil, it is true, but some of us wither there, and some of us thrive. In time, you learn," he adds, eyes dropping to the trinkets layered at her throat, "which of us makes better monsters."

Sabine's mouth twitches in a smile. She is glad to be a thorn.

Renata calls out from down the road, drawing restless circles around a lamppost, skirts flaring gently in the breeze.

Soft red petals, she thinks as Hector drifts away.

Sabine watches him go as she tugs the rose from her hair, barbs catching on the strands, carrying threads of copper with it.

"Espina mía," she murmurs, bringing her thumb to a thorn, pressing down until the skin splits, and sluggish blood wells up. A drop runs down her wrist.

"Sabine!" calls Renata, one arm hooked through Hector's and the other reaching out, toward her. She smiles, licking the blood from her skin.

"Coming," she calls, dropping the flower to the street.

V

Córdoba, Spain
1557

One by one, the books fall down, each landing with a dull thud on the rug.

"Latin. Latin. Greek. Parable," mutters Hector, pulling them from the shelf.

"What are you looking for?" asks Sabine from the low sofa where she lies, sprawled like moss across the velvet cushions.

He tugs another from the shelf, studying its contents before flinging it aside. "Something I haven't *read*."

Sabine rolls her eyes. Hector and his books.

It's been decades since she first eyed the folios in the Olivares house, since she sounded out the names on the bottles in the widow's shop. A lifetime, and in that time, she has learned to decipher the marks well enough, can make sense of what she reads. But she has never understood the draw of doing it for pleasure.

She mentioned, once, that the whole pursuit seemed tedious, and Hector lost his head, went on such a tear about how she simply hadn't found the right story, how when she did, she'd understand. Sabine only shrugged, and said she was content to amuse herself in other ways.

"How many scriptures does one house *need*?" he snarls, casting the good book across the room. Sabine may not spend her hours reading texts, but she has had fifteen years in which to read Hector and Renata, front to back. Has studied both enough to know that Renata can be as cruel as she is ardent, always burning hot, while Hector swings like a pendulum between sulking and exuberant, uncanny stillness and sudden bursts of movement.

Tonight, he is restless.

He paces, sits and rises again, a sea churned up, as if possessed, ignited.

It is beginning to annoy her.

Sabine does her best to ignore his manic air, turning her attention to the ceiling overhead. She studies the seven beams that run from wall to wall, each the width of a well-grown tree, until she finds it, in the grain of the centermost log: a face. The whorls, like eyes, the darkened groove like a disapproving mouth. The fire cracks and spits in the hearth, and by its unsteady light, the mouth flickers between indifference and anger.

Sabine scowls back as another book lands on the floor nearby with a muffled thud.

"He gets like this sometimes," says Renata, drifting through the doorway, "after he's indulged." The only evidence of her time upstairs is a single smudge of red across her bottom lip. "One craving begets another."

She sweeps her arm across the room as she says it.

It is an elegant room in an elegant house, fit for the family of six who lived there, and who now lie strewn about like cast-off clothes, linens wrung dry after a wash. A man and woman both slumped against the wall. Another lying in the hall, the gold rope of her hair creeping along the bottom of the doorframe. The children, now upstairs in their beds.

Sabine has never had a thirst for such small prey, but Renata seems to savor it, likes to sit them on her lap as if they're hers, rock them to sleep before putting them to bed for the last time. To each their own, she thinks.

There were six at the beginning of the night.

Now, there is only one.

A man, robust and in the flush of youth—perhaps that's why he's managed to hold on so long, despite the loss of blood. He's sitting on the floor, shoulders propped against the side of a chair.

He called her *bitch, demon, whore.* So many invectives spilling from his bloodied mouth. Now it opens and closes without a sound, and his chest hitches with every shallow breath. Sabine might have killed him faster, if he hadn't been so rude.

Renata sinks into the cushioned seat and rests her hand on the crown of his head, begins to play with his dark curls as if he were a pet. But his eyes are trained on nothing, his sluggish heart fighting against the downward pull of death.

Hector has finally abandoned the pursuit of books and instead found a fiddle. He begins meandering through a song with the air of someone plucking the notes out of thin air. His fingers stain the bow.

The face on the ceiling smiles. Frowns. Smiles. Glares.

Sabine sits up, and the room sways, the way it did sometimes when they were on the ship. The hearth light blooms in her vision, and it's been so long since she felt unsteady or unwell that it takes her a moment to recognize this feeling.

Her bare feet land on the rug, and she declares, with equal parts annoyance and amusement, that she feels *drunk*.

"It's in the blood," explains Renata. "What they take in, so do you. At least to some degree."

Hector stops playing, props the fiddle on his knee. "Blood is blood," he says, "and yet, that is like saying food is food, whether it be vegetable or venison." He gestures with the bow. "Yes, it all serves to nourish, but that does not mean it satisfies the same."

"A difference in the details," says Renata. "Here, I'll show you."

A bottle of Calvados sits half-empty on a side table. With one hand, Renata takes it up. With the other, she knots her fingers in the dying man's hair, draws his head back and forces the bottle to his lips.

"Drink, my darling," she says. "I'm trying to make a point."

He struggles, throat bobbing against the liquor, but soon his protests are forced down. Liquid conquers air.

"Think of it as a decanting," says Renata cheerfully.

Hector chuckles and rests the fiddle back beneath his chin.

"Come," she says, twitching her free hand toward Sabine, who has never enjoyed being given a command, and yet, in Renata's mouth, the word turns playful. In Renata's mouth, it is soft, and coaxing, and Sabine gives in and goes to her, the room rolling gently beneath her feet.

"Drink," she says, and that is an easy order.

Sabine kneels, brings her mouth to the man's straining neck. Skin breaks beneath her teeth, the blood pours in, and there is the heartbeat on her tongue, the drumming in her chest, the only part she's ever focused on. But now, as she drinks, she reaches past it, and finds, folded in the metal tang, the sharp sweetness of winter fruit.

Sabine forces herself to stop, to pull away, not because she wants to, no, only because Renata is at her ear, asking softly, "Well, what do you taste?"

The man's head slumps against his chest, the neat crescent of her fangs already fading. His skin has taken on a ghoulish pallor, and yet somehow his stubborn heart clings on. Sabine closes her eyes and swallows, the taste retreating with the pulse.

"Apples," she says, with a delighted, dizzy laugh.

That laugh, a sound so foreign in her ears it seems to come from someone else. Renata grins, and rises, drawing Sabine with her. The room rocks, and tilts, the heady mix of blood and liquor buzzing through her, but Renata keeps her on her feet.

Hector has taken up his melancholy song again, but she insists on something cheerful. Obligingly, he changes to a folksy tune. And then they are dancing, Renata and Sabine, twirling barefoot across the rug, careful not to trip on fallen limbs.

It is a moment to press in amber.

A lightness she has never felt.

Until Renata twirls her once, too hard, and then lets go, and Sabine loses her balance, her quick senses rushing to catch up with her slow limbs.

She stumbles, not on a body, but a short wooden stool that breaks beneath her when she falls. The fiddle skids to a stop as the stool snaps, and splinters beneath her, a thick shard piercing her back.

There is pain, but it's a ghost, a pale echo of the things she once felt, and Sabine thinks little of it as she reaches back, wraps her hand around the wood. She draws it out, sighing in relief, and annoyance. After all, her dress is ruined.

She scowls at the offending stick, then looks up to find Hector's face contorted, Renata's hand at her mouth. Twin pictures of shock, horror. As if a bit of wood could fell Sabine.

"What?" she asks, dropping the shard onto the pile. The blood has already stopped, the skin knitting clean. "It is nothing."

"But it could have been . . ." whispers Renata.

"What have *I* to fear from a bit of wood?" she answers blithely, but the room's easy cheer has melted, replaced by something heavy. Hector's expression darkens.

"I forget, sometimes," he mutters, shaking his head, "how little you know."

Sabine bristles, opens her mouth to bite back, but just then the man on the floor summons the last of his strength, and makes a final, doomed effort at escape. He drags himself across the rug, makes it barely an arm's length before Hector strolls over and uses his boot to nudge the man onto his back. Crouches and splays a hand across the man's heaving chest, though his attention lands solely on Sabine.

"What have you to fear?" he echoes darkly. "Let me show you."

His fingers dig in, sinking through shirt and skin. The man's rib cage gives with a sick crunch, the scent of blood heavy on the air, his mouth yawning in a scream that dies somewhere around his throat as Hector tears out his heart.

The body twitches, and goes still, and Hector rises, and walks over to Sabine, and drops the organ in her lap.

If Hector meant to horrify her, he has failed. She is hardly squeamish.

Sabine looks down, weighs the bloody mass in her palm. She has never held a heart before. It is small, but dense, at once heavier and lighter than she imagined. This lump of flesh made lifeless without its host.

"Behold," he says, "the sole source of our fragility."

Her fingers tense around the heart, as if willing it to beat. But her grip is too strong, and it emits only a trickle of blood before collapsing inward. Fragile.

Nothing about her is supposed to be fragile now. And yet—

"If that bit of wood had driven deeper, you'd be dead."

Sabine flinches.

"Are there other ways to die?" she asks, thinking of the widow, crumbling to ash against her dress.

"Yes, and no," says Renata. "Your bones will set. Your skin will mend. But the heart alone stays mortal. It is the seat of life, and death. If it is ruined, or removed, severed from the head or drained of all its blood, there is no mending to be done. When the heart collapses, so do we. If you must die," she adds thoughtfully, "a blade or stick is quick, a bite is kind, but fire is a bad end."

Sabine looks up. "Why is that?"

It is Hector who answers. "Because the heart burns *last*." He fetches up a bit of broken stool, a slice of wood the length of his forearm, and wags it like a finger. "Fire, steel, wood, it does not matter. Destroy our hearts, and we are destroyed as well. So, I suggest you learn to guard yours better."

With that, he flicks his hand, and sends the wood slicing toward her chest.

Sabine catches it, of course, he knew she would, but the point is close—too close—and the look in his eye is full of scorn, the air taut as a cord, and there is a moment, only a moment, when she wants to stand and drive the shard up beneath his ribs, just to end this lecture.

Just a moment, but then Renata is on her feet, gliding between them.

"Easy, my love," she coos at Hector, though she reaches for Sabine. "She didn't know. And now she does." Renata is still looking at her *love* as she grazes Sabine's wrist, gently takes the stake from her hand and tosses it into the hearth. Her head never turns, and yet, that touch is like a small but knowing look, a silent warning.

And then it's gone, and she is focused solely on Hector. She strokes his back and says something in his native Catalan. He sighs and rakes his fingers through his hair, leaving flecks of dry blood in their wake. And by the time his hand falls back to his side, the pendulum has swung again, the air loosening as he sweeps up the fiddle and begins to play, neither the dirge nor the dance, but something brighter.

And it would be easy to forget, to believe that nothing happened, except the evidence is everywhere.

The broken stool.

The decimated corpse.

The heart, cold and lifeless in her hand.

Later, she will think about this moment as a turning of the tide. The beginning of the end. But for now, Hector finds the melody, and Renata folds herself back into her chair, and Sabine tosses the ruined heart into the fire, and watches as it burns.

VI

Winter becomes spring, and spring becomes summer, and summer once again gives way to fall. They tangle like weeds, the three of them, and yet there is an order to it. Sabine on one side, Hector on the other, Renata squarely between, keeping them together, holding them apart.

Sabine and Hector bicker now and then, but she is not one to flinch, or shrink from a fight, and he enjoys her boldness—after all, she is not a petal, but a thorn—and if he can feel her occasional urge to push him from the nearest cliff, well, it doesn't seem to faze him much.

They pass the days in the houses that they've emptied, in rooms rented to men and women who vanish in the night. Doors locked, and curtains drawn against the sun, Hector and Renata sleep together in the largest bed. More than once, they invite Sabine to join them there, but she still relishes her own space, retreating to a second room, a private refuge.

But she doesn't go far—admits, if only to herself, that she does not mind the nearness of them, the way the solid silence of their bodies takes up space.

And then one night, Renata climbs out of Hector's bed, and into hers.

Renata, whose touch has always sparked something in her. Whose fingers wake her now, tapping like rain against her skin.

Even half asleep, Sabine no longer pulls away. She rolls toward the touch, finds Renata staring at her, eyes like darkened panes, small candles burning behind glass. A silent question. A silent answer. Then, Renata's mouth on hers.

They have kissed a hundred times, but this is different.

Perhaps it is the way Renata's bare limbs wind around her body, or the fact Hector isn't watching, but heat plumes beneath her skin, and her heart seems to turn over in her chest. A smile pressed against her lips, and then Renata's mouth begins to travel, leaving a trail of kisses down her throat, over her breasts. The skim of teeth against her skin makes her entire body kindle, light.

Renata's hand drifts lower, hooks the hem of her nightgown, plays up over her thigh. Then it slips between her legs, and Sabine catches her wrist as something clamps inside her. A ghost of that old rebellion. A pair of doors flung shut against impending siege.

"No," she says. "Not that."

But when Renata begins to pull away, Sabine's grip tightens on her wrist, unwilling to let go. Renata halts, hovers, trying to read her expression in the dark.

"Tell me," she whispers, "what do you want?"

That is the problem, isn't it? She doesn't *know*. Sabine is full of knowing what she does *not* want, but even after all these years, she hasn't found the words for what she *does*. The air must be filling with her longing and frustration, because Renata shifts, brings her mouth back to Sabine's.

"You lead," she says. "I'll follow."

Something comes loose then. Something clicks.

Sabine rolls over, pressing Renata down into the bed—a memory rises up, of Andrés struggling beneath her—but Renata only smiles. Small as she is, there is no human weakness. She has that stony strength, a mirror of Sabine's, disguised by supple skin, curving hips.

Renata reaches up to touch Sabine, but she *tsks*, and takes her hands and guides them onto the cushion above her head.

"Stay," she says, and Renata does, her arms raised, her fingertips against the headboard, her body a map, waiting to be charted. Her stillness, an invitation to explore.

Sabine straddles Renata and surveys the smooth terrain, first with her eyes—eyes that capture every slope and line, even in the dark—and then with her hands.

She takes her time exploring, as if trying to memorize the contours of Renata's collarbones, her hips, her navel. Until Renata starts to shift again beneath her, not restless but eager, body arching, and Sabine lays a palm flat against her stomach and pushes her back down into the bed.

"I said, stay," she orders softly.

Renata bites her lip, and whispers, "Please," the words too faint for human ears. Whispers, "I want this." Whispers, "I want you."

And yet, it's clear, she will not take what she wants. Will let Sabine decide when and how to give it to her. Sabine, who is getting bolder now.

"Do you?" she whispers back as her hand slides down Renata's stomach, and then, lower still, between their bodies, coming to rest in the shadow between Renata's legs. Stroking the soft folds. "Do you want me?"

She studies Renata's face, sees the candles brighten, her mouth part, the air clouding with a hunger she doesn't try to hide.

"Yes," she pleads, and Sabine's fingers slip inside.

Renata's body answers instantly, warm, and wet, her head tipping back, her throat long and her mouth open, fangs glinting in the dark. She looks the way Sabine feels right after she bites someone. Like she's the one who's breaking open.

Her fingers curl, and Renata lets out a small gasp, and this time, Sabine doesn't stop her when the other woman reaches up, fingers snaking through her copper hair, grasping the back of her neck, pulling her closer.

Sabine catches Renata's mouth with hers, teeth skating along her bottom lip. Doesn't know she's broken the soft skin there until she tastes the blood, earthy, sweet.

Her senses flare. Her body comes alive again. And even though there's no one between *her* legs, she feels her own pleasure mounting with Renata's.

In her marriage bed, she'd been nothing but a site where pleasure happened to someone else, but as Renata's body clenches around her hand, Sabine feels *awash* in pleasure.

Renata is panting louder now, and Sabine, sure that Hector will hear them, presses her free hand over Renata's gasping mouth as her pleasure crests and her whole body tenses beneath Sabine.

As her limbs go slack, Renata laughs against her palm. Sabine withdraws, and lies beside her, expecting her to leave. But she doesn't, simply winds her limbs like roots around Sabine, and crashes into sleep.

Sabine lies there, folded in Renata's arms, her scent, her own limbs heavy in the aftermath, until she drifts off, too.

When Sabine wakes, it is night, and her bed is empty.

She rises and finds Renata and Hector dancing lazy circles in the sitting room as he teaches her something called a waltz.

Sabine sits on the edge of a chair and braids her hair, and watches, sure that he will take one look at her and know, and this life of theirs will fall apart.

But that whole night passes, and Hector makes no mention of it.

He knows, of course he knows. Sabine is certain of it.

There are no secrets between the three of them, and even if Sabine could keep what happened to herself, Renata seems determined to put it on display. More than once, she abandons Hector's side for Sabine's, as if staking claim there, one arm snaking around her waist. More than once, she kisses her outright. More than once, she fondles, strokes. And every touch makes Sabine tense a little more beneath Hector's watching gaze, until her whole body is coiled and bracing for the fight.

And yet, it does not come.

Hector only smiles, and carries on alone.

She cannot fathom it. Andrés was such a jealous man. And so she watches him all night, trying to read the air around him, trying to grasp at his mind, his mood, his thoughts, trying and failing until at last, he turns on her and snaps that he can feel her knocking at the door, and it is grating on his nerves.

"If you have something to say," he scolds, "just say it."

It's a relief to be confronted, and she lets the truth spill out. "I bedded Renata."

Hector doesn't plunge into one of his moods, doesn't strike out at her, doesn't rant or rage. He just cocks his head to one side. "And?" he asks, confirming her suspicions. He knows. He knows, and yet—

"You are not mad."

He only shrugs. "Why should I be? Because she is *mine*?" His mouth twitches. "Renata does not *belong* to me, Sabine. And even if she did, forever is a very long time. She is free to amuse herself however she likes. Sometimes that means she wanders off, into someone else's bed."

His tone never darkens, but his eyes do.

"You thought I would be threatened. By you. But I am her *maker*, Sabine. Renata will never look at you the way she looks at me. You will never mean as much to her as I do."

He might as well have struck her, the words stinging like a handprint on her cheek. It makes her feel foolish and small. It makes her want to break something. Someone. But Hector has not finished breaking *her*.

He shakes his head and says, "Perhaps one day you will understand what it means to truly matter to another. Until then, just remember, little thorn." He smiles, with not so much as a candle's worth of warmth. "You may be her plaything. But I am her *god*."

That night, Sabine thinks of killing Hector.

Of fleeing Spain.

Of slaughtering a town, and leaving the two of them to be discovered in the bodies' wake.

But then, Renata climbs back into her bed, and pulls her close, and makes Sabine promise not to leave. And she does not understand the look in the other woman's eyes, the sheer weight of the request.

"I won't," she promises.

She does not feel the words wrap around her heart like chains until the next time, when her bed is empty, and she tries to leave, and learns the hard way that, among their kind, promises are *binding*.

And so she has no choice.

She stays.

VII

That next year, they sweep through Spain like a sickness.

Whole villages reduced to graveyards in their wake.

For weeks, the church bells seem to ring relentlessly, carrying news of death across the countryside. They are thorough monsters, careful to leave no survivors in their wake, no one to carry word, or warning. And so their play repeats the next night and the next, and the next, until the scale of death is news enough, and fearing its contagion, people begin to stay inside their houses.

That spring, they dress as plague doctors and walk ahead of their destruction.

In summer, they masquerade as members of the Inquisition, the stitched crosses enough to make gazes drop to the dirt.

By fall, Hector has set his mind firmly on churches, insisting he's developed a taste for clergy, and will only feed on members of the house of God. As if the blood is somehow blessed, the pews better than a soft down bed.

Sabine has never been devout, never put much stock in any but herself. Still, she thinks it's reckless, and dumb, to target a place with so much power.

But Hector will not be dissuaded. She has always found him moody, but there is a new edge to his temper, a manic glint that bothers her, especially since her fate is tied to theirs.

Renata does not seem concerned.

"It's like a storm," she insists. "It will pass."

Foolish, thinks Sabine, even as she follows. Careful to avoid the churchyard soil.

The chapel itself holds no power over or against them. It is a common structure, open to all, so there is no trouble crossing the threshold, taking shelter within. It is the burial plots they must avoid.

Sabine learned this the first time she drifted toward the stone markers, and Renata caught her hand, hauled her back onto the path.

"Death calls to death," she warned.

Now, Hector places his palms against the wooden doors and throws them open, ushering his rose and thorn inside the church.

Sabine considers the swept stone floor, the vaulted roof, the hollow cavern of the space. It is late, and the hall is dark, save for a cluster of votives, a lamp beside the altar, casting shadows up against the cross.

Hector passes a darkened candelabra and neatly tips it over, shattering the silence with a clanging crash.

The echo trails away, and shortly after, a door opens and a priest appears, disheveled but awake, straightening his robes as he approaches, looking from one of them to the next to the next. His gaze snags first on Sabine's loose red hair, coiled round her shoulders like a snake, then on Renata's dark skin, draped with strands of gold, before landing at last on Hector's tunic, lifted from a Templar.

"My children," he says, the air around him clouding with confusion. "What brings you to the house of God?"

"Are we too late for Mass?" Renata asks, a giggle in her voice.

The priest glances at the windows, the sun long set. "It was at Vespers," he says. "You may come back tomorrow."

He begins to turn away, when Hector clears his throat.

"But I have sinned," he declares, laying a hand to his chest, the symbol there. "And it weighs heavy on my heart."

The priest turns back. Hesitates, then nods toward the confessional. A cabinet with two doors, two separate chambers. The priest goes in first, and Hector follows. Sabine leans against a pillar, picking at her nails as Renata dances up the aisle. Inside the cabinet, there is a muted struggle. A muffled gasp. And then, moments later, Hector emerges, pulling on the priest's attire.

"How do I look?" he says, smoothing the white robe over his tunic, a smudge of red like a kiss on the collar.

"Blasphemous," Sabine says dryly, and Renata laughs, the sound ringing like bells through the empty church.

"Now what?" she asks, and Hector grins and says, "We wait."

The next evening, the parishioners come pouring in.

Sabine counts them as they enter, the way she always does, no matter the size. It's important to be thorough, to know how many were there when you started, so you know how many should be left behind.

Today, the numbers rise. Five, ten, fifteen, twenty. And four more. Two dozen bodies in the church. Two dozen heartbeats. Two dozen lives.

Renata bolts the doors, and Hector takes his place before the altar. The three of them exchange a knowing look. The air draws tight, coiled with their hunger. Renata winks, and Hector smiles, their good mood bathing her like moonlight.

In these moments, it is easy to forget that Sabine is shackled to them.

It's strange, but ever since her promise, the knowledge skirts her thoughts, as if she cannot look straight at it. When she tries, her mind goes blank. As if the promise not to leave has become a want, and she's aware that the want does not belong to her, exactly, and yet, she feels it just as keenly. There are cracks, moments of remembering, but they seal up again before Sabine can fit her fingers in, pry open the gaps and reach the thoughts within.

There and gone.

At the altar, Hector raises his hands, his voice, and begins.

"Pater Noster, qui es in caelis . . ."

Renata was right. He does enjoy an audience. Voices murmur, bodies shift, confusion rising like steam, and by the time the congregation understands that this is not their priest, it is too late.

What happens next is a slaughter.

A gruesome banquet. Two dozen bodies thrown into wild motion, like a herd of startled animals. Frantic beasts, bleating in terror. The blessed air stained red with panic.

And the three of them, like wolves, upon a kill.

The sheer scale of death turns Sabine savage, makes her edges fray and her mind go blank. She is not drunk so much as wild. A *feral rose*, she thinks, the phrase looping in her mind as she falls upon the fleeing prey. Gone are her thoughts of risk, her thoughts of anything but blood.

She drinks, and drinks, sure that here at last she will finally feel glutted, finally feel full, finally find the limits of her hunger. But she doesn't. Instead, it only opens wider, each bite like a stitch unpicked until the darkness is a chasm.

And she is falling in.

At some point, the screaming stops, the pounding, too, no one left trying to escape.

Silence washes over everything, heavy in the slaughter's wake.

Hector sinks onto the step at the front of the room, his white robes painted crimson. Renata sits beside him, and Sabine stretches out along the top stone stair, her head resting in Renata's lap, lost inside the dreamy drunken aftermath, the subtle notes of sacramental wine that laced the blood. Everything feels loose and quiet, a bolt of ribbon come unrolled. She wants to stay there, right there, forever.

But the corpses are already cooling.

So they rise, abandoning the church and the bodies within.

Twenty-four.

Sabine knows. After all, she counted each one as they entered. But that night, drunk on blood and freedom, she doesn't think to count the bodies as they leave.

If she had, she would have noticed that now—

There are only twenty-three.

VIII

The night they die, the world is white.

It snowed, sometime during the day, just enough to coat the dead grass, and skim the gravestones, dust the roofs of the small crypts that sit like houses off the path.

In the distance, chimneys heave smoke and the windows are all shuttered, bodies drawn in against the winter chill. Nearly the shortest day of the year, and so the darkness falls early and lands thick as they make their way up the road to the waiting church, the promise of another slaughter.

Hector and Renata stroll arm in arm, ahead, while Sabine drifts in their wake, her hood drawn up against a cold that brushes her skin, but never settles there.

She passes beneath the low branches of a tree at the same time as a breeze, its limbs shaking off a fresh layer of snow. She pauses, holds out a bare hand, watches the flakes settle without melting on her skin. There is a strangeness to the air, she thinks, but cannot place it. A held-breath silence that could simply be the snow.

She lets her hand drop.

Renata and Hector have drifted farther ahead, or rather, she has fallen farther back. They have nearly reached the church. She is about to follow, when something makes her look over her shoulder.

There is no twitch of movement, no sudden sound, no warning in the air, only the subtle tap of someone's gaze. She glances back down the path and sees a window with the shutters thrown, a small face pressed to the fogging glass.

A child, watching.

Sabine tips her head in question, and the child lifts a finger to their lips. Eyes flicking past her. To the church.

It is her only warning.

She turns at the sound of wood doors groaning inward, sees Hector and Renata step into the empty church. Only it is not empty. Voices erupt, shouting not in fear, but rage, and Sabine's body takes a single lunging step forward before her senses drag her back. For a second, she's pinned, caught between the two forces, the fact she cannot leave Hector and Renata, and the knowledge she cannot save them either, not from what waits inside the church.

Instead, she darts sideways, into the shadow of the tree. Presses herself flat against the trunk and watches as a crowd spills out—ten, twenty, thirty men—wielding torches, pitchforks, spears, and shackles, Hector and Renata thrashing in their midst. Metal chains wrapped tight around their limbs, their throats. The night air thick as smoke with the sudden rush of rage and violence. Calls of *devil, demon, monster.*

Sabine watches as Hector is forced to his knees. He springs back to his feet, throwing off his captors, fighting with all his feral strength—but then he is brought down again, blades driven into calf, and shoulder, the chains tightened and locked.

A man thrusts a spear into Renata's side, and she cries out, less in pain than fury, fear, her eyes searching the night, her mind open wide and calling for Sabine before a hood is forced over her head.

Sabine watches, coiled.

She cannot leave them, even now, but she stands transfixed by the scrape of wood on stone as caskets are dragged onto the path before the church.

Three caskets, not two, and *that* detail is enough to make her come unstuck. She pushes off the tree, and flings herself, not into the town, whose doors are flying open, but into the cemetery lot that runs beside the church.

One step between the graves, two, and suddenly she gasps, and buckles to the frozen ground as if impaled. Twists round, expecting to find an attacker, but there is no one there. And yet, the pain rolls through her. Brighter than the pitchfork, or the wooden stool, pain that wraps like a fist around her fragile heart.

She scrambles forward, body going weak, hands shaking as the skin begins to wither on the bones.

Death calls to death, Renata warned.

Renata, who is now being forced down into a coffin, while Sabine drags her own failing limbs over the ground.

Renata, who showed her how a body could bloom in the right hands, how welcome the right company could be—back when it was a choice. Before she tricked, and trapped, and bound Sabine to herself, and Hector.

Hector, who's clawing and screaming oaths as he's nailed into a box. A gruesome end. And one Sabine refuses to share.

She forces her body forward, through sickness worse than sunlight, vision blurring as she claws her way to the nearest crypt. She fumbles at the frozen bolt and forces in the rotting wood, stumbles into the tomb, gasping, her lungs straining for air they have forgotten they don't need, and slumps back against the door.

There is a body with her in the crypt. Long dead, she thinks, just from the age of the tomb, but death calls to death, and the corpse calls to her, the slab of stone between them providing only scant relief. She imagines rot rising, reaching up, trying to drag her down.

After everything she's been through. After all that she's endured.

Sabine curls against the stone, presses her hands against her ears.

There are no windows in the crypt, but she can hear them calling for her. She can hear the crowd's voices swallowing Hector's and Renata's, can hear the jostle and scrape, the anvil swing of hammers driving nails.

And then something else.

The crack and snap of fire catching, chewing its way through wooden boards.

After that, Sabine stops listening.

Lets the sickness fold over her like sleep.

The men stay with the burning coffins until dawn.

And so, Sabine stays hidden in the crypt.

She drifts in her fevered state, curled on that stone floor, dying, but not dead. Weak from sun, and sick from hunger and grave soil. Sometimes she is there, and sometimes she is somewhere else. Back in Santo Domingo, perched on the stable roof and spitting cherry pits onto her brothers' heads. But when she leans back to look at clouds, she finds Andrés looming over her, his weight squeezing the air from her lungs, crushing her beneath him, the way she then crushes the widow in her arms, one of them turning to ash and the other to stone.

On and on it goes until at some point, she comes back to herself.

It is dusk. The sun is gone. The voices have gone with it. Somehow, she finds the will to rise and stumble out of the crypt, but then, her legs give way, hands splayed against the frozen ground. The dead calling her down.

She tries to stand, and can't, and wants to laugh, or rage, at the idea that she has survived so long, so much, only to be felled by *dirt.*

It is not right. After all, her heart is still inside her. It has not been ruined or removed, wrung dry or cut out, and so, she tells herself, she will survive. Somehow. If she can just get up. But her limbs refuse to listen. To obey her mind. She sits, growing roots in the dead ground.

From here, Sabine can see the church.

The coffins on the ground before it, reduced to mounds of smoking ash.

It is a bad way to go, she knows. After all, the heart burns last.

She felt it, when Renata died. She felt the binding break between them, felt the promise sever, slough away. She is no longer bound, and yet, here she is, unable to leave.

And Sabine is tired.

For the first time in her life, she thinks, too tired to go on.

The earth feels oddly soft beneath her. She imagines herself sinking.

Bury my bones, she thinks as her body topples over, one cheek pressed to the soil, as if listening. And there. There it is. The steady beat of a heart. She shuts her eyes and listens as the sound gets closer, and closer and—

"Señora?" She drags her eyes open, and finds a boy, his voice barely dropped, his limbs stretched long by later youth. "Are you all right?"

Sabine struggles, finds just enough strength to sit up. "No," she says in a raspy, hollow voice.

He kneels beside her. "Who did you lose?" he asks, taking her for a mourner, her body bowed by grief.

Sabine looks to the smoldering ash before the church and answers. "Everyone."

"Come," says the boy, offering his hand. "It is too cold to grieve tonight."

She meets his gaze. His expression is kind, the air around him humming with concern.

"You're right," she says, taking his hand. But when he goes to pull her up, she pulls him down. Against her. Fangs slicing down to bone.

The blood pours in. His young heart hammers boldly in his chest. And then in hers.

And by the time it stops, Sabine is just strong enough to reach the cemetery's edge, to claw her way out of this realm of death. As soon as her feet land on the path, the graveyard lets go its hold, and her strength comes rushing back. Her senses sharpen, and her world steadies, and the night around her flares into stark relief again.

She looks one last time at the remains before the church, her mouth twitching with the ghost of a smile.

Hector and Renata may be dead, but Sabine is not.

She has been resurrected. Alone, but alive.

Snow begins to fall again, dusting the fresh corpse as she turns, and disappears into the dark.

ALICE

(D. 2019)

I

The bottle shatters into stardust.

Catty is thirteen, and Alice is ten, and they're in the gravel lot behind their granddad's pub, the baseball bat resting on Catty's shoulder as she sets another empty on the wooden stump that no one could be bothered to haul up when they made the parking lot.

(Not that it stopped them from cutting down the rest of the tree, and Alice has never understood why they didn't finish the job, or leave it alone. It makes her sad every time she sees it.)

Alice sits cross-legged on the hood of someone's car and watches as her sister winds up again. She swings, and the bottle shatters on impact, the sound as high and bright as bells, and Alice winces, even though she saw it coming, a kind of automatic flinch, because it's one of those sounds that means trouble. It's a rock pitched through a kitchen window, a pint knocked off a counter, a pair of glasses crunched under a clumsy foot, a girl taking out her heartbreak with a bat.

Catty lines up another bottle on the wooden stump.

A swing. A crack. For one brief, beautiful second, the glass dust hangs suspended in the glow from the streetlight, glittering like mist before it falls. Alice looks back over her shoulder, ready for the door to swing open, for *someone* to come out and tell them off, but the game is on—

(*which* game doesn't matter, it's usually rugby or football, but she's seen snooker, darts, cricket, just so long as it's tuned to something that gives them an excuse to lift a pint in the general direction of the screen and shout cheers or mutter disapproval)

—so no one shows.

Catty fetches up another bottle from the crate by the pub's back door.

And even if they were doing something wrong, no one would stop them because they're "Harry's girls"—Harry being short for Harold Moore, who *owns* the Port of Call.

(She's always thought it's a silly name for a pub, seeing as Hoxburn is nowhere near the sea, and the only vessels rolling in, their granddad likes to say, are the men who stay docked at the bar, and the tourists floating by. Even though *tourist* is a pretty generous word, since Hoxburn is the kind of place people drive through on the way to somewhere else. Somewhere better.)

Before their gran up and left, Alice heard her saying that towns could die as sure as people. Only sometimes people die fast, and places usually die slow. But Alice figures that if Hoxburn does die, the pubs will be the last to go.

Pubs, plural, because there's two.

(Funny, how Hoxburn has only one petrol station, and one grocery, and one laundromat, but *two* pubs, the Port and the Maudlin. They have the decency to be at opposite ends of the main street, not facing down like duelers, and on days when one is closed, you'll find the owner drinking in the other, to show there's no bad blood.)

Catty winds up again, curses sliding through her teeth like steam.

"Fucking numpty eejit *bawbag*," she seethes, a string of words collected like fine stones, her accent going thicker, the way Granddad's does whenever the tourists in the pub are English.

She swings, and the bottle shatters into light.

Alice is honestly surprised Catty and her first boyfriend made it a month, let alone three. Will was two years older, fifteen to her thirteen, which carried its own glow, but otherwise he was . . . *dull*. A weak candlelight against her sister's glaring torch, so she just kind of assumed Catty would be the one to break his heart—but then he went and kissed some fifth year and word got back, it always does, and here they are, her sister furiously shattering bottles while Alice stares at the glitter they leave in the gravel.

Catty lines up another bottle. Alice's butt is falling asleep, so she hops down from the car's hood, the lot crunching beneath her shoes, and Catty mistakes the motion for a want and offers up the bat.

"Go on," she says. "Give it a go."

Alice's hand responds before her brain, reaching to take the thing just because Catty held it toward her. Because that is the power of big sisters, the urge to take anything they offer.

The bottle stands waiting on the stump, a finger of backwashed beer at the bottom. She flexes her fingers on the wooden bat, tries to summon a shadow of her sister's passion, but feels no urge to swing.

"Picture someone you hate," offers Catty, and Alice can see her pulling up the mental list, from the girls at school to poor dumb Will to Eloise, always Eloise—

(Eloise, who finally moved in six months ago, who didn't change a single thing about the house for weeks, and even then, made sure to ask them both about each and every item to see if it held meaning, and Catty stood there saying *yes, yes, yes,* about the potholders and the pillows and the kitchen plates out of spite.)

But the truth is, Alice has never felt an anger strong enough to be called hate. Oh, she feels plenty of other emotions—worry, and panic, sadness, and fear—but they make her want to hold on to things as tight as she can, keep them together. She doesn't understand the urge Catty has to break them instead.

Her sister watches, arms crossed, and waiting, and even though she seems more annoyed than wounded now, Alice remembers the look on her face when she first got home, before Catty realized Alice was there, on the couch, before she knew she was being watched, before she saw Alice, and wrestled the pain into anger.

When she thought she was alone, she just sat there, looking small, and sad, and hurt, and the thought of Catty hurting—of someone hurting her—*that* makes Alice angry. It lights a fire in her heart, a burning heat that spreads across her ribs, over her shoulders, and down her limbs and she winds up, and swings at the bottle, the impact sending a jolt through her wrists as the glass explodes. Her heart skips, a thrill when it breaks, a rush when it shatters, a nervous laugh escaping like steam from the kettle.

Shards rain down onto the gravel, and Catty whoops, and grabs her shoulders.

"Sláinte!" she says, her anger dissolving into pride. They are in this together now. The distance between them collapsed, lives folded like paper.

And Alice wants to go again.

She reaches down into the crate, hand closing around another bottle, realizes too late the lip is broken, sharp. Pain flashes, shallow and bright, and she gasps, recoils as if bitten, the blood welling up across her palm. A sound escapes, part yelp, part cry, and she knows the cut isn't deep, knows that hands and heads bleed badly, but she can feel her pulse in the meat of her palm, and the spreading ache and the sight of the blood still make tears spring to her eyes.

And then Catty is there, grabbing her wrist, twisting the cut to the light the way Eloise does when studying a splinter, and Alice knows she's looking for glass. There isn't any—no glint, no glitter.

Catty pulls her hand right up to her face.

And runs her tongue through the blood.

And just like that, the pain's forgotten, replaced in an instant by disgust.

"Ewwww!" shrieks Alice.

But Catty only laughs and licks her lips. "Yum."

Alice shakes her head. "Disgusting."

Catty shrugs. "It's just you," she says. "And whatever's in you is in me. We're made of the same stuff."

She passes Alice's hand back the way she passed the bat, as if it is an offering, a secret, something to be shared, and Alice stares down at it, watching as a fresh line wells from the cut. The blood is smooth and black as oil in the dark. She can smell the iron in it as she lifts her palm to her face, that rusted penny tang.

And this is a memory, so Alice knows what happens next.

Knows that, for just a second, she thinks of licking her hand but doesn't, scrunches up her nose and wipes the blood on her jeans instead, and Catty leans the bat on the stump and tugs the headband from her hair and ties it round the cut, and they go home.

That's how it happened.

But that's not how it happens now.

Now, Alice doesn't move. She just stands there, hand halfway to her mouth, as Catty watches, her eyes dark and lips stained red, and the night around them sharpens and blurs at the same time, till the pub is nothing but a smudge, but the blood on her hand is so vivid she can see the light from the streetlamp bouncing off. The bead becomes a ribbon that rolls down her wrist, glitters like the glass on the gravel, and the sight of it doesn't repulse her anymore.

It looks wonderful, candy bright.

She wants to know what it tastes like.

And Catty says, "Go on," and her mouth begins to water, and her teeth begin to ache, and there is a hungry coil in her stomach, and Alice wants to bring it to her lips,

But she can't—

It's like the air has turned to stone, or she has—

And she can't move—

Can't close the small distance between her hand and her mouth—

Tries so hard her whole body shakes—

And feels like it will shatter until—

"Son of a bitch!"

Rachel's voice tears her out of sleep.

And just like that, Catty's gone, and the pub and the lot and the bat and the blood are gone, and all that's left is the hunger, Alice's whole jaw hurting, and her stomach clenched tight.

Rachel swears again, so loud Alice thinks she must be standing right beside her head, only she's not, she's at the other end of the suite. And yet, somehow, Alice can hear her ripping the sheets from the bed two rooms away, shoving them into the laundry bag and bitching to herself.

Alice puts a pillow over her head, pushes down as hard as she can to block out the sound, would worry about accidentally smothering herself but that doesn't seem to be a problem right now.

The curtains are drawn, but light still pries at the edges, and Alice wants to burrow deeper, find her way back to Hoxburn, but it's Monday morning and she has class and Rachel is still cursing. She forces herself up, opens the door in time to see her suitemate dragging the laundry sack into the common room.

"What's wrong?" she asks hoarsely.

Rachel kicks the laundry bag and mutters, "Hate it when I'm early," and Alice should have stayed put, because she can smell it now, the blood on the sheets, and everything inside her gives a vicious twist, teeth sharpening in her mouth, and she has just enough time to close the door before Rachel glances up.

Alice shudders slightly, slumps back against the door, but the thin boundary of wood is not enough, and the blood is still there and the dream is still there and before she knows it, she's biting into her own hand. The blood slicking her tongue tastes sweet and wrong, like rancid honey, but it steadies her, at least.

"Are you feeling better?" Rachel calls through the door, and Alice forces her jaw to loosen, watches the puncture marks heal like a time lapse in reverse as she swallows her own blood and lies through her clenched teeth.

"Yeah," she manages, "a bit."

"Want me to grab you anything?" Rachel must be leaning against the door because Alice swears she can hear the other girl's heart rapping like knuckles on the wood before she tells her no.

Mercifully, Rachel and her soiled laundry leave, and Alice slides down until she's sitting on the floor. Her laptop lies discarded at the foot of her bed, the Post-it stuck on top.

She digs her palms into her eyes.

Last night, Alice found exactly zero Lotties in the school directory, but back home, Lottie is a common nickname for Charlotte, and she found twelve of those spread across four years in the record. Each one had a photo, and none of them were *her*. (Of course, it never occurred to Alice to ask Lottie if she was even a student, because by that point, her mind was blank, and her mouth was busy.)

After hitting that dead end, she spent the next few hours scouring social media, trawling for any pictures from the party. There were plenty of those, though most were either tilted shots of bodies in neon light, close-up selfies, or artful pics of disembodied limbs, and she was just beginning to suspect that Lottie wasn't there, wasn't real, that Alice might simply be losing her mind, when she saw her.

It was almost dawn when she found the photo. One and only one, and in it, Lottie's face is caught mid-turn, violet curls lifting off her cheeks as she flashes the corner of a dimpled smile, the edge of a brown eye. But it's her.

Alice knows, beyond a shadow of a doubt, because even through the screen, she found herself tipping forward toward the other girl's gaze, had to look away before she fell in.

Alice saved the candid to her phone, and after that, went crashing into sleep.

But now she's awake, and it seems like such a narrow lead. She still has no idea what to do, how to turn a single out-of-focus picture into a flesh-and-blood girl who can explain what's happening to her, who can tell her *why*, and there's a voice in her head saying that it won't make a difference, that it's already *done*, that no matter how far she goes, how far she's come, there's no escaping—

Class.

That's it. Alice needs to go to class.

Sure, it feels a bit ridiculous, given what's going on, but she knows how easy it is to fall behind, and then how hard to catch up. She gets back to her feet, pulls on a top and a fresh pair of jeans, and as she does, she tastes Lizbeth's detergent wafting from her drawers, smells the dregs of Jana's perfume, which she dabbed behind her ears before the party, feels the scrape of her own hair against her face, the whisper of cotton as it shifts against her skin, and the warmth of her gold pendant where it rests against her sternum, all of it so sharp it's overwhelming.

A heartbeat quickens in her ears, and Alice gasps and presses a hand flat against her chest, relief welling up like tears until she realizes the pulse isn't coming from behind her ribs. It's that familiar eight-count beat, and soon the voice kicks in.

"*When I was a child / I got lost in the woods . . .*"

Alice digs the phone out from under the covers and silences the song, and the pulse, plunging herself back into that uncanny silence. Only it's not *really* silent, is it, because if she listens, she can hear the footsteps in the hall and the groan of the pipes inside the walls and the tinny ghost of speakers playing somewhere on the Yard.

So many noises stacking, overlapping, tangling inside her head.

Alice drifts to the window, studying the blade of light between the curtains. She chews the inside of her cheek and reaches out, letting the sun graze her fingertips, bracing as she does for the sear of a hand on a hot stove, ready to recoil as her flesh begins to burn.

But it doesn't.

There's a strange sensation, sure, like ants crawling across her knuckles, a dizzy wrongness, like vertigo. She steels herself and pulls the curtain back, wincing as the too-bright light sends a lance of pain behind her eyes, like the onset of a migraine.

But she doesn't go up in flames.

Alice: 1, common lore: 0, she thinks, even as she hauls the curtain shut, plunging the room back into relative shade.

Relative, because even with the blinds drawn, she can see everything in sharp relief, from the lines of tight script in the open textbook on her desk, to the wrinkles in her sheets, to the silver rings and bracelets adorning Lizbeth's jewelry tree.

(All of it real and not sterling, Alice knows, because her roommate made a point of telling her as she was unpacking that her skin rejected alloys, so she simply couldn't wear anything unless it was pure silver or real gold, even made a joke about her body having expensive taste.)

Now Alice reaches out and lays a questing finger on the nearest bangle, waits to see if it will singe her. This time, she doesn't feel the wrongness of it, doesn't feel anything at all.

Alice: 2.

And maybe she's feeling bolstered by those two points stacked in her favor, or maybe it's the fact that her first class is econ and one of the students in her section lives at the Co-op (which means he might recognize the girl in the photo on her phone) but Alice shoves on her shoes, nicks a pair of shades from Lizbeth's desk, and sets off.

Halfway across the Yard, she has regrets.

Even with the shades, the sun is piercing, and though the daylight doesn't *burn* her, it plants itself like a hot wet hand on the back of her neck, reminding Alice of the time her family went out on the open water. The waves were rough, and she spent an hour retching over the side, and that's how she feels now, off-balance, her stomach rising in her throat, only this time she is the ship and the girl and the rolling sea all at once.

By the time she reaches the nearest gate, her limbs are shaking, and when she finally stumbles into the safety of the building, she sags against the wall, waiting for the sickness to retreat.

A steady current of students fills the hall, headphones on, heads bowed, one of those grim reminders that your life is small and the world is big, and even when it feels like it's falling down, it's only falling down on you. To everyone else, it's just going on as usual.

The scent of coffee reaches Alice from a kiosk. Her throat feels like it's made of sandpaper, and she pushes off the wall and orders a straight coffee, simple, black, hoping to rack a third point in the game of Alice versus common lore. She takes a cautious sip, and shudders in relief when it doesn't come back up.

But it doesn't taste right, either.

She adds one sugar, two, three, but it's like spraying air freshener over rot—all it does is add a second, noxious layer, a film on her tongue, and after that she gives up, dumps the contents from the cup, thirstier than ever as she heads for the econ auditorium.

The room is filling up, and she scans the growing crowd, until she finally spots the guy from the Co-op, manages to dredge up his name (Sam) right before she reaches his seat.

"Hey," she says, and he looks up at her, starts to smile, and Alice swears she can feel his interest piquing, before she shoves the phone into his face.

"I'm looking for this girl," she says, and his shoulders slump, before he even glances at the screen.

He shakes his head and mumbles, "Sorry, never seen her."

"She was at the party."

He shrugs. "So was half the class." His mouth twitches. "Didn't get her number?"

Annoyance prickles in her chest, but then the professor is clearing his throat, and everyone is taking their seat. Alice sinks into an open desk, stares down at the face on the screen, wonders if she *should* actually paper campus with flyers asking, *Have you seen this girl?*

She shoves the phone in her pocket, pulls the notebook from her bag, and tries to focus on the teacher's voice—

(so loud she can hear the echoes trailing in its wake)

—his notes as they appear on the glaringly white screen—

(Has it always been that bright?)

—as the sights and smells and sounds around her mount—

(the scratching of pens, the typing of keys, the girl chewing gum two rows ahead, and the guy, four seats over, jiggling his knee, or the cell phones buzzing in backpacks on the floor, or the sweat and sweetness hanging in the air, thickened by stress, and sleeplessness, and strong caffeine)

—until it gets to be too much, and she puts her earbuds in, plays white noise as soft as it will go, hoping to muffle the people, the room, but it's just like the coffee from the kiosk—

(one thing atop the other, coating it instead of canceling)

—and she's trying to focus on the class, but she can't because there are six bodies in her immediate vicinity, one to either side, two in front and two behind, and she can hear six hearts beating in six chests—

(can smell—taste? *feel?*—the blood inside those organs)

—and then the guy beside her rolls his head atop his neck, the muscles cording, and her mouth goes dry, and her vision tunnels and her teeth begin to ache, and she doesn't realize she's digging her fingers into the desk until she hears the crack, looks down expecting to see broken nails and finds splintered wood instead.

Alice shoves up to her feet.

A dozen heads turn, but for once in her life she doesn't care what anyone else thinks. She escapes into the hall, and then, into the nearest bathroom, bracing herself against the sink.

Her reflection stares back from the mirror, and it has the gall to look like nothing's changed, and fuck the two points in her favor, fuck the whole game of Alice versus common lore, because isn't she entitled to some kind of cosmetic recompense? Where is the beauty meant to offset the horror of what's happening? The suddenly clear skin, the perfect hair, the glamour and the grace?

The only thing Alice sees are the hollows beneath her eyes. Her eyes, which are still neither blue nor green nor gray but that same old muddy in-between, and if there *is* a fevered light behind them now, that's hardly enough to make up for the rest of this.

For the fact that even in this tiled room she can *hear* the crush of bodies through the walls, living breathing eating laughing bodies, and hers isn't making any fucking sound, and how ridiculous and wrong that her chest is tight and she still feels like she can't breathe, even though she doesn't seem to need the air, and her heart still feels like it's trying to claw its way out of her chest, even though it isn't even beating, and Alice wants to scream, but she can't bring herself to do it, even now, doesn't want to make a scene, so instead she bends her head and splashes water on her face, and tells herself everything will be all right, even though she knows she's lying.

And she's still slumped forward at the sink when she hears the door swing open, the smack of bootheels on the tile, the twang of Hannah's voice.

"Don't tell me you're still wrecked," she drawls.

Alice drags her head up to the mirror, looks at herself instead of Hannah, focuses on the narrow streams of water running down her face, her jaw, her throat.

Hannah folds her arms across her chest. "How hard did you party at the Co-op?"

"Too hard," says Alice, aiming for a wan smile and falling short into a grimace.

She tries to straighten, but feels her body clench around that dull, pervading hunger. "Cramps," she adds, folding over again.

Hannah digs around in her purse, pulls out a bottle of pills. "You need some ibuprofen?"

She takes a step toward Alice as she says it, and her perfume is overwhelming, a vanilla-and-peach-scented cloud that hangs in the air and tastes like soap on Alice's tongue. But beyond it, behind it, *beneath* it, she hears that steady pulse. Picks up the iron scent of blood.

Her throat tightens. She doesn't move.

Hannah rattles the bottle. "Well?" she snaps impatiently.

Alice pushes off the counter, turns, and reaches for the pills—or at least, that's what she means to do, but as she starts moving toward the other girl, she can't seem to stop, the distance between them collapsing, until Hannah is pressing the bottle into Alice's chest. She looks down, watches her fingers curl around Hannah's, the pills nested like a doll inside their hands.

"Thanks," she says, and this is the part where she's supposed to let go, but she can't seem to find the will to pull away. She can feel the pulse through the other girl's skin, the heat of her body, imagines warming herself on this little fire of a life.

"Um, yeah, you can keep them," says the other girl, trying to drag her hand free.

But Alice doesn't let her. Her *body* doesn't let her. She doesn't blame it— her skeleton hurts, her muscles and tendons hurt, her skull hurts, all the way down to her teeth, the kind of pain these pills can't touch, but maybe Hannah can. Like Colin, in the Yard last night. Alice remembers how much better she felt afterward.

She looks up into Hannah's face, her dark eyes narrowed in a confusion that Alice swears she can taste. The thin flick of eyeliner over each, eyebrows raised, her lips pressed into a line, a combined force that would have once made Alice shrink back, embarrassed.

Alice, who sits at the back of the lecture halls because she hates feeling like she's being watched, or *seen*.

Alice, who's the barnacle on the party wall, not the center of attention.

Alice, who doesn't know how to take up space without apologizing for it.

That same Alice meets Hannah's eyes and holds her gaze, trapped like the hand beneath her own. And she's pretty sure she's seen something about compulsion in those TV shows, and Alice has no idea if it's real, but Hannah is still standing there, a new flush of color in her cheeks.

Stay, thinks Alice. *Stay right there.*

She closes the last sliver of space between them, their hands knotted between their bodies, her teeth sharpening, her mouth starting to ache, and Hannah is just staring at her, lips parted and eyes wide, and it's working, Alice honestly can't believe it's working—

Which is exactly when it stops.

Hannah blinks, and recoils, the air around her suddenly heavy with disgust.

"Ew, no," she snaps, wrenching backward. Alice lets go, and the pill bottle drops, rolls, forgotten, beneath a stall, as Hannah scrunches up her nose and says, "I'm not a *dyke*."

The word bounces off the tile walls.

A single vicious syllable.

(Alice remembers the first time a boy called her that name, the sting of it like a slap, the way it made her cheeks burn hot and her eyes sting, the way Catty walked straight past her and broke his nose, and somehow that was worse, and afterward they walked home in silence, Alice brushing away tears, until she finally asked, "Why did you hit him?" and Catty shot back, "Why didn't you?" Said nothing else till they reached the steps outside their house, and then she turned and took her by the shoulders and said, "When the world pushes you, push back.")

The word echoes through the bathroom.

Alice feels her face go hot again, but this time, it isn't shame.

It's rage.

Rage, at all the Hannahs of the world, convinced the worst thing a girl like Alice can feel is want, and at this particular Hannah, for looking at Alice and seeing a monster, just not the one she thinks.

The kind of rage that made Catty take a bat to the bottles in the parking lot.

Alice gets it now. Why her sister was always breaking things.

Because rage shatters out, not in.

She looks at Hannah, a tight smile tugging at her lips. "What did you just call me?" she hears herself ask, but doesn't recognize the edges in her voice.

Those are new.

Sharp.

And maybe Hannah couldn't feel her sorry attempt at compulsion, but she does feel *this*, Alice is sure, watches the girl's face crumple as she backs away, one step, then two, until her shoulders hit the dryer on the wall, and Alice can taste her fear, the way she tasted the menace on the guy last night, his violence surrounding them like smoke. She can hear Hannah's racing heart, and it makes her teeth hurt, and in that moment, she wants Hannah to turn and *run*.

Not so she will get away.

So Alice can go after her.

But Hannah doesn't move, and after a second—a minute, an hour—the world steadies, and Alice feels her senses steady, too, reality rushing back, and she shoves past the girl and out of the bathroom before she loses herself again.

II

Alice plunges out into the harsh light.

She flinches as she puts the stolen sunglasses on, shielding her eyes, resisting the urge to beeline back toward the Yard and the dorm and the safety of the curtained dark, only because it will not solve the clawing problem of her current hunger—thirst? She doesn't know which to call it (because it feels like both). Her mouth is dry, and her stomach is empty, and her whole body feels like it's ringing like an empty chamber.

A glass, waiting to be filled.

She could keep pretending that maybe there's a food or drink that will ease the hollow feeling, but so far, only one thing seems to help—one point in the column of common lore that might as well rig the rest of the game, because it's the one that matters most.

Alice needs blood.

The thought alone is enough to make her throat go dry, and she's suddenly aware of how many students are drifting up and down the path she's on, their heartbeats heavy in her head—but last night was a mistake, one she just nearly made again with Hannah, and this is her new life. She's not about to ruin it.

So Alice turns, and heads off campus.

She puts as much distance as she can between herself and the storied buildings and the tree-lined streets and the faces she is just starting to know well enough to recognize. And to be recognized.

She walks, hugging the shadowed side of the road until she reaches the river, and then keeps going, along the tree-lined banks, walks until with every single stride, she can feel the strain spreading through her body, her ligaments tight, her bones stiff, tries to think of where to go, a movie theater, maybe, somewhere dark, if not exactly private; it's not perfect, but right now nothing is.

Alice sinks onto a bench in the shade, puts her head in her hands.

Maybe if she knew what—or who—she's looking for.

She remembers a popular serial killer show about a guy (it's always a guy) who targeted bad people, found a moral way to feed the urge to hurt, to kill, and as Alice gets back to her feet, she tries to figure out what makes a person bad enough to deserve that kind of thing. And then she passes a construction site, and hears the rise and fall of a whistle pointed her way.

Sees three men, perched round the wheels of a machine, one with his fingers still in his mouth, and for once instead of making herself smaller, hunching in, hurrying on, Alice slows and straightens, turns to meets their gaze. She doesn't smile, doesn't say anything, just stares, and they must see *something* there, because they draw back, duck their heads and shrink away, and it feels good, or it would if she weren't so fucking hungry.

If there were one of them instead of three.

But it gives her an idea.

Alice looks down at herself, in her T-shirt and black jeans, her high-top sneakers, wishing she'd picked something more suggestive, even though she knows it doesn't really matter. That the simple act of *having* a teenage body, no matter how it's dressed, has always been enough to justify a man's attention.

She tugs her hair out of its ponytail and slows her stride, unpicks a decade's worth of warnings as she lowers her guard, thinks *Look at me, see me, want me.* Part of her feels like a fool, but the rest is too hungry to care. She walks to the end of the block, then lingers, fingers looped in the straps of her backpack. The sun slips behind a cloud, and she shivers in relief.

She turns and starts back down the same stretch of road.

And halfway down the block, she sees him.

Feels him, really. A middle-aged guy in a decent suit, rolling a set of car keys round his index finger as he ambles toward a sleek sedan. And here's the thing—Alice probably wouldn't have noticed him if he hadn't been looking at her first. Staring, really, that way some men do, as if looking is fair game, because in their minds, all girls are just asking to be looked at.

So yeah, he's staring at her, with a canted head and a crooked smile, eyes tracking in a way that makes her stomach twist, that old familiar fear welling up, the warning pressed into every inch of a girl's skin until it lives there. She forces herself to smile back, tucks the borrowed shades up in her hair (even though the light is brutal) and bites her bottom lip just a little as she walks over to him.

"Excuse me, sir?"

Flirting with other girls is a long game, a drawn-out con of longing, and guessing, toeing the edge of a pool before finally, sometimes, in a moment of weakness or exasperation, flinging yourself in.

But Catty always said that guys were easier.

Just let them think they're in control.

There's a moment, as Alice gets right next to him, when she's worried that he'll look at her and see what those construction workers did. That he'll pull back, hurry away. But the only thing rolling off this man is confidence.

He is so sure which of them is predator, and which is prey.

"Yes, honey?" he says, and all the old parts of Alice say *No*, say *Wrong*, say *Get away*, but the new part says, "Think you could give me a ride?"

The air around him tastes like sugar burning, and she makes a mental note, that acrid scent seems to go with arrogance, and appetite.

"Sure thing," he says as his gaze wanders up and down, slow as brushstrokes. "Where to?"

Alice swallows, feels her old self welling up, like sabotage, but she bites the inside of her cheek until it bleeds, and reminds her what she wants. What she needs.

"Well," she says, trying to make her voice soft, a secret in the space between them. "Where can you take me?" And even as the words leave her lips, she has to fight the urge to roll her eyes, because this will never work, she should have made another go at compulsion instead—but his smile just splits into a grin, as if God has handed him a treat. As if it's all too easy.

"Hop in," he says, holding the car door open for her, and as she slides onto the leather seat, the door swings closed, the steel shell and tinted glass blocking out the worst of the sunlight. Her head clears and her vision steadies, and for a moment Alice sighs in pure relief.

Then the man gets in, and the car starts, and the locks click, and she stiffens, fingers twitching toward the door on instinct, and Alice has to remind herself, over and over, that it's going to be okay. That she doesn't need to be afraid, because nothing bad is going to happen.

At least, not to her.

She leans back into the leather as the engine growls, and the car pulls into traffic, and the man's hand finds her knee, and she tells herself to go somewhere else.

And she does.

Piece by piece—

Until the car is gone—

And the man is gone—

And his hand is gone, and—

She is flying on her bicycle, pebbles crunching beneath the tires.

Up ahead, Catty's hair sways as she runs, gold hair hacked short to the shoulders with a pair of kitchen shears, the ends dyed stop-light red. She's fourteen now, and *fast,* a runner on the school's track team—the only sport she was keen to play, because it didn't involve any teamwork or chat—but that's not why she's running now.

Alice pedals faster, trying to close the gap.

She's eleven, a head shorter than Catty and still waiting for that spurt of growth everyone keeps promising, the one that will unfold her into something more, but it hasn't shown up yet, so when her sister took off, she had the sense to grab her bike, the only way to catch up now.

And she *has* to catch up.

Because for once, Catty is running from *her.*

She's not heading up the hill behind their house, but down the road out of town. Away. Away. And it's Alice's fault.

Even though it's not, not entirely, some of it has to fall on Dad, and El—

(El, who Catty still insists on calling *Eloise,* even though it's been three years, Eloise, as if she's a visitor, an unwelcome guest, or worse, an intruder, an imposter, a usurper, a gas leak, a slow poison.)

—but *Alice* is the one who smiled, and threw her arms around El's shoulders when she heard the news that she was pregnant. Alice is the one who made the mistake of saying *Congrats* and *That's wonderful* and then made the unforgivable error of adding the word *Mum* to the end, and even though it felt right she knew it was a mistake, as soon as it was out, tried to suck the word back behind her teeth, but it was too late, Catty flinched back as if struck, and took off.

Alice catches up on the bike, slows to pace Catty, says "Please," says, "I didn't mean it," but her sister only speeds up, trainers pounding and blue eyes red from winter cold and rage.

(Catty only ever cries when she is angry.)

"Go home, Bones," she snaps, and that word—*home*—comes out sharp enough to hurt. Alice flinches.

"I'm sorry," she says, and she is, and she isn't, and it's all a mess in her head. Because Eloise is a kind of mum, the only one she remembers, the one who leaves notes in her pockets and packs her lunch and holds her when she's sad, or sick, or scared.

And Catty is the one who leaves.

Who runs.

They reach the edge of town and Catty keeps going, Alice trailing in her wake, till Hoxburn is behind them, out of sight, and Alice is just starting to worry that her sister won't stop, when something inside Catty finally seems to break. She draws up short, sinks into a crouch, and digs her hands into her hair—

And *screams*.

A banshee wail that rolls through the hills, snagging on the gorse and moss. A violent, visceral sound that would have brought neighbors spilling from their homes if they were still in town. If this weren't the kind of countryside that dampens everything.

Catty screams until there's no air left inside her lungs, and then her body just kind of deflates, slumps back onto the grass, knees drawn into her chest. Alice ditches the bike, but doesn't go up to her, not yet, can practically feel the anger wicking off her sister in waves, like gas fumes waiting for a match.

That week, in chemistry, they'd learned how to douse a flame, not with water but the shiny fireproof blanket behind the teacher's desk, watched as he unfurled the sheet and let it fall, tamping it down over the blaze, and Alice wishes she could do the same to Catty's temper, wishes she could fall on her sister and smother the heat. But she can't, so she just sinks into the grass a few feet from Catty as she glares into the distance. "*Pregnant.*"

She spits the word between her teeth like a watermelon seed.

Alice chews her lip and wonders what bothers Catty more, the idea of being outnumbered, her father moving on, or the fact someone in the house will finally have a *reason* to call Eloise *Mum*. (A small, traitorous part of her thinks it could be nice, having a little brother.) But of course Alice can't say that so she says nothing, just sinks her fingers into the frigid earth instead, imagines she is growing roots, tendrils reaching down and out until she can touch Catty without touching her.

The silence stretches heavy, settles cold, until Catty says, "We have a mum," and Alice says, "I know."

"We don't need her."

And Alice says, again, "I know," trying not to think about Eloise wrapping a fresh towel around her shoulders last week, after they got caught in the rain.

Catty digs a cigarette out of her hoodie, nicked from Dad's stash even though he told Eloise he quit when she moved in. She's got a book of matches, too, swiped from Granddad's pub, and it takes her three tries to get a light, but then the matchstick catches with a hiss. Catty lifts the flame to the tip, inhales, and doesn't even cough, just holds the smoke inside and then lets it come spilling through her teeth.

Alice wrinkles up her nose, but then Catty holds it out, and it might as well be a sacred offering. As good as saying *I forgive you* but also *It's us and them* and Alice is so relieved to still be *us* that she takes the cigarette and drags in until the tip flares red, and a whole fireplace kicks off in her lungs. She coughs, and coughs, and when she finally stops, she feels dizzy, and doesn't know if it's the smoke or the nicotine or the lack of air, and Catty just pats her on the back and puts the end between her lips again, looks up at the cloud-strewn sky.

"You remember her, right?"

There's a tremor in her voice, and Alice realizes she's not angry, she's afraid, of being the only one who does.

Alice nods, but here's the thing: she doesn't.

She knows Mum was a journalist, the kind that went all around the world. There are photos tacked on Catty's wall—Mum reading on a beach in San Diego, sipping tea in a pastry shop in Tokyo, smiling, eyes closed, beneath a turning maple in Boston.

(That last one has always been her favorite, because of the leaves; she didn't know they could turn that shade of yellow, a crown so bright it blurred.)

She knows these things, but there are no memories to go with them, and the few she has are like tea bags used too many times, all the flavor fading till it's just tinted water. Alice wishes she remembered the cadence of her mother's laugh, the scent of her shampoo, what she said when she tucked her into bed.

A plane slips overhead, leaving a tiny chalk trail. Catty watches it go. "Remember when she told us about her trip to New Zealand?"

Alice nods. "Yeah," she lies. "But tell me again."

And Catty looks at her—

A sad smile playing on her lips as she takes a breath and—

The man's hand tightens on Alice's knee.

A playful little squeeze that flings her back into her body.

Makes her want to crawl out of her skin.

He smiles, and Alice wonders if he can feel her fear the way she tastes his want, if it is a predatory gift.

They've crossed the bridge, and the Boston streets are whizzing by, and she just wants this to be over, wonders where they're headed, and as if he can read her mind, his dry mouth twitches and he says, "You're awfully far from home."

Alice shivers, thinking he somehow knows where she goes to school, until he ventures, "Scotland?" And of course, he's just referring to her accent.

Alice nods. "Needed a fresh start."

Before and after. Then and now.

"Is that so?"

She hates this strained attempt at small talk. Every word feels like it's pulling too much weight. But soon enough he pulls into a high-rise's resident garage. He parks, and unbuckles his seat belt, and she expects him to unlock the car, open the door for her again, lead her up to some minimalist loft with harbor views.

But instead, he just turns toward her, waiting, as if she's supposed to know what happens next, only she doesn't, which he seems to like even more. He takes her hand and guides it toward his crotch, and she can't stomach the thought of *that*, the recoil strong enough to spur her into motion.

Alice swallows, and then climbs over the center console, and onto his lap, and up close, he smells like money on display. Expensive metal and too much cologne, and beneath it, want, and need, and blood. She can feel the hardness of him through the too-thin layers of his suit, and he starts murmuring a breathy stream of "Good girl" and "There you go" and "You like that?"

And she doesn't.

The only thing she *likes* is that he's there beneath her, his head lolling back as she shifts her weight against his lap, exposing the pale column of his throat, the only throbbing part of him she cares about, met by the only part of her that answers—teeth going sharp inside her mouth, denting and then pricking into her bottom lip.

She leans forward, but before she can reach his neck, his head drops down again, his face level with hers, as his left hand vises around her thigh, and the other reaches between their bodies for the button of his slacks.

He starts to unzip, but her hand clamps down on his.

"Wait," she says, and the panic in her voice makes his eyes narrow, annoyance flickering across his face.

"Don't get shy on me now," he warns, knocking her hand away. "What, you need a little coaxing?"

He grabs her waistband, pulling her flush against him, fingers worming down the front of her jeans as he frees himself with his other hand, and the car is too small, the space too tight, and Alice can't get back, so she goes forward, falls against him and hits the recline lever on the side of the seat. It gives, and they tumble backward, and in that off-kilter moment, she sinks her teeth into his throat.

Blood sprays into her mouth, like a gulp of air after too long below water, and this time there is no moment when the world drops out, no lapse in time, just Alice, and the blood spilling across her tongue, and down her throat, lining the inside of her skin as the man beneath her fights, rakes at her face, kicks the car horn, and he is twice her size, and strong, but she is stronger, and as she drinks, his pulse becomes her own, a heavy beat, and it's like the lights come on inside her, and she feels right again, good again, as his heart pounds inside her chest.

He grabs her by the shoulders, tries to force her off, and there, at last, is his terror (like a grace note on her tongue). Her fangs sink deeper, jaw clenching until she feels the give of cartilage, hears the scream through his vocal cords, teeth humming like a tuning fork.

Alice doesn't let go.

She drinks until her body loosens, every twisted cable in her going slack, drinks until the man's pulse stops sprinting and begins to limp. A song hitting the last chorus. She drinks until at last he slumps, lifeless, in the seat beneath her, teeth sliding free as if on instinct, jaw loosening the moment the pulse drags its feet to a stop.

And even then, the stolen heartbeat lingers in her chest, so long she thinks that maybe it will stay, beating behind her ribs.

But finally, it trails off, too.

And she is plunged back into stillness.

Alice looks down at the body beneath hers, his eyes open and empty, his mouth ajar, and waits for the shock of what she's done to pass, waits for the swell of horror to come rushing in its wake.

The revulsion. The guilt.

But the truth is, the only thing she feels now is relief. Because the thirst is finally gone. The headache is gone. And even though the heartbeat is gone, too, she feels alive again. Revived.

As the seconds tick by, Alice understands that she is not okay.

This isn't something that will pass, like a sickness or a storm.

That whatever's happened to her, there is no going back.

She climbs off the body, and into the passenger seat, the scratches on her face already healed. Beside her, the man's throat is a bloody mess, a ragged seam. But as she watches, the skin there begins to knit, and close, leaving nothing but a few wayward drops of blood along the collar of his shirt.

She forces herself to reach back toward him, freeing the leather wallet from the pocket of his slacks, takes three twenties, and gets out, careful not to leave any prints on the billfold or the handle (she's seen enough detective shows).

As the door swings shut, she catches her reflection in the tinted window.

And for the first time, she sees the change.

There's no sudden beauty. No clear skin, or shining curls.

But the Alice who looks back is undeniably new.

SABINE

(D. 1532)

I

Venice, Italy
1679

Two nights until Carnevale, and the city is bursting at the seams.

Carts rattle down the narrow roads and clog the bridges. Carriage wheels clatter over stone, the roads and houses overrun, voices filling the air as tents are raised and piazzas made ready.

The collective noise is more than enough to hide the sound of the girl struggling against Sabine.

She has just arrived, carried on the tide of traffic from Verona. Cities, she has found, make perfect hunting grounds. Places so busy, a handful of deaths will almost always go unnoticed. Still, she is careful. Never leaves more bodies than she can count.

Sabine's fingers tighten on the back of the girl's neck as her teeth sink deeper. She used to tell them not to be afraid, but that was so many, many years ago, before she learned how much she liked the taste of fear.

Bright, and bittersweet.

In her arms, the girl stops fighting.

Her heart grows sluggish before finally it falters, fails. Sabine sighs and lets go, watching as the body lands with a soft splash in the canal below, the sound swallowed by a commotion on a nearby bridge.

There is a blue silk ribbon in her hand, freed from the girl's hair as she was drinking. Sabine curls the fabric around her finger, savoring the last echoes of the heartbeat in her chest.

"Quanta avventata," says a voice behind her.

How reckless.

She turns to find a man she's never met, leaning, arms crossed, against the wall. At first glance, he is a gentleman, his clothes rich and tailored to his form, broad shoulders, tapered waist. His eyes deep gray, like chips of slate, his black hair neatly combed, a mustache curling like a second grin over his upper lip.

She didn't hear him coming. A mystery, until the side of his mouth tugs up, flashing a pointed fang.

Ah, she thinks.

He is not the first of her kind that she's met since Hector and Renata. There was a man with snow-white hair in Barcelona. A woman thin and coiled as a rope in Athens. A pair of sisters in Marseille. The older ones Sabine could not read, but the sisters were younger, their curiosity plain as pipe smoke on the air. And Sabine knew that if she crooked a finger, as Renata did that night, so long ago, they would follow.

But she didn't.

The time for friends has come and gone. On the rare occasion when she covets company, she finds it, and afterward, the blood tastes brighter for the time they've shared.

But Sabine prefers to hunt alone.

And so, each time their paths have crossed, she's kept her distance. And each time, she felt their presence long before she saw them.

But this one has caught her by surprise.

And he does not seem intent on leaving.

"Posso aiutarla?" she asks—*Can I help you?*—the Italian rolling off her lips. She has been told she speaks it well, almost as if it were her native tongue. It is not hard to learn, when one has time. And Sabine has plenty of it.

His eyes flick past her, to the canal. The girl's body vanishing beneath the surface.

"It is considered rude," he says, "to make a mess in someone else's house." Sabine looks around. "And yet, I do not see a house."

Casually, the man unfolds his arms, and abandons the wall, rising to full height.

"You do not see four walls," he says. "You do not see a roof. A door. But do not be mistaken. You are standing in *my house*."

He ambles toward her as he says it, and as he does, a strange thing happens.

Sabine feels herself retreat. Not out of choice, or even fear. The air around her thickens, then goes solid, that telltale hook of trying to cross a threshold through which she hasn't been invited.

Again the man steps forward, and again Sabine finds herself forced back, until she feels the street drop out beneath her heels, the water sloshing against the canal walls below.

Indignation rises in her, but fascination, too.

"How?" she asks, boots balanced on the edge.

The stranger doesn't answer, only looks up at the sky, as if considering the moonlit clouds. And then he turns his back on her and sets off down the road. The air relaxes, and Sabine takes a careful step from the edge when she hears him call out, "Venga."

Come.

She laughs, a cold sound sliding through her teeth, is halfway through telling him just where he can go without her, when the man glances back and smiles at her, almost warmly, and says, "That was not an invitation."

A hand, invisible as the doorway, and just as firm, plants itself between her shoulders and she feels her body moving forward before her mind can think to hold it back.

Sabine understands then, that despite his easy manner, he is *old*.

Old enough she never heard him coming.

Old enough to lay claim to streets and open air.

Old enough to move her like a puppet.

The knowledge makes her skin prickle with a primal kind of fear. It has been such a long time since she was made to feel like prey, and she detests it, wants to tear this stranger open crotch to crown, wants to get away.

But more than either one of those, Sabine wants to understand.

To know how he has done it. So she can do it, too.

The moment she starts forward on her own, the hand retreats. But she can feel it, hanging just behind her, like a draft. Knows that if she stopped, or turned, or tried to leave, it would be there to catch her.

So she does not stop, or turn, or try to leave.

She catches up, and walks beside the man instead of in his wake.

To a passerby, they would appear a happy, handsome couple, on their way home. Sabine, in her fine dress, her hair a loose curtain of molten copper. And him, with his broad shoulders, fingers clasped behind his back.

A handful of men stroll down the opposite side of the canal, and when they spot Sabine and the stranger, one calls out, lifting the bottle in a way that is half greeting, and half toast.

"Don Accardi!"

The man beside her smiles, waves, bidding them good night.

"Don *Accardi?*" she asks as they walk on. "Is that your name?"

"It is how I'm known, in Venice," he says, "But you may call me Matteo. And what shall I call you?" he adds politely.

"Why ask? Surely you are strong enough to pluck it from my mind."

Matteo shrugs. "Perhaps," he says. "But that would be rude."

"Oh, *that* would be rude?" She sneers. "But forcing me to follow you—"

He tuts. "Am I such loathsome company? You are the one who came into my house—"

"It isn't *yours*—" she counters as they cross a square.

"—and tossed a corpse in my canal—"

"Bodies are found floating every day."

"The least you can do is be a decent guest," he continues, leading her around a corner, "and walk with me—"

"I do not even know where we are going."

"To my home."

Sabine cocks a brow and says, "I thought all of Venice was your home."

And there it is, again, that odd, affable smile. As if the entire thing amuses him. They pass beneath an arch, into a columned courtyard, a riot of wisteria blooming in the corners.

"Here we are," he says, coming to a stop at last.

Sabine stares ahead. And then up. It is less a house than a palazzo. Three stories tall, its front as ornate as a church.

"Do you live alone?" she asks. "Or are there more of you?"

Matteo seems to weigh the words before he answers. "There are no others like us here."

"Let me guess," she says. "You scared them all away."

"No," he says. Then, "Only some."

His boots echo softly on the courtyard stones as he approaches the front door, which is its own grand affair, wrought iron forming a half circle overhead, tendrils thrown out like rays of sun.

It swings open at his touch, and he strolls in, but as Sabine goes to follow, her body snags on the threshold. She finds herself pinned, unable to go forward, unable to retreat. She grits her teeth, good humor withering.

"You brought me all this way," she says, "only to leave me at the door?"

Matteo tips one shoulder in the entryway. "Ah," he says, clicking his tongue. "I was afraid of that."

"Do you intend to let me in?"

"I would, but I cannot." And before Sabine can point out the absurdity of laying claim to an entire city but not the house in which he lives, Matteo lifts his voice a measure.

"Alessandro?" he calls out. "We have a guest."

A moment's silence, followed by the soft tread of bare feet, and then a second man appears at the far end of the hall. Elegant and young, honey-blond hair ribboning around his face, his eyes a shocking shade of azure blue—but it is the *red* that draws her gaze. His fingers are coated crimson, the color splashing up his arms, across his tunic, leaving flecks like freckles on one cheek.

"Did we interrupt?" Matteo asks, to which Alessandro gives a languid shrug.

"No," he says. "I was just cleaning my brushes."

So that is what he's covered in. Not blood. *Paint.*

As he ambles toward them, Sabine realizes two things.

He is handsome, in a doll-like way.

And he is unmistakably human. She can hear the soft and steady turning of his heart, can taste his caution wafting down the hall.

"Have you brought home a stray?" he asks, at the same time Sabine mutters, "So you have a pet."

Matteo looks between the two of them and laughs. "Alessandro Contarini, this is . . ." He trails off, waiting for her to introduce herself.

"Sabine."

His mouth twitches. "How odd," he muses.

"Is it?"

"I knew another Sabine once." The words are a chip of ice between her shoulders, but, small mercy, he seems content to leave them there. "Go ahead," he says, shrugging off his cloak. "Let her in."

Sabine's attention slides to the mortal in the hall. Matteo's pet. "Yes," she purrs, fingers rapping against the air, where they land as if on wood. "Go ahead and let me in."

The young man, *Alessandro*, studies her.

Not as a mouse studies a cat, but as an artist studies a subject, deciding how best to capture it. Then he bows, one hand billowing outward in a flourish. "You are most welcome here."

As he says it, the threshold melts away, and in a single stride, Sabine is in the foyer, and has him up against the nearest wall. Blood pounds beneath his skin, and she is still deciding whether to tear open his throat or use his little life for leverage when he is out from under her grasp, twisting behind her, as fluid as a banner in the wind.

By the time she turns, there are two lengths of steel against her skin, the first a blade beneath her jaw, the second a pistol just below her ribs. Sabine looks from the weapons to his azure eyes, so full of life.

Matteo hasn't moved. He simply stands there, looking on, amused.

Then, as easily as he was on her, Alessandro steps away, the weapons vanishing into a holster at his back. And Sabine must admit, she finds herself impressed. Or at the very least, intrigued.

"Well," says her host, "now that you've met . . ."

And with that, he strolls off into the house, leaving them both to follow.

Sabine trails Matteo up the palatial stairs, which give way onto a wide hall, studded with open doors. He gestures to the first one on the right. "This room, I think, has the most extraordinary views."

He leads them into a salon, high-ceilinged and marble-floored, lit by an ornate chandelier. A massive multipaneled window fills one wall, and paintings fill every other, some portraits, and others scenes of life, and while Sabine has never taken much interest in the arts, she can see the talent in the movement of brush, the light that seems to bloom behind the canvas.

Alessandro gestures to the red splashed across his front, and excuses himself so that he can go clean up, while Sabine drifts to the windows. Her host was right about the view. From here, all of Venice seems to stretch out at her feet. At the same time, if she turns her head just so, she can see Matteo, ghosted in the glass, the good mood dropping from his face.

"I meant what I said, Sabine. This is my home. And I will not have you make a mess of it."

He drifts forward as he speaks.

"If you wish to stay, then you may do so as my guest, and I will be your gracious host. But you will live as I do, by a certain set of rules. There will be no skulking about in shadows, no victims stolen from the street and cast in the canal. I will show you how to savor every soul you take. How to claim space, and bend minds, how to enthrall, enchant, and masquerade. How to be the last one they think of when the bodies go missing."

His hand settles on her shoulder.

"I will show you how to *live*, better than you ever have before."

Sabine lets her gaze slide back to the water, the bridges, the city's sculpted buildings like shadowed prints against the sky, a handful of windows lit even now by candlelight.

"A rousing speech," she muses dryly. "But if I refuse your patronage?"

Matteo sighs and reaches past her, rests his hand against the window glass. Beyond, the first light has just begun to tint the sky.

"Then you best go now," he says, "and be on the road to Rome by dawn."

There is neither hope, nor menace, in the words. As if he does not truly care which path she takes, only that she takes one. As if the choice is hers. And it is—at some point, the spectral hand has vanished from her back, and Sabine knows then that if she turned to go, there would be nothing to impede her.

Matteo withdraws as a shape twitches in the doorway.

Alessandro has reappeared, dressed in a clean open-collared tunic, the paint scrubbed from his hands and face, the skin there pink from scouring. Matteo goes to him and lays a kiss gently on his shoulder, a gesture at once so simple and so intimate.

So unlike Sabine, who found the shape of her own urges in the dark and thought that was the only place a truth like hers could live. That it was something to be shrouded. Yet here these two men are, together, and she does not need the ability to feel Matteo's mind to know that there is more than simple lust between them. She sees it, in the way her host's expression softens, the way his gaze lingers on the other man.

Love.

As terrible and bottomless as hunger.

She wonders what it's like.

"Good night, Sabine," says Matteo absently as he and Alessandro slip into the hall, but his voice, soft as it is, wafts back toward her as he goes. "If you do decide to stay, it is a spacious house. I'm sure you'll find a room that suits you."

Moments later, she hears a heavy door swing closed. An old lock turn.

And she is alone.

It is nothing—she has been alone a hundred years, has managed well enough, forgone every chance, when it arose, to fall in step with others like her. And yet, she lingers at the window, watching dawn creep forward as she considers what to do.

Whether to stay, or go, or spite him. She should go, of course. Her curiosity *is* piqued, but she is not one to bend beneath the weight of other people's rules. Least of all a man's. And who is he to be making such demands on *her*? To drag her here and then deliver ultimatums?

But the *air*—in the end, it is the air that sways her. The way it bent around her in the street, turned solid as a door. The way she was forced back, over a threshold that wasn't even *there* save for his whim, his will. Sabine wants to know how Matteo did it.

I will show you, he said, and she will hold him to his word.

And then, she will do whatever pleases her.

After all, he exacted no oath, made her promise nothing. Besides, she thinks, as she turns her back on the glass and crosses the elegant salon, fingers trailing over curtain and molding and painted wall, she has only just arrived in Venice, and does not have a place to stay. At least, not one as fine as this.

She finds three bedrooms, besides the one whose doors are locked, the one with a human heart beating beyond, and chooses the largest at the end of the hall. Its walls are stamped with wild vines, their edges filigreed in gold, its curtains thick enough to blot out every trace of light. And a four-poster bed seems to grow straight out of the floor, dark wood branching at the top into a kind of canopy. It is extravagant. Ornate.

It is exactly to her tastes.

Sabine slips off her boots, and lets her bare feet caress the silk rug, kiss the marble floor. A small plume of dust rises around her when she sinks onto the lavish bed, but she does not care. And by the time the sun rises, she is not on the road to Rome, but instead buried under fine sheets, and dreaming of doors that all give way beneath her touch.

II

The sunlight tears her out of sleep.

For an instant, Sabine is somewhere else—pressed into the corner of a barn, curled on the stone bench of a crypt—before the room takes shape around her. Beyond the bed, a crack where the curtains don't quite meet, the harsh sun forcing its way through.

She rises, cursing softly at the intruding light as she pads over to the window. Discovers it is not as early or as bright as she first thought—what she took for midday sun is actually late afternoon, the low light glinting off the surface of the water. An hour or two until dusk.

She pulls the curtains shut, sighing as the darkness is restored. But there's no point in going back to bed, now that she's awake.

Instead, Sabine decides to explore the room she's chosen.

After all, despite the dark, her eyes can pick out every detail. The carvings on the bedposts. The ribbons of pink running through the marble floor. A hand mirror and a brush. A low velvet settee. A comb studded with small jewels. The gold trim on the painted ivy and, hidden there, a pair of golden leaves, extending into handles. A cabinet, disguised to blend in to the wall.

Inside, she discovers half a dozen dresses, each neatly folded and wrapped in paper. Parcels of honeycomb and emerald and aubergine. She draws them out, fingering the layers of silk skirts, the perfect stitching and lace trim. All finely made, though a few years out of style.

Still, Sabine tries them on, until she finds one she likes best: a bodice and skirts the indigo of a freshly rising bruise. She slides the jeweled comb into her hair, and then abandons the safety of her darkened room for the muted light of the hall beyond.

By day, the house seems even grander.

It is quiet, too, the sounds of the city muted by the heavy walls, but she can feel the others in the house, one a weight, solid and silent, the other thinking, breathing, disturbing the air like a tremor, simply by being alive.

She moves toward the second, is halfway down the stairs when she picks up the soft scrape of a palette knife, the whisper of a brush, the telltale sigh of breath. Matteo's human pet. She finds him in a room that might once have been a small salon and is now a studio.

Alessandro sits in a pool of late-afternoon light, attention hanging on his canvas. From the doorway, she cannot see what he is painting, but she can see the pallor of his skin, the hollow in his cheek, the veins like blue ribbons at his throat.

"Have you come to spar again?" he says without turning his head. "I suppose I can always use the practice."

Sabine folds her arms. "You have keen senses, for a mortal."

"I know," he says, dipping the brush. "Mateusz taught me well."

"*Mateusz?*" she echoes, the name odd, heavy on her tongue. "I thought he was Matteo."

A shrug. A small, half-private smile. "He is both. But Mateusz came first. It was his name back in Staropolska. But if you ask him, he will tell you it belongs to another man. Another life." Alessandro's brush moves like an extension of his hand, gesturing across the canvas. "Besides, most Venetians can't pronounce it. But I learned, because I like the way it sounds. Even more, I like how his face changes when he hears it, like a pebble thrown into a pond."

"So he prefers it to Matteo?"

Alessandro laughs. "No, he hates it. It drives him mad. But that can be fun, sometimes, as well."

Sabine's mouth twitches in amusement. "How did you know it was me, and not Matteo?"

"He makes sound," he says. "I know he does it on purpose, to put me at ease. But I would know, even if he didn't. There is an air to him. You have one, too, but yours is . . ."

"Colder?"

"No," he says, "just different." He glances toward her for the first time, and the air catches in his chest. Sadness sweeps across his face, spills into the air around him.

"Ah," he says. "I see you found my sister's clothes."

Sabine runs a palm along the skirts, wonders if it is the sight that upsets him or only the memory. "She is dead?"

A short nod. "Three winters back. So I fear they are a little out of season now." Then, recovering himself. "But of course, you wear them well."

His gaze escapes back to the canvas, but if it's meant as a dismissal, she ignores it. Drifts into the room, sinking into a chair against the wall, where the sun doesn't reach, as Alessandro begins mixing a new color on his palette. From this angle she can see the canvas, and is surprised to find her own face staring back.

Not a perfect match—he has been painting her from memory—but still. He has captured more of Sabine than she'd expect. A sense of movement in the eyes, the light behind them, the edges of her foxed just so, as if she is emerging out of shadow.

"It was just an exercise," he says. "I can do far better, if you would sit for me."

She knows he means another time, and yet, as she perches in her chair, he begins to glance from the piece to her and back again, making small adjustments to her jaw, her brow, the incline of her head.

There is something purposefully imprecise about the way Alessandro paints, as if the spirit is more important than the details. Layers of color transform, blend, contrast, and as Sabine watches, she finds herself enthralled. By the work, and by the way he's lost in it.

His guard is down, the air around him tinted not with fear, or want, or violence, or any of the things Sabine has come to expect from mortals in her midst. Only a calm intent. A steady focus. If she listens, she can hear the soft pacing of his heart, and she is hungry, and he is right there, and the next time he pauses to rinse a brush, she muses, almost idly, "If I wanted to kill you, do you think you could stop me?"

He dips a small brush, then pauses, as if considering. "It is hard to know what one is capable of, until it becomes a matter of necessity. But I hope I'm not forced to find out."

She studies him, perplexed, not by the arrogance in his words, but the absence of it. "You are not afraid."

Those bright blue eyes find hers across the room. "Of death?" asks Alessandro. "Or of you?"

Sabine arches a brow. "Consider us the same."

He hums thoughtfully. "I have no fear of death, nor any urge to court it. In fact, I am quite fond of living."

Sabine props her chin on her palm. "And yet," she says, "you are still mortal. Does Matteo refuse to make you as he is?"

"Not at all," he answers cheerfully. "He has offered many times. But I refuse to let him."

She frowns. "If you are so fond of living, why reject the gift of life?"

"Is it life," he counters, "if there is never death to balance it? Or is its brevity what makes it beautiful?" The words spill out in such a practiced way, she's sure he's made the point before.

"Besides," says Alessandro, raising his hand as if to cup the waning sun that bathes his corner of the room. "What good is an artist without his light?"

Sabine stares at the handsome youth, bemused. "You say this now, when you're still young and life seems endless. But one day, your beauty will wither, and your flesh will sag—"

"And my bones will be buried in the family plot," he says, returning to his work, "and if God sees fit, something good will grow from them. But it won't be me."

Sabine shakes her head, exasperated.

"Don't bother," says Matteo from the doorway, and even though he's just risen, he looks ready to take the town by storm, in his finely tailored vest, his polished boots, an emerald pin at the collar of his cloak. "He can be shockingly stubborn when he wants."

Alessandro flashes him a grin. "And yet, you love me."

"And yet, I do." Matteo turns his attention to Sabine. "I'm glad to see you are still here."

"Well," she says with a shrug. "I was tired, and it was almost dawn."

"Indeed," he says, and thankfully, he doesn't make her swear an oath, declare herself subject, run through his list of rules. Only says, "Follow me."

At least there is no hand against her back, no will but her own. She rises, leaving the painter to his work as she trails Matteo into the hall.

"Your pet looks a touch unwell."

He makes a dismissive wave. "He insists he paints best after I have fed. Claims it makes him light inside. Lets his mind quiet and his fingers lead."

Sabine cannot stifle her surprise. "You drink from him?"

"When he allows it."

"And yet, you do not claim his heart."

"No, Sabine," he says impatiently. "It's called restraint."

She rolls her eyes. "How boring."

It is then she realizes Matteo is not leading her up the stairs, or into one of the adjoining rooms, but to an outer door at the end of the hall. She slows.

"It is still light out."

"And yet," he says, reaching for the iron handle, "we are going out."

Before she can protest, the door has been flung open, and she is assaulted by the sun. Orange shards leap off the water, send pain lancing through her head. She tries to retreat, into the shadowed safety of the house, but Matteo is there, one arm around her waist as he forces her forward onto a wooden dock, a gondola waiting below. A man stands at the prow, leaning on his pole.

"Why?" she growls, jaw clenched against the dizzy sickness that rolls through her as Matteo leads her down the steps to the waiting boat.

"Because," he says, only the faintest strain in his own voice, "some things we do for pleasure, and others for purpose."

A thin canopy has been erected over the back half of the gondola, but it does little to shield them against the setting sun. Still, she folds herself beneath it, clings to the meager shade as Matteo instructs the gondolier to take the route around San Polo, says he'd like to give his friend a tour.

He then joins her beneath the canopy, lets out a small sigh as he settles on the seat across from her. Sabine closes her eyes, her discomfort matched only by the anger at being subjected to it.

"A tour?" she mutters. "Is this really necessary?"

When Matteo speaks, his voice is low enough that only she can hear it. "It is important to be seen, so that you are seen as one of them. When the bodies go missing, the first suspects are the strangers."

Pain radiates from her temples to her teeth, and Sabine struggles to think of anything, let alone Hector's warning about keeping corpses in one's wake. But after a moment, she manages. "That is why you leave before they're found."

"A fine strategy," Matteo says, "if you're content to spend your whole life running. But why run when you can put down roots and grow?"

As if to prove a point, he waves to a couple strolling by above. Exchanges pleasantries with a gentleman on a bridge just before they pass into the brief respite of the tunnel. Sabine wants to melt into the damp stone arch. The only mercy, she thinks, is the fact that dusk is quick approaching. But Matteo doesn't even flinch when they emerge into the light again.

"How can you stand it?" she asks through gritted teeth.

"I am old," he says simply. "I have had a long time to learn my limits."

To every side, snatches of music and laughter fill the air, the streets packed for the first night of Carnevale, but the canals are glutted, too. Gondolas passing close enough to touch, voices washing like fog around them.

Desperate for some distraction from the discomfort of the sun, Sabine continues talking. "What is old, to those who do not age?"

"Oh, but we do," says Matteo. "It may not show in the luster of our hair, the smoothness of our skin, the strength of our bones. But do not be mistaken. *All* things are touched by time, and we are no exception."

Sabine frowns. "I do not feel changed."

"You are still young," he says, and she snorts. She does not feel it, has by now lived far longer than a human ever would. Matteo registers her doubt.

"For them," he says, gesturing at the busy city, "age takes its toll in decades. For us, it is the work of centuries. And it is not measured in wrinkles, or gray hair. Where others rot without, we rot within." He raps his knuckles against his chest. "We are hollowed, bit by bit, as all that made us human dies. Our kindness. Our empathy. Our capacity for fear, and love. One by one, they slough away, until all that's left is the desire to hunt, to hurt, to feed, to kill. That is how we die. Made reckless by our hunger. Convinced we are unkillable until someone or something proves us wrong."

It has been decades since she thought of Hector. Now, she thinks of him for the second time that *day*. Standing at the altar in the church, a wolfish grin on his stained mouth, his stolen robes splashed red. Renata, assuring her it was nothing but a stormy mood, that it would pass. The sound they made as they were chained and burned inside their coffins.

"You say you're old," she says, forcing her mind back to the gondola, "yet you still seem to have your senses."

A rueful smile. "Give me time."

At last, the sun slips behind the buildings, the sickness withdrawing in its wake. Sabine feels herself uncoil.

"Oh look." Matteo leans back smugly, rests an elbow on the gondola's edge. "You have survived."

She shoots him a withering look. Matteo only chuckles, though she thinks she can make out the slightest strain at the corners of his eyes, the line of his mouth, even as it melts away.

"We are none of us immune to the nature of decay, Sabine. But I believe its effects can be . . . delayed. With a semblance of control." His gaze drops to her neckline as he says it, the baubles hanging there. "You kill too often and too easily."

She shrugs, thumb skating over the tokens. "What can I say? My hunger runs deep."

"Perhaps," he ventures. "I'm sure it *feels* that way. The hunger lives inside us all. To some it is an empty bucket. To others, a yawning pit. And yet, no matter how shallow or how deep it feels, here is a truth that will either drive you mad, or bring you peace." He sits forward. "There is no filling it. You will never be sated. It does not matter whether you drink a carafe or drain a city. The hunger will not ease."

Matteo leans back, elbows resting on the gondola's rim, but his eyes never leave Sabine. He stares at her with that gray gaze, as if she is a pane of glass, and he can see straight through her, all the way back to the frenzied night she nearly lost herself, the slaughter in the church. As if he knows what happened there, how the more she fed, the emptier she felt. How the hunger never waned, but opened in her like a chasm, so wide it nearly swallowed her as well.

"You must learn to master it," says Matteo, "or it will master you."

Sabine's hand drifts to the charms around her throat. "Let me guess," she muses. "You intend to show me how."

The boat slows to a stop before the house again. Her host rises to his feet. "I do," he says, offering a hand. "And who knows. You might even enjoy it."

III

By night, Venice is transformed.

The Piazza San Marco, the city's grandest square, with its colonnade of arches, has been remade by joyful revelers. Jesters and acrobats, flame-eaters and musicians. Torchlight burns to every side, carriages jostle, and spilled wine makes rivers on the ground. People lean out of windows, their arms flung wide, dried petals raining down onto the crowd. Ordinary clothes have been abandoned, traded for costumes at once ornate and absurd.

It is a spectacle unlike anything Sabine has ever seen.

For human senses, the scene must be a feast. For hers, it is cacophony. So many bodies pressed together, the air clouded with their urges and intents, and their faces hidden behind masks. Some sprout feathers, and others horns, tricorne hats perched over plaster or porcelain brows. A handful of rictus grins and garish scowls flash among the horde, but most are strangely expressionless, their painted lips pressed together as if holding back a secret or a smile.

Sabine's own mask rests against her face, gold and white and framed by pearlescent peacock eyes. Beside her, Matteo has opted for one with the jet-black feathers of a crow. Alessandro strolls at his other side, his mask ornamented with the pristine plumage of a swan.

A set of mismatched birds who've flocked to the festivities.

Sabine studies the crowd like a guest arriving at a banquet. She is hungry. She is *always* hungry, of course, but she has not fed, not since last night when Matteo accosted her on the canal, and their time in the sun has left her feeling hollowed. No bother, she thinks, she will soon be satisfied. It is only a matter of choosing who to take. There are so many revelers, one or two will surely go unnoticed.

But Matteo looms like a jailer at her side, that invisible hand hovering behind. Perhaps, if they had lingered in the crowded square, she might have found a way, but he leads them across it, to the Palazzo Ducale, produces a gilded card, and a pair of servants at the doors, clad head to toe in white, ushers them inside.

And so they trade one Carnevale for another.

Here, the dresses are far finer, the masks ornamented with real gold instead of paint, the jesters and jugglers replaced by acrobats who twirl in rings suspended between the chandeliers, while music ricochets against the stone.

Servants drift through the ballroom, their masks like phases of the moon, and ferry trays of glasses fizzing with Prosecho, while dancers fill the center of the room, and Alessandro murmurs something in Matteo's ear, and peels away to join the throng.

And when Sabine insists that she can easily amuse herself, suggesting that he follow in his lover's wake, Matteo's expression darkens. "Some things are frowned upon," he says, "even during Carnevale."

Instead, he slips his arm through hers, suggests they take a turn around the room. It is less crowded than the piazza outside, but not by much, and so they skirt the very edges of the hall, while the revelers spin and twirl and laugh within. Their faces may be tucked away behind their masks, but Sabine can smell their wealth, taste the ostentation of the air, along with the heady scent of wine, knows that if she bit into any of them she would instantly feel drunk.

The thought makes her teeth feel sharper in her mouth.

"Pick one," says Matteo, his voice so low it reaches only her. "And let us play a game."

"A game?"

"You may stalk your prey, hunt them, seduce them, learn as little or as much about them as you like—"

Sabine's mood brightens, her hunger rising with it.

"—but you cannot take their life till Lent."

Her good humor shatters into a brittle laugh. "*Lent?*" She scoffs. It is *ten days* away.

"Take heart," he presses on. "There are other ways to occupy your thirst. To satisfy the urge. Direct your hunger, and draw the pleasure out far beyond the moment of the kill." His slate eyes shine behind his mask, and for the first time, she glimpses something darker there, understands that no matter how well he plays the part of gentleman, there is a monster in him, too.

And yet. Ten days? Sabine has never gone more than a night or two. She shakes her head. "It is too long," she says. "I'll starve."

"How do you know?" he asks. "Have you ever tried?"

"Why would I?" she says, nodding at the bodies crowded in the ballroom. "When there is so much to eat?"

Matteo's grip tightens a fraction on her sleeve. "Because every corpse that falls in the canal makes ripples. And I know for a fact you will not starve. I did it once. I promise, it took *much* longer than a fortnight. And I learned a valuable lesson."

"Which is?"

"We need less than we think."

Sabine purses her lips. "Desire and necessity are different things."

Matteo clucks his tongue. "Then you refuse to play?"

"Do I have a choice?" she asks.

"The road to Rome is always open."

She frowns, surveying the crowd as one song ends and another starts, this one faster, brighter than the last. The dancers spin and she glimpses a flash of crisp white feathers just before they turn away. "What would Alessandro think of your game?"

"He is my partner, not my prey. As such, there are certain urges he cannot understand. Ones he cannot satisfy."

They have made a full turn of the ballroom now, are right back where they started.

"As entertaining as it sounds," says Sabine, "I have never been a fan of other people's rules."

"Alas," he says, "the world is governed by them." He bends his head toward hers, black feathers tickling her cheek. "The difference is that *games* have prizes."

Her interest kindles. "Oh? What would I win?"

"Besides the knowledge that it can be done?" He hums softly, as if considering. "If you can last till Lent, I'll show you how to lay claim to any place, and make it yours."

Her mouth twitches. At least it is a worthy prize. "And if I lose?"

"Then you learn nothing," he says coolly. "But you do not strike me as the losing type."

He is right, of course.

"Well then," says Sabine, surveying the crowd. "Let the games begin."

Another turn around the room, and they have each chosen their mark.

Matteo selects a man similar to him in build, broad-shouldered and square-jawed, though his dark hair, where it shows at the edges of his stark white mask, is shot through with strands of gray.

Sabine chooses a woman with a narrow waist but ample curves, a cascade of black curls spilling down her back. Her whole face is hidden behind a white mask, a gilded lily blooming on one side.

How tempting it is, to walk right up to the woman, under some invented pretense, draw her away into the dark. And yet, she cannot rush. Nine more nights stand between this one and Lent.

Between Sabine and victory.

And so instead, she dances. With Alessandro first, and then Matteo, and all the while watching the white lily. Sees the moment when the woman turns and slips out of the ball, is swallowed by the swell of costumes in the dark, and in that instant, the game begins to feel at once thrilling and impossible.

It takes three nights just for Sabine to spot her mask again amidst the crowds of Carnevale.

Three nights, and all the while the hunger is a rising beat beneath her skin, and the glaring absence of one. The too-still space behind her ribs. *She wants. She wants. She wants.* It is hard to think of anything else, and so she doesn't. Instead, she spends three days, three nights, holding the image of her prey like a cherry on her tongue. The way she did a century ago, when she was a girl named María, when the season was ending, and the fruit almost gone, and she let the last few morsels go soft between her teeth as she resisted the urge to bite down.

Back then, she never lasted very long.

Now Sabine chews the inside of her cheek until she tastes the bitter sweetness of her blood. And carries on.

Three nights, three different gatherings, and then, at last, she spots the gilded lily mask, surrounded by that raven hair, and the relief is so bright

Sabine has to stop herself from rushing over and clamping a hand onto the woman's arm before she can disappear again.

But there are still six nights till Lent, and so instead, she watches. Notices the way the woman holds her glass, the way she lifts her mask, just so, to steal a sip of wine, revealing the edge of a round face, a dimpled cheek. How she stands rapt, right in front of the performers, as if the show they're putting on is just for her. How she chats cordially enough with those around her, and yet belongs with none of them.

Sabine watches, and notices when her prey leaves, just after midnight.

And this time, she doesn't simply watch the woman go.

She follows. Slips off her shoes and walks, barefoot, down the cobbled road, silent in the woman's wake. And the game might have ended then and there, her hunger is so sharp, so great, but a group crashes drunkenly between them, and by the time Sabine has woven past, the woman is ducking through a door into a darkened house.

And so, Sabine walks back to Matteo's place alone.

On the fourth night, she skips the celebrations altogether, and returns to the same road, and waits. It is nearly midnight when she sees the door swing open, and the gilded lily steps into the dark, alone. Sabine bows her head, waits until she's close before crouching over and swearing softly at her shoe.

"Oh dear," says the lily, stopping by her side. "It looks as though the heel is broken."

Sabine feigns annoyance, as if she did not break the shoe herself. She sighs, and tugs off her mask as if in need of air. The lily gasps.

"Your hair," she fawns. "What a magnificent shade. Did you color it for Carnevale?"

Sabine shakes her head, but the woman is already reaching up to touch a coil, and her skin smells of lilies, too, the veins pulsing on the inside of her wrist. They are alone, and she is right there, and Sabine's mind is going blank with thirst, her will splintering beneath the weight of want. The only thing that holds her back is the fact she is sure Matteo will find out. Will smell the failure on her. And Sabine refuses to give him the satisfaction of it. She clamps her jaw shut and tallies the remaining nights till Lent.

And then, as if to mock her hunger, the gilded lily points back at the nearby house and says, "I'm staying right there. You should come in. I'm sure I can find something that will fit."

Sabine almost laughs. She is making it so easy. Too easy. It takes all her strength to shake her head and kick off her ruined shoes and say, "Thank you, but it's all right. I don't live far." Sweeping them into her hand, before wishing the woman she will kill a pleasant night.

At dawn, when Sabine falls into bed, she dreams about her prey, the pieces she has so far glimpsed: her narrow wrists; her dimpled cheek; her long, smooth throat. The way the milky skin will tear beneath her teeth. The sound the heart will make inside her chest.

Sabine wakes hungrier than ever.

She stands before a mirror in the hall and examines her reflection, convinced that she'll find herself wasting away. She expects to be confronted by sunken cheeks and hollowed eyes, her skin shriveling around her bones as it did in the graveyard all those years ago.

But somehow, she looks exactly as she always has.

Which is to say, unchanged.

Matteo, meanwhile, seems engaged with his own quarry.

To keep it fair, he has agreed to abstain from Alessandro's blood, and soon the color returns to the young artist's face, though his *mood* worsens by the day. It is not only that he cannot seem to paint, but that Matteo has apparently eschewed his bed as well.

"I thought you were the picture of control," she chides her host when she finds him emerging from another chamber.

Matteo lifts his chin. "Control is knowing yourself well enough to know your limits." His eyes drift toward the stairs. "Better to avoid temptation."

As if on cue, the studio door slams shut below.

Sabine rolls her eyes and says, "You'd think he is the one who's starving."

IV

On the fifth night, Sabine finds her prey strolling with a man.

One who reeks of gluttony and greed, his attention drifting everywhere but to the woman on his arm, in her gilded lily mask. Sabine's mood darkens, even as her hunger peaks. She wonders if she'll need to handle him as well.

But on the sixth night, the woman is alone again.

Sabine follows the lily from her front door to San Marco, watches her weave between the crowds and carts, buy a bag of candied fruit, and stop before a living statue on its pedestal. A woman dressed as a marionette, a wooden mask with a puppet's face, and pale ropes running from her wrists and ankles to a wooden frame above her head.

Her prey clearly has a penchant for performers.

The lily drops a coin into the bowl and the puppet jerks to life, moving through the motions with a wooden gait. Sabine cannot see the expression on her face, but she's sure it is a mix of curiosity and wonder.

Sabine surveys the square and chooses her own performer, this one dressed as a jester. She strolls up and drops a coin into his cup. It lands with a heavy clink, and he springs to his feet and begins to juggle for her.

She watches, feigning interest, until she hears the rustle of skirts, feels the lily drift up to fill the narrow space beside her. Sabine smiles behind the painted safety of her peacock mask and turns, pretends to startle in recognition.

"Hello again," she says, making her voice sweet and bright. "I found a better pair of shoes." Then, nodding at the jester, who has finished his play, and is pretending to be made of stone again, "Isn't it delightful?"

"Indeed!" says the lily. "I wonder how they stay so still."

"I don't know," says Sabine. "I can barely sit through dinner." She is rewarded with a laugh like little bells. She turns away from her prey, scans the square as if taking it all in for the first time. "I wonder, are there any others?"

And just like that, the gilded lily hooks her elbow through Sabine's and says, "Come, I'll show you. There is a great one, over here."

On the seventh night, she learns the woman's name.

Bianca.

Bianca, whose voice is high and sweet, and always on the verge of laughter.

Bianca, who is twenty-two, and recently engaged, to that oafish man Sabine saw her with two nights before.

Bianca, who seems excited to be wed, which is enough to convince Sabine that she has chosen well, will be doing her a kindness, sparing her the horrors of a marriage bed, the burden of being a wife.

Bianca, who is not from Venice, but Modena, and though her fiancé brought her here to experience the spectacle of Carnevale, he seems to care less for the balls than the corners where bets are placed and cards are played, and so, Bianca has been left largely to her own devices.

It is all wonderful but, she must admit, it is a little lonely, too.

How lucky she feels, then, to have made a friend.

How grateful, to have met Sabine.

By the eighth night, Sabine is ravenous.

And yet, there is a new shade to her hunger. A clarity, a brightness, every sense sharpened by the single-minded focus.

She paces the house until dusk, eager to resume the hunt.

On the ninth night, they return to the Ducale, she and Bianca, and perch like birds on the upper colonnade, making up stories about the dancers below. They spin messy yarns of sordid affairs and murder plots, Bianca's contributions fueled by her love of novels, Sabine's drawn from memory.

At the end of the night, Bianca insists that Sabine come with her the next and final day, to witness the menagerie they've gathered in the square, a caravan of birds and monkeys, tigers and bears. Sabine is already making her excuses when Bianca's hand comes to rest on her arm, her eyes twinkling behind her mask as she says, "Please, say that you'll come."

And Sabine finds herself saying yes.

Until now, she has only seen the Carnevale by night, imagined it rising up like mushrooms after dark.

How strange, then, to see the costumed masses revel in the sun.

The daylight ushers in another kind of torment: children. They dart between skirts and horses, stalls and carts, their faces painted and their voices loud.

Sabine wishes she were in her darkened chamber, safe within her bed.

Her feathered mask provides a small shield against the light, but she is tired, her head pounding from hunger and the sun's vicious glare, even sheltered as she is beneath the parasol that Alessandro gave her when she left. Meanwhile, Bianca throws her arms out and delights in the arrival of the spring. How bleak it's been, this winter past, she says. So much rain, so little sun.

Sabine grimaces behind her mask, and lets Bianca draw her toward the crowd, and the cages, and the creatures kept within.

Her mood lifts at the sight of them, prowling behind their bars, these creatures larger and fiercer than she has ever seen. A bear rises on hind legs and towers overhead. A red-faced monkey grips its cage with human-looking hands. A bird with every-colored feathers squawks and settles on its perch. But it is the cats that most enchant her. Mouths wider than a man's head, and teeth as long and sharp as talons. Fur in shades of black, and white, and even red. Like her.

Sabine approaches the ginger beast, steps right up to the bars, and in response, the lion growls, retreats, as all beasts do, sensing danger.

Behind her mask, she smiles, showing teeth.

Once, Bianca gets too close to a cage, and the tiger within lets out a warning roar. She leaps backward with a delighted yelp, and clutches at Sabine as if escaping peril. As if she has not fled one predator in favor of another.

Sabine laughs, softly, to herself, and holds Bianca tighter.

~⌇~

Ten days.

Ten days that seem to last forever.

And then, somehow, are gone.

Suddenly, it is the last night of Carnevale, the most extravagant one yet. It is the feast before the famine, the entire city gorging on its pleasure. The hours wilt and drop away. The sky over Venice explodes with light as fire-works ring in the final hours, the blasts echo like thunder, and beside Sabine, Bianca lets her head fall back and gasps in childish delight.

It is magnificent.

And then it is over.

Bells toll across the square, and Sabine walks her companion home. Along the way, Bianca sheds her mask, lets it dangle on its ribboned backing from her wrist. Her cheeks are flushed, her eyes glassy with wine.

Her head lolls on Sabine's shoulder as she murmurs sleepily, "I wish it did not have to end."

"So do I," she lies.

If her own heart could beat, it would be racing now, giddy in anticipation. Instead, there is only the coiled silence. The hollow waiting to be filled.

They are almost to Bianca's when Sabine leads her off the road, into a narrow gap between the buildings. Bianca giggles, the sound bubbling up, her limbs off-balance from the night of drinking and dancing.

Sabine takes off her mask, and Bianca studies her face, then reaches out and curls a copper lock around her finger, the air above her nothing but curiosity and trust.

It has already happened.

Sabine has killed her a hundred times.

Has let her imagination feast on the inevitable act.

In some of her fantasies, Bianca struggled.

In others, she was so surprised that she went still.

But in none of them did the woman's fiancé come stumbling around the corner.

Bianca startles, turning toward the sound, but Sabine presses her back against the wall. Holds a finger to her lips, makes sure to smile as if it is a joke.

A *game*.

The man walks straight by the narrow alcove, never once glancing into the dark.

And then he's gone.

Sabine drops her hand, and Bianca takes a breath, lips parting, perhaps to make a joke, or ask a question, but the words die on her lips as Sabine bows her head and brings her mouth to rest against the woman's throat.

Bianca stiffens in surprise, and Sabine wonders, briefly, if she would welcome this, if it were just a kiss. But her pulse is a desperate beat, her skin so thin a barrier, and Sabine has waited long enough.

Her teeth sink in.

Bianca gasps, and Sabine's grip tightens, blood spilling through her lips, the heartbeat heavy on her tongue.

And it is *exquisite*.

Every pulse repays a minute, an hour, a day, nine days of waiting, ten nights of wanting, of unremittent hunger, every agonizing moment hoping her restraint would be rewarded. Hoping the suffering endured would be worth it when she reached the end.

And it is. It is worth it for the heady rush alone, the dizzy thrill, the lifeblood pouring in, soaking through Sabine's body like deep water on dry earth.

Bianca whimpers, and Sabine's teeth drive deeper still, pinning her prey to the wall as she closes her eyes, and drinks, and drinks, until there is nothing left but a body, abandoned, and a stolen pulse cradled in her chest.

A heartbeat that blooms within Sabine.

And lasts all the way home.

V

Matteo arrives at the palazzo an hour after she does.

Sabine sits in the salon, thumbing her prize—a single fabric petal, painted gold, peeled from the lily on Bianca's mask—when he sweeps past the door, his clothes stained red, and his eyes dark, his mustache plastered to his cheeks with blood. As if he did not drain his prey so much as tear them limb from limb.

Her host says nothing, only vanishes down the hall into his borrowed room. When he emerges half an hour later, he looks so hale and put together that Sabine begins to doubt herself. To wonder if the man she glimpsed so briefly in the doorway was someone else.

His clothes are clean, his face is washed, the easy air returned and the affable smile fixed neatly on his face as he crosses to the grand windows, watches the last embers of Carnevale burn to nothing.

"So," Matteo says at last, turning back to face Sabine, "you did not starve." He inclines his head. "Tell me, did you enjoy the hunt?"

"It was *diverting*," she admits, fixing the gilded petal on a cord around her neck. "I've come to claim my prize."

"Tonight?"

Sabine rises to her feet. "Why wait?"

She expects him to put it off, offer some excuse, but Matteo only nods and strides into the center of the room. There he stops, and spreads his hands.

"Bricks and boards may build a house," he says, "but it's a man's *intent* that makes it his. The conviction that a place, any place on this green earth, can be laid claim to. The strength of will behind the word *mine*." His hands glide through the air. "Take this room. I have allowed you in, but it does not change the fact that it is mine. And if I decide you are no longer welcome—"

Matteo barely moves, nothing but the slightest incline of his head on that last word, and yet Sabine finds herself thrown backward by that sudden

unseen force. She gasps as her body moves against her will, a terrible sensation, the air before her turned to stone, the air behind a dragging weight, like
hooks sunk into her skin.

Before she knows it, she is up against the wall, half expects for it to crack
and crumble, the bones inside her body grinding from the force.

"You've made your point," she growls through gritted teeth, but Matteo
simply folds his arms, and she realizes that he does not plan to welcome her
again. He is waiting for her to find her will. To claim the space herself. Or be
forced out. Sabine tries to shake away a spike of panic, and focus.

Mine, she thinks desperately.

But nothing happens.

"This room is *mine*," she says aloud, to no avail. Sabine can barely think
through the dragging force, the crushing pressure of Matteo's will, his smug
amusement churning up her temper. She squeezes her eyes shut, focuses not
on the house, or even the salon, but the small square of stone against her
back, the floor right beneath her bare feet. *This, right here*, she thinks, *is mine*.

The weight against her weakens. The hooks release. She sags a little in
relief.

"Congratulations," mocks Matteo. "You own roughly a dinner plate of
space."

And sure enough, when Sabine tries to take a forward step, the wall is
there again. The whole wretched process must be repeated. She focuses on
the floor just before her toes and thinks, *Mine*, the word a little stronger in
her head. The air gives way another foot.

And another.

And another.

Inch by inch, she carves her trench back through Matteo's salon until she
is right there, before him, close enough to see the wax in his mustache, the
filaments behind his eyes, the way one brow quirks up slightly as if to say,
What now?

Sabine looks down, focuses on the floor beneath *his* boots, and thinks,
with every measure of conviction she can muster: *Mine*.

Matteo's amusement falters.

To her delight, so does his stance. She has not laid a hand on him, and
yet, he stumbles slightly, as if pushed, retreats a single heavy step.

Sabine lets out a delighted sound. Matteo grins.

"Well done," he says as the air in the salon goes slack again. He turns to leave. "Enjoy your room."

"Wait," she says as he turns to go. He pauses in the doorway. "You promised to show me how to lay claim to any space, no matter the size."

"I did," he answers wearily.

"Then how did you lay claim to all of Venice?"

Matteo meets her gaze. "The same way," he says, with a shrug. "Stone by stone, and step-by-step."

Sabine thinks that is the end of it.

She's won his game and claimed her prize. She considers leaving, but the next night, Matteo strolls into the salon and says, "Shall we play again?"

And to her surprise, the words stir something in her, anticipation rising at the prospect of another game.

It is harder, during Lent.

The masks are gone, the shroud of drunken revelry removed. The city draws in on itself again, and in response, Matteo draws her out. Introduces her as his niece, and his ward. Widowed young, so sad, he knows.

Sabine plays the part as her gaze slides over these gatherings, searching for her newest mark. She has been warned never to pick the oldest children of the wealthy, or the public faces, anyone whose death would cause a scandal or a scene.

Matteo's rules are cumbersome, but she does see the merit in them, the freedom they afford, and the thrill of hunting in plain sight.

One night he hosts a dinner in the courtyard, the doors of the palazzo flung open on the summer air. Alessandro plays the part of friend, except in certain, trusted company. And when Sabine's attention is not hanging on the guests, it is on Matteo.

How easily he moves among them.

How well he's known, and liked.

How casually he lifts a glass, as if to sip, and makes the food vanish from his plate.

How seamlessly he blends into this world, as if it's his.

Two weeks, he announces when they play again, then three, pushing the threshold of her thirst a little more. Each time, Sabine expects to find her limit, and each time, she is surprised, and glad to learn it isn't there. That she is stronger than she thinks.

Each victim is a kind of courtship.

A prelude to pleasure.

And she does take pleasure in them all.

Again, they play. Again. Again.

Until Alessandro throws a fit at the prospect of losing his lover to another game, of being forced into a celibacy he did not choose, and after that, Matteo does not always join her in the play. But he does reward her every time.

And so Sabine discovers not only how to appease her hunger with the hunt, but how to bend a human will, both the way it wants to go, and then, the ways it doesn't. How to close her mind, and pry open someone else's.

Matteo's lessons, doled out like laurels.

Back in the courtyard, the guests around his table chat and drink. Sabine lets the sound wash over her as she twists a token around her finger, thinking of her latest prey.

In time, the charms around her neck have taken on a special air, each a memory no longer of a moment's kill, but a month's slow pursuit. A stranger courted into friendship, into trust.

Her host meets her eye across the table. He lifts his glass toward her as if to toast.

"Does it never make you hesitate?" Matteo asked the night before. "Getting to know your mark so well? Spending so long in their company? Do you ever think to let them live?"

But Sabine smiles now, as she did then.

Because the truth is, the knowing never holds her back.

If anything, it makes the killing sweeter.

ALICE

(D. 2019)

I

Metal rattles on metal as the train slides through the dark.

Alice sits on a hard plastic seat, teeth clenched and arms wrapped around the backpack in her lap. She'd had enough sun for one day, opted for the T to take her back to campus, thought it would be safe, considering it's just after 2 P.M., and the car's half-empty, a handful of bodies scattered across two dozen seats, and the memory of the man's heartbeat still echoing behind her ribs.

She doesn't want to think about him, so instead, she thinks of Lottie. Or Charlotte. Whatever her name really is. Wonders how the hell she's supposed to find a stranger in a city of more than half a million, a girl she knows fuck all about beside the fact she clearly isn't human. If she'd been a fellow student maybe, but Alice doesn't think she is, which means she has a Post-it Note and a single blurry party photo and she can't exactly post the two online with the caption *Do you know the girl who killed me?*

Alice groans, and grips the backpack tighter as the train pulls into South Station. The doors open, and two get off, and four get on, and she finds herself searching the strangers' faces, as if Lottie might suddenly walk back into her life as easily as she walked out of it.

There's a kind of logic to that, right?

Sure, the odds are a million to one, but then again, when you stop and think about it, what were the odds of Alice meeting Lottie in the first place? How many times did she think of bailing on the party at the Co-op? More than once while getting ready, a handful on the way, and even after she was *there*, how many times did the path split? How many choices did she make? If she had gone back early. If she'd turned right toward the front door instead of left toward the hall. If the line for the bathroom hadn't been so long. If she hadn't gone past it to the bedroom? If they'd never met. If they'd never danced. If she hadn't taken Lottie home.

If, if, if, and she knows that way lies madness but once she starts, she can't stop her mind from going down the hundred ways it could have ended instead of how it did.

If, if, if, the road branching so many times—if she had been assigned a different suite, gone to a different school, if she hadn't left Scotland—has taken so many turns she might as well be a different Alice, living a different life, and she can't even remember why she's gone down this road, has to turn around, pick her way back through the splitting paths until she finds the place it started.

Odds.

That's right.

The odds of Lottie stepping onto the train she's on right now are slim to none, but it doesn't stop Alice from hoping every time the T comes to a stop, doesn't stop her from staring at the doors every time they open with that low hydraulic hiss, searching each and every face as the people pile on.

But none of them are Lottie.

Alice finds fragments of her—the tan skin, the brown curls, the bow-like bottom lip—but the first belongs to a guy twice her size, the second a girl of ten, the third a woman old enough to be Eloise. They're tall and short and large and lean and most obviously, human.

They fill the car with heartbeats, like overlapping drums, and now Alice has another problem. She thought she'd be safe enough, taking the train, because she wasn't hungry anymore.

But as the T slides into Park Street, Charles/MGH, Kendall/MIT, and the car begins to fill, she realizes that's not exactly true.

The hunger is a pale shadow of itself, a whisper instead of a shout, but somehow it's *still there.*

Not a capital H, the way it was before, not an *all Alice can think of, teeth aching and tongue heavy, heart rattling like a can of loose change in her chest* kind of need, but a quiet nagging, an emptiness, a well, and she can't help but wonder what it would take to fill it up—

(which makes her think of Catty, the way she was always famished from running track, how everything she ate just seemed to burn away without ever sticking to her)

—and that makes Alice think of the time she and Catty got too stoned and she had the munchies so bad she kept forgetting the way food tasted as soon as she had swallowed, so kept going back for more.

And then Alice remembers the man in the suit in the sedan, remembers the heat of his blood spilling down her throat, remembers the iron taste as a woman and her little girl take the nearest seats.

And the hunger *flares*.

It sharpens like a knife, and Alice surges to her feet, fast enough that heads are turning. She thinks of saying she's not feeling well, but she's afraid of what will happen if she opens her mouth, so she just clings to the pole nearest the door, closes her eyes and waits for the train to stop again, and as soon as it pulls into Central, she gets off, even though it's one stop shy, and the sun is like a hammer, her skull a sheet of glass.

Alice forces herself up and out onto the street, braving the shivers and the headache for the last few blocks, cutting through campus buildings to keep the worst at bay. She propels herself on with the promise of a darkened room, a heavy duvet blocking out the light, finally reaches the dorm and the third-floor suite feeling like Odysseus at the end of his long quest, limbs shaking and soul wrung dry.

All she can think about is her bed, the dark, but Alice knows the second she walks in that something's wrong.

Lizbeth and Jana and Rachel are huddled together on the couch, the air around them slick with shock and sadness, and for a moment Alice thinks they know where she's been, and what she's done, that her crimes have somehow rushed ahead of her.

But then Lizbeth looks up, and frowns, and says, "Are those my sunglasses?"

"Sorry," Alice answers, plucking them from her head. "I felt a migraine coming on."

She drifts toward the couch, where Jana perches next to Rachel, rubbing circles on her back.

"What's wrong?" she asks, and Rachel's head swings up, eyes red from crying, opens her mouth only to snap it shut again as fresh tears come spilling down her cheeks.

"You haven't heard?" says Lizbeth. "They found a student in the Yard."

Her eyebrows arch in that knowing way, as if to say the word without saying it.

They found a student *dead*.

Alice's stomach tightens, and she was right, wasn't she? It was one of hers, just not the most recent one, and she really should have seen this coming, knew it was only a matter of time before they found the body.

"It was *Colin*," says Rachel between sobs, and the name ricochets inside her skull.

("Come on, let's get you home.")

And she remembers, then, why he looked kind of familiar, where she'd seen him once, his arm slung round Rachel's shoulders at the latest student mixer.

("I've got you.")

Why she'd trusted him enough to let him hold her up, walk her to the Yard.

Alice swallows. "Do they know what happened to him?" she asks, feeling a little dizzy, a little sick, and it might just be the sun but she's always been a shite liar, the blood rushing to her cheeks (though she can't help but wonder now if that's still true, wants to reach up to touch her face and see, but that would probably look suspicious, so she doesn't), and then to her relief, the girls all shake their heads, mismatching metronomes.

"No official cause," says Jana.

"Which means it was an overdose," adds Lizbeth. Rachel scowls, and she hastily adds, "It was probably an accident. Drugs these days are laced with god knows what."

At which point, Rachel starts to cry again, her sniffles interrupted by half-hiccupped words about how nice he was to her, how he could have been *the one*, and Alice wants to lunge across the room, take Rachel by the shoulders, and say, *I did you a favor.*

But she can't, so she leaves the girls to their grief, and instead slips into the welcome dark of her room, and crashes down onto the bed, and sleeps.

II

Alice wakes after dark to an empty suite and a group text telling her the girls are all headed out to Colin's vigil, and she's welcome to join them if she's feeling up to it.

Which, of course, she's not.

Instead, she's sitting in a cocoon of sheets, staring at the laptop balanced on her knees, the Post-it tacked in the corner of the screen.

Goodbye, Alice.
xo Lottie

Her fingers hover over the keys like she's waiting for them to take charge.

The cursor blinks in the search bar, willing her to use the word, the one she doesn't want to type, or think, because it feels like taking a step out of the world of the sane and the grounded and the human, as if the taste of blood isn't echoing behind her teeth.

Alice takes a breath—she knows she doesn't need to, but it helps—and then she forces her fingers to the keys, spelling out the word.

She hits Search, and sure enough the first two pages of results are filled with costumes, notices for parties being hosted round the city, despite the fact that Halloween is still a month away. *Creatures of the night, rejoice,* announces one site, featuring figures in high-collared capes, red contacts. Another offers a variety, shrink-wrapped or slutty or sparkly. A third, capsules of fake blood that break between fake teeth.

Alice runs her hands through her hair, and adds the word *real,* and for the next hour, her econ reading and her problem sets both sit neglected on her desk as her search history fills with the stuff of bad fiction, and she's all too aware that she's sitting in the dark with her screen's light turned as low as it will go, searching for monsters.

Or more specifically, places they might meet.

Eventually she ends up on a subreddit that leads her to a forum that leads to some kind of off-brand Yelp page for clubs in the Boston area, and it's pretty impressive, considering there was so little in the way of culture back in Hoxburn, let alone *sub*culture, just the rugby boys and a handful of punks who carpooled to the nearest concerts, which were usually in Glasgow, but a city this size seems to have something for *everyone*, from BDSM meetups to dungeons to goth clubs, every site rife with disclaimers that what happens is roleplay between consenting adults.

Only two of the places listed show a shred of promise. Neither uses the word, but both talk about *alternative fare*, the language just cagey enough to make her think she *may* be onto something. After all, she thinks, the real thing probably doesn't announce itself. Hiding in plain sight and all of that.

One of the places doesn't even have a website, only a handful of photos uploaded over the last few months. Moody shots taken in a darkened club.

The other is full of vague promises, declarations for the lost and the damned, which admittedly is a bit dramatic, but what else is she supposed to do?

She can't just sit there, going to class and killing men in cars.

She needs to find answers.

Needs to find Lottie.

So Alice gets up, and gets dressed.

Which is harder than it sounds. She doesn't know what look she should be going for, only knows she feels absurd aiming for true goth—she doesn't own any leather or lace, and a quick look through Lizbeth's drawers confirms that she doesn't, either—so ends up opting for dark-wash jeans and a vintage black hoodie nicked from Catty's closet and never returned, the front emblazoned with a crow, the graphic faded to a pair of ghostly wings by years of washing.

She notices as she heads for the door that the volume on the hunger is creeping up again, which feels mortally unfair, given what that last meal cost her. The nearest of the two clubs is way over in the North End, and Alice doesn't trust herself in the closed chambers of the T so she orders a ride, using the cash she swiped from the man in the sedan.

She slips through the nearest gate and into the back seat of the waiting car.

Which turns out to be a bad idea. The driver is blaring eighties shout rock, refuses to turn the radio down, and she can taste his cologne on the back of her tongue as if he bathed in it. She digs her nails into her knees, ends up riding with the windows open, the sounds of the street surrounding her until it makes a kind of white noise in her head.

The car finally spits her out on a road she doesn't know, and drives off before she even finds the entrance to The Dark Side (yes, that's really what it's called). It turns out to be a black door studding a black wall, no sign, nothing but a hammered approximation of a handprint dented in the steel. She fits her hand into the mark, as if the door might open like a secret, but it doesn't, the door is locked, and there's no bouncer, no crowd, no sounds of life within, and Alice pulls the place up on her phone again, and sees the vital detail that she missed the first time round.

The Dark Side isn't open on Mondays.

Alice groans, and knocks her head against the cold steel door.

She kicks the metal, not hard, or at least, not hard enough to hurt her foot, is shocked when it leaves a noticeable dent. She kicks the door a second time, puts some real force behind it, and the metal actually bends. Alice marvels at the damage before it occurs to her that there are probably security cameras, and then she backs away, and turns, hurrying down the block.

When she's a safe distance from the dented door, she slows and pulls out her phone, glares at the out-of-focus picture of Lottie for a few seconds before swiping over to the map.

It's a solid mile to the second club (which is definitely open) but Alice can't bear the thought of calling another car, and besides, the night air feels good; not just good, but the exact opposite of the way she felt all day, the limb-shaking wooziness of the sun, and people talk about the way a place changes depending on the weather, but she's always felt the same way about day and night. Like they're two entirely separate worlds.

A different smell, a different taste, a different energy.

Now, in the dark, her mind calms and her body uncoils.

Her head is clear and her legs feel strong, so she decides to walk.

Never walk alone at night, they tell you, if you're a girl.

And it isn't fair.

Because the night is when the world is quiet.

The night is when the air is clear. The night is wild and welcoming and

Alice lets her head fall back, until all she sees is the sky, not black, as it should be, given the time, but a twisting tapestry of blue.

A color that will always make her think—

Of summer days—

And wedding bells—

The day Eloise Martin marries Dad, *everything* is blue.

From El in her azure sundress, to Dad in his twilight suit, Catty and Alice both in robin's egg, and baby Finn, perched on Granddad's lap, in a onesie the same shade as Catty's eyes (minus the anger). Outside the church, even Hoxburn is showing off one of those rare summer days where the rain comes and goes before noon, taking all the clouds with it.

"We are gathered here . . ." says the priest in the church beside the graveyard where Mum is buried, and here's the thing, it's a hard day, it was always going to be a hard day.

But maybe it will be a good one, too.

Or maybe Alice is a fool for ever hoping, because Catty's been spinning for a fight since El first walked into their lives, and even though they waited *years*—till after Finn was born, till El has been around almost as long as Mum was, for Alice at least—to tie the knot, and Catty's fifteen now to Alice's twelve, it turns out there's no expiration date on pain.

(And it breaks Alice's heart that Dad's happiness and her sister's hurt go hand in hand, or worse, that they are angled at each other, like pistols, or blades, and all she can do is put herself between them.)

And Catty *did* make a scene, three months ago when Dad made the announcement. She scoffed and said she didn't see why they bothered with white dresses and rings, since they clearly hadn't waited to do the deed, and Dad had raised his hand like he might lay it on her, but he'd never been that kind of man, so it had come back down again, and he'd chided her for being crass, said her mother would be ashamed, and that was enough to send Catty fleeing to Granddad's for a week.

(And Alice knows why she goes, because Granddad never shouts back, doesn't treat fights like a contest, or a challenge to see who can make the most noise, which probably comes with running a pub as long as he has, and dealing with his fair share of the drunk and the mad.)

But even after all of that, Alice keeps thinking, keeps *hoping* that maybe it will be okay, especially after they get through the *Do yous* and *I dos* and Catty glares at the ground but doesn't object (though Alice sees her fingers tighten on the small bouquet they've each been given, and she's just glad the rose stems had their thorns snipped off), and afterward her dad relaxes visibly, smiles and kisses his new wife, and even then Catty holds her tongue, and she might have kept on holding it, gotten through the rest of the day in stoic protest.

If not for the gift.

It's after the vows and before the reception, and they're in the little room at the back of the church, just Alice and Catty and El.

"A moment, just for the girls," El said to Dad before closing the door gently in his face, and when he's gone, she takes out a pair of small blue velvet boxes—this blue so deep it's almost black—hands one to each of them. Inside, Alice finds a gold bauble on a chain. Not a charm or a locket, but a small cylinder.

And her first thought is that it looks like a gilded bullet.

But her second thought is that it's beautiful. The surface is stamped with little flowers, and there's a lightness to it, as if the chamber's hollow. Catty's frowning as she lifts her pendant from its box, and Alice didn't know it could be opened until Catty finds the lid, thin fingers twisting, the contents spilling into her palm.

At first, it looks like dirt. Fine as sand, but twice as dark, and Alice doesn't understand, even as El tells them for the hundredth time that she's not trying to replace their mum.

It's not until she says, "This way, wherever you go, she'll be with you."

The hammer falls. Alice realizes what it is.

Catty's fist slams shut over the grave dirt, her face contorting with disdain.

Catty, who could never take anything without bending it. Who could turn any olive branch into a sharpened stick.

"That's nae me mum," she seethes, her accent going thick with hate. "She's not out *there*, rotting in the ground." She knocks her fist against her chest. "She's not a fucking bit of glaur to wear around my neck."

Catty flings the golden vial down, flecks of dirt raining in its wake, and storms out of the room, and maybe it's the swell of grief on El's face, or maybe it's the fact her legs, her heart, her bones are tired of being pulled both ways, but for the first time since the first time, Alice watches Catty go.

And doesn't follow.

She stays, glued to the spot. Swallows around the rocks in her throat as she cradles her own small pendant in her palms, as if the precious thing might fly away.

"Thanks, El," she says, her voice full of cracks. "It's really nice."

It's not even a lie. Alice loves the little talisman. It's not her *mum*, of course it's not, but she likes the weight. The object, filling the space of memory.

She looks up and meets her stepmum's eyes, soft and brown and full of pain, and she just wants to make it go away.

"Would you help me put it on?" she asks, holding out the golden chain, and El dashes the tears from her cheeks, and nods.

"Of course," she says.

Alice lifts her hair out of the way, and El's touch is light as feathers as she slides the chain around her neck, fastens the clasp, kisses the back of Alice's head before she pulls away.

Alice touches the pendant again, then tucks it under the hem of her dress, where Catty won't see, the gold warming there against her heart. And by the time she's turned toward Eloise, the color's back in her cheeks.

When they step out of the little room, Alice is shocked to find Catty standing in the hall, next to Dad, his hand on her shoulder and her arms crossed tight.

Alice will never know what he said to get her to stay, whether he threatened or begged, but you can see it, in the wedding photos taken after.

The emptiness in her eyes—

Like a house packed up—

The tenants already gone.

———

Alice reaches for the necklace as she walks, turns the gold vial between her fingertips, brings it to her lips the way she does sometimes when home feels too far away.

Then she turns the corner, and the second club comes into sight.

At the very least, it isn't closed.

The entrance is halfway down an alley, the door propped open, spilling darkroom red light onto the road, and the guy outside has more studs than an upholstered chair.

He looks Alice up and down. "You in the right place?"

"No idea," she says, holding up the phone. "I'm looking for this girl?"

The bouncer doesn't even give the screen a proper look, just shrugs and says, "Maybe you'll find her," nods his head toward the open door, but when Alice starts forward, his arm swings up to block her way.

"You got ID?"

She does, but there's no point in showing it, since she's nearly three years shy of twenty-one. The moment seems to stretch, his expectation warring with her need. And this is the part where Old Alice would fumble, and fall over herself with *sorrys*, apologize and walk away, but New Alice is on a mission.

New Alice isn't going back to campus, not until she has a lead.

She remembers the way her hold settled over Hannah, how it only faltered after Alice herself did, so she meets the bouncer's gaze, holds it, as if it is a pool, something she could dive right into, as she says, "I'm old enough."

The world doesn't shiver with her voice. There's no ripple, no vibration, no way to know the difference between a simple statement and something stronger. The words hang between them, and all Alice can do is wait and see what happens next.

"Are you?" he asks, but there's no attitude, no leering look, only the smallest furrow in his brow, as if he's trying to listen to his mind as well as hers. Alice holds his gaze and nods.

"I am. Now let me in."

He blinks, then shrugs. "Go on, then," he says, and Alice wants to preen, to crow, to pump her fist because it worked, it worked, but she's afraid it will somehow break the spell, and maybe there was no spell, maybe he just didn't care, but either way, she heads in.

Only she's halfway through the door when he blocks her way again.

"Wait," he says, and Alice grits her teeth, expecting trouble, but he's just holding up a pair of paper wristbands, one red, the other white.

"What's that?"

"Everyone is either predator," he says, waving the red one, "or prey," he adds, then snaps the white one round her wrist without asking which she is, which she wants to be.

Alice rolls her eyes, and goes inside.

III

The music pulls her in and under.

A heavy beat that pulses through the club, too loud to hear, to think.

Everywhere Alice looks she sees bodies pressed together, most of them dressed in black leather and black cotton and black lace.

Chalice.

That's what the place is called.

It's straight out of a paranormal romance, dark velvet swallowing the corners and mirrors draped with cotton shrouds. Lamps with crimson-tinted bulbs and alcoves running down the walls like cubbies in a crypt.

Alice skirts the crowded club, searching for Lottie.

She passes through a pool of black light, and suddenly her hands are splattered neon in a way that makes her want to rush into the nearest bathroom and start scrubbing at the skin. But no one seems to notice the blood spray on her skin, or if they do, they don't care.

To her right, two guys are locked together against the wall, limbs tangled, hands, too, a band of red, a band of white, the air around them thick and sweet, and Alice tenses when their mouths break apart and she sees the tips of pointed teeth. There and then gone, as he buries his head in the curve of the other guy's neck.

And maybe, just maybe, she's found the right place, the real thing. Hope rises in her as she hooks her finger under the white wristband, and snaps it off, then heads for the bar.

No stools, so she leans her elbows on the counter and flags the bartender down, a wiry woman with contacts that make her eyes look black from edge to edge. Alice slides her phone, face up, across the bar.

"Have you seen this girl?" she shouts over the blaring beat.

And maybe it's the contacts but the bartender doesn't even seem to look, just shakes her head and says, "You gonna order something?" jabbing a pointed crimson nail at the board behind her head, where everything has a name like Violence or Heartbreak or Hunger.

Alice orders a Heartbreak, ends up with a shot glass of something that looks like blood but smells like sugar. Tastes like it, too. She gags, spits the contents back into the glass, squeezes her eyes shut and realizes that she is, of course, an idiot, that this place might as well be the film set for a teenage urban fantasy, that there's nothing real about the people here, it's clearly another dead end and—

"First time?"

Alice opens her eyes, and turns, and for a second, she's looking right at Lottie.

Lottie, leaning an elbow on the bar, her smile cocked and her curls now tinted red instead of violet. But then Alices blinks, and it's not her, just another curly-headed girl, her skin too fair, and her eyes a lightless, ordinary shade.

Ordinary, but pretty all the same, ringed the way they are in black, tiny jewels winking at the inner corners. A white band loops around one wrist, and gold rings glint on every knuckle, catching the club's odd light as she reaches out and brushes a fingertip along Alice's cheek. A dark bead hovers on her skin, as if she's pricked her finger on a thorn.

Alice stares down at the smudge, and frowns.

She didn't realize she was crying.

The girl looks down, too, perplexed, then lifts her finger to her lips, as if to lick the blood away—bur Alice is racked by the sudden fear that it will do something to this girl, hurt her, change her, so she snatches her hand before it reaches her tongue.

The girl flinches. "Your hands are cold."

"Are they?" asks Alice, and she could have wiped her blood from the girl's skin, but she doesn't. She can't. The sight of it churns the hunger up, and before she knows what she's doing, Alice lifts the girl's fingers to her lips, and when she doesn't resist, Alice puts the index finger in her mouth and licks it clean. Her blood, which doesn't taste the same, but still rings her hunger like a bell, and she doesn't mean to bite the girl, but as her teeth skim the soft meat of her fingertip, her jaw commits a small, defiant act, and tightens. Alice has barely bitten down, but she feels the skin break, easy as a peach under a paring knife.

The girl gasps, lets out a nervous laugh.

"Wow, those are sharp," she says as she draws her hand back, but she doesn't seem mad—if anything, her pupils have gone wide, the air around her tinged with want, and then she's drawing Alice away from the bar, away from the twisting bodies in the center of the club, away from the throbbing beat and into a corridor, and then her mouth is on Alice's mouth and her hand (the one with the white band) is sliding beneath Alice's hoodie, and her heart is pounding through her ribs when she brings her lips to Alice's ear and says, sincerely, "Bite me."

And maybe it's the way she says it, or maybe it's the club lights, turning the world crimson, but Alice feels a trapdoor fall open deep inside her as she brings her mouth to the waiting slope of the girl's throat and lets her teeth slide in.

Blood wells and breaks across her tongue. The girl gasps, and that sound unlocks a deeper kind of want. Alice turns, pressing her back against the nearest wall. Ringed hands grip Alice's arms, and she says something Alice can't hear, not over the heartbeat flooding back into her chest, and even though it's only been hours since she fed, she is ravenous, a broken vessel trying to fill itself up faster than it leaks, and maybe if she just drinks enough the hunger won't be able to catch up with her, maybe her heart will keep beating, maybe it will be enough and—

Someone wrenches Alice backward.

She stumbles, straightens in time to see the girl's legs go out, her body sliding down the wall before a guy with spiked black hair shoves past Alice and steadies her.

Alice stares in horror. What has she done?

The heartbeat trails off in her chest, and in its wake, the club comes rushing back, all that bad techno and cheap red light. The guy is sitting the girl who isn't Lottie down in a chair, and the mean bartender is rounding the counter, asking if she's all right, and he's saying, "Yeah, she just had too much too fast, you know they always forget to eat."

And Alice is still dazed, unsure what she's done, and how she could have lost herself so quickly, and she's staring at the girl, the one who wanted to be bitten, but she looks pale, and frightened now. Before Alice can ask if she's okay, the guy with the spiked hair has Alice by the arm, and he's leading her away, past the covered mirrors and the black-clad crowd, past the two guys from earlier, who are still kissing, only this time she's close enough to see the way the plastic fangs flex when the one with the red band clenches his teeth.

Fake.

All of it's fake.

But she's—

"You're in the wrong place," snaps the spiky-haired guy as he steers her toward a back door, and out, into the quieter, colder night.

And Alice wants to say *No shit,* but she's still blood drunk and a little dazed, so it takes her a moment to realize what he just said, and what he *didn't* say, because if there's a wrong place, then maybe there's a right one, too. He's already turning away when she calls out, "Wait!" She catches the door before it closes. "Where do I go?"

The guy looks back. "No idea," he says. But that's not good enough.

"Please," she grabs his wrist, and he stiffens a little, either because her hands are cold, or because he knows, and if he met her eyes, she'd try to make him tell, but he doesn't, just looks past her into the alley and says, "Try following the music."

She lets out an exasperated sigh. "What is *that* supposed to mean?"

"No idea." The guy shrugs. "But it's what I was told to say, if someone like you came round."

The words hum beneath her skin.

Someone like you.

Meaning, there are people like her somewhere.

He pulls free of her grip and turns away.

"Hey," she says, digging the phone from her pocket. "Have you seen this—"

But the back door is already swinging shut, taking the club's red lights and low beat, and leaving Alice out in the cold.

SABINE

(D. 1532)

I

Venice, Italy
1709

Years pass, and as they do, Sabine finds herself at home.

In the palazzo, yes, but that is simply walls and windows, rooms and floors. It is her host and his lover who make it something more.

They build a life together, Alessandro, Matteo, and Sabine. They form a novel kind of family. She sits for the mortal and his art, and spends late nights talking with her host, each of them trading stories of the years before they came to Venice.

She and Matteo are so different, and yet alike.

Alessandro says they are like two blocks of granite: headstrong and stubborn. But he is wrong. They are not the same. Sabine watches Matteo and his mortal love, sometimes with envy, and others with disdain, and while she understands Matteo's many rules, she also loses patience with them, and finds herself longing for a change of scenery, or pace. And so Sabine begins to venture off sometimes, to Tuscany, or Rome.

She goes intent on savoring a night or week or month of freedom, of solitude, the ability to kill as often as she pleases, only to discover that she's come to crave the drawn-out tension of the hunt. That without the prelude to the pleasure, it comes and goes too quick, leaves her unsatisfied.

Not that she will admit it to Matteo.

More than once, she wanders farther, knowing that when she does return, whether it is in a month, a season, or a year, she will be welcomed back.

Welcomed *home*.

Inside the palazzo, time goes by, marked only by the paintings added to the walls, the shift of styles in the wardrobes, and the slow alteration of Alessandro's face, his countenance.

A new century is ushered in, and while Matteo and Sabine look exactly as they always have—as unchanging as the palazzo, the lagoon, the very bones of Venice—Alessandro's youth is long behind him now.

His once-gold hair has turned a paler shade, his skin now thin enough to see the skeleton beneath. Some of his edges have grown sharper, while others are made soft by age. He walks with a cane, and each season seems to lean more of his weight on the polished wooden stick.

He is still lovely, in that doll-like way.

And Matteo is still in love. A ruinous thing.

He claims he has long made peace with Alessandro's choice, his inevitable decay, and insists they still have years, that even mortal life lasts far beyond the blooms of youth. Makes jokes about how he will always be the older of the two, while insisting Alessandro only grows more elegant with age.

It is maddening to witness, and Sabine wonders whether Matteo is lying to Alessandro, or himself, or if he thinks saying things can make them real. If that is a power he has, one he has not shown her yet, or if he's simply in denial, unwilling to accept the truth.

And then, one winter, Alessandro's chest begins to hurt. His lungs are rattling by spring, and Matteo loses his composure, begins to beg his lover to reconsider their arrangement. To let himself be planted in the midnight soil.

Quiet as they are, Sabine hears the conversations, rooms away.

Stay with me, he pleads, but Alessandro will not waver. If he did not want to be young forever, why would he choose to be old? Life is meant to end. It is not for man to decide when.

Sabine listens, and seethes.

What is the point, she thinks, of loving something you are doomed to lose?

Of holding on to someone who cannot hold on to you?

It is Matteo's fault. His folly. And yet, somehow, the pain echoes through her, too. Because she has come to like Matteo's pet, to enjoy his company, mortal as it is, to consider him a *friend*, and now she feels like she's been slowly poisoned. She didn't want to care about him, but she does, and the impending loss doesn't make her sad.

It makes her *furious*.

That last week, Alessandro spends every waking moment in the sun, his tired face tipped up to catch the light.

More than once, Sabine drifts into the courtyard after dusk to find him sleeping in his garden chair, thin limbs crossed beneath a blanket.

More than once, she has to listen for the quiet murmur of his heart, the soft drawing of breath, to make sure he hasn't left.

More than once, she thinks of putting an end to all this nonsense. Of taking care of him herself. Plant him in the midnight soil, and be damned. Let Alessandro hate her, as she has begun to hate him, for casting this shadow on their happy life.

But then his blue eyes drift open, and he looks at Sabine the way he did on the first night, with that artist's crisp gaze, as if trying to decide exactly how to paint her.

He has tried a dozen times in these intervening years, but though she does not change, he cannot seem to capture her. And now, she knows, he never will.

"Come to keep me company?" he asks, a faint rasp behind the words.

"Actually," she says, "I've come to spar. You look in need of practice."

A soft, unsteady chuckle. "Tonight," he says, "you might just have the upper hand."

The humor drops out of her voice. "You are a fool," she seethes.

He smiles, and closes his eyes. "I know."

⌒‿⌒

She is not there the night he dies.

She is out, walking the streets, unable to bear the sound, his heart, like a clock someone has failed to wind, the beats slowly losing pace.

She is not there, but she knows, the moment she returns.

It is not just the stillness in the house. It is the *air*, stained black with pain. Not Alessandro's, but Matteo's. Matteo, who has kept his mind well guarded all these years, who to her has always been opaque. But now his grief is splashed against the floor, it slicks the walls like paint. It is all Sabine can smell. All she can taste.

She hovers at the bottom of the stairs as the minutes turn to hours. She has held a hundred humans as they died, felt them turn to corpses in her arms. And yet, she cannot bring herself to go upstairs and see this body for herself.

She sleeps in Alessandro's studio, surrounded by his art. Two days and nights Matteo stays inside his room. Until the house begins to smell of rotting flesh as well as pain. Until Sabine can't stand it anymore, and sends word for the physician, who comes to take the corpse away.

Alessandro Contarini, fifty-nine, and buried in his family plot.

In the nights and weeks that follow, Sabine avoids the house. Leaves Matteo to his misery, sure that it will pass.

And yet, it doesn't.

Matteo acts as though he's died as well. He is a specter. A ghost. He moves out of their room. And into another. And another. And another. Searching for a bed that will hold one instead of two, before at last he abandons the pursuit and takes over the salon instead, pulls the curtains and blocks out the light of Venice before collapsing on the couch.

"Come on," she says. "Let's play a game."

But he will not.

Visitors come by day and night bearing their condolences, but the knocks all go unanswered, flowers left to wither on the stoop. Gone, too, are the gondola rides, the public demonstrations, all effort at keeping up pretenses.

At night Matteo sits so still out in the courtyard that it's a wonder the wisteria does not begin to grow around him. Sabine wonders how long it will take for him to starve.

That year Carnevale comes and goes without a single mask, or ball, or game, and Sabine grows tired of his sulking. If only he would rant, or rave, rampage through the house, break the furniture and rend the curtains, tear the walls apart, do something, *anything* to clear the air, to let it out. Instead, he seems to calcify.

Matteo does not eat.

He does not sleep.

A month, and the whole place still hangs thick with sorrow. And she cannot bear it anymore.

"Enough," she says.

"Get up," she says.

"We're going out."

But Matteo is lost inside himself. And it is maddening. Another month of this, a season, two, and Sabine has had enough.

"You chose to love a mortal man," she snaps. "You refused to change him."

You knew what would happen. You knew, and you brought it on yourself. What right have you, then, to be surprised by grief? To be so undone by it? If you cannot rouse yourself, you might as well go lie down beside him and let the grave dirt take you."

Sabine knows that she is being cruel.

She does not care.

Once she starts, she cannot seem to stop. The words come spilling out like bile. Perhaps she is only trying to rouse Matteo from his grief. Perhaps she needs to purge her own as well.

"*Mateusz*," she snaps at last, and that, at least, earns some reaction. The name lands like a blow, and he winces, turning toward her, the pain in his eyes so black and bottomless that she recoils.

But he says nothing, and Sabine cannot stand it anymore.

She leaves. Spends the winter in Verona, shaking off Matteo's grief. Watches the old year die and the new one begin with flower-strewn effigies carried through the streets, the air full of church bells and candle smoke and hope.

In February, Sabine returns to Venice, unsure what she will find.

She steels herself against whatever ruin waits within the walls of the Palazzo di Contarini. Decides that if she must, she will drag Matteo out. She is surprised, then, to find the windows lit, the courtyard swept, the ivy freshly trimmed, thinks perhaps Matteo has abandoned the house, sold it and fled. But the door swings open under her touch, and no one else's will is there to meet her on the threshold, push her back.

Sabine steps into the carriage hall, braced for the fetid gloom she left behind, but it is gone, Matteo's pain no longer hanging in the air. She slips off her shoes, lets her bare feet settle on the marble floor, starts toward the staircase when she hears it.

The shift of a body in a chair.

The crack of parchment turning.

Sounds that reach her not from overhead, but down the hall, the room at the end, which was Alessandro's studio, until it wasn't. That door has been shut fast ever since his burial, but it hangs open now, a soft glow spilling out.

Sabine stops short in the doorway, her whole body snagging there as if repelled.

But it's only surprise.

At seeing Alessandro.

The blond curls unspooling down his face. The long, pale lashes, over eyes that shocking shade of blue. His body stretched on the low sofa, long fingers paging through a book. Alessandro, restored to beauty, youth.

He looks up at her and grins, flashing pointed teeth.

And it is not him. Of course it's not. Alessandro is still dead.

The knowledge hits her like a dull blow.

"You must be Sabine," he says, this interloper, abandoning the book and leaping to his feet. The easel has been put away, but the smell of paint lingers, ghosted onto every surface, and her first thought is that he shouldn't be here. In this room. It isn't his.

"Matteo has told me much about you!" says the stranger with a manic cheer, and as her shock fades, so does his resemblance. It's true, he has Alessandro's features, but they've been arranged in a different way. His body, moving with a different tempo.

When Alessandro was alive, he had a smooth and steady manner, as if anything too quick might startle them. The stranger's voice is louder and lower at the same time, his movements sudden and halting, as if he isn't used to his new strength, or speed. His thoughts are just as messy, tumbling into the air around him, clouds of want and interest and amusement. And of course, hunger.

"Ah," says a voice from the doorway, "I see you've met Giovanni."

Sabine turns and finds Matteo, as he was the night they met, thirty years ago, hale and hearty, shoulders broad and back straight.

Gone is the man made haggard by loss. The thicket of unkempt curls has been combed back. The mustache neatly groomed. The wrinkled linens replaced by black breeches and a pale tunic with pearl buttons, polished boots, an emerald cloak pin at his throat.

"I have indeed," she says, arching a brow as if to ask, but his eyes are flat, his mind shut fast, the air around him silent. Giovanni flings an arm around Matteo's shoulders, less like a man staking claim and more like a pup longing for attention.

"We are going out," announces Giovanni. "You must come, so we can celebrate."

"Celebrate what?" she asks.

"That you are here, of course! Matteo will stop sulking now that you are back, and we are all together."

Together. It shouldn't chafe, and yet it does.

Matteo hands Giovanni a coat, but he waves it away.

"It is supposed to snow," he chides.

"E allora? I am not cold."

"It is not a matter of your comfort," he says with the exasperated air of a parent explaining things to a small child. "It is about other people's notice."

Giovanni sighs, and holds out his arms, and Sabine shakes her head, watches in bemusement as Matteo dresses his new pet. Watches as he bows his head and plants a kiss on Giovanni's shoulder, the way he did Alessandro's so many times. But that was love, and this something else. It has the hollow motions of performance. An actor going through his marks.

Giovanni pulls away instead of leaning in.

"I am so hungry," he declares, his good mood suddenly replaced by a dramatic sulk.

"You just ate," says Matteo placidly.

"That was last night! When I was mortal, I ate two times a day, sometimes three. Surely it's the same."

"It isn't, I promise you."

"But I feel like I will starve!" he declares.

Sabine and Matteo share a look. An almost-smile.

They step out into the courtyard, and Giovanni—Gio, he insists on being called—loops an arm through hers as he complains that Matteo has so many *rules.*

"He does," Sabine agrees.

"I do not see the point of them."

"The point," says Matteo, "is to survive."

"How boring!" declares Gio, sucking in a breath he doesn't need, just to blow it out again. "But Sabine is here now. And surely *she* will be more fun."

II

"I'm relieved," she says, a few nights later, "to see you looking so *revived*."

They are out again, on another evening walk, Venice glittering by lamplight.

Matteo smiles, but it doesn't reach his eyes. "It is our nature, isn't it? To persist. Continue on when others can't."

"You do seem to be persisting." She nods at Giovanni, who now strolls ahead, hands in his pockets and head thrown back. "I'm sure your new companion helps."

Matteo's smile flickers, briefly becomes a grimace. "I thought—"

"Don Accardi!" call out a pair of women, strolling toward them, arm in arm. "How glad we are to see you."

Sabine searches her memory, knows they've met before. Sisters, she recalls, though she didn't bother to learn their names, since she could never separate the two. Either in her mind, or in person.

"I was beginning to think you'd abandoned Venice," says one.

"Though I can't blame you," adds the other.

"The winter is so bleak."

"I fear I was unwell," he says, despite the fact he is, has always been, the very picture of good health.

"Truly?" says one.

"You'd never know it," says the other.

"Indeed, you do not age a day."

"Neither do you, Carmina," he counters gracefully.

Her sister snorts. Carmina sours, then says, "My mirror disagrees."

"The fault is with the glass, then, and surely not with you."

Matteo's charm, infallible as ever. He turns to his companions. "You recall my niece, Sabine."

"Who could forget such a beauty?" says the first, Carmina, the air stained with an envy that buoys her own mood.

Matteo gestures to his other side. "Allow me to introduce a new acquaintance, Giovanni."

"Piacere di conoscerla," says Gio brightly, bending low to kiss each of their gloved hands. But on the second one, he lingers, head bowed, his grip shifting just enough to turn the hand palm up, exposing the inside of her wrist, the veins just beneath the skin. Sabine can feel exactly what he plans to do before he does it. Not that she intervenes.

But of course, Matteo does. He lays a hand on Gio's shoulder, a simple gesture, save for the tightness of the grip.

Gio drops his hand and straightens as the women blush and say good night. As soon as they walk on, Matteo wrenches Gio round to face him.

"What have I told you?"

Gio holds up his hands in mock surrender. "I did nothing."

"Only because I stopped you."

He rolls his blue eyes, which Sabine has decided are in fact a duller shade than Alessandro's. It is only the strange light in them that makes them seem so bright. "Why shouldn't I have eaten them?" he whines.

"We do not hunt our neighbors," scolds Matteo. It has the air of a recurring quarrel. "We do not kill those whose death would cause an uproar."

"Rules, rules, rules," he moans. "I do not *care.*"

"You should. You must."

"What does it matter if they're of noble blood or common stock? What is the difference in the end?"

Sabine doesn't say that Gio has a point. She doesn't have to. It must be written clearly on her face because Matteo takes one glance at her and mutters, "Oh, *don't.*"

"You are an elitist," declares Giovanni, crossing his arms.

Sabine snorts.

Matteo flings his hands out in frustration. "It is not about which lives have worth. Only about which ones will be *missed.*"

"How is that different?"

"Don't be naïve," he snaps. Then sighs, and cups his new lover's face. Sabine studies them. Matteo, who believes all lives have worth. And Gio, who seems convinced that the same logic renders all lives worthless. She wonders which will give in first.

In the end, it's Giovanni. Perhaps because he does not want to fight, or perhaps because he finds the quarrel boring. A waste of a perfectly good night. Either way, Giovanni deflates, and rests his head against Matteo's.

"Bene," he murmurs. "Show me then who I *can* eat. I'm really very hungry."

Matteo softens.

Shortly after, it begins to snow.

A light dust that frosts the lamplight and lands in small drifts on the empty gondolas.

Matteo and Sabine walk arm in arm, Gio trailing in their wake. A handful of flakes land on Matteo's hair. The only flecks of white.

"The sisters have a point," she says. "How old are you supposed to be?"

She asks this, and not how old he *is*, knowing that he will not tell her. Matteo has never made more than passing mention of his early life, and on the rare occasions she has pressed, he's changed the subject.

She wonders now if Alessandro knew. If so, the stories died with him. Her only token is the name, *Mateusz*, which she keeps as if it were a talisman around her neck, a coin she can neither trade nor use.

"I know I cannot stay both *as* I am, and *where* I am, forever," he admits. "People start to notice. And then, they start to talk. And then, it is only a matter of time before a life must be given up, or lost. But I will miss this city dearly. And all the memories it has."

Ahead, a couple pause halfway across a narrow bridge, stopped to appreciate the way the snow falls between the buildings, melting when it hits the water.

Their backs are turned, and their attention held. An easy meal. Too easy for their tastes, but not for Giovanni. Perhaps Matteo thinks the offering will put an end to his new lover's whining.

He turns, as if to signal his assent.

But Gio is not there.

"Merda," Matteo curses softly, doubling back as a new smell cuts through the cold night air. Blood. The odor lurches through her—metallic, sweet. It's been three nights since her last meal, and the scent sends an ache from her temples to her teeth.

They find Gio in an alley two blocks back, folded over the body of a man beside a cart. Matteo pulls him off, but it's too late.

The man lies crumpled on the ground, his eyes open and his throat torn wide, the last beats of his heart sending a weak trickle of blood onto the stones beneath.

Two hundred years, and the sight still tightens something in her. A feral hunger. The same one she sees in Gio's face, the bottom half of which is painted red.

"I chose a commoner," says Gio, wiping his mouth on the sleeve of the coat he doesn't need. Now that he has slaked his thirst, he seems to have regained his senses enough to register Matteo's anger. "He was alone . . . I thought you would be glad."

Matteo rakes a hand through his black hair, looks like he wants to push his new love into the canal. Instead, he orders Gio out of the way, and kneels beside the body.

Sabine folds her arms, tips her shoulder against the wall, watches as Matteo attempts to arrange the dead man's limbs beside the cart. Most bite marks close after the fact, but the wound at his throat is so wide it will never mend in death. The violence, unerasable.

"Every corpse makes ripples," she recites.

"Not now," mutters Matteo.

"Where is *Gio's* ultimatum?" she wonders aloud. "Somehow I doubt you will threaten to banish *him*. Tell me, is it because you made him or you bed him?"

Matteo straightens. Pinches the bridge of his nose.

"He is young," he says that night.

"It will get easier," he says the next.

"He will learn."

But of course, he never does.

Sabine has walked the earth long enough to know that not all flowers grow well in the garden.

Some thrive, and others wither.

And a wretched few must be dug up before they ruin everything.

She has been home less than a week when the first bodies are discovered.

A well-known merchant. And his wife. The two of them found dead inside their courtyard.

After that, the sisters—the ones they met together that first night.

The bite marks fade, but the other signs of Gio's butchery do not.

What he was like in life, Sabine will never know, but she can guess. After all, what grows in the midnight soil is not a different flower, only a bolder bloom. He is by nature passionate, and *reckless*.

Matteo tries to turn his rules to games, as he did once with her, but it doesn't work. Gio cares less about rewards than slaking his relentless thirst. He has no patience for the slow pursuit of prey. Instead, everyone he passes becomes a potential meal.

And he is making an ungodly mess.

Each and every corpse makes waves, and the waters of Venice soon begin to churn.

Word of a killer spreads, and when the body of a magistrate is found propped against a column in San Marco, some take to their homes, and others to the streets. Men patrolling day and night, the air around them humming with the hunger for justice, for blood.

It is inevitable. Like standing at the top of a steep hill, the valley laid out below, the knowledge that if you point yourself down, it's only a matter of time before you reach it.

Sabine is not surprised when she comes home one night and finds Matteo standing on the balcony, looking over the lagoon. His shoulders tense, his head bowed low. She knows, before he says it.

"Gio is dead."

The words fall, and keep falling. She waits for them to land, searches herself for sadness, dread, but finds only dull relief. Knows that Matteo can smell it on her, and braces for his mood. Wonders if he will plunge himself again into grief. But he doesn't, only shakes his head and says, "If the mortals hadn't killed him, I might have done it myself."

A grim confession.

He turns toward her as he says it, and he looks so . . . tired. As if the nights with Giovanni have worn on him, much longer than the centuries without.

"What happened?" she asks, though she can guess.

He was caught attacking a man. Found with the body. There was no judge, no court, no sentence. They fell on him right there. Drove him through with spikes. Cut off his head.

A gruesome act, but Matteo recounts it in a weary voice. He crosses to a chair, drops into it. Rakes his fingers through his hair.

"It was a mistake," he says softly. "I knew when I did it. It was selfish. I was grieving. After you left, I finally forced myself outside. I was walking when I saw him and I thought . . ." He trails off, shakes his head. Then, "Have you ever taken a companion?"

"Now and then," she says, and it is true. She has indulged that hunger when it rose. "But only for a night."

"Perhaps one day you'll find someone you want to keep for longer."

"I doubt it," says Sabine.

She does not tell him she has thought of it, a few times over the years, watching Alessandro and Matteo. The bond they had. The life they shared. But while she envied what they had together, its aftermath was bleak enough to put her off.

He manages a wan smile. "Only because you have not met them yet."

He rises slowly, as if bearing a heavy weight. "If you ever do decide to turn a lover, make sure you know their temper well. This life can be a kindness, or a curse." His gaze goes to the window. To Venice. The buildings, lit like floating candles in the dark. "This city. If I stay here any longer, I may as well lie down by Alessandro and let the grave dirt take me, as you once said."

"We are made for many things," muses Sabine. "But surrender isn't one of them."

He nods. "That is why I'm leaving."

A strange tug behind her ribs, though she cannot tell if it is toward him, or away. So many years now, she has been the one who comes and goes, while Matteo stayed, anchored to Venice.

"Where will you go?"

He has passage on a ship, he tells her. Bound for the Americas.

"You're welcome to come with me," he adds, though they both know she won't.

It is not just the time aboard the ship she dreads. The thought of so many weeks at sea, trapped in a rocking vessel beneath the scorching sun, surrounded by passengers who have been counted, whose every absence would be missed.

It is Alessandro—or at least the absence of him, and the knowledge that he will follow Matteo wherever he goes, from now until the end, like a shadow, a ghost. And Sabine has no desire to be haunted.

When Matteo boards his ship the following night, she knows she will never see him again. Watching it sail, she feels a shallow swell of grief. A ripple. But then it's gone, he's gone, and something shifts inside her, crumbles, falls, taking the wave of sadness with it.

Where others rot without, we rot within.

Sabine suspects that it is starting: that some small piece of her has died, as Matteo said it would. She thought she would feel frightened, or at least disconcerted by the loss, but there is only a visceral relief, like shedding layers on a too-hot day, the absence like a breeze against bare skin.

She exhales, feeling lighter than she has in years.

III

The widow arrives on a Monday. A Thursday. A Sunday.

Steps out of a carriage in Paris. Athens. Berlin.

Descends from a riverboat in Vienna. Onto the banks of Budapest. Belgrade.

Ventures as far as Krakow. Amsterdam. Algiers.

On a map, her path would resemble roots, questing outward. In person, she feels like she is drifting, without a destination, a beginning or an end.

She travels alone, and yet, each of her old companions are still with her. In a way.

Now and then she relies on the freedom of the widow's mourning garb, the shelter of the veil. And when she feeds, she savors every meal the way Renata taught her, picking out the notes as well as the beat. When she's on the road, she follows Hector's rule, careful to stay ahead of the bodies she makes. And when she finds a place to spend a fortnight, or a season, or a year, she puts Matteo's teachings to good use, folds herself into society before she picks her prey. Makes herself at home in villas, manses, pieds-à-terre. Becomes a friend, a neighbor, a familiar face.

The years die, and she does not.

Now and then, she wakes to find another little corner of her emptied, some aspect crumbled away in sleep. Perhaps it was a shard of insecurity. A sliver of regret. Sabine probes her mind, trying to find the nature of the absence, like a tongue searching for a missing tooth, but never does.

It does not bother her.

It is a welcome kind of loss.

Especially when other, keener urges move in to fill the space.

In Prague, she lets a man go, not to spare him, simply because she craves the chase. The thrill of watching someone flee. He runs, as if she will not catch him. As if one of her steps is not three of his. As if there was ever a chance of getting away.

The hunger is a constant. It never leaves her. Never fades.

But as the decades pass, her delight at independence does. The novelty of solitude wears off, and Sabine finds herself aware that she's alone—not *lonely*, that is too strong a word—but longing, perhaps, for company.

Someone to look at her the way Renata looked at Hector.

To love her as intensely as Alessandro did Matteo.

To be what María's maid would not, what the widow might have been if she had survived, all those years ago.

Someone to share this life.

Someone to make her feel *anything* more than hunger. Or at least, a different kind.

Sabine has her prey, of course, the subjects of her games, with whom she passes nights, sometimes even weeks, before the play reaches its conclusion. Though more and more, she begins to wonder what it would be like to spare one. To keep instead of kill, to make them as she is.

But when the moment comes, they scream, they fight, they run, and hunger always gets the best of her. Perhaps, if in that vital, final beat they looked at her with want or love instead of terror.

But they do not.

So she carries on, alone.

IV

London, England
1823

The rain hangs in the air, but doesn't fall.

It is a damp dusk as Sabine glides down the street, sheltered from the mist and the last dregs of light beneath her parasol, her veil pinned up into her hat.

She has just arrived, but already she is quite fond of London.

It is a messy, sprawling city, and no matter how many bodies find their way into the Thames, she doubts anyone will notice.

Sabine thumbs one of the pendants around her neck—a Polish grosz— and slows before a dress shop window, a gown the color of honeycomb on display beyond the glass. Her reflection hovers just beside it. With her red hair bundled discreetly against her neck, she is a somber ghost in gray and black. The bleak armor has served her well as a woman traveling alone, but she must confess she misses the jewel-toned gowns she used to wear. The honeycomb one calls to her, lit by a lamp still on inside the shop.

Sabine looks up and down the road.

At this hour, most of the businesses are already closed.

She assumes this one is as well, despite the lamp, but then the door swings wide, and a mother and daughter come tumbling out, the latter chittering about lace and the former nagging her to stand up straight. Sabine catches the door as they pass by, is still holding it when a voice within the shop bids her to come in. And to close the door behind, before the damp spoils the silk.

Inside, a middle-aged modiste kneels before a half-made dress, tacking a hemline with metal pins, which she plucks from between her teeth, all the while muttering to herself. The English, Sabine has noticed, seem to do that, as if quiet is a thing that must be banished, lest it settle in.

"I'll be with you in a moment," says the modiste, and so Sabine looks around the narrow room, considers the selection. The shop is full of headless bodies, each wearing a different dress. The colors, all paler than she would prefer, pastel shades of pink and green and blue. Watered down, she thinks, just like the London air.

She grazes a ribboned waist, the fabric cinched just below the bust.

After a century of bustles and big skirts, the new fashion seems designed to pour down the body in thin liquid layers. Far more to her taste.

The modiste spits the last two pins into her hand. "Have you come to collect a dress?" she asks, groaning a little as she gets to her feet.

"No," says Sabine, drawing out the skirt to see how wide it flares. "I've come to buy one."

"You're too late, miss," says the modiste, turning toward her as she says it. She draws up short, taking in the somber dress, the veil. "Oh, I'm sorry for your loss."

Sabine's mouth twitches. "Yes, well, that's why I'm here. I think I've spent long enough in mourning. I find myself in want of something brighter."

A slight grimace. "I'm afraid all the dresses in the shop are spoken for."

Sabine lets the skirt slip through her fingers, nods at the honey-colored gown in the window. At a glance, she knows that it will fit. "Even that one?"

"*That* one is reserved for Lady Fletcher's eldest daughter," says the modiste, as if the name means anything.

"How long, then," asks Sabine, "to have a new one made?"

"Weeks," answers the modiste bluntly.

Sabine sighs through her teeth. She has never been a patient woman, and now that she's decided to rid herself of her dreary mourning palette, she cannot wait. She considers persuading the modiste, but it's one thing to bend a mind the way it wants to go, and another to force it the other way, and hers is clearly set, so Sabine tries a new approach.

"Money is no object," she says, reaching for her coin purse. But there's no greed in the air around the modiste. Only a harried energy.

"To you, or any other member of the ton," she says, waving her hand. "If you had come to me a month ago, perhaps, but now, with the season about to start . . ."

Sabine frowns. These days she thought she had a decent grasp of English, but the conversation is studded with words she's never heard before, or ones she has, but snipped and dropped into new context. "Season?" she asks. "Do you mean spring?"

The modiste bustles past her toward another half-finished dress. "You must be new to London," she says. "The season, when England's most eligible daughters descend on the city to be presented here at court. Every mother in the ton hoping to secure a worthy match." She stabs a pin into a ruffled sleeve. "Three months of teas and balls and God forbid they wear the same dress twice."

Sabine's mood brightens as the woman speaks.

This *season* sounds diverting. A wealth of prospects. A perfect place to occupy her time, her mind, her urge to hunt.

"You know," says the modiste, looking her up and down. "I do have something from last season that might fit." She turns toward a curtain at the back of her shop. "It won't be the latest fashion, of course, but beggars can't be—"

She never finishes the thought.

"What a wonderful dress," says Lady Pollard barely a week later, as she takes her seat in Sabine's parlor.

"Why thank you," she says, running a hand over the honey-colored skirts. She was right—it did fit perfectly.

And so does London.

The first thing Sabine did, after procuring the new house—it belonged to an old baroness who died in her sleep, or so it's said, and had no living heirs—was to send out invitations to the ladies on her street.

After all, it is important to be seen.

Three women sit around her table now, and in the wake of Lady Pollard's compliment, the other two make cooing sounds of warm agreement. Sabine smiles and pours from a teapot made of painted porcelain, grateful that the late baroness shared her expensive taste.

It is early afternoon, the light reaching through the gauzy curtains, but the surrounding houses interrupt the sun, and the windows all face south, and Sabine has arranged the chairs so that hers sits safely out of reach, regardless of the hour.

"Speaking of dresses," says Madam Harris. "Have you heard about the modiste on Earl Street? Dropped dead in her shop. Pins still in her mouth, and a dozen dresses left unfinished."

"And so close to the start of the Season," says Madam Thatch.

Sabine knows now that in context, the word is pronounced with a slight emphasis, as if it is a proper noun. English is a fickle language, but she is learning.

She contorts her face in mock horror as she takes up her cup. "What a loss."

The women coo, and nod, and soon talk of loss invariably turns to talk of *her*.

She is a widow, after all, despite the honey-colored dress. She is just out of mourning, she explains. The air around her swims with a fresh hunger, not for blood or food but *gossip*.

Who was her husband?

Well, she says, she was married to a Spanish viscount named Andrés.

How easy it is to lie when you can use the truth to do it.

A viscount! they exclaim. *Goodness me. What was he like?*

And here is where history invites revision. And a hefty bit of flourish. In Sabine's hands, Andrés becomes a kind and loving husband, his family known for wine as well as wealth. And she, a noble daughter in her own right, raised mostly in Spain, but with a fondness for the trappings of the British court. They had just moved here, for her, in fact, when he perished. Suddenly.

How tragic, the women echo, sitting there with hands to breasts, and tea forgotten.

They are horrified, of course. And just as rapt. Their curiosity bleeds into the air, circling the room like smoke. They want to know more. Want to know everything. But Sabine lets the silence hold. Forces them to break it.

"You are so young," says Lady Pollard, reaching for her hand, which has been warmed by the teacup she's been holding.

"And *so* lovely," adds Madam Thatch.

"Surely you could make another match," offers Madam Harris.

Sabine arranges her features into something like sadness, softened by time. "He was the love of my life," she lies. "I do not think I want to find another."

Murmurs of understanding.

"What about your family?" asks Lady Pollard.

Sabine shakes her head and says, "Mine, I'm sad to say, were gone before I wed. And his are back in Spain."

"Then you are all alone!" says Madam Harris, aghast.

"And yet," she says, letting her gaze skate from one face to the next, "I do not feel that way." A small but hopeful smile playing on her face.

"Don't worry," they say with bobbing heads.

"We will make the introductions."

"You'll never want for company."

"You will fit right in."

Sabine smirks behind her cup of tea.

"You are too kind."

The Season. What a concept.

That first night is like the opening of Carnevale. Less debauchery, perhaps, or so it seems, but everyone is so well fed and watered, pampered and dressed and paraded through the ballrooms. She watches, considering her options. It is a feast of choice, and though Matteo is not there to play, she sets the game, the rules, the prize.

Never the girls being presented to the court. Nice as they are to look at, bundled like presents in taffeta and lace, Matteo's voice still has a way of nagging from inside her head. *Not the ones who will be greatly missed. Whose death would bring catastrophe.*

Still, Sabine is not so strict as her old friend, and a Season is a long time—too long, she thinks—to go entirely without a meal. She tends her hunger like a flame, stoked just enough to keep the coals blushed, the heat from going out. But the bulk of her excitement, her attention, goes to the prey.

That first year she contents herself with a lady's maid.

The next, a daughter who's made the rounds three times without a match.

The third, a visiting cousin, already wed.

More than once, Sabine catches the eye of a male suitor, thinking to court *her* instead. More than once, she's forced to pause her game, to clear the board of this unwelcome piece. But it is never satisfying. She forgot the bitter way their blood tastes. Like unripe fruit.

Matteo would call it cheating, but it's not as though it slakes her thirst.

And then, the fourth year comes around, and perhaps it is just that she has put down roots, sown and grown herself into the London soil, but Sabine finds she is no longer content with choosing scraps.

She wants a greater challenge.

After all, the Season is full to bursting with young women and their suitors. They are all hunting for something, someone. Why shouldn't she?

Perhaps she craves the risk as well as the reward.

After all, the danger is what makes the prize so sweet.

She stands on the balcony that first night, at the presentation ball, and instead of searching the wings, as she has in years before, she lets herself survey the banquet streaming by below. A river of young women, all in shades of cream.

By the end of the ball, she's made her choice.

A lanky girl with white-gold hair, and blushing cheeks, and blue eyes that remind her of Matteo's lover back in Venice.

Sabine is giddy with the promise of a proper hunt.

But at the next ball, as she searches for her chosen mark among the couples dancing in the hall, Sabine sees *her* instead.

A new face. Dressed in gold and growing like a vine against the wall.

Her complexion, not the pale shade called English rose, but sun-kissed, nearing bronze. Her hair a mass of brown curls, twisted and pinned, but clearly fighting to escape. Tendrils climbing free around her heart-shaped face. Her mouth, like a slice of peach, and her eyes, wide and bright with wonder.

"Who is that?" Sabine asks lightly, and Lady Pollard lifts a pair of looking glasses to her nose, and squints across the hall.

"Oh," she says. "That must be Amelia Hastings's newest ward."

Sabine finds herself intrigued. "She wasn't announced."

"No, not this year," says Lady Pollard. "Word is she's a bit rough around the edges. Though I'm sure Amelia will set her straight." Her voice dips low beneath the weight of gossip. "I heard there was an incident, back at her estate." She leans in closer still. "Something involving another girl."

Sabine feigns shock, even as her interest sharpens. "You don't say."

"But of course," chirps Lady Pollard, fluttering a fan, "I'm sure that was only idle talk."

The woman takes her leave, but Sabine stays where she is, attention hooked on this new girl, the one with the white-blond hair and pale blue eyes already slipping from her thoughts.

It is her game after all.

She is allowed to change the rules.

She watches as the girl plucks at the dance card on her wrist, as if it were a chain, and even though the ball is full of bodies, their thoughts a whispered tangle, her mind seems like it is reaching out, the air around her full of hope and fear and *life*. A longing to be seen, set free.

A lovely girl.

A perfect mark.

Sabine has no way of knowing that this one night will tip the balance of her life.

That this one girl will be both the beginning and the end of everything.

ALICE

(D. 2019)

I

"Follow the music," said the bouncer, like the world's most unhelpful white rabbit, and now here's Alice, stuck in Wonderland.

She has no idea what he meant, or why everyone in America has to speak in fucking riddles instead of just telling her what she needs to know.

Follow the music, like it's a sign post, a street name, like there aren't a thousand overlapping sources of sound in a city like Boston. Songs spilling out of every bar, and every car, and every pair of headphones. Lyrics fighting for space with every other kind of noise, the grumble of traffic, and below that the grate and hush of the T, and over the top, talk radio spilling from cracked windows, and laughter from restaurants and the din of the sports games on the televisions and the hush of tires on damp streets and the rustle of dead and dying leaves and a hundred other sounds converging on her, smothering any one track that might otherwise stand out as music.

Alice walks, and listens, or at least she tries—straining to pick the sounds apart, tease some singular song from the many tangled threads, but how is she supposed to make out a melody, to find the song she is supposed to follow, when there are a hundred channels playing in her ears? How is she supposed to—

Alice's legs lurch to a stop.

Because she hears it.

Something that definitely qualifies as *music*.

There and then gone, but Alice is listening now, really listening. She stands perfectly still and inclines her head, and as she does, the sounds shuffle in her ears, some getting brighter and others falling back until she catches the faint timbre of an organ playing, the lifting voices of a choir. She closes her eyes and turns slowly, until she can make out the direction of the melody.

Follow the music, he'd said, so that's what Alice does. She follows it, down two blocks and over one, the high sweet sound getting stronger, clearer, with every step until she finds herself in front of a church.

The door is ajar, warm light spilling down the stairs.

One minute she's standing there in the narrow pool of lamplight and the next she finds herself wading through it, climbing the steps, and the next her hand is on the wood and the door's groaning open.

Her boot scuffs the threshold but there she hesitates, recalling something about damned bodies being unable to enter the house of God, and she's suddenly afraid that if she tries to step inside, she'll be expelled by the crosses on the wall, or lit ablaze by some force's holy wrath, driven back into the dark.

But then her foot lands, and the floor is just a floor, and the crosses leave no mark, and she's standing well within the house of God, untouched, unharmed.

So much for common lore.

Alice puts another mental tally in her column as she slips into an empty pew and listens to the choir sing. Thinks about all the Sunday mornings her family spent in church, less out of faith and more because it was the thing to do, everybody moving through the motions, and even though Alice never got caught up in the sermons, she always loved the songs. The way music filled the hall, bouncing off the glass and stone, liked the fact that their family sat together, and all the memories she has of those moments are nice ones, which is probably why they didn't stick.

Only one comes back to Alice.

Her head on Catty's shoulder, her sister tracing secret words onto her palm with a chipped blue fingernail, bitten to the quick. *Promise. Always. You and me.*

Now, Alice sits alone and listens as the choir ends. She has figured out that this isn't the song she was supposed to follow, the place she was meant to find, but it's still hard to make herself stand up. To leave the wooden pew and the memory behind.

But she can't stop now.

She has to find the music.

As the priest glides up to the lectern, Alice rises and slips down an outer aisle, and out a side door, into a little garden that runs along the church. A handful of squat stones crowd the path, and she notices the graves only as her boots cross from paving stones to grass, and her entire body *buckles*.

Alice gasps as she goes down and at first she thinks she must have tripped over some rock or root, but when she tries to stand again, she *can't.*

It's not a spasm, or a cramp, but the pins-and-needles of legs gone suddenly to sleep, of laughing so hard your limbs go weak. But her body isn't sleeping, and nothing about this is funny. She is on her hands and knees, trying and failing to get up, fingers sinking into the grass, and she watches in horror as a gray pallor creeps across her skin, like something vital is leeching out of her.

And she is terrified.

The fear she should have felt but didn't, not when she came to in the shower, not when the driver struggled beneath her, not when she saw the fangs in the mirror and couldn't find her pulse—every ounce of it hits her now, with crushing force.

Alice tells her body to get up, but it refuses, seems to sink a little deeper into the ground, and panic flares like light behind her eyes, and her head swims, and she can't breathe. Her lungs have clamped shut, and for the first time she *feels* the absence of the air in her chest, the lack of blood in her heart, a need she can't fulfill. She is a body in distress, and then on top of it comes the same fluish haze she felt standing in the sun, but this is worse, because then, every inch of her said to get away, into the safety of the nearest dark, and here, only half of her is fighting. The other half is already giving up. It's *dying.* A cold hand on her face, telling her to stop, to lie down, to lay her cheek against the soil and let it take her.

It washes over her, begins smothering the panic—a fog too heavy to see or think through, and would it be so bad? The ground is soft and cool beneath her, welcome as a bed, and Alice has never been so tired.

Get up, get up, says a singsong voice in her head, the same one Catty would use right before she tore the blankets off and dragged Alice by the ankle out of bed. But there is no blanket now. There is no bed. And yet—

Get up, Bones. Catty's voice, louder now inside her skull.

Alice drags her eyes open. Her vision slides in and out of focus, then holds just long enough for her to see the little garden gate, the street beyond. It's not far, this little cemetery no more than a narrow strip in the shadow of the church.

Alice locks all her focus onto that gate. She gathers the last of her strength, and reaches for the nearest tombstone, using it to lever herself up, forcing herself away from the ground. She shuffles, stumbles, makes it from the grass onto the nearest paving stone, which seems to rock beneath her like a too-small raft, the deep, dark water sloshing to every side, threatening to tip her over, turn her back. But she is up, on her feet, and somehow, she lurches toward the gate. Legs buckling a little with every step, until at last, at last, her hands meet the metal. It's old, and rusted, and groans under her weight, before the gate finally scrapes open, and Alice is out.

She is free.

She makes it to the curb and doubles over, retching into the gutter. Nothing comes up, but her lungs suddenly inflate, her heart gives a single stubborn beat, and she watches the color, what little there is, slide over her hands and up her wrists.

Alice looks back at the pretty little garden with its headstones, and thinks, *What the ever-loving fuck was that?* Puts a point squarely in the enemy column, because apparently the sun won't do her in, but the burying ground will.

Fuck this, she thinks, and then because that doesn't help, she says the words aloud.

"*FUCK ALL OF THIS!*" she shouts.

Across the street an older woman frowns in disapproval as she totters by, and for once, Alice doesn't fucking care. Her nerves are jangling and she can't find the music she's supposed to follow, and if she had a bat right then she'd take it to every post and pole on this street. But she doesn't, so she turns and kicks the nearest trash can as hard as she can. It buckles beneath the force, and Alice stares at the damage, feels a laugh rising in her chest, the kind that's more hiccup than humor, a sad, overwhelmed sound.

She slumps onto the nearest bench and folds forward until her forehead rests against her knees. Thinks about calling it a night, going back to the dorm, but then what? Rinse, repeat? And the thought of repeating this day is enough to keep her pinned in place.

Alice sits there for five minutes, maybe ten, and as the fear retreats, the anger settles, the night steadies, bending around her like she's a rock in a pond. The air ripples, carrying a hundred scents, and feelings, and sounds.

Slowly, she cocks her head and tries to listen.

It's like turning on a faucet, again the noise comes rushing in, but this time she doesn't fight the tide, tries instead to let the noises mingle and wash over her, to float instead of drowning.

Alice listens, hearing everything and nothing and then—
Something.

At first, she thinks it's a trick of her senses, a string of music conjured by her desperate overloading mind, but the longer she listens, the more certain she is that it's real. Not a beat, or a ballad, but the bell-like tinkle of piano keys, a melody at odds with the sounds of the city. A song.

Hope stirs, stubbornly, inside her.

And Alice gets to her feet once more.

II

Alice follows the music.

It's a brittle strand of notes amid the city's crowded symphony, and she moves with cautious strides, afraid that one wrong turn will cut the cord, send the melody skittering away. But with every block it grows a little brighter, a little louder, rising by degrees, one meager decibel at a time, until she turns onto a narrow street in Beacon Hill and finds a set of short brick steps, leading down to a sublevel door.

Not the steel door of an alley club, but a wood one, painted green.

A ribbon of fairy lights wraps along the iron rail, and a small sign mounted on the brick wall by the door reads WHITE THORN BLACK ROAST.

And standing there, halfway down the steps, the hope goes right out of Alice's sails, because it's obvious that this is another dead end. It's a *coffee shop*—she can smell the beans roasting from the street—and she wants to sit down on the stoop and cry, but she can't even do that now without causing a scene. She should probably just turn around and walk the three miles back to campus, but she can't bring herself to do it. Her legs are stuck, not the way they were back in the graveyard, but leaden, as if they've simply lost the will to listen to her. Maybe it's the fact she's come this far, and she has no other leads, or that this place feels familiar in a simple, human way, a nod to the girl she was before, the one who constantly found refuge in café corners, fingers curled around a mug of tea, or the fact she can still hear the music, spilling softly through the door.

But Alice goes forward instead of back. She reaches the bottom of the steps, and the cheerful green door, and goes in.

A little bell chimes above her when the door swings open, and she steps into a place that feels more like a cluttered living room than a public café. It's cozy, a mishmash of furniture, sofas and chairs circled up around low tables, interspersed with four-tops, a handful of booths, and between the bearded guys in beanie hats, and the girl sipping a latte and scrolling on her phone, Alice feels like she's back on campus.

Like she's just ended up here on a study break, in the midst of a long night.

She looks around, some small but desperate part of her still hoping for a sign, a back curtain, the promise of a second hidden space, but there's only the counter, and the barista behind it—a middle-aged woman with a short brown bob and a pair of pink librarian glasses.

The woman is saying something, low, under her breath, either chatting with someone Alice can't see or maybe just talking to herself. Either way, Alice feels like she's interrupting, so even though there's no one else in line, she waits, until the woman's attention finally cuts toward her, a bemused look as if she's the strange one for just standing there.

"You want to order something?"

Alice hesitates—the barista's gaze flicks away, and back—but the bell has chimed again, and there are two people in line behind her now, and in the end, she asks for a menu, feels like an idiot when the woman points up at the hand-drawn board over her head. Just the usual fare, and her dad always says there's nothing a strong cup of tea won't fix, whether it's a cold or a pair of wet shoes or a bad day at school, so that is what Alice orders, and the woman makes it right, at least, with a boiling kettle and a healthy scoop of leaves, even if it comes in a mug instead of a pot. She carries it to a corner table and sinks into a cushioned chair, wraps her fingers round the mug for a warmth she doesn't need, but habit is its own kind of comfort.

The tea smells earthy and bitter and right enough that Alice thinks, just maybe, this is the place her old life and her new will meet, this small allowance, that it will taste like home instead of rot, but the illusion crumbles as soon as the liquid crosses her lips, her throat vising closed against the sip.

She spits the tea back into the cup, then folds her arms and lays her head down on the wood and decides this is a good enough place to give up. She wills the table to reach up and swallow her the way the graveyard tried to do, but the wood holds firm.

"That bad, huh?"

She drags her head up to find a guy, perhaps a little older than she is, but not by much. He's lean, verging on thin, dirty-blond hair just long enough he has it tucked behind his ears. His fingers are dotted with silver rings, and he's cradling an espresso cup in one hand, a notebook in the other, and she's about to tell him that she's really not in the mood for small talk right now when he asks, "What did you hear?"

Alice stiffens, frowns, uncertain. "What?"

"You followed the music, right?" he says, as if it's not a secret at all, and the air contracts around her, tight with warning and hope. She is sitting upright now, so thrown by the easy way he asks the question, and also by the thought that she might have actually done something right, that maybe, just maybe, she's actually found what she was looking for.

"Um, yeah," she manages.

"Well?" he asks, lifting the espresso to his lips. "What did you hear?"

Alice blinks, and looks around the café. It's fainter here, inside the shop, but it's still there, the piano rising and falling like a tide. "I don't know. Bach?"

The guy shakes his head. "Kids these days," he says. "Not everything good is old as well." He leans forward, resting his elbows on the back of the chair, and smiles, as if to himself, but she sees them—the tips of two teeth, sharper than the rest—and Alice wants to fling her arms around his shoulders out of sheer relief that she is not alone.

But her head is still spinning and she doesn't exactly know the etiquette for things like this, and—

"For your information, it's Einaudi."

She drags her thoughts back. "Huh?"

"The composer." He nudges her tea aside, setting the espresso in its place. "Go on. Try this."

Her stomach turns at the sight of the dark sludge, the memory of the over-sugared coffee in the econ hall, but she watched him take a sip, and it didn't seem to hurt him, so Alice lifts the small cup to her lips, and as she does, she catches the scent of iron beneath the coffee's edge. She drinks, feels her throat tighten once, and then unlock as the unmistakable taste of blood hits her tongue, and it's—

—weird.

There's no pulse, no bloom inside her chest, but it still goes down, warmth trailing in its wake, the trapdoor inside her falling open onto nothing but empty space, as if she never drank from that girl back at Chalice, or the creep in the nice car, or the guy on the Yard. She gulps it down, the contents little more than a swallow, and for a moment, the floor beneath her steadies and her mind goes clear—but then the cup is empty, and Alice feels wrung out, that sudden urge to cry again, though in frustration, fatigue, or hunger, she honestly doesn't know.

"Still thirsty?" he asks, then offers her a wan smile, a soft chuckle escaping like a sigh. "Silly question, isn't it? Black and red," he adds, and he doesn't raise his voice, but she can tell, somehow, he's not talking to her now, and sure enough the barista glances over, and he holds up two fingers, and she nods and gets to work.

Alice looks into the empty cup, her mind racing till it feels like it will trip itself. "Then this place really is . . ."

"Oh, it's just a front," he says, voice dropping at last. "We keep the bodies in the back. Blood orgies on Sunday nights. The password this month is *pineapple*."

Alice stares.

The guy stares back.

And then, after a painfully slow moment, one corner of his mouth goes up. He's mocking her. Gently, but still. Alice isn't in the mood.

"Ha ha," she offers dryly, and it must sound even sorrier coming out, because his expression softens as he takes the seat across from her. The barista drifts over, sets two espressos down, and wanders off again, her lips still moving as she talks to herself.

"The vast majority of the customers are, in fact, ordinary people," he says, "but it's true, my doors are open to all kinds."

Alice wonders what that means as she takes up the cup.

"Angel, demons, psychics."

She nearly chokes on the drink, but when she looks up, there it is again, that little, teasing smirk. Like this is all a game, a joke. As if she hasn't spent the whole night searching for proof, and going slowly mad. He seems to feel the annoyance wicking off her, because the smile drops away, leaving something earnest in its wake.

"Ezra," he says, holding out a hand.

"Alice." She slides her fingers into his, and the touch feels both right, and wrong, and it takes her a moment to figure out why—there is no pulse beneath his skin, no warmth, and nothing of him on the air, no emotions or desires clouding up the room like smoke. He is a pool of silence, a small oasis in the chaos, and when she meets his gaze, she sees his eyes are pale, and steady, like flecks of frosted glass, but there is a kindness in them.

"What are you doing here, Alice?" he asks gently.

She blinks, remembering her night, her search. She drags the phone from her pocket and swipes over to the photo.

"I'm looking for a girl," she says, nudging the screen toward him, and even now, she's braced for disappointment, for him to take a passing glance and shrug and say sorry, but he's never seen her.

But that's not what Ezra does.

He stares down at the screen, a small crease taking shape between his brows.

"Lottie," he murmurs, half to himself, and the way he says it, so full of knowing, makes Alice's hands begin to shake, her own voice trembling as she says, through gritted teeth, "You *know* her?"

Ezra drags his gaze back up. "I do," he says. "I have, for quite a long time."

"Where is she?" demands Alice, but the venom in the question makes him frown, and cross his arms.

"Why?" he asks—and that right there, the wall he puts up, protecting *her*—it's the final fucking straw.

"Why?" she snarls. "Because she *did this* to me." Alice's throat tightens around the words. "She ruined my life. She made me this way. And then she just *left*."

Ezra frowns and shakes his head. "That doesn't sound like her."

Alice stares at him, aghast, anger rising like bile in her throat. She wants to sweep the cups from the table, to say it doesn't *fucking matter* if it sounds like something she would do, because she did, she stole Alice's life, right when it was starting.

But before she can lash out, Ezra holds up a hand.

"Tell me what happened."

The anger in her does a strange thing then. It hardens.

Catty always burned hot. But now, Alice feels herself go *cold*. Cold enough it *hurts* her skin, her bones, her throat as she forces the words out, tells him about the party, and the aftermath, the Post-it Note, and the bottomless hole in place of answers, or explanation.

Alice tells him everything, And Ezra listens, arms folded and eyes cast down, until she's done, or at least until the story catches up with where she is, right here and now, and there's nothing left to say.

Then he runs a hand through his hair. "Something doesn't add up," he says, "but it's not your story." He shakes his head. "The Lottie I knew would never do something like this."

"Yeah, well," mutters Alice. "People change."

"They do," he says, his voice dipping as he adds, half to himself, "all things wither in the end." He sighs and sits forward. "We need to find Lottie."

"Great." Alice is already on her feet. "Let's go."

He cocks a brow. "Where exactly?"

"You know her. Lottie. Charlotte. So then, you know where to find her. Lead the way."

Ezra shakes his head. "I don't know where she is."

Alice feels her spirit start to buckle again. Until he raps his knuckles on the table and stands, adding, "But I know someone who might."

Alice follows Ezra across the coffee shop, picking past sofas and chairs to a back corner, where a Black girl in a BU sweatshirt sits cross-legged in a booth, large pink headphones clamped over her ears, blasting hard rock loud enough for Alice to hear the reverb. She's typing furiously, empty espresso cups and a small pile of philosophy textbooks spread in a half circle across the table, like a barrier that says *Keep out.*

Ezra leans his arms on the side of the booth.

"Melody," he says in a singsong voice.

"Studying," she singsongs back, her fingers never slowing on the keys.

"I need a favor."

"I need good grades."

"I haven't charged you for the last three—" He glances back toward the counter, and the barista holds up four fingers. "—*four* espressos. And I'm feeling generous enough to clear your tab. For the week."

The girl—Melody—sighs, fingers hovering until one twitches and taps a key. The music cuts off in her ears, and she plucks the headphones off, and settles them around her neck. "What do you want?"

Ezra smiles. "I'm looking for someone."

"I take it they don't have a phone?"

Ezra shakes his head. "Afraid not."

Alice watches them volley, wondering how the hell this girl is going to help them find Lottie—this girl, who smells like cinnamon and soda bread, whose heart is a steady rhythm in her chest, who is undeniably, unmistakably human, until she rolls her neck and cracks her knuckles and says, "I'll need something she's touched."

At which point, Ezra nudges *Alice* forward.

Melody studies her. "I see."

"I don't," says Alice.

"I told you," says Ezra. "White Thorn Black Roast caters to a varied clientele. My favorite customer, Melody, in addition to being a reliable patron, has certain sensitivities."

She rolls her eyes and shoots a look at Alice. "He means I'm psychic."

Alice stares, unsure if this is another joke. In her defense, it's been a long few days, and the girl doesn't exactly look like she spends her free time staring at a crystal ball.

"Yeah, well," says Melody, with a withering stare. "You don't look like a vampire."

Alice recoils as if struck. The girl's mouth twitches in amusement. "Take a seat." She glances at Ezra. "I'll need a large coffee. Black. And a plate."

He gives a small salute and strides away, one hand in his pocket, as Melody starts to clear the semicircle of cups and books out of the way.

"Philosophy?" asks Alice, trying to fill the awkward silence.

"I wanted to go into law," she says. "But it's hard when you already know who's innocent and who's guilty."

"So you read minds? See the future? Speak to the dead?"

"I'm not a medium," says Melody, nodding toward the barista, whose lips are still moving, pausing now and then as if listening. "I don't speak to the dead—present company excluded."

That word rings through Alice like a bell.

"I'm not—" she stammers.

"Sorry," Melody says quickly, "didn't mean to offend."

Then Ezra is back, depositing the cup of coffee and the plate on the cleared space between them.

Melody takes a sip, then promptly upends the rest onto the dish. The dark liquid spreads, running edge to edge, but doesn't go over the sides. It settles into a shining black pool.

"All right," she says, as if steeling herself. "Give me your hands."

Alice hesitates.

It's not *just* the fact that, an hour ago, she didn't know psychics were real, or that two days ago, she was a first-year student whose biggest concerns were keeping up with coursework and trying to make friends. It's that the last time she let a stranger in, she woke up dying (*Dead.*) and now her life has been turned upside down, and she's sitting in a coffee shop she found by following a song too soft for human ears with some girl who can read her mind, and Ezra made jokes about angels and demons, too, and how is Alice supposed to know what's real, what's right, what's happening to her, when every door that should have answers opens onto questions and who knows what anyone would even see if Alice let them look into her mind and—

"Alice." Melody's voice is steady, but kind, somehow in the booth and in her head at once, calling her back into her body. "Trust me," she says. "I'm not looking for anything I don't need." And then, in a lower voice, "And don't listen to Ezra, he's full of shit."

"I heard that," he mutters, leaning against a nearby post.

Alice manages a brittle smile, then swallows, and reaches out, and lays her hands on top of Melody's. Cold on warm, and she can feel the heartbeat through the other girl's skin, and she clenches her jaw as the hunger stirs again, like a beast waking from a shallow sleep, and forces her gaze to the still, black surface of the coffee on the plate where Melody is staring, too.

"Okay," says the psychic. "Think of the last time you were with her."

Alice tries to meet Melody's gaze, but her brown eyes have taken on a kind of fog, pale wisps curling over the irises, and it makes her think of standing in the yard back home, when the moon was bright enough to light the low clouds so they looked like they were glowing, Finn's small voice calling to her from the doorway and—

"Focus," urges Melody, squeezing her hand.

Alice swallows, forcing herself to remember. She looks down at the still black surface, and lets her vision blur as she thinks back, retracing her steps until the other girl's pulse becomes the beat of the music through the walls, and then she's coming out of the bedroom, and there she is, as if she's been waiting there all night, just for Alice. She stands, and drifts forward, until she's close enough to kiss, and that's when Melody's hands vise around hers.

The memory gutters, going murky in Alice's mind, a black-on-black ripple before Lottie springs back into her line of sight, only now the party is gone, the violet dye is gone, her curls glossy and dark, the short silver dress replaced by black slacks and a black-and-white-patterned blouse, a silk bow cinched at her throat. She's striding up a spiral staircase, heels sinking into a plush blue rug, and fingers trailing a blue-patterned wall, and Alice's heart lurches as Lottie looks back over her shoulder, right at her, with those eyes like strong tea, and that coy smile, dimple flashing in one cheek.

And in that moment, Alice wants to surge forward, grab her and pin her to the wall, but she can't. This isn't her mind, this isn't her memory, and Lottie isn't looking at Alice, because Alice is someone else. Their fingers are tangled, and the hand that isn't her hand is darker, the nails painted autumn shades of gold, and amber, and red, and as Lottie leads her up the stairs, she does the only thing she can.

She follows.

The two of them walk up and up, past gilded sconces to a landing, and down a hall to a room, where Lottie grabs her—not her—by the waist, pulls her—not her—back against the door with a breathy laugh, the same sound that made Alice's knees go weak the night she killed her.

And Alice tries to say something, to say *No*, to say *Wait*, to say *Run*, but the two of them are already tumbling back into the room, and the last thing she sees is the number—139—etched into a gold plate on the door, before Melody lets go of her hands, and the vision crumbles, and Alice is left feeling like someone slammed the door in her face.

She recoils, back in her body in the coffee shop booth, Lottie lingering like a camera flash behind her eyes, repeating every time she blinks. She sits there, caught between the two places, two selves, shivering with anger.

"Well?" asks Ezra, who's perched backward on a chair.

Melody rubs her eyes, as if clearing away sleep. "She's at a hotel."

"Oh good, there are so few of *those* around."

Alice shakes her head, locks her hands in her lap until her knuckles ache.

"There was blue," she says, trying to force the tremble from her voice. "On the stairs. Blue runner. Blue walls."

Ezra's expression brightens. He snaps his fingers. "The Taj."

Alice feels her chest tighten, not with panic, but hope. "You know it?"

He nods, already on his feet. "It isn't far. Thanks, Mel."

"Anytime," she mutters, pushing the now-cold coffee aside and settling the headphones back over her ears.

"Really?"

"No," she says dryly, hitting a key so the wall of bass guitar springs up between them. Alice feels like she should say something, thank her for her help, but Ezra's already shooing her toward the door.

"You don't have to come with me," she says as he shrugs on a coat.

"I could use the fresh air. Besides," he adds, "I meant what I said. The Lottie I knew wouldn't do this."

But she did, thinks Alice as they leave the café, the little bell chiming in their wake.

III

As they head down the block, Ezra digs a plaid scarf out of his coat pocket and loops it around his neck.

He catches Alice staring. "What? It's cold."

She frowns. "Is it?" She's only wearing the black hoodie and jeans, but she doesn't *feel* cold, realizes she hasn't, not since she came to in the shower, icy water soaking through her clothes.

"Not to us, maybe," says Ezra, nodding at a huddle of people across the road, shuffling, heads bent, against the wind, "but to *them*."

Alice shrugs. "I'm Scottish," she says, "maybe we're just more resilient."

"Maybe, but the fact is, when Boston winter rolls around, they'll notice if you're going about with a thin sweatshirt and no hat. So it's better to blend in."

As he says it, he drags air into his lungs, exhales a thin plume of fog, rubs his hands together, as if trying to get warm. A convincing pantomime. He's clearly had a lot of practice, and even though he looks twenty, maybe twenty-five, there's an ease to his stride, as if he's had a long time to settle into his skin.

"How old are you?" she asks, wondering as soon as the words are out if it's rude to ask, but Ezra doesn't seem to mind.

"Older than I look and younger than I feel," he says, "especially for being so long in the midnight soil."

Alice frowns. "What's that?"

"The midnight soil? Oh, just a turn of phrase." He shoves his hands in his pockets and spins so that he's walking backward, facing Alice as he recites the words from memory.

"Bury my bones in the midnight soil,
  plant them shallow but water them deep,

and in my place will grow a feral rose,
soft red petals hiding sharp white teeth."

Something about the words makes Alice shiver, and yet, she finds herself turning them over and over in her mouth as Ezra falls in step beside her, hooking his arm through hers.

"For warmth," he says, and she doesn't pull away.

They walk side by side in silence for a while, Alice's head spinning, and her heart a still weight in her chest, and every time she blinks, she sees Lottie, ghosted on the inside of her lids.

Lottie looking back, and smiling.

As if she knows exactly what she's doing.

Exactly who she is.

Alice squeezes her eyes shut—

Until the image fades—

And the cold wind picks up in her ears—

And just like when she looked into the shining black surface, her mind goes somewhere else.

The air whistles around them, as if the night is full of ghosts.

Alice has always had a love-hate relationship with Halloween. Most places take it to a foolish place, all shop costumes and cheap scares, but here in Hoxburn, the holiday holds on to a shade of its old witchy self. A reminder that Scotland was a pagan place before it was a Christian one, a land that still rings in the changing of the seasons and the years with lanterns and bells and wooden effigies burning off the dark. Sure, jack-o'-lanterns grin on porch steps, and paper ghosts sway from the trees, but there is a somber air to it, and even the children usually dress up not as astronauts or fairies, but ghouls and witches and ghosts, guising as spirits let loose for the night.

Alice is thirteen now, too old for all the candy and knocking on doors, but the night still has a power over her. The wind is full of whoops and howls, and even though the only ghosts are kids in sheets, eerie eyes cut out of cotton, the air smells like woodsmoke and dying leaves, ripe with mischief, and magic, and more than a little menace, and if she were alone, it might get to her, but she's not.

Catty's there, one elbow hooked through hers as they march together down the moonlit road. Catty, like an anchor and a buoy all at once; like a bonfire, burning back the dark, so Alice feels only a pleasant thrill, a fun kind of fear, like watching a scary movie from the comfort of the couch.

They're on the way to a party.

It's at Catty's secondary school, to be fair, but Alice still can't believe Dad and El agreed. She thinks it's probably because they feel bad, that Catty's been spending so much time at Granddad's place over the pub instead of home, ever since baby Finn was born, while Catty says it's because they're too tired to care—which is true, they're not even up for handing out sweets, just set a bucket on the step and a sign warning people not to knock or they will set a banshee loose.

It doesn't really matter why.

The point is that Dad and El said yes.

(With instructions, of course, to be back before midnight, and a weighted look at Catty as they said it, as if Alice isn't more than capable of keeping time.)

Someone's smashed a jack-o'-lantern on the curb, and Catty kicks a piece that might once have been a nose, or eye, down the road. They take turns punting it as they walk, the lump getting smaller and smaller as it skates along the concrete until it's not worth kicking anymore, which is fine because they're almost there.

Up ahead, the school's lit with amber lights, orange balloons painted to look like pumpkins bobbing in the breeze. But instead of heading up the steps, Catty nudges Alice on, past the school and its chaperoned dance, shooting Alice a wicked grin, as if that was the plan all along.

"Where are we going?" she asks, trying to sound like the answer doesn't matter, like the thrill isn't turning to cold dread in her gut. Catty offers a cheeky look, made slyer by the feline whiskers slashed across her cheeks.

"To a party."

Catty's elbow is still hooked through hers, so Alice doesn't have much choice; when Catty keeps walking, so does she, until the school's nothing but a lump of light behind them, the sounds from the town's center fading, too, and Hoxburn isn't that big, and they're running out of roads, and for an awful second, as they near Friar's Way, Alice thinks they might be heading for the graveyard.

But Catty wouldn't do that to her. Not ever, but especially not tonight.

Two years back, a boy in Catty's class dared her to go in, on Halloween of course, and Alice can still remember the horrible creak of the old iron gate, the shape of her sister growing smaller between the graves. Alice counted to seventy-two before Catty came back again, her eyes red with tears and black with rage.

"What's the matter, Catty?" the boy had drawled. "You see a ghos—"

Only he never got to finish because as soon as she was through the gate, she split her knuckles on his face. And on the walk home, blood tracing between their locked fingers, Alice didn't ask Catty what she saw, if she saw anything, but she always wondered, still doesn't know, if she was sad because she *saw* Mum's spirit, there beside the grave, or sad because she didn't.

And sure enough, they turn off before the graveyard, onto a narrow lane called Maple Cres, and Alice thinks how strange it is that they live in a town so small, and yet there are still roads she's never really been down.

Soon new sounds start creeping in, music being played too loud over shitty speakers, and voices tangling with shouts and laughter, and then they reach the house where the party is.

The front door hangs open like a mouth, full of silver streamer teeth, the edges of the building traced with orange light, like there's a fire burning somewhere beyond.

Alice tightens her grip on Catty's arm, or tries, but she slips free, jogging up the steps.

Alice follows.

Inside, the music is more bass than sound, heavy as a pulse, the front room full of zombies and witches and devils, and she feels suddenly silly in her blue dress and white apron, dressed as that storybook Alice, curious and bold. She would have been a witch but the other party, the one at the school, had a bookish theme, and Catty was supposed to be her Cheshire cat. But with only the whiskers drawn on her face and a tail pinned to the hem of her jeans, her sister looks effortless amid the other costumes.

While Alice just looks like a kid, tagging along.

There's an old slasher film playing on mute on the TV, and Alice watches a man with a saw silently prowling through the dark while Catty beelines for a table littered with open bottles. The whole walk, something in her bag made a glassy thump every time it hit her hip, and now she knows why. Catty produces a full bottle of gin, nicked from the pub, and adds it to the lot on the makeshift bar before pouring two cups of punch from a bowl ringed by empty bottles of vodka and rum and half dancing her way back to Alice.

"Where are we?" she shouts over the beat, and even though the song picks right then to get louder, she can see Catty shaping the name, tongue against the roof of her mouth.

"Derrick's."

Alice wants to roll her eyes. Derrick. Of course.

Catty met him at school (only *met* is the wrong word because in a town as small as Hoxburn, everyone is already tangled up) and Derrick is two years older and only one grade ahead, but he plays the drums in a friend's band and has a tattoo of a compass in the center of his chest, and the one time he met Alice, he called her a wee lass nipping at her sister's heels, so as far as Alice is concerned, he can go get fucked (which is a thing she heard her classmate Eddie say, and she likes the way it sounds, even in her head).

"Relax!" Catty mouths, handing her a plastic cup.

Alice takes a sip, only to discover it's more water than whatever alcoholic punch Catty's downing as she scans the crowd.

Stay here, she mouths, gesturing with her hands. *I'll be right back.*

And then she and her empty cup are gone, ducking through a doorway into another room, obviously looking for Derrick.

Someone knocks into Alice, a guy with a face painted like a skull, made creepier by the fact he's somehow stained his whole mouth black as well. Alice scrambles back, presses herself into the wall to get out of the way. Decides to stay there as a trio in hooded black cloaks drift by.

She takes another, smaller sip of her drink, the sweet burn somehow going both down her throat and up into her head. She closes her eyes and leans into the wall, feels the bass beat against her spine, hum along her ribs, tells her body to relax, and it's starting to listen when a hand jerks her back into the room, and there's Catty's whiskered face, her tilted grin, her fingers like a bracelet on Alice's wrist as she drags her off the wall.

"Come on, barnacle."

She leads Alice through a kitchen—past another skeleton, a girl painted like a porcelain doll, a guy with fake blood running down his face—and then out, into the cool night of the backyard, where the music isn't deafening and a bonfire blazes in an orange peak against the dark.

Alice sighs in relief, fills her lungs with the fresh air as Catty tugs her toward the flames.

A group of teens stand ranged around it, chatting and sipping from their own red cups, the light splashed against their faces, and for a moment, neither of them talks. Catty's attention has disappeared into the flames, the way it does when she's looking through something instead of at it, so Alice copies her, stares right into the fire even though it's hot and bright, and burns her cheeks. She closes her eyes, can see the whole thing ghosted on her lids.

"Let's get out of here," says Catty.

Alice blinks, hopes rising for a moment because she thinks Catty's talking about the party, but then she adds, "Once you finish school," and Alice knows she means *after*. After, that weird nowhere word that can mean an hour or a day or a year or never but not *now*.

"Where?" asks Alice.

Catty keeps her eyes locked on the blaze. "London. Madrid. Tokyo," she muses, listing all the places in Mum's photos. "What about America?"

"How will we get there?" asks Alice. "What will we do?"

Catty shrugs, as if the questions aren't important. "You're smart, Bones. You can go to one of those big fancy schools, and I'll—I dunno, I'll take photos. Or make drinks. Be a bartender. Or a model. You always hear those stories about girls getting discovered. That never happens here. But out there, it could."

She stares into the fire, and Alice can see the future taking shape in Catty's mind, the way it plays like light across her face. She tips her head, just so, as if she's already on some fancy set, limbs gracefully arranged like she's waiting for someone to snap her photo.

That's why Catty likes Derrick. Or at least, that's what she claimed, when Alice asked. She didn't insist he was handsome, or clever, or even kind. She just shrugged and said, "He *sees* me."

As if he's the *only* one, or even the first.

As if Alice didn't come into this world with both eyes focused on her sister.

Catty catches her staring, so Alice makes a camera of her hands, and Catty rolls her head toward the imaginary lens, and winks, and Alice clicks her tongue and prints it on the back of her mind, and then Catty brightens, and Alice smiles, till she realizes it's because Derrick has shown up, a piece of gray plastic perched on his dark hair.

Alice cocks her head. "What are you supposed to be?"

He flicks the plastic down over his face, smug expression vanishing behind a wolfish mask, spreads his arms as if waiting for applause, then says, "But wait, there's more," and pulls out a red umbrella, opens it over his and Catty's heads.

"See? Now we're raining cats and dogs."

Alice rolls her eyes because wolves and dogs aren't even the same thing, but Catty cackles with delight, and Alice can't help but wonder which one of them she dressed up for, and the whole thing leaves a bad taste in her mouth, and then as if on cue, Derrick reaches behind his back and produces a bottle of something neon blue.

He spins the cap off and takes a swig, then points the lip toward Alice, as if to say, *You want a sip?* And she would have probably shaken her head, scrunched up her nose, half because it's the kind of booze their granddad wouldn't even stock on the lowest shelf of the pub, and half because he's just had his mouth all over it. But before she can, Catty waves him off.

And Alice knows there's no malice in the gesture, but something about the way her sister does it, the look in her eye, like Alice is still a kid who needs protecting, makes her snatch the bottle from Derrick's hand and take a long swig.

She nearly chokes as the liquor stings her eyes, and strikes a match inside her throat, going down like a mouthful of hot tea.

Derrick whistles, and Catty swipes the bottle off her.

"Whoa, slow down," she says, and isn't that ironic, given all the times Alice has said those same words to her big sister.

Slow down, slow down.

Alice doesn't know she's laughing until Catty frowns, sends Derrick to fetch a glass of water.

Catty turns to Alice, hands on her hips. "What's gotten into you?"

"Nothing," she says, because how can she explain this pit inside her, the way she wants to either shrink or grow, go back to when they both were kids, or fast-forward to when they're both grown up, that either one's better than this feeling, like the gap between them's somehow growing, and Alice can't catch up.

"I just—" She falters. The swig was two shots, maybe three, but her head is already spinning. The sounds around her rise and fall like she's on a roller coaster instead of standing, boots on grass. "—I want to be like you."

She wants Catty to smile, to hook an arm around her shoulders and say *You are,* say *We're two of a kind,* or some silly shit, but she doesn't. Her expression changes, like someone pulled a curtain down.

"No, you don't," she says, cupping Alice's face. "Don't be me, Bones. Just be you."

The bonfire crackles. Alice swallows. "But I don't know who that is."

"That's okay." Catty cracks a smile. "You've got all the time in the world to find out." And maybe that's true, but Alice can't help but think about the fact that Catty's always known exactly who *she* is. And then, her sister shrugs and says, "But I know who you are."

And it's probably a joke, a trick, but Alice feels her heart lift anyway. "Really?"

"Yeah," says Catty, light playing in her eyes. "Want me to tell you?"

Alice nods, and Catty leans in close, puts her mouth right against her ear, and Alice holds her breath and listens as Catty starts to speak, but just then someone lobs a firecracker into the fire and it goes off with a sudden, deafening shriek, and then Derrick is back, putting a glass of water in her hands as he pulls Catty away,

And Alice is left standing there, alone—

With no answers—

Only a ringing in her ears, and—

Her toe hits a jutting piece of sidewalk, forced up by a nearby tree and—

Alice lurches, and her eyes fly open, and there is Ezra, his arm looped so casually through hers, his head tipped back as if considering the night, but there is a studied air to it, like a head turned tastefully away to give a person privacy, and she can't help but wonder if somehow he felt or heard what she was thinking—if her mind, her memories, are just spilling out, painted on the air around her, and the thought makes Alice queasy, she wants to pull them back, tuck them under the collar of her shirt with the little golden pendant, but he just clears his throat and says, "It's not far now."

They are almost to the Commons, the park stretching like a shadow up ahead.

Ezra slips free of Alice, and tugs a flask (of all things) from his coat pocket, and when he opens it she can smell the penny scent of blood. Her throat tightens as he takes a swig, teeth aching as he hands it to her. She drinks, and it doesn't even touch the edges of her thirst, knows that she could drain a dozen flasks and it wouldn't make a dent, but can't stop herself from swallowing, feels guilty for how light it is when she hands it back.

But Ezra just slips it back into his coat.

"Where does it all go?" she asks, exasperated. "No matter how much I drink, the thirst is always there."

"That," he says, "is one of the great questions. The bigger one is, if you *know* that it won't fill you, why bother drinking at all?"

"Don't we have to? Won't we starve?"

"Starving," he says, "is far harder than you think. Go on," he says, as if he can hear her racing thoughts, the way they trip and tangle. "I'm sure you have more questions."

"How long can you go?"

"Some go months. Others years."

"*Years?*" She can't seem to go more than a day without unraveling.

Ezra nods. "Madness will take you before hunger ever will."

Alice chews her bottom lip, as gently as she can. There is so much she wants to ask. So much she doesn't know or understand, but the question that pushes to the front is this.

"Why a coffee shop?"

Ezra laughs, clearly expecting something else. "The coffee shop's fairly new. Before that it was a bar. And before that, a bookstore. And back during Prohibition it was a speakeasy. I change it around every ten to twenty years, to keep from standing out, or ending up on a historic registry."

"Why bother, then?"

He considers. "After a while you learn, it helps to have a purpose. Besides, keeps me from getting lonely. I get to meet all kinds of people."

"Like angels and demons and psychics."

He snorts. "Exactly. But normal people, too. After all, if I only catered to a certain clientele, I'd be out of business. There's not that many of us."

Us. The word feels like an ill-fitting coat. She resists the urge to shrug it off. Instead asks, "Why not?"

Ezra exhales another plume. "Fickleness, I suppose. And folly."

He lets his head fall back, and she follows his gaze up, past the buildings to the night sky, amazed that there are *stars.* Alice knows that there are always stars, but before, they would have been too faint, her eyes too weak to make them out, and now, she can see them, scattered like diamonds in the sky, and for the first time, she makes a new column in her mind, of things that maybe aren't so bad.

The lack of fear—that one goes at the top, but right beneath it, she puts this.

But then she starts to wonder how many stars she'd see if she were back in Hoxburn, and then she remembers that if she were back in Hoxburn, she'd never have crossed paths with Lottie, she'd still have a future, a life, a pulse, and that's enough to tear the mental paper from her mind as Ezra clears his throat again.

"Here is something you should know. We think ourselves immortal, but we're not. All things get hollowed out by time," he says. "Including us. For some it will take centuries, for others only a mortal life, but one way or another, eventually, pieces of us die. The parts that made us human. Till all that's left is hunger, and rot."

Alice swallows. "What happens then?" she asks.

Ezra's head drops, his eyes pale but bright. "One way or another, we meet our end."

"Sounds pretty grim," she says, wondering if that's what he thinks happened to Lottie, if that's why he's coming with her now.

To save his old friend—or bury her.

She scuffs her boot. "You don't seem rotten, Ezra."

He flashes her a crooked grin. "Don't be fooled. I'm just going slower than the rest."

There is so much more she wants to ask, but at that moment, his steps slow to a stop, the Commons to one side and a row of buildings to the other, and Alice looks up to find the entrance of the Taj Hotel.

Suddenly, her limbs go heavy. She feels rooted to the pavement, torn between the urge to go in and the urge to turn and run—until she remembers that she can't go back, not far enough, not to her old life, because it isn't there anymore, because Lottie took it from her, and that is enough to break loose.

Ezra holds the door and Alice forces herself over the threshold, through the entrance, and into the hotel.

Inside, a marble floor stretches through the lobby, and the perfume of fresh flowers fills the air, so strong it's almost cloying. To the right, there's a candlelit bar, but to the left, the stairs—the same bright blue ones she saw in her vision.

Alice starts toward them, only to be interrupted by the appearance of a concierge in a trim black suit.

"Can I help you?" he asks, hands spread slightly in a way that could be a welcome or a wall, and before Alice can think of what to say, Ezra is there, fingers resting gently on the concierge's sleeve.

"We're visiting a friend," he says, his voice steady, and there's moment of tension, when the concierge looks like he might pull away, but then his eyes flick up to Ezra's and he sees something there that makes the rigidness go out of him.

"Shall I call up for you?"

"No need," says Ezra cheerfully. "We know the way."

He drops his hand, but the effect seems to linger, because the concierge stands there, like a puppet waiting for someone to tug on his strings.

"Anything else, sir?"

Ezra smiles. "No, thank you," he says, "but you have a wonderful night," and the way those words wash over him, they might as well be an order, a spell, because the man smiles in genuine pleasure and assures Ezra that he will.

The concierge drifts away across the lobby.

"How did you do that?"

"Conviction," he says, as if it's that simple. As if Alice hasn't struggled with that all her life, as if she didn't have to hide in a bathroom and dare herself just to be a little bolder for one night, as if that need for false bravado didn't lead her here. To this.

"You know," he muses, watching the concierge drift out of the lobby and into the bar, and order a drink. "One thing you learn when you live as long as we do, is that nothing's permanent. Who you were isn't who you have to be."

With that, Ezra nods toward the stairs. "After you."

He trails behind her now, instead of leading.

But she is glad he's there. A shadow at her back. A steady hand.

Alice puts her foot on the first step. She runs her fingers along the rich blue paper on the wall, feels her boots sink into the soft blue runner on the stairs.

There was a moment, when her plane hung suspended over the vast Atlantic Ocean, nothing but blue below and blue above, when she looked out at the in-between, stomach in knots, and told herself that her heart was pounding with excitement instead of fear.

This is your life, she thought as the plane sailed on.

This is how it starts.

There are eighteen stairs between the hotel lobby and the landing. Alice counts them as she climbs—eighteen moments of before and after, then and now, eighteen chances to go forward, or move back. Only there is nothing behind her anymore, nothing ahead, the whole road has been erased, and she wants to know why.

She *needs* to know why.

Alice passes a mirror on the stairs, an ornate thing in a gilded frame, and as she locks eyes with the girl in the glass, she is back in the bathroom at the Co-op party, makeup smudged and body coiled stiff with nerves, trying to make a deal with herself, a bet, a game.

Old Alice for New Alice. Just for one night.

She touches the surface of the glass, her fingers no longer warm enough to leave a mark, then drops her hand, and forces herself up, and up, and up, until she's standing in the hall. Until she's right there at the door.

The numbers stamped into their small gold seal, just as she saw them in the vision.

139.

Alice looks down at the placard looped around the doorknob—*Do Not Disturb*—and she doesn't even have to press her ear to the wood to hear the sounds beyond, bubbles of soft laughter, mouths on skin, whispers of pleasure and—

She grits her teeth and raps her fist against the wood, waiting for the poetic moment when the door will swing open, and the girl who came into her life (and left with it, like a prize), will have to look her in the eyes, to see what it's like when your past comes back to haunt you.

But the moment doesn't come.

The sounds of pleasure don't stop, even though there's no way they didn't *hear* the knocking. Alice stares in disbelief at the door, and Ezra waits for her to try again, but she's apparently used up all her nerve, because her hands are now hanging limply at her sides, all the strength gone out of them.

Ezra doesn't knock, just clears his throat and leans a little toward the door and says, "Lottie, it's me. We have a problem."

And even though he didn't raise his voice, the movement in the room shudders to a stop. Alice can hear a murmured *Stay there,* and then the weight of a body rising off a bed, bare feet across the floor, and this is it, the lock turns with a soft click, and the hotel door swings open, and there she is.

Lottie.

The same girl who perched at the edge of the bed in the dark, who danced with Alice surrounded by colored lamps and saved her from the stampede of bicycles and ran with her through the rain, and made her come apart.

Lottie, standing in the doorway, her blouse unbuttoned and her heels cast off, curls wild and cheeks flushed as if *her* heart's still beating in her chest.

"Ezra?" she says. "How did you—"

And then she finally sees Alice.

She sees Alice, and those eyes of hers, those candle-bright brown eyes go wide, and at least she has the decency to look surprised. That part goes to plan. But not what happens next, not Lottie stepping into the hall and catching Alice's arm, her whole face twisting with concern as she says, "Alice?"

Her name on Lottie's lips, her voice, so sad and sweet, so full of caring that it makes her reel.

"What happened?" she asks, as if she can't feel the lack of heat, the absence of a pulse, the silence pooling inside Alice where there should be sound, and the worst part is that even now, *even now*, Alice feels the pull, like gravity, the urge to lean into Lottie's touch instead of wrenching back, away, so she does, lets it carry her forward, until her hands connect with Lottie's front. She shoves her back as hard as she can.

"What *happened?*" snaps Alice as they both stumble back into the room. "You should know."

"Char?" comes a dreamy voice, and another woman appears, the one with the warm skin and the autumn nails, wearing nothing but the bedsheets. "What's going on?" she asks. "Who are these people?" and Alice can't drag her gaze from the thin ribbon of blood running down the side of her neck, the wound itself already healing, but she can taste the pulse from here, like a penny on her tongue.

Lottie—Charlotte—Char, whatever she's calling herself, goes to the woman and cups her face and says, in that too-steady voice Alice is starting to recognize, "Go into the bathroom. Take a long shower. I'll join you when I can."

The woman manages a sleepy nod, and goes, closing the door behind her, and Alice feels like a tightening spring. "Is that what you did to me?" she snaps.

Lottie turns toward her.

"No," she says. "I wouldn't." And she has the nerve to look *wounded* by the accusation. Alice watches as she sinks onto the edge of the bed, fingers actually trembling as her hands go to her mouth, and she looks like she might cry, and Alice bristles because this isn't right, it isn't fair. Where is the wicked grin, the monstrous smile, the villain's monologue? Lottie doesn't deserve to look so hurt when *she's* the one who did this.

She's the monster here.

"I didn't compel you, Alice," she insists. "I didn't have to."

"Bullshit."

"You wanted me there," she says softly, almost to herself. "It was just a bit of fun."

"*Fun?*" snarls Alice. "Was that before or after you killed me?"

Lottie flinches. "I *didn't*," she says, and Alice grabs her by the shoulders, forces her to look her in the eyes.

"Then how do you explain the fact I'm *dead?*"

Dead. The word gets stuck halfway up her throat. She has to tear it out like roots, leaving the taste of rot behind.

But Lottie only shakes her head. "It wasn't me."

She says that last part to Ezra as much as Alice—Ezra, who's leaning, arms crossed, at the spot where the hall becomes the room, as if *his* opinion somehow matters more, as if he's the one whose life is over.

"It wasn't me," she says again, tears now sliding crimson down her cheeks. "It's not my fault."

"Then whose is it?" demands Alice, and Lottie whispers something, a single word, too soft for even her to hear.

"What did you say?"

Lottie clears her throat and says the word again.

"Sabine."

CHARLOTTE

(D. 1827)

I

London, England
1827

In the house on Merry Way, there are two kinds of sitting rooms.

The first is put to use—the cushions worn, the hearth soot-stained. The second is more a staging ground—a place for fine things on display. Charlotte stands in the second kind of room, every lamp and vase and pillow arranged just so, and holds her breath, certain that the slightest breeze will upset everything.

Her kingdom for a book—she brought a stack, of course, but they were taken straight to her room with the rest of her trunks, and she was sent to the salon.

Charlotte has been waiting here for nearly an hour, hands clasped before her like a prisoner waiting for their sentence, heart rattling with nerves inside her chest. She stares out the window, longing for the rolling grounds of Clement Hall, but all she sees is London proper, stone and brick as far as the eye can see. Here and there, the briefest glimpse of grass or tree, a bit of nature under siege. On the street below, carts and carriages clatter by, and women stroll beneath bright parasols, past men with top hats perched like chimneys on their heads. Charlotte has been to the city several times, though never alone, and it's always struck her as grand, yet rather bleak. Oh, there's plenty of color, in the dresses, the furniture, the rugs, but every ounce of it has been imported, as if to offset the dreary backdrop.

More than once, Charlotte hears the soft bustle of steps beyond the salon door, and turns hopefully from the window—but no one comes. She sits (on the very edge of a pristine chair). She rises (careful to smooth the cushion). She paces, and sits again. Restless, nervous, and uncomfortable. Six hours over dirt and cobblestone have left her stiff and sore, and desperate to stretch her legs.

Exhausted, and impatient, she slumps down onto the sofa.

Right as the door swings open.

Charlotte lunges back to her feet as her aunt strides in, tugging off her gloves and passing them to a maid, along with a brisk command for tea. Amelia Hastings, a terrifying breed of high society, at once round and sharp, pale hair pinned up in an elegant bun, and shrewd blue eyes that land squarely on Charlotte. Eyes that could unpick her, stitch by stitch.

"Aunt Amelia," she says, trying to sound cheerful as she comes forward to embrace her father's sister. But there are no open arms, no kind kiss planted on her cheek. Instead, Amelia catches her outstretched hands and draws them apart, studying the girl between.

"My, my," she says, "how you've sprouted up."

She drops Charlotte's hands and steps back to continue her inspection.

"Eighteen," she muses, "though you wouldn't know it by that dress. And this hair," she adds, "tell me, has it ever met a brush?"

"Oh, it's met many," quips Charlotte. "And bested every one."

Her mother would have smiled. Her brother would have laughed—at least, he would have back before the garden and the book and Jocelyn. Aunt Amelia does neither, only purses her lips, and says, "Wit is like salt, my dear. Best in very small doses."

Charlotte feels her cheeks go hot. She's never been good at hiding her emotions, the way other girls do, not when they seem intent on hovering just beneath the surface of her skin.

And it is her skin that Amelia goes for next.

"How *tan* you are," she notes, with a small but telling tut. "Your mother's side, no doubt." Charlotte cannot hide her frown, but she manages to hold her tongue and doesn't say that it's hardly *her* fault the current fashion is for such a sickly shade. It's as if every one of them has recently survived a brush with scarlet fever.

Amelia nods to herself and says, "There is a kind of country beauty to you." Which Charlotte *almost* takes for a compliment, until her aunt goes on to say, "Don't worry, that can be refined."

A tray arrives, bearing a teapot and four cups, the porcelain rattling slightly as the maid sets it down. Amelia's attention swivels, shooting the maid a stern look, and Charlotte savors the brief reprieve, steels herself as the scrutiny swings back her way.

"My brother has let you run roughshod over the estate, romping and roaming like a second son. And your mother. Good breeding, of course, but well, she's always been *eccentric*."

Surely, Charlotte thinks, there are worse things one can be, but she doesn't say it, only bites her tongue and curls her fingers around the tiny bundle of dried flowers hidden in her skirt, recalls her mother's parting words.

You are the kind of bloom that thrives in any soil.

And as if Amelia can hear the memory, she says, "Wildness is like a weed. If it's not plucked out, it will take over everything. But don't worry," she adds, "you're here now, and we shall set you right."

With that she lowers herself into a chair, and gestures for Charlotte to sit, which she does, as gracefully as possible. Her aunt watches, eyes narrowing a little when Charlotte's back touches the pillow. She quickly straightens.

Her aunt begins to pour the tea, the gestures delicate, precise, doesn't spill a drop, and Charlotte is just beginning to wonder who the other two cups are for when they arrive.

Edith and Margaret. Amelia Hastings's current wards. Edith reminds her of a tulip, tall and thin with a large head, made larger by the arrangement of her auburn hair. Margaret is softer, rounder, a blushing rose. They move with a fragile kind of grace, and each performs a perfect curtsy, like a flower wilting in the heat, before drawing themselves up again.

"Charmed," says Margaret in a breathy tone.

"How nice to meet you," says Edith, her voice sweet as syrup.

When they sit, they perch delicately on the edge of the seat, arrange their limbs, their hands, their chins, as if sitting for a portrait, their backs never once touching the cushions. How exhausting it must be, thinks Charlotte, even as she tries to hold herself a little straighter.

"As you know, I have something of a reputation," continues Aunt Amelia, stirring milk into her tea, "for polishing girls into gems. But first"—she sets the spoon aside, lifts the cup, only to pause halfway to her mouth—"I must know the kind of stone I'm working with."

She takes a sip, then, clearly intending for Charlotte to speak, but there's a right answer, and she has no idea what it is. When she says nothing, her aunt lets out a small, exasperated sigh, and returns the cup to its saucer.

"My dear," she says plainly, "what makes you shine?"

It is a clumsy metaphor—after all, according to Amelia, *she* will do the shining—but Charlotte understands—she is being asked what sets her apart. My *heart*, she wants to say, but of course, her heart got her into all this trouble in the first place. So instead, she replies with a tally of expected talents. She has been schooled in pianoforte, drawing, and French (though, the last, admittedly, she learned from reading novels).

Her aunt seems unimpressed.

"If I had known," she says, "I would have hired proper tutors. Alas, your father hardly gave me warning. As it is, we'll fit in lessons in decorum when we can. He tells me you are a quick study. Of course, the Season is already underway. I couldn't present you this year if I tried. But that's for the best," she adds, "we'll need the time. For now, you'll have Edith and Margaret to look to. With any luck, their training will rub off."

And then her aunt is rising, and so are her wards, the other teacups returned to their tray before Charlotte's even had a sip. She stands, too, nearly spilling her tea as the woman walks past, slowing only to cast a last, shrewd look over her niece.

"Don't worry, Charlotte," she says, the words less like a promise and more like a threat. "We'll make a proper Hastings of you yet."

II

Clement Hall
Two weeks prior

Laughter blew through the garden like a breeze.

A giddy shriek, a cheerful shout, bare feet racing over lawn, and stone, and earth, and step.

The gardens at Clement Hall were like a painting still in progress, the center perfectly finished, the edges devolving into rough lines, unkempt clusters of apple trees and patches of wild rose. Her mother's sculptures dotted the landscape, clay animals tucked between bushes or perching on gates, a menagerie of silent spectators.

Jocelyn reached the fountain first, cutting one way and then the other, Charlotte on her heels, the two chasing each other like hands around a clock. Jocelyn let out a startled cry as Charlotte splashed her hand through the pool, made a mad lunge for the other girl, but she was already breaking away, disappearing down another path.

She darted beneath a wooden trellis and then stopped, as if crossing some imaginary finish line. She twisted back toward Charlotte, who came to a breathless halt on the other side and grinned wickedly as if to say, *What now?*

And for a moment, they stood like that, coiled, flushed, each studying the other, each on the verge of movement, like a girl and her reflection, though they looked nothing alike.

Jocelyn Lewis was a study in contrasts, green eyes and raven hair framing skin so pale that the slightest effort puts roses on her cheeks. Charlotte Hastings, on the other hand, was shades of brown. Eyes the color of tea before the milk goes in, hair a mess of chestnut curls, skin that spent the winter tan, and darkened by degrees in summer, freckles dappling her face year-round, like flecks of paint.

At that moment there was, of course, one other crucial difference.

The journal, clutched in Jocelyn's hands.

Charlotte's journal.

"Joss," she said slowly, one hand raised as if creeping toward a skittish cat. "Give it back." Her pulse quickened as she said it, her friend's green eyes going bright with mischief as she unwound the leather cord.

"And sacrifice this glimpse into the brilliant mind of Charlotte Hastings?" Jocelyn smiled, teasing, toying. Charlotte wanted to throw herself onto the girl, the book. Instead, she inched forward, but her friend danced back in turn.

"Jocelyn," she warned, trying to sound stern instead of terror-stricken.

"I wonder," mused her best friend. "Have you been writing about *me?*"

At that, Charlotte—who could keep a secret off her tongue but not her face—made the fatal mistake of flinching, and Jocelyn cackled in delight and flipped open the book, but before she could skim, Charlotte flung herself forward. Jocelyn yelped, and turned to flee, made it almost to the line of fruit trees when Charlotte caught her around the waist, and they both tumbled down into the grass.

"You feral thing," said Jocelyn, giggling.

"You wretched thief," countered Charlotte, winded and giddy. The journal lay face down, several feet away. Neither of them bothered making a grab for it. They sprawled on the lawn at the edge of the orchard, limbs tangled and dresses stained, a tree root digging into Charlotte's back, but it was worth it, for the dappled shade, the weight of Jocelyn beside her.

Jocelyn, whose hand found hers, fingers knotting in the grass. "I only wanted to know your thoughts."

Charlotte's heart leapt inside her chest, even though it was nothing, they'd known each other since their bodies were shapeless, edgeless, they'd shared beds and woken with their limbs entwined, hair grazing each other's cheeks.

And yet.

The words were a spark against Charlotte's already burning skin. She rolled onto her side to look at Jocelyn. "You could have simply asked."

"You could have lied."

Charlotte scoffed. "Such slander!"

Jocelyn rolled toward her, head pillowed on her hands. "All right then. Tell me what it says."

Charlotte swallowed, her throat suddenly dry. It would be easy to say no, to scoop up the journal and go marching back to the house. But Jocelyn's green eyes were wide and waiting, and the words came spilling up from memory.

"*'Sometimes, when I'm with Joss, I forget who I am.'*"

The other girl blushed, and so did Charlotte.

"*'I forget who I am meant to be.'*"

Charlotte reached out and tucked a loose black lock behind Jocelyn's ear.

"*'And all I know is that I want—'*"

At that moment, something cracked, came free. Jocelyn's mouth found hers, or hers found Jocelyn's. She didn't know which of them closed the gap between their bodies, only that the kiss was softer than she would have dreamed it, because it was *real.*

If they had stopped, right there, it could have passed for chaste, a glancing kiss between old friends—but it didn't. There was the sound of Jocelyn's breath catching in her throat, and Charlotte's heart skipping with a nervous speed, her skin alive with heat, as if she'd grazed a patch of nettles, and their hands—their hands—two of them still tangled, and the other two now searching, Charlotte's on her cheek and Jocelyn's on her waist, fingers knotting in the fabric of her dress. Pulling Charlotte forward, closer—

And then, suddenly, firmly, away.

Their mouths broke apart, Charlotte gasping as if coming up for air, a laugh already rising like bubbles in her throat. But they were no longer mirror images. Jocelyn's cheeks were flushed, her breathing quick, but her face was drawn, and when she spoke, her voice was thin and tight and scared.

"We shouldn't have done that," she whispered, and Charlotte flinched as if struck, but before she could say anything, another voice joined in.

"No, you shouldn't have."

James.

His hair windblown, a riding crop tucked under one arm.

In the time it took Charlotte's older brother to bend down and collect the discarded journal, the two girls had flung themselves apart. But it was too late. They were in such a state of disarray, their faces flushed—Charlotte's with shock, and Jocelyn's with something worse. Shame. She looked like she might cry.

"James—" started Charlotte, surging to her feet. But before she could say any more, her father was coming down the path, asking James about the filly, how she was adjusting to the saddle. He startled at the sight of them.

"Charlotte, Miss Lewis. What are you doing out here?"

Jocelyn was standing now, every ounce of her attention fixed on her skirts, and her attempt to set them right.

Her father looked around, perplexed. "Where are your maids?"

Charlotte found she couldn't speak, the air was all sucked out of her, and she was afraid to try and force it in again, in case she came apart. How had it all gone so wrong? Moments earlier, she had been so full of hope and joy, and now her best friend wouldn't look up, and neither would James. She knew she had to beat her brother to the answer, but when she tried, she found she couldn't breathe, and in the end he got there first.

"I wanted to show Miss Lewis around Mother's garden, now that everything's in bloom," lied James. "Charlotte was kind enough to chaperone."

It was the best excuse he could have given.

And the worst.

At twenty-one, her only brother had been notoriously fickle when it came to matches. Now, at the mere mention of a prospect, especially one so well-known and well-liked, a light kindled in their father's eyes, his attention flicking between his son and Joss in a way that made Charlotte's stomach ache, made her want to scream, to plant herself between her brother and her friend, as if staking claim. But she was not a fool, and she knew she would owe her brother dearly.

"Darling, are you well?" her father asked, and Charlotte realized then that she was shivering. At some point, the sun had disappeared behind the clouds, and it looked like it would rain.

How quickly the English weather turned.

"I should be getting home," said Jocelyn. She looked at Charlotte's brother. "Thank you, James." Charlotte, she ignored.

Her brother nodded grimly. Her father held out his arm.

"Come, Miss Lewis," he said. "I'll walk you to your carriage."

Charlotte watched her best friend go, held her breath and hoped that Joss would glance back, that those green eyes would find hers and they would say, *It is all right, we are all right.*

But she never did.

The moment they were gone, she heard James draw breath to speak, but Charlotte could not bear to hear the words, and so she turned, and hurried home. She didn't run, but walked as briskly as she could, chest heaving with pent-up tears as she rushed back through the trellis and around the fountain, rewinding the path of her chase, wishing she could reverse the time as easily. How far back would she go? Before the interruption, or before the kiss, or before she glanced up from her journal to study Jocelyn across the blanket they'd spread on the lawn, and the look on her face gave away too much of what she'd written.

The first drops fell as Charlotte reached the back steps of Clement Hall, James trailing like a shadow in her wake. He reached her, of course, and they stood in silence as the rain came down—a sudden downpour, the kind unique to spring.

He met her gaze, and Charlotte forced herself to hold it. He took after their father, his complexion lighter than her own, his eyes darker, his hair content to fall in loose, elegant waves. She thought for a moment he'd leave it at a look.

Please God, let him leave it at a look.

But God was not on her side today.

"Lottie," he began, almost gently.

"It wasn't—" she started, shaking her head, but he cut her off.

"You are not a child anymore."

She scoffed. Three short years between them, but he treated the time like a chasm.

"You cannot . . . that is, you mustn't . . ." James, who never struggled for words, could not seem to find the right ones now. She wanted to melt into the stone beneath her, or rush inside, escape upstairs into the safety of her room.

But he was still holding her journal.

That damning book.

"It was a lark," she lied with a brittle laugh. "Nothing more."

Please believe me. Please believe me.

But the look on his face was unconvinced.

"Be that as it may," he answered cautiously, "you are nearly grown, and there are certain games you can no longer play." James rapped his fingers on the journal. "Surely you understand. There are rules. Expectations."

"*You* don't play by them," she shot back. James Hastings, unwed, unwilling to even entertain the idea, attached as he is to his independence.

He arched a brow and said, "We are not equal, Charlotte."

There was no malice to the words, and still they stung. "In intellect, perhaps. In willfulness, surely. But the simple fact is that you are a woman, and I am a man. And yes, it does afford me certain freedoms. But even so, one day I *will* need to take a wife, just as you will need to take a *husband.*"

Husband. What an ugly word. A rock tossed in a clear pool, muddying the water. She tried—and failed—to keep the thought from showing on her face. Perhaps that was what damned her in the end.

James extended his hand, and the journal with it, but when Charlotte reached to take it, he held on a moment longer.

"Be careful, sister," he said, before letting go.

He disappeared into the house, left her clutching the book to her chest as the rain fell heavy as a curtain, the garden lost from sight.

That night, Charlotte tore the last ten pages from the journal and burned them in her hearth. Tears slid down her cheeks as the paper curled, the words devoured one by one.

But as the fire cooled to embers, she sighed with something like relief, and told herself that it was done.

III

London, England
Spring, 1827

Charlotte Hastings cannot *breathe*.

Though she suspects it has less to do with nerves and more the ruthless way her corset has been cinched. The carriage hits a crack in the cobblestones and the boning cuts into her ribs, and now she knows why Edith and Margaret move so carefully. Why their voices are so faint.

Edith and Margaret sit across from her, gloved hands folded neatly in their laps, and looking less like girls and more like Roman busts, lovely and pale and draped in pastel shades of satin. Somehow, small as their waists are, they find the air to talk, reeling off names that mean nothing to her as they toy with the dance cards looped around their wrists.

Charlotte fidgets with her own, turning the ornate slip between gloved fingers.

Aunt Amelia fills the bench beside her, bound in sturdier fabric with a higher neck, to hide her ample bosom. She has spent the last five minutes delivering a lecture about the hierarchy of court, and how it's decided who will host the balls each night. Charlotte assumes the speech is meant for her, but she is too busy trying to breathe.

Perhaps she *is* a bit nervous. After all, this is a first, and those are always frightening.

The carriage hits another bump, and she winces, one hand going to the front of her dress. It was a gift from her mother, a gold so pale it shimmers beneath the flowers embroidered down the front. A dress her aunt declared *passable,* only because it was too late to get another, though she dislikes the way it makes her niece's skin look even darker.

But Charlotte loves the way the fabric glitters, matched by the trio of gemstones at her throat, her wild curls bound up beneath a net of pearls. In truth, when she saw herself in the hall mirror, she did not know whether to smile or flinch at the sight of such a pretty stranger.

Though she doubts the image will survive the ride.

The carriage is stuffy enough that she can feel her hair trying to escape the hundred pins her aunt's maid forced into it. Her feet are already aching in their shoes, and a dread is rising to snuff out what little air she has.

At last, the carriage stops, and they descend, and for a moment she drags in giant gulps of air, and even though London air cannot be called fresh, it soothes her aching lungs. She closes her eyes and pretends that she is standing on the garden path, chin lifted to the night.

And then a firm hand plants itself in the small of her back. Aunt Amelia chides her for clogging the walk and nudges her forward toward the waiting house. Music wafts through the open doors, along with the sounds of laughter, delicate as glass. The bubble of voices. The rustle of skirts. A dozen overlapping sounds that reach like hands into the night and drag her through.

But as Charlotte steps into her first *proper* ball, a strange thing happens.

Her aching heart, her fear and worry, which have been with her step for step, are overwhelmed by something new. A kind of awe, or wonder.

The house is not a house. It is a *wonderland*.

A thousand burning tapers cast a veil of golden light that seems to land on everything. The marble floors and polished sconces, the vases and crystal cups, and the girls in all their finery. The gems in their hair, around their throats, the beads sewn into their gowns.

Charlotte has always had a dreamer's heart, an artist's eye, the kind of imagination that unspools itself at the slightest touch. And in the few short days between arriving at Aunt Amelia's house and this first ball, she has had time to make use of it, to conjure scenes from books she's read, stitch together swatches from Edith and Margaret both.

And yet.

They do not hold a candle to the truth. *Lovely* is not a bold enough word for such a spectacle. It is *dazzling*. Extravagant, and ornate, grander than anything she's ever seen, and for a moment, she feels giddy, wrapped in a childlike delight, the kind she felt when she saw a glowworm for the first time, igniting in her mother's palm, or a star come loose, tumbling across the night. The rushing joy of doors flung open, and oh, if only Jocelyn were here—

Charlotte's ribs begin to ache inside their corset. Her feet hurt in her shoes. And perhaps it is the pain that brings her back to earth, dampens her momentary wonder, and reminds her she is just a girl, and the ball is just a house, and both of them are simply playing dress-up.

Pretending to be what other people want.

Instead of what they are.

Clement Hall
One week prior

The letter came at breakfast.

It was always Charlotte's favorite meal, not for the food, which was plain enough—a pot of tea, a tray of toast, half a dozen soft-boiled eggs perched in porcelain cups—but for the easy way her family sat, ranged around the table, at once together and apart, each engaged in their own quiet morning rituals, the only sounds the occasional trill of birdsong, the chime of porcelain, the whisper of pages turning.

She could lay her family out like hours on the clock.

At three, her father perused a paper, one of the weeklies sent from London.

At six, her brother made notes in the margins of a ledger (he was newly apprenticed to a bank).

At nine, her mother stared out the window, her mind on some corner of the garden or her latest block of clay.

And at noon, Charlotte sat with a novel in one hand and a toast point in the other. She had mastered the art of balancing the two without smudging the book or missing her mouth.

She was on the last chapter when the mail arrived, a single piece delivered to her father's elbow. Charlotte didn't pay it much mind as she popped the toast point in her mouth, read the final pages of *Udolpho*, and felt beset by the strange mix of pleasure and grief that came with finishing a book.

She sighed and set the novel down.

"Done already?" asked her mother.

"You go through them so fast," observed her father as he broke the letter's seal. "At this rate, we'll run out."

"Good thing, then," she said, reaching for another piece of toast, "that more are always being written."

It was true, Charlotte had made a fair dent in the library at Clement Hall, though the shelves were mostly filled with Swift, and Diderot, and Goethe, and she preferred the works of Austen, and Defoe, and Radcliffe.

This last one came from Jocelyn.

Jocelyn had never trusted Charlotte, not since she gave her *Frankenstein*. Her friend had come storming in the next day, looking absolutely haggard and claiming she hadn't slept a wink, because it was so frightening. From that moment on, she insisted, she would read only romance.

As if love and horror could not go hand in hand.

Jocelyn read less than half of *Udolpho* before she declared it *far too grim*, with its haunted houses and restless ghosts, and practically hurled the book at Charlotte, saying, *You'll likely love it.*

She couldn't wait to tell Jocelyn that she was right. Only, Charlotte hadn't seen her since the incident in the garden, nearly a week before, and every time she thought of it her stomach gave a vicious little twist. It had been such a perfect day, until it wasn't. And when she tried to call to mind the kiss (which she did, again and again, despite herself), it came with the bitter aftertaste of Jocelyn's expression. But she knew that when she saw her friend, everything would be all right again. It had to be. They could go back to how they were before.

If that's what Jocelyn wanted.

Charlotte realized she'd been dipping the same toast point in the same egg cup for far too long. Realized, too, as she set it down, that something about the room had changed without her noticing. That at some point, her father and brother and mother had all stopped engaging in their own pursuits. That her parents were now exchanging a wordless look, and James was looking, rather pointedly, at his empty plate.

"Charlotte," began her father, and the tone of his voice made her heart quicken, her skin tighten over her bones. Something had happened. Something was wrong.

"What is it?" she asked, scanning the table for a clue, seeing only the letter lying open by his plate. "Has someone died?"

"Hardly," said her mother with a brittle laugh.

Her father cleared his throat. "We need to talk," he said, "about your education."

Charlotte relaxed then, just a little. She was a sturdy enough pupil. Which was to say, she bustled through the work as one might through a lengthy meal, eager to be excused. "If it's about the tutor last week, I wasn't *hiding* from him. I simply lost track of time."

James snorted under his breath.

"It's not," said her father, tapping the paper. "I've been speaking with your aunt, Amelia. And we think it would be a good idea for you to visit her . . ."

Reading as much as Charlotte did, she knew there were words, and words *between* words, ones that hid in the spaces, the pauses, the breaths. They hung on sentences, weighed them down with all the things that were not being said.

Her aunt, Amelia, lived in London with her husband. They had three daughters, raised and wed, but their house was never empty, thanks to her aunt's talent for navigating court, and the myriad girls who passed through every Season to be groomed, and presented as her wards.

"Visit her?" said Charlotte, dread coiling around her ribs. "Surely she is too busy."

"I was worried about that," replied her father, "which is why I wrote. But she assures me there is room for you."

Room for you.

Her heart started drumming in her chest. "Why must I go at all?" she asked, her voice threatening to break. "You and Mother didn't meet at court."

Charlotte had heard the tale a dozen times, of how *he* was touring a friend's estate, of how *she* came by chance to visit the same day, how her mother tipped the world beneath her father's feet. It always sounded wonderfully romantic. As if their meeting was destined. Fate.

"But we both went," her mother chimed in now. "There's more to it than finding matches. It will be good for you to make some friends. To meet other girls your age, as well as suitors."

"Besides," added her father, "no one is expecting you to make a match *this* Season."

A *match*. Her head began to spin.

One day I will need to take a wife, just as you will need to take a husband.

"You won't be formally presented," her father went on. "It's simply a chance to watch, and learn, so that next year you'll be ready."

Charlotte swallowed. "You always said it could wait."

"I did. But your brother has convinced me otherwise."

And there it was, the words between the words. The reason for the layered speech. Charlotte glared at James. He had the decency to flinch.

"I simply said it might be a good idea. A chance to see what life will be, beyond the confines of Clement Hall. I thought perhaps you might be growing bored."

How could she be bored, with so much space? With Mother's garden and with Father's books? With James for talk, and Jocelyn for company—

But that was the problem, wasn't it?

There are certain games you can no longer play.

Charlotte felt tears sting her eyes.

"Goodness, Lottie," James added with a cheerful huff, "you act as if you're being *punished*."

Am I not? she almost snapped. But it would be as useless as asking *Why now?* It was obvious. Perhaps her brother had not betrayed her secret. But he would, if she forced him to. And to give it words would damn her.

Her mother reached out and took her hand, giving it a gentle squeeze.

"How exciting it will be," she said, "to spend the spring in London."

A spring away from Clement Hall.

Away from the gardens.

Away from Jocelyn.

"Just wait," her mother added cheerfully. "By the end, you'll be writing home, begging us to let you stay."

Charlotte chewed the inside of her cheek to keep from crying. Her brother looked away, as if the very prospect were undignified.

"It's settled then," said her father, rising to his feet. He kissed the top of Charlotte's head, and gentle as the gesture was, it had all the weight of a door swinging shut.

IV

London, England

One moment, Charlotte is surrounded by people, and the next, she is alone.

Her aunt peels away to join a cluster of women chatting by a grand bouquet, and soon after Margaret and Edith are called to dance, and both stroll off without a backward glance, and just like that, Charlotte finds herself at her first ball without a chaperone.

Small mercies, she thinks, grateful to be free of Amelia's constant scrutiny.

She claims a glass of lemonade and drifts from room to room, slowing now and then to take in the splendor of the ball. More than once, Charlotte feels herself drawn to a halt by the sheer grandeur of it, but every time she feels like she is in the way or underfoot, so she retreats, until her shoulders meet the curtained wall, and watches the servants pass with silver trays, the men and women talk and dance, the whole thing like a play until—

Her gaze snags on another girl, across the room.

It is the color of her hair that catches Charlotte's eye, her breath. Or rather, the *lack* of color, her curls the same glossy black as Jocelyn's. The same lily-white skin, so pale it glows against the rose tone of her dress.

Her head turns, this phantom friend, and just before their eyes meet, Charlotte is convinced they will be green—but of course, they're not. They're dark, and just like that, the resemblance mercifully dissolves. And yet, she does not look away, and neither does the girl. The moment stretches like a rope between them, and then the girl's mouth twitches, tugs into the kind of secret smile that makes Charlotte's face go hot, and her heart quicken . . . until she realizes that the look, the smirk, are meant for someone else. A young man who strolls up and bows, asking her to dance. The girl curtsies, offers him a white-gloved hand, and lets herself be drawn away.

And Charlotte wishes she could melt into the floor.

Instead, she claims another glass of lemonade and escapes, out of the room and across the intervening hall to the safety of the stairs. She is halfway up before her pulse finally slows, and so does she, one hand on the glass and the other clutching the rail as if for balance.

She sighs. From here, at least, she can absorb the ball in peace, see the couples dancing in the hall below. Her own card hangs from her wrist, the lines still mercifully blank.

She watches the partners move in time with the music, drifting together and apart, their hands grazing, elbows hooking for an instant before they separate. On the girls, the dresses glitter, like sunlight glancing off a pond. And every movement sets them shining, the candlelight glancing off their hips, and hands, their collarbones, and breasts.

Charlotte swallows and forces her attention to the other half.

To the young gentlemen, dressed in their coats and tails, their combed-back hair and white cravats, each there to court and find a match, secure the future of their house.

She studies them, and tries to summon *something*. To understand what the girls find so alluring about this other sex. What makes their hearts quicken and their faces flush. Charlotte has read enough romance to know the way she *should* feel in their presence, and yet, while more than once the heroes in those books stirred her, reality does not.

She watches, *wanting* to want them, the way she wanted Jocelyn. Wanting to feel that mix of fear and hope, a hunger for their gaze, their touch, wanting her heart to flutter in their presence.

And when that fails, she tries a new approach—pretends that they are sculptures instead of flesh, breaks them down into their component parts and tries to admire the neat lines of their shoulders, the curl of their hair.

There is an elegance, to some of them. A poise.

But the longer she looks, the more the vision cracks, the charm rippling like a mirage until they are reduced again to awkward limbs, jutting chins, their posture so stiff she pictures them as paper dolls mounted on sticks, or—

"Like show ponies, prancing," says a voice behind her, and the image makes Charlotte snort into her drink. She gasps, and wipes her nose, imagining Aunt Amelia's horror, after the week of etiquette, as she turns to face the speaker.

And her whole world stops.

Later, when Charlotte looks back on this moment, it will take on the air of the impossible. In her mind, the ball will come to a grinding halt, the music stopped, the bodies frozen in their poses, some dancing and others with glasses halfway to their lips, the moment suspended on a breath.

Of course, that is not how it happens.

And yet, that is how it feels.

Like time is splintering, her whole life split into before and after. And who knows what might have happened, if she hadn't kissed Jocelyn that day in the grass—if she hadn't been sent to her aunt's house that year—if she hadn't been on those stairs at that ball on that night—

But she did. She was. She is.

The woman at her side is pretty. And yet, *pretty* is too dull a word.

She is tall and slim, with features more like a Grecian bust than an English rose. There is a sharpness to her edges that sets her apart, but then, so does everything about her. She is dressed in purple. Not lavender, or mauve, or lilac, or any of the other pastel hues that are in vogue this spring, but a much darker shade, one closer to bruised plum, or grape. Her skin is fair and smooth, and her hair. Her *hair*. Ropes of copper bright enough to burn the air around her head where it's been coiled.

She is a few years older than Charlotte, at a guess. Or perhaps she only seems that way. All the other girls have a restless air, as if caught in a constant, nervous breeze. But this one stands, arms folded loosely across her waist, one gloved hand cupping her elbow, while the other twists a pendant at her throat.

Charlotte knows that she is staring, but she cannot help it.

And then the woman's gaze, which until now has been leveled on the dancers, slides toward Charlotte, her eyes an ochre medley of gold and brown. And there it is, that feeling the men have tried and failed to stir in her, that heady, ground-tipping mix of hope and fear, the hunger to move closer, and to shrink away. Charlotte cannot bring herself to do either, so instead she forces her attention back to the dancers.

But the men have all been transformed into colts, with their odd, cantering gait.

"Oh no," she groans. "Now all I see are horses."

"You're welcome," teases the woman, and this time, Charlotte hears the faint touch of an accent, the very edges of her English foxed, as she gestures to the crowd below. "Well," she muses, "anyone you'd like to ride?"

The sound that escapes from Charlotte is half gasp and half laugh, so sudden

and so loud that a few heads around them turn, and she can practically hear
her aunt Amelia *tsking* from somewhere down below. She claps a hand over
her mouth, mortified, but the woman only smiles, mischief dancing in her
eyes.

"I'll take that as a no," she says, slipping a gloved hand through Charlotte's
arm. That touch, so easy, so familiar, Charlotte never thinks to hold her
ground, simply melts into it as the stranger draws her up the stairs.

"You're new to town."

"Is it that obvious?"

"No," says the woman, "but I have a knack for noticing. For instance," she
adds, nodding toward a pair at the bottom of the stairs, "*that* is Lady Pen-
dleton's eldest, Eleanor. Pretty enough, but as interesting as paint. Unless,
of course, you *enjoy* hearing someone spend an hour talking about curtains.
There, beside her, is her brother, Albert, who has made the rounds three
years now and refuses to propose."

"Is no one to his liking?"

"On the contrary, they all are. He cannot seem to pick." Next, she gestures to a gentleman at the edge of the dance floor, a pale mustache like a
line of cream across his upper lip. "Frederick Hanover, likes to promise, never
delivers, and on the way has ruined the purity of countless prospects. You
don't want anything to do with him."

As they make their way around the balcony, several guests nod warmly at
the woman on her arm. She answers each with passing charm, but her attention never strays from Charlotte.

"Henry Castle," she continues, gesturing to a slender young man with a
crop of dark curls. "If looks were wealth, he would do fine, but alas, his family's estate is crumbling."

Charlotte tries to pay attention, but it's hard to notice anything but the
scent of roses wafting from the woman at her side, the way her breath tickles
the curls at Charlotte's neck.

"That girl there, the one in blue," she says, nodding at a figure in the
doorway, "is Lisbeth Rennick. She was supposed to debut last Season, but
she spent seven months up north instead. For her *health*." A knowing pause.
"And that one, with the white-blond curls, is Olivia Finch. One ball in, and
her card is full. Apparently, she's as kind as she is pretty."

"And *you?*" asks Charlotte, unable to hold her curiosity at bay.

Those hazel eyes widen a fraction. And then, she laughs. A soft, low sound.

"Forgive me," she says, "I've skipped straight to the part where we are already friends."

With that, she pulls back, drops into a brief but elegant curtsy. "My name," she says, "is Sabine Olivares."

Sabine.

That name. Charlotte does not know, then, how many times over the years it will spill out of her, as a longing, or a plea, or a curse. In that moment, all she knows is that she finds it strange and beautiful and fitting.

She feels a little giddy as she presents herself.

"Charlotte Hastings," she says, bobbing in her dress, "but my family calls me Lottie."

And there it is again, that smile, like a secret, or an inside joke. "First strangers to friends, and now friends to family? It appears we *both* are skipping steps."

Charlotte knows she's imagining the coyness in the woman's tone, but her heart still gives a little flip, and she knows that if she were to pass a mirror at that moment, the color would be there, like a signal on her cheeks.

She is glad when Sabine begins to walk beside her once again. And yet, it's strange, the easy way their bodies fit together, as if molded by years instead of minutes, and Charlotte finds she is far too aware of the places they meet, so she forces her attention back to the ball.

"How do you know so much about them all?" she asks as they descend the stairs.

Her new companion shrugs. "Sharp eyes, keen ears, and a gift for going unnoticed."

"But surely you don't," she says. "I mean, how could anyone not look at *you?*"

The moment the words are out, Charlotte feels her face go hot, wishes she could take them back, not because she didn't mean them but because she did, and what is wrong with her?

But Sabine doesn't cringe, demur, or even blush. Only lifts a single brow to show she's heard the words, then carries on straight past them. "Ah, but you see," she says, "there is one thing that renders me invisible."

"What's that?"

"I am a widow."

Charlotte's heart sinks on her behalf. "Oh," she says as they reach the bottom of the stairs. "How dreadful. I am sorry."

Sabine leans in, her voice barely a whisper as she says, "I'm not."

The words are at once so soft and yet so jarring that Charlotte wonders if she even heard them, but before she can ask, or even stop to study Sabine's face, a young man strides up to them. His hair is a shock of honey blond, his face long and narrow. Charlotte assumes he's come for Sabine, but then he bows to her.

"Miss Hastings," he says. "How nice to find a new face at the ton. I am George Preston. Of Barrington. I was hoping to have the next dance."

"With me?" she asks, vaguely stunned.

George looks from her, to Sabine, and back again. "Yes. I mean, if your card has room, and Mrs. Olivares does not mind."

"Nay," says her new friend, and only Charlotte hears the slight trill at the end of the word, making it sound like *neigh* instead, and she has to stifle a grin. And before she can think of an excuse, Charlotte feels Sabine's hand come to rest against the small of her back, light fingers nudging her forward, into George's outstretched palm.

Charlotte has no choice. She lets him lead her out onto the floor.

More than once, she glances back, expecting to find her new companion gone, but every time she looks, Sabine is still there, those hazel eyes fixed on Charlotte, until the music swells and the dance carries her away.

V

Clement Hall
The last day

Charlotte had written to Jocelyn, of course.

Told her of the impending trip, and got back a single page in her friend's neat hand, wishing her a pleasant spring. No mention of the garden, no explanation or excuse for withdrawing in its wake. A half-blank slip of folded paper. As if nothing had happened. And yet, if nothing had happened, she surely would have rambled on the way she always did when talk turned to the city and the Season, would have told Charlotte to come back bearing stories and gifts. If nothing else, she would have come to say goodbye.

But she didn't.

And less than a week later, as the tulips and hyacinth were giving way to rosebuds, Charlotte Hastings left for London.

The luggage was loaded, the horses waiting, a six-hour ride on bumpy roads.

Her father stood waiting in the foyer, and wrapped her in a firm but brief embrace.

Her brother met her at the door, laid an arm around her shoulders as he told her that the time away would clear her head. She did not trust herself to speak, so she said nothing, shoes crunching as she walked across the gravel drive, each step a small but audible protest as her legs carried her away from Clement Hall.

Her mother was the last to see her off.

"I don't want to go," whispered Charlotte. It was the first time she said the words out loud, and her voice broke beneath the weight of them.

Tears slipped down her cheeks.

"I'm sorry," she said, trying to brush them away. But her mother caught her hands.

"Never be sorry," she said, "for who you are."

Charlotte understood then that burning the pages of her journal had done nothing. Her mother already knew. She looked back at her husband

and son, standing on the steps. "Some people keep their heart tucked so deep, they hardly know it's there. But you," she went on, turning back toward Charlotte, "you have always worn it like a second skin." She ran a hand down her daughter's arm. "Open to the world. You feel it all. The love and pain. The joy and hope and sorrow." She pulled Charlotte close, carrying the scent of the garden. Of home.

"It will make your life harder," she said into her daughter's hair. "But it will also make it beautiful."

Already one of Charlotte's curls has escaped its hold. Her mother reached up to tuck it back. Her hand lingered, came to rest against her daughter's cheek, her palm soft from years coated in clay and earth.

"Time is a funny thing," she said. "It goes racing by right under our noses. I close my eyes and you are eight and climbing trees to get the highest fruit, perching up among the birds to eat your prize. And then I blink, and here you are, all grown, and I don't know how." Her brown eyes—the same shade as Charlotte's—shimmered with feeling. "We've kept you at Clement Hall too long."

"But I am happy here," pleaded Charlotte, hoping her mother would be the one to give, to let her stay.

But her mother only smiled and shook her head. "You will be happy there as well," she said. "Do you know why?" She took something from her pocket, a small bundle of dried flowers, the ones that grew wild at the edges of the yard. "Because you are the kind of bloom that thrives in any soil. And who knows, perhaps you will meet a worthy gardener."

Charlotte winced at the thought, but her mother only pressed the bundle into her hand.

"And barring that," she went on, "think of all the stories you'll have to tell when you get back. After all, there is no art without life to inspire it." She tapped her finger on the very tip of Charlotte's nose. "So go, and be inspired."

Charlotte nodded, spirits lifting a little as she climbed up into the carriage.

It was only a season, she told herself, thinking it was true.

She had no way of knowing then.

It would be fifty-two years before she returned to Clement Hall.

VI

London, England

Charlotte sits at the table the next morning, wishing for a book.

She had one with her when she stepped into the dining room, but her aunt gave her a withering look over her tea and proclaimed it indecent to read at a shared table.

"The greatest gift," her aunt declared, "is one's attention."

A rule that doesn't seem to apply to her uncle, Alfred, who sits at the head of the table, half-deaf and wholly content to be ignored as he reads the morning paper. But quarreling is also frowned upon, so she resigns herself to buttering toast and listening to Margaret and Edith, whose delicate façades have crumbled, giving way to giddiness as they chirp like birds about the ball, recounting each and every dance.

Margaret paints a thin coat of jam on her toast and announces that she wouldn't be surprised if a suitor came to call that very day.

"*Already?*" demands Edith, her poise cracking beneath the weight of envy.

The other girl flashes a smug little grin and takes a bite, but Amelia cocks a brow and says, "In that case, you best stop eating and go make yourself presentable."

Margaret almost chokes on the bread, tries to swallow as daintily as possible before rising and rushing from the room.

Aunt Amelia turns toward Charlotte. "Well, my dear," she says, "how did you find your first London ball?"

And even though her ribs are bruised and her feet are sore, the truth is, she found it lovely. But before she can answer, Edith cuts in.

"She only danced one time, and spent the rest of the night with a woman on the stairs."

Her aunt's expression narrows. Edith chomps on her toast and Charlotte wrings the napkin in her lap. "That's true," she says. "It was, I admit, an overwhelming night, and Edith and Margaret were both so busy, and I didn't want to bother *you*. Sabine was kind enough to keep me company."

She's braced for a rebuke—but her aunt brightens at the name. "The young widow Olivares? Well, I see no harm in *that*. As far as new friends go, you've chosen rather well. She is the picture of propriety."

Charlotte chews her cheek to keep from smiling. There are a dozen words she'd call on to describe the friend she made, but *proper* isn't one of them.

Not that she'd ever say as much to Aunt Amelia.

"A widow?" asks Edith, crinkling her brow.

"Indeed," says her aunt. "Her husband was a Spanish viscount, closely favored by the crown. I believe his family was in the business of wine—or maybe it was silk?" She shakes her head. "Either way, good breeding, both of them, and newly wed. They had just come to London when he died." She tuts. "A tragedy, to be alone so young."

"She looked pretty enough," says Edith, in a grudging way, as if her own looks could hold a candle to Sabine's. "Why doesn't she remarry?"

"I'm not one for gossip," says Aunt Amelia briskly, and then, without a moment's pause, "but from what I've heard, he was the love of her life."

Charlotte frowns at the image, but it's soon replaced by another. Sabine, beside her on the stairs. The odd light in her eyes when Charlotte said that she was sorry for her loss, and Sabine leaned in and whispered back, *I'm not.*

"I've heard her say she will never take another husband."

"What a sorry life," says Edith. But she's wrong.

The woman Charlotte met at last night's ball struck her as neither sad nor lonely.

Only free.

The bell rings and a servant arrives, announcing a suitor for Margaret, and with that the day plunges into motion, the subject abandoned with the breakfast plates, forgotten by everyone save Charlotte.

Three days later, and she is at her second ball.

The dread of that first night has been overtaken by a nervous hope, while the pale gold of her first dress has been replaced by a new one in a slightly warmer shade, on Aunt Amelia's orders—God forbid she not be lighter than the silk—and thanks to the mercy of a maid who agreed not to cinch the corset *quite* so tight, she can even breathe.

It is a lovely, cloudless night, rare enough for London in the spring, and the ball seems to be spilling out from the hosting house like spokes of light, into the courtyard behind the property. Lanterns hang from branches. Candles perch on walls, and the overall effect is rather wonderful, as if the stars have come down from the sky to shimmer just above the heads of every guest.

Charlotte finds a place along an ivied wall, content to watch the ball unfold from there, but as she scans the mingled guests and dancing couples, the young men in their coats and the girls in their dresses, she finds herself searching for a specific face, a coif of copper hair.

She doesn't see Sabine arrive.

But she feels it.

One moment, the wall just beside Charlotte is empty, and the next, it is not, and her heart picks up, and she knows, even before she turns her head, that it's her.

She's dressed in a gown the color of caramel, her hair a burnished cloud around her head. She leans back against the wall, arms folded loosely and eyes on the dance, as if she has been there all along.

Charlotte brightens. "I was just thinking of you." The words come tripping out of her, heat rushing in their wake. Jocelyn would have blushed, or looked away, embarrassed for them both. But Sabine's mouth only twitches in a catlike smirk.

"What a coincidence, Miss Hastings. I was thinking of you, too."

The same words, simply echoed back, and yet Charlotte feels a little dizzy, wonders if the corset was tightened after all.

"Oh," she says, finding her breath, "if I am to be Miss Hastings, then you must be Viscountess."

Sabine's expression cools. "If I had wanted you to call me that, I would have told you."

"Still," says Charlotte. "If I had known that you were titled—"

"It was another life," she says with a shrug. "Believe it or not," she adds, lowering her voice, "I have had more than one."

There is an invitation there. A door, ajar. But before Charlotte can reach for it, Sabine brightens, and breezes on. "Besides, we are already friends, and therefore, we have no need for family names and foreign titles. I am simply Sabine."

"Very well," says Charlotte with a smile. "Then you shall call me Lottie."

But to her surprise, the other woman shakes her head, and she feels a little wounded, until Sabine says, "If it's all right, I'd rather call you Charlotte."

She frowns, confused. "Why is that?" she asks.

Sabine turns toward her, one shoulder tipped into the wall, and even though they're both on their feet, in the middle of a ball, it reminds Charlotte of stretching in the grass, nose to nose with Jocelyn.

But *Sabine* doesn't look away.

She studies Charlotte with those unblinking hazel eyes, and it must be the many candles that make them look like they are burning.

"A name is like food," she says. "It has a flavor. Some are bland, and some are bold, some bitter and some sweet." She nods at a passing woman, and then, as soon as she is gone, tips her head toward Charlotte's and says, "Take that one. *Mary*. Plain as milk."

"What about *Margaret*?" she asks, summoning her aunt's first ward.

Sabine purses her lips, as if tasting the letters. "Like tea without sugar."

She bites her lip to keep from smiling. "And *Edith*?"

Sabine scrunches up her nose. "Burnt toast."

She cannot stop herself. "And *Charlotte*?"

A smile tugs at the corner of Sabine's mouth. The smallest thing, and yet, she feels like she is falling toward it.

"There you are," declares Amelia, sweeping up impatiently, as if Charlotte is a shawl that she's misplaced. "I hope you don't intend to spend all night like a weed growing from this w . . ." Her aunt notices Sabine and her whole demeanor shifts. "Viscountess!" she says brightly. "I do hope young Miss Hastings hasn't been imposing on your time."

Sabine's smile changes, too, takes on a practiced air.

"Not at all," she says. "She has been the picture of politeness. A testament, no doubt, to your instruction."

Charlotte can practically see her aunt's mood lifting at the praise. "Kind words indeed, coming from someone so esteemed."

Sabine lifts her chin, and Charlotte marvels at the change as the widow and the aunt exchange their pleasantries, the way Sabine has slipped into this other self, her coy smile and her teasing air replaced by something smooth and cool and distant.

Then Aunt Amelia peels Charlotte from the wall, nudging her on and talking about someone she just has to meet. Sabine nods blandly, as if she doesn't care, and it's such a small, convincing cruelty that Charlotte almost flinches as her aunt leads her away.

But when she looks back, Sabine is herself again, head cocked and arms crossed.

One gloved hand flutters in a wave.

And then they turn the corner, and she's gone.

That night, as the maid tugs the pins from her hair and frees her from her dress, Charlotte turns her own name over on her tongue, guessing at the taste.

VII

In fairy tales, big things happen in threes.

Three children. Three beds. Three roads.

The third bite is poison, the third gift is great, the third door always leads home.

It makes sense, then, that when Charlotte looks back on this time, it is the third ball she dwells on most.

The one that changes everything.

That night it's held at some lord's city manor, and there appears to be a *theme*.

The ornate interior of the impressive house has been transformed into a blooming garden: a well-manicured one, of course, every leaf and petal in its place, but the massive bouquets grow from every corner, and pale green gossamer spills down the walls, stitched with bits of glass that catch the light like dew on grass. It is a wonder to behold, and Charlotte is surprised to find she wants to share it—not with Jocelyn, but with *Sabine*.

Alas, there is no sign of her new friend.

Charlotte has been at the ball the better part of an hour, more than enough time to be abandoned by her aunt, and then Edith and Margaret in turn, enough time to search the chambers and accept that the widow Olivares isn't there. Charlotte has finally resigned herself to braving the rest of the ball alone when someone touches her shoulder, and she turns, hopes rising, only to find George Preston.

The young man who asked to dance with her three nights before.

He bows, blond hair flopping into his face, then straightens with a sheepish grin.

"Miss Hastings," he says, voice cracking a little around the words. "I was hoping I would find you. May I have the pleasure of your company, for this next dance?"

Her fingers close reflexively around the card at her wrist, the lines still blank. She is about to make some excuse when she spies her aunt watching from across the room, shrewd eyes narrowing with interest, and knows that she is trapped.

"Of course," she says, managing a tepid smile as he leads her out onto the floor.

Their hands lift and meet, waiting for the music.

In the books Charlotte has read, the men all smell of leather or wood or winter air. But not George Preston. He smells like soap and sweat, his hand clammy even through his glove and hers. She is grateful that the dance keeps them apart as often as it brings them together. But every time they do link arms, he rushes to tell her how glad he is they've met, how lovely she looks, how fine her dancing is, praise doled out in hurried snatches, and she knows she should feel flattered by the words, the breathless way he says them, but the truth is, they go right through her like a breeze.

The music quickens, and Charlotte does her best to keep up, trading partner for partner until she is returned to Mr. Preston's side again, and just as the song charges toward its breathless end, she sees her.

Sabine, growing like a wild bloom, her copper hair wound into a braided crown, her dress a mossy green. She catches Charlotte's gaze and lifts a glass, the crystal winking as it strikes the light. Charlotte nearly stumbles, but George is there to steady her.

The song ends, and the dancers all applaud, and Charlotte offers her partner a hurried curtsy and a thank-you, before fleeing to her friend.

"There you are," she says, still breathless from the dance. "I was beginning to think you might not come."

"I wouldn't miss it," says Sabine. And yet, she doesn't look happy to see Charlotte. Her expression is stern, almost severe, and Charlotte cannot help but ask if something's wrong.

In response, those hazel eyes land on her, heavy and unblinking.

"Indeed," she says. "I've discovered something troubling . . . about you."

Charlotte feels her stomach lurch, the floor tilt dangerously beneath her. "Oh?"

But instead of going on, Sabine takes her by the arm and leads her out of the main hall, and into an adjoining parlor. She pulls the doors shut in her wake, and the rest of the ball is swallowed behind gossamer and glass.

Sabine folds her arms, as if waiting for a confession, and Charlotte feels her heart trip inside her chest, the blood draining from her face, afraid that she has done something untoward, or somehow overstepped.

"Whatever it is—" she begins, when Sabine cuts in.

"You don't know how to dance."

The air comes rushing out of Charlotte's lungs like steam, and she finds herself laughing out of sheer relief. "Of course I do," she says.

And she *does*.

That is, she'd learned—with James and Jocelyn and Joss's cousin Anthony, the boys in coattails and the girls barefoot, twirling on the polished wooden floor of Clement Hall. The four of them turning and crossing and handing each other off like parcels, while their tutor plunked the keys.

But now in the parlor, Sabine shakes her head. "You are merely going through the motions."

"Isn't that the point?" she asks, to which her new friend clicks her tongue.

"Perhaps," she says, "if you're content to secure a husband with no taste," and Charlotte almost says she'd be happier still to secure no man at all. Catching herself at the last moment, she crosses her arms and says instead, "Well then, how am I supposed to dance?"

Sabine holds out a gloved hand. "I will show you."

The words make Charlotte shiver. It is not that she doesn't want to take the offered hand. It's that she does, and does not trust herself. She bites her lip and looks around. "We have no music."

"Of course we do," says Sabine, inclining her head. And sure enough, she can hear it, coming through the door, a little muted, its edges furred, but there. The musicians picking up again. A new song just beginning.

Charlotte brings her gloved hand to rest atop Sabine's, only their fingers hooked together.

"When you dance," she begins, "imagine there is a wind."

She moves, and so does Charlotte.

"A force that you must push against."

She turns, and Charlotte turns, too.

"The wind does not want you to reach your partner."

Sabine retreats a step, holding Charlotte at arm's length.

"But the wind is the only thing holding you back, and without it—"

Sabine draws Charlotte suddenly forward.

"—you would reach your prize."

Charlotte flushes, off-balance, but Sabine steadies her, and says, matter-of-factly, "You are too stiff. Relax. Close your eyes."

A nervous laugh. "I'll trip."

That teasing smile. "Don't you trust me?"

And funnily enough, she does.

Charlotte closes her eyes and, after a few awkward paces, she surrenders, lets herself by moved by feel alone. Guided by Sabine's hand on her arm, her back, her waist, Sabine's voice, saying *Good*, saying *Better*, saying *There you are*. In the absence of sight, her other senses brighten, her skin humming with the nearness of another body.

Not just any body, but Sabine.

Sabine, whose hand is cool and dry, who does not smell of soap and sweat, but fresh-turned soil, and melting sugar, night air, and ripe stone fruit.

"Now," says her teacher. "Let's try again."

Charlotte opens her eyes and they dance, the precise order of the steps abandoned, replaced by the rhythm of the music and Sabine's whim as she leads. They move together like a girl and her shadow. Linked one moment at the elbow, the next, the tips of their fingers. Bodies that briefly overlap, and tangle, only to break apart again, and every time they do, Charlotte feels as if a rope's drawn tight between them, the almost physical urge to catch Sabine's hand, to draw her close again.

"When did you learn?" she asks as they lock elbows.

"Another life," says Sabine as they tangle, turn.

"How many have you had?" asks Charlotte.

"More than most . . ."

The song ends to polite applause beyond the door. In the parlor, Charlotte stands inches from Sabine, their arms still raised, fingers laced in the space between them, and Charlotte cannot bring herself to pull away, so she waits for Sabine to lower her hand. To break the cord humming in the air. Instead, she holds the pose, the slightest smile tugging at her lips, as if it is a test.

Or worse, a game.

The thought is enough to make Charlotte drop her hand. She retreats a step, and smooths her skirts and says, "I suppose we should get back. I wouldn't want to keep you from any suitors."

She waits for Sabine to nod and turn to the doors. But she doesn't. Instead, her eyes burn into Charlotte's.

"Alas," she says, "none of them are suited to my tastes." And surely it is just a bit of clever repartee, but Charlotte's stubborn heart still quickens for a moment at the thought—the *hope*—of what could live between those words. "You, on the other hand," she adds, "will have your pick."

Charlotte's stomach twists at the memory of George Preston's clammy hand.

I do not want them, she thinks. *I do not want their gazes on me. I do not want their hands. I feel nothing when they touch me. I feel nothing when they speak. And when I dance with them, it does not feel like this.*

"Well," she says, clearing her throat. "I doubt I'll find someone who leads as well as you." She forces her body toward the door, but it betrays her halfway there. "Why are you helping me?" she asks, turning back. "Surely there are better ways to spend a ball."

Sabine's mouth twitches. "I have been at court long enough to know how dreadful it can be." She drifts toward Charlotte once again. "And how pleasant," she adds, "in the right company."

She reaches up and for a moment, Charlotte thinks she is about to stroke her cheek. She holds her breath, and hopes, but then the hand slides past, to fix an errant curl.

Beyond the parlor door, the music lifts. Another song begins.

"Well?" says Sabine. "Shall we rejoin the ball?"

Charlotte shakes her head. "Not yet. I think I need more practice."

Sabine smiles. "As you like," she says.

And so they dance again.

VIII

Back at Clement Hall, time always took Charlotte by surprise.

One day it seemed that spring had just arrived, and the next autumn was rushing in, the sun no longer warm enough to burn off the morning chill.

London is no different.

One moment April stretches as far as she can see, and the next, somehow, it is behind her. Days trip into weeks and the balls roll out in even stride, a steady cadence of affairs, each followed by a short reprieve. A chance to catch one's breath, and have a new dress fitted, to rest and ready to do it all again.

In the intervening days, the parlor fills with suitors—not for Charlotte, of course, as she has yet to be presented—but Edith and Margaret both entertain a string of them, bland smiles fixed firmly on their faces as they pour tea, and talk of weather, and country homes, and strolling in the park, as if that is enough to build a life on.

Charlotte, meanwhile, suffers through lessons on etiquette, posture, speech, and grace, punctuated by Aunt Amelia's nagging voice.

"Charlotte, sit up straighter."

"Charlotte, cross your ankles."

"Charlotte, stop frowning."

The sheer relentlessness of it makes her look forward to the corsets and the pins, the sore ribs and heels, the nights in other people's houses. And, of course, the company.

"Charlotte, pay attention."

"Charlotte, did you hear me?"

"Charlotte, are you *listening*?"

She is, but only because she doesn't have a choice. Still, as her father said, she is a quick study, and by the end of the month, Charlotte has become a decent mimic of the girl she's meant to be. But it is only ever that, a posture, a charade. Playing dress-up for a life she does not want.

It is worth it, though, for those evenings with Sabine.

Sabine, with her biting wit, her wicked humor, two things seemingly concealed from everyone save Charlotte. They pass whole nights strolling arm in arm, or with their heads tipped together in a corner, their voices tucked beneath the music.

How easily they've grown together. How right it feels.

How nice, to have a friend.

And that is what they are, Charlotte tells herself, *friends*. Even though, when she thinks back on those half a dozen balls, what she remembers are not the gorgeous venues, or the young men in their fine suits who now and then ask her to dance, but the widow Olivares and her many dresses. Each one tailored perfectly to fit, and each two shades darker than the sea of other girls. Honey when the rest are cream. Garnet when they are rose. Forest when they are mint.

Eventually, to her surprise, Charlotte's dance card begins to fill.

She doesn't think much of it—after all, this is not her year—and so she dances with a carousel of young men named Henry, Philip, George. She smiles and nods and lets them lead her through the motions, does her best to be polite without encouraging them more, never accepts the offer of a drink, or an invitation to take the evening air, or walk arm in arm around the room. And if she blushes when they dance, it is only because she knows Sabine is watching her. As if her hand's right there, at Charlotte's back, guiding her across the floor.

Now and then Sabine herself agrees to dance, and though her partners usually leave looking flustered, Charlotte still feels an odd pang at the sight of her in someone else's company. Once, Sabine even steps outside with a handsome young man, and Charlotte is shocked by the force of her own jealousy. Even though she is only gone for the length of the next dance, a well-lit turn around the garden, the sight of her walking away makes Charlotte want to cry.

But then Sabine is back, and slipping an arm through hers. "How tiresome men are," she says, and then, with that crooked little smile, "Did you miss me?"

And Charlotte doesn't want to lie, so she makes her voice teasingly bright. "Far too much. You mustn't abandon me again."

"Don't worry," says Sabine, and in that softer tone, the one that seems reserved for her, "I far prefer your company."

And just like that, the momentary grief is gone.

The words make Charlotte feel as if she's bathed in light.

It is not only Sabine's beauty, or her charm.

It is the fact that when she is there, the rest of the world seems to fade. What dazzled suddenly goes dim when compared to the weight of her presence, the force of her attention.

Sabine arrives and Charlotte's heart begins to race.

Her eyes leave trails of heat on Charlotte's skin. And when Sabine laughs, it's like the first hasty gulp of champagne, the fizz gone straight to Charlotte's head. Intoxicating.

She finds herself thinking of something her father said about her mother— that on the day they were first introduced, it felt like a reunion. As if they'd known each other all their lives, and forgotten, until the moment when they met again.

But that was love, and this is friendship.

Don't you see, it *must* be friendship.

She would be a fool to ruin things, as she did with Jocelyn.

So it is enough, she tells herself, just to share this Season with Sabine.

It is enough, just to spend these evenings in her company.

It is enough.

Until—

IX

She's standing at her window when the letter comes.

It's been raining for days, and the sudden break in the clouds, the arrival of late-afternoon sun, feels like a blessing. She closes her eyes and lets it warm her, turn the inside of her lids rose gold, and for a moment, she is lying on the green at Clement Hall with a volume of Blake, or Keats. Summer days were made for poetry. Daydreaming in verse.

"Charlotte."

She blinks, and turns to find her aunt standing in the doorway.

"Come away from the window," she tuts. "You hardly need the sun."

At this hour, the light is barely strong enough to take the chill off the glass, but Charlotte bites her tongue and withdraws into the sitting room. Her aunt studies her, taking in her hair, neatly bound, and her dress, a creamy satin, and, finding nothing else to chide, she gives a short, satisfied nod, and turns to go.

But halfway to the door, Aunt Amelia draws up short.

"Oh," she says, producing a letter. "I almost forgot. This came for you."

The wax on the seal is a rich, inky blue that Charlotte knows at once, since she is the one who gifted it to Jocelyn.

Her heart begins to race.

Jocelyn, who has not written since she first left Clement Hall.

It takes every ounce of Aunt Amelia's teaching to keep from lunging for the paper, to stand and smile politely as it's put into her hands, to wait until her aunt is gone to open it.

Charlotte doesn't realize her hands are shaking until she tries to break the seal without damaging the wax, and fails. She doesn't care. She sinks onto the stool, heart soaring at the sight of Jocelyn's curving script.

Dearest Charlotte—that is how it starts, and just like that, she is back in her mother's sun-drenched garden, laughter ringing with bare feet on the stones, Joss on one side of the trellis and Charlotte on the other. And they're both smiling.

And Charlotte realizes how badly she has missed her.

Dearest Charlotte—

She reads on, hungry for more of Joss's voice, her words.

I write to you with happy news.

Charlotte rushes on, but her eyes trip over the lines that follow.

Your brother James . . .

She stumbles.

I have said yes . . .

Pitches forward.

I hope you will be glad for us . . .

Falls.

How grand it is, when friends become family.

They are no longer at the trellis, no longer lying in the grass. Joss is on her feet, hands clasped and eyes cast down in shame.

Your future sister.

A tear hits the parchment, followed by a second, and a third, smudging the last three words.

Charlotte reads the letter a second time, and a third. Over and over, until the words sink in, coil through her, spread. Until the urge to scream gives way to something worse. Cold and hard and miserable.

She doesn't know how long she sits there, staring at the paper. Only that when she finally looks up, the sun is gone, and her aunt is calling her downstairs.

Darkness has settled over the room, and yet, when she rises, it moves with her.

A loathsome fog that follows Charlotte out of the house, and into the waiting carriage, and through the first hour of the ball, stealing all the color and the sound.

It finally lifts a measure at the sight of Sabine moving toward her through the room, but even still she cannot shake it, and it must be a physical thing, because Sabine takes one look at her and says, "Come, this will not do."

The next thing Charlotte knows, she is being ushered up the stairs.

"Where are we going?" she asks as Sabine draws her through the mazelike rooms, the sounds of the ball snuffed out by the intervening doors and walls, before they reach some far-flung corner of the house surely off-limits to the guests.

Sabine moves as if she knows the place, and when Charlotte says as much, she looks at her, bemused, and says, "I should hope so." A hidden door gives way onto a private study. "After all, this is *my* house."

The words are enough to dislodge Charlotte's grief.

"*Your* house?" she gasps, looking around.

Surely Aunt Amelia would have mentioned that night's ball being hosted by her friend? Then again, perhaps she *did*. The carriage ride was brief, and her aunt kept up a steady stream of words. Charlotte simply wasn't listening.

On the heels of understanding, horror. She wheels back toward the door. "I cannot keep you from your own ball!"

Sabine brushes the words away. "Just like a ball, once it's been set in motion, no one needs me there to keep it rolling. Besides," she adds, going to a cabinet on the wall, "some nights aren't made for dancing."

She emerges with a pair of crystal cups and a bottle of sherry. She pours, filling each nearly to the brim.

"Now tell me," she says, handing Charlotte one, "what has you in such a dour mood?"

Charlotte looks down at the ruby contents of her glass. She takes a sip, surprised by the sweetness, but as soon as she's swallowed, her eyes begin to prick with tears.

Dearest Charlotte.

How grand it is.

"A friend of mine is to be married." Her throat tightens around the words, and she feels like she might choke, so she downs the sherry, warmth rushing in its wake. "I am happy for her," she makes herself say. The right words, but they ring hollow. "I should be happy for her."

"But you are not."

Something splinters inside Charlotte. She tries to draw breath, and feels like she might shatter. "I thought—that is, I hoped—"

But she cannot bring herself to say it, because she knows how foolish it will sound. How silly she must look. A child, caught up in a child's crush. She should have known, the moment Joss pushed her away, the way her face went red with shame, the fact she never wrote. But despite it all, some stubborn part of Charlotte was holding on to hope, shielding it like a candle in a breeze.

Now she shakes her head forcefully, as if to banish all of it.

"Oh"—dashing a stray tear from her cheek—"don't let me bore you."

"You have not bored me yet," says Sabine, refilling her glass. "I doubt you ever will."

The warmth turns to heat in Charlotte's cheeks. The wretched fog begins to finally withdraw, retreat.

"Come," says Sabine, leading her to the center of the study, where two low velvet chairs sit before an inlaid table. Sabine lowers herself into one, and then, to Charlotte's surprise, kicks off her shoes. From a hidden drawer, she withdraws a pack of playing cards. Charlotte cannot help but laugh a little as she sits.

"What would my aunt say," she muses, "if she knew I was trading suitors and balls for sherry and cards?"

"The greatest gift," declares Sabine, in almost perfect mimicry of stiff Amelia, "is a well-rounded education." She gives the deck an expert shuffle. "Now," she says in her own voice, "what shall we play? Cribbage, euchre, or whist?"

They decide on whist, and soon Charlotte has abandoned her own shoes, stockinged feet tucked up beneath her in the chair, the ball safely locked behind the intervening doors. They pass the first hand in silence, but as Sabine deals the second, Charlotte can feel her thoughts begin to turn, the darkness rolling in.

Across the table, Sabine reclines, cradling her glass in one hand and her cards in the other. She looks perfectly at home. Which, of course, she is.

"I envy you." The words slip out, and then Charlotte cannot stop them. "I know it came at such a cost, but still, I envy you. Your freedom. The way you get to live."

Sabine glances up, over the tops of her cards. "What would you do with it, I wonder?" She sets her hand aside and leans forward in her chair. "Your life. If it were yours, to do with as you please?"

Charlotte's gaze drops to her hand.

The room flickers, and for an instant she is back at Clement Hall.

She is crouching to plant a new rose in the garden, bare knees sinking into the soil.

She is at the breakfast table in the dining room, a book in one hand and a toast point in the other.

She is twirling barefoot across the parquet floor of the salon.

The scenes flash by, brief as cards being shuffled, but in them all, she's not alone. A second figure flickers at the edges of her sight. It kneels beside her in the garden. It sits across the table. It spins her in its arms.

And then the scenes are gone, blacked out by her brother's face, her journal in his hand.

Charlotte shakes her head. "But that's just it," she says, her vision blurring. "My life is not my own. It never will be. I already know how it will go. In a matter of weeks, I will return home and watch my best friend wed my brother, and next year I will be forced back here, paraded about until some stranger deigns to claim me for a wife." She knows she's being maudlin, but she can't help it.

Sabine takes up her hand again. "You don't sound keen to make a match."

"I don't have a choice," says Charlotte, frustration welling up. "So why pretend? The exercise has no point, except to hurt."

Sabine shrugs and says, "Everyone has choices. They only have to make them."

"You make it sound so simple."

"Simple? No." Sabine discards one card and draws another. "But you cannot *have* what you want until you *know* what you want. And once you do know," she adds, "it's only a matter of what you're willing to do to get it."

"Yes, well," snaps Charlotte, "we are not all lucky enough to be widowed." Her hand flies to her mouth. "I'm so sorry," she says, wishing she could take it back. Fresh tears well behind her eyes, and she shakes her head, cheeks burning hot. "What a horrid thing to say."

But Sabine doesn't seem wounded. If anything, she looks *amused*.

"The night we met," she says, resting the cards on top of her still-full glass of sherry, "do you know what drew me to you on the stairs? What has drawn me to you, every night thereafter?"

Charlotte shakes her head. In truth, she does not know. Has never known. "My quaint pastoral charm?" she quips, even as a tear escapes.

Sabine's mouth twitches. "It's the way you cannot hide your feelings. If they do not spill out of your mouth, they shimmer on your skin. They fill the air around you, so loud they almost shout."

Charlotte colors. "I have always been this way." She reaches up to wipe away the tear. "I cannot help it."

"And you shouldn't have to," says Sabine, leans across to stop her hand so the tear continues down her cheek. "The world will try to make you small. It will tell you to be modest, and meek. But the world is wrong. You should get to feel and love and live as boldly as you want."

Charlotte grits her teeth. "*Should* is not *can*. And the world makes the rules, not me."

"Does it?" Sabine's hand drops back to her cards. "Oh look," she says, laying them face up on the table, "it seems I've won again."

Charlotte looks from her hand to Sabine's. There are five aces between them. "How . . ."

"Isn't it obvious?" says Sabine, leaning back in her chair. "I cheated."

A twitch of her fingers, and another ace appears in her gloved hand. She flicks it onto the stack. "The wonderful thing about luck," she says, "is you can make your own." Her gaze drifts toward the study door. "Alas, it seems the ball is winding down."

Charlotte startles. "Of course." She rises to her feet, too fast, the sherry going to her head, forcing her to grip the chair for balance as she says, "I've kept you far too long."

"Charlotte—"

She fumbles for her shoes, gets them on, and hurries toward the hidden door.

"Charlotte, wait."

She never saw Sabine stand up, let alone cross the narrow room, but as Charlotte's hand reaches the handle of the door, Sabine's slides past her, comes to rest against the wood.

It is not the closest they have ever been—there were moments when Sabine was teaching her to dance, their bodies tangled briefly—but Charlotte startles at the nearness, the sliver of space between their bodies, Sabine's like a shadow, close but not yet touching hers.

And perhaps it's the sherry, or the talk of freedom, of chance, that is making her so hot, or perhaps it is knowing how easy it would be to close the narrow gap, as Charlotte had done in the garden, certain if she did, that *Sabine* would not pull back in shame.

And yet, she does not turn, is still facing the door when Sabine dips her head, lips brushing Charlotte's ear. "Your dress," she murmurs.

It is a finicky gown, with a dozen hook and eyes running in a column down the back, and the top one, it seems, has come undone. And before Charlotte can reach to fix it, Sabine is drawing off her gloves. "It's a lie, you know, that you only get one story." Charlotte's breath catches as Sabine's fingers—cool and steady—graze the bare skin between her shoulders. It takes only a moment to hook the clasp, but Sabine doesn't pull away.

Her touch lingers, then begins to drift down the line of closures, cold fingers burning the satin in their wake. Charlotte bites her lip as Sabine's hand slides around her waist, splays between her hips.

There is nothing chaste about that touch, their bodies flush against the wood. Charlotte tips her forehead against the door, breathes into the wood as Sabine's hand ventures lower, her mouth coming to rest at Charlotte's temple. She can feel the woman smiling against her skin.

Then, that voice, sliding like fingers through her hair.

"When you discover what you want, come tell me."

And then her hand is gone, her weight is gone, Sabine is gone, slipping out past Charlotte, her dress vanishing through the door and down the stairs.

X

A girl bends at the waist as she pours tea.

Another stands with a box balanced on her head.

A third perches primly on an ottoman, a placid smile on her face.

Charlotte turns page after page, each with its own picture of propriety.

Around her, the sitting room is humming. Nearly a week ago, Margaret made a match with a fine gentleman named Reginald, and Edith expects her own proposal any day now. The Season is racing toward its end, and the whole house has taken on a nervous energy, a held-breath kind of hope, but Charlotte feels herself weighted down by dread. She dreads the imminent parting with Sabine, dreads returning home to James and Jocelyn, and a life that no longer fits.

She wishes she could curl up on the sofa, but Aunt Amelia caught her once, in those first days, and now Charlotte doesn't dare. Instead, she sits stiffly on the sofa's edge and pretends to read. As if she hasn't had enough of etiquette.

She turns the page and sees a pair of women strolling arm in arm.

Like show ponies prancing . . . anyone you'd like to ride?

Charlotte smiles at the memory.

Another page, and here she finds a man and woman dancing, their arms locked at rigid angles as they turn.

You are merely going through the motions.

And here they are, the steps laid out on paper with little printed feet. But as she stares, the drawing twists, the stiffness gives way to looser limbs.

Imagine there is a wind . . .

She turns the page again, and again, twisting each image in her mind until the brittle lines give way to memories. It is not hard. She finds her thoughts are always going to Sabine. Her eyes. Her hair. Her mouth. Her hands.

She turns the page, half expecting to see a picture of two women playing cards, shoes kicked off and sherry glasses at their elbows.

Charlotte shifts at the thought of that last ball. Sabine's body humming next to hers.

She presses her knees together, an ache pooling like heat.

When you discover what you want . . .

But Charlotte knows.

She lies awake and burns with it.

She twists and turns with it.

Last night, when she could not sleep, her hand found its way between her legs, and she let herself pretend it was Sabine's. Could almost hear the breath against her neck, the voice in her ear, whispering her name as if it were a secret, and—

"Aren't you a picture?"

Her aunt comes bustling in, and Charlotte sits up even straighter, trying to smother the flush that's crept across her face.

"I must say," continues Amelia, tugging off her gloves, "I had my doubts, but you *have* come a long way these past few weeks."

And that much is true. Charlotte no longer protests at the cinching of the corsets, or the stiffness of the shoes, or the hundred pins the maid stabs in her hair each night to tame it. But she has submitted to these discomforts knowing they are temporary discomforts, and she will fling them off again the moment she is home.

"Thank you, Aunt," she says, conjuring the same tepid smile as the faces in her book. "I've had good teachers."

Amelia absorbs the compliment like light, and drifts toward a round table, laden with gifts for Margaret and Edith. She surveys the offerings: a small bouquet of roses, a handful of cards, a box of candied fruit, a dish of chocolates.

"Next Season, I've no doubt, the offerings will be for you."

Charlotte ducks her head to hide the grimace as her aunt plucks a chocolate from a dish (she has a sweet tooth, though she'll deny it, seems to think that if the sweet is small enough to swallow in one bite, it does not count).

Just then, the bell rings.

"Finally," sighs Aunt Amelia, as the house surges into motion.

Edith arrives, and for once the roses on her cheeks look more from stress than pinching. And yet, by the time she arranges herself on the divan and snatches up a bit of needlework, every curl is in its place, her hands steady and her face as smooth as milk.

Charlotte closes her book and stands, eager to absent herself for the proposal, is halfway to the door when the butler arrives with the news that the caller is for *her*.

Edith's expression turns to ice, and Aunt Amelia's warms with something like delight, and Charlotte simply laughs, knowing there must be some mistake.

But then the man walks in, and her amusement dies.

It's George Preston.

George, with whom she's danced half a dozen times, and spoken to far less.

George, who was a pleasant enough partner, a way to pass the time.

George, who stands in the good sitting room with a bundle of flowers in one clammy hand and his hat in the other, a nervous smile tugging at his mouth.

As if he isn't there to ruin everything.

"Miss Hastings," he begins, and she wonders if he even knows her proper name until he clears his throat and croaks out, "Charlotte," and it sounds wrong, harsh, nothing like Sabine's soft purr, and then to her horror he begins to talk about how deep his feelings run, how surely she cannot be surprised, given that he's been quite bold in his affection.

Charlotte feels herself inch backward, until the sofa's arm abruptly stops her. She opens her mouth to speak, but cannot seem to find the air. George has stolen it all. The room and everyone in it is so far away, their voices little more than echoes, and George is still going on and on about how certain he is that she will make a good wife, a good mother, that they will have a happy life.

And all Charlotte can think is that, if she had known, she never would have danced with him. If she had known, she would have fled from that first ball. This wasn't supposed to happen, she isn't even *here*. She was just playing dress-up, after all.

She is not a lily or a rose. Not a flower ready and waiting to be picked.

She is still growing wild at the edges of her family garden. She is not ready. She will never be ready. This isn't what she *wants*.

George has finally stopped speaking, and everyone is looking at her now, as if waiting for an answer, and Charlotte finally drags in a great, heaving breath.

"If you'll excuse me," she says, too loud, the words crashing through the fog, "I just need a moment's air."

She hurries past them, toward the door, and George is trying to follow, and she is saying, "No, no, please stay, I'll be right back," and her aunt is calling after her, but it's too late, she is already escaping from the parlor and the hall and the house on Merry Way.

She sees a hansom cab parked along the road, and she climbs in, asks the driver to take her to the widow Olivares.

Ten agonizing minutes later, she arrives.

Ten minutes to practice what she wants to say, and yet, as she steps out onto the curb, she feels her courage falter. She stands before a house that last night looked so inviting—the doors open and the windows lit, a row of tiny lanterns burning like fairy lights along the walk—but now looks dark, forbidding even.

But the image of George, standing in the parlor, spurs her up the path, and to the door. She knocks, but no one answers. Panic winds like weeds around her ribs.

She knocks again.

"Miss?" asks the driver from the road. "Shall I wait?"

Charlotte hesitates, uncertain, knows only that she cannot bear the thought of turning back, not now, so she presses all the pocket change she has into the driver's hand and sends him on his way, begs for his discretion, and whether it is the shillings, or the panic in her eyes, he bobs his head, and flicks the reins and goes.

Charlotte returns to the door, and knocks again, and this time when there is no answer she tries the handle, and finds the door unlocked. Before doubt can overwhelm again, she plunges in. She pulls the door shut behind her, and turns, expecting to cross paths with a butler or maid, some kind of staff. The house was full of help the night before.

But today, there is no one.

The house sprawls around her, hollow, vacant.

"Sabine?" she calls out, softly first, and then in a voice that echoes off of marble, tremors over wood.

"Sabine!"

The whole house feels so empty, so still, that a sudden terror grips her, that Sabine has up and left, abandoned London and her, or worse, that she was never there, some phantom haunting her these past few months, a figment of—

"Charlotte."

The word wafts through the air like smoke, and there she is.

Sabine stands at the top of the stairs, dressed in nothing but a black silk robe, parting to reveal a pale dressing gown. Her hair, no longer up in an intricate braid or bun, hangs loose, burning trails down her front, and the sight of her is striking enough that for a moment, Charlotte forgets.

She forgets the horror of the last hour, the forces that sent her running from her aunt's salon, and thinks only of her words that first night on the stairs.

How could anyone not look at you?

Sabine drifts toward her down the stairs, her bare feet padding over marble. She looks drawn, as if she's been in bed for days, fighting some long sickness—but that's not possible. Charlotte saw her just the night before.

"Are you ill?"

A slow blink. "Only resting," she says, her voice fogged with sleep, even though it's the middle of the afternoon. Sabine reaches the bottom of the stairs and frowns. "What's wrong?"

And just like that, it all comes rushing back.

In one violent exhale, she remembers.

"*Everything.*" The word tears from Charlotte like a sob. "I'm sorry," she says, shaking her head. "I know it was thoughtless to come unannounced—I shouldn't have—but George called on me today. He asked for my hand. My hand!" Her limbs begin to tremble, and so she paces as she talks. "And what he said beyond that, I don't know. From the moment he opened his mouth, all I could hear was my own heart, hammering to get out."

"So you came here. To me." Sabine sounds bemused, as if it's such a strange idea. As if she has not been the sole source of Charlotte's comfort these past two months.

"I know it's wrong to simply show up. But I did not know what else to do, or where to go—"

Sabine holds out a hand to halt her nervous movement, and it stops her, as sudden as a cage door swinging shut. And now there is nowhere else to look except Sabine. Her gaze is flat as glass, her expression unreadable. "Would you marry him?"

Charlotte recoils at the question. "I did not attend those balls for *him*. I did not dance each night hoping *he* was watching. I did not lie awake and hunger for *his* company. I—oh, do not look at me like that."

Sabine inclines her head. "Like what?"

"Like I'm some foolish child. A silly girl who's spent the entire Season clinging to your skirts." For the first time, she is brave enough to find Sabine's burning gaze, and hold it. "You told me to come find you, when I knew what I wanted. Well, I do."

She swallows. How hard it is to say the words, even when they're true. How much it feels like standing on a precipice, like the smallest wind will either push her back, onto solid ground, or forward, into an abyss.

"I want you."

Sabine's cool hand settles on her cheek, and she holds her breath, waiting to see which direction she will fall. "Do you?" she asks, and there is a faint barb to the question, a challenge in her voice that fills Charlotte with fury.

"Yes!" she snaps, her voice ringing through the empty house. "I have wanted you since the night we met, and every moment since. I want the life you speak of, that belongs to no one else. I want to feel and love and live as boldly as I please. I want to be like you." She closes the gap between them, lifts her hands to cup Sabine's face, is shocked again by the coldness of her skin, but she doesn't pull away. "But most of all, I want to be *with* you."

Sabine's expression clouds, as if the strange light in her eyes is guttering. "I do not know if you are ready."

Charlotte feels her balance falter. But then, a strange thing happens. Anger comes rushing up to steady her. "How dare you—I am *here*! I have just fled my own proposal to lay my heart bare at your feet."

"There are things you do not know."

Charlotte glares defiantly. "I know there is nothing you could tell me that would make me love you less, nothing that would make me want to leave." She swallows. "Nothing, save that *you* do not feel the same. That you do not want me, too. Is that it?"

Sabine's brow furrows. "No."

"Say it, then," demands Charlotte.

Sabine's mouth twitches. She lifts her cool hands and rests them over Charlotte's on her face. "I want you," she says, the light rekindling behind her hazel eyes. "I have wanted you in ballrooms and in parlors, in crowds and behind closed doors. I have wanted you since before we ever met."

Charlotte feels like a window flung open. Fresh air rushing in.

And then Sabine turns away, toward the stairs, but she is drawing Charlotte with her. They have wandered through a dozen houses arm in arm, but every time the halls were crowded with bodies, with music, with life. Now as Sabine leads Charlotte up the stairs, there are no onlookers, no pretenses. They are together. And they are alone. No gloves, just their laced fingers, Sabine's cold, and hers hot. Her heart hammering inside her chest with fear and hope and want and wonder, and maybe Sabine was right, and her feelings are so loud that they spill out of her, because she looks back and smiles as if she can hear every single one.

Sabine leads Charlotte to a chamber with the curtains drawn.

The room is plunged into such a heavy darkness that even with the light spilling in from the hall, Charlotte can barely make out the outline of the furniture, the bed. She crosses to the window, reaching for the curtain's edge to draw it back, but Sabine is there to catch her wrist.

She twists round, breath catching at the sudden closeness, Sabine's body tangling with hers, as it did the night before, only this time, they are face-to-face, her mouth inches from Sabine's, the air between them humming with want, and at last, Charlotte closes the distance and kisses her. Their lips brush, and this is the part where Jocelyn pulled away.

But Sabine doesn't.

Instead, she answers, deepening the kiss, pressing Charlotte back against the curtained glass. Her lips part, teeth skimming Charlotte's bottom lip. A pricking pain.

She flinches, and draws back, touching her lip. Even in the dark, she can see the stain against her fingertips before Sabine brings them to her mouth and swipes her tongue over the blood. And smiles. Not the secret smile, the ghostly tugging of her lips. She smiles showing teeth, two of them sharper and longer than the rest.

Something flashes through Charlotte then, something that is and isn't panic. Something that is and isn't fear.

There are things you do not know.

Everyone has choices.

They only have to make them.

You make it sound so simple.

Simple? No.

Sabine doesn't let go of Charlotte's hand. Instead, she turns it, exposing the soft inside of her wrist, the pulse visible beneath her skin.

"Do you trust me?"

How easy it is, to see danger once it's passed. But she is young, and filled with dread and want, both warring in her chest. And she has come this far. "Yes."

"You're afraid," says Sabine, bringing her hand closer to her face.

"Yes," says Charlotte. Then, "But not of you."

Sabine's smile widens, right before her teeth sink into Charlotte's wrist.

She gasps, stiffens at the brightness of the pain, the way it lances through her flesh, followed by the sudden animal urge to tear free, to pull away. But to her surprise, she doesn't. This moment, she knows, is a kind of test. The pain spreads up her arm, leaves her feeling dizzy, faint.

Years later, she will ask Sabine what would have happened, if in that moment she had fought, or screamed, or fled, and her love will only stroke her cheek and say, "Why dwell on things that did not happen?" and Charlotte will know, then, with grim certainty, that one way or another, she'd have never left that room alive.

Sabine's teeth slide free, a strange ache pooling in their wake, and when she looks up, her eyes are burning brighter than they ever have, candles behind painted glass. How could Charlotte have ever thought that they were *human*?

"What are you?" she asks at last, and Sabine's mouth twitches in that old familiar way.

"What am I?" she muses, almost to herself. "A widow."

She tugs Charlotte forward, turns her in her arms as if they're dancing. "A feral rose."

She lets go suddenly, and Charlotte stumbles, catches herself against the bedpost. But in the next breath, Sabine is there again, cool hand cupping her chin. "I am free." Those lantern eyes, the only thing she can make out in the dark. "Free from pain. Free from rules. Free from death. Free to live as I want.

Free to take what I want. Free to be who I want. With whomever I want." Her fingers slide through Charlotte's hair, come to rest at the nape of her neck. "Is that what *you* want, Charlotte?"

The word leaves her, as easy as air. "Yes."

It is all she wants. All she has ever wanted.

Sabine's eyes flick to Charlotte's injured wrist. "There is a cost," she says, but when Charlotte looks down, she finds the wound closed, the bite marks fading, the pain already gone.

Her skin is still hungry. Her heart is still racing.

"I understand," she says, even though she doesn't, *can't*. "I want more. I want this. I want you."

Sabine draws her close, lips brushing Charlotte's as she says, "Remember that."

And then Charlotte is being pressed back, and down, into the bed, and Sabine is on top of her, her hand where Charlotte's was the night before, making its way beneath her dress, and up her thigh, and then at last, between her legs. Her thumb grazes the darkness there, and Charlotte gasps, her entire body bright with longing.

She grips Sabine, not to push her back, only to drag her closer, digging her fingers into the woman's arms, clutching at her as the heat builds between her legs. She arches in pleasure, clenching around Sabine's wrist, and every time her mouth grazes Charlotte's skin—laying kisses on her shoulder, her collar, her breast—she braces for a bite that doesn't come. Sabine only smiles, her fingers sliding deeper, and when Charlotte finds the breath to speak, the word that rises to her lips is *please*.

And perhaps this is all it is, she thinks. This is how to take what you want, to live as you want, this is how to be free. And then, right as the heat crests, Sabine's mouth finds the curve of Charlotte's neck, her lips part, her teeth grazing skin.

And she bites down.

Charlotte shudders, the pleasure rolling through her first, and for an instant, she has two heartbeats, one at her throat, and one between her legs. But then the latter fades, and in its wake, she feels the pain, that heavy ache spreading through her limbs, behind her ribs, around her heart.

And it *hurts*.

Worse than the teeth biting into her wrist, because this time, Sabine doesn't stop. If anything, her teeth sink deeper, and Charlotte whimpers, the pain no longer hidden in the shadow of the pleasure. Fear steals through her, then, sudden, and animal, and sharp, but even if she wanted to fight back, it is too late. Her heart is kicking but her limbs are leaden, and Sabine is made of stone, and the fear is already fading with the edges of her sight.

And her heart, her heart, which has gotten her into trouble all her life, her heart, which feels too much, and beats too hard, now falters. It trips, and stumbles, weakly, to a stop. And Charlotte feels like she is falling—no not falling, *sinking*. Down through the bed, into someplace quiet, empty, dark, like the stillness at the very edge of sleep.

And too late, she understands that it is death.

That she is dying.

And she doesn't even feel betrayed.

This is what she asked for, isn't it?

After all, death is another kind of freedom.

At least, she thinks, she's not alone.

Sabine is with her, in the dark.

And then, distantly, she feels the weight of something against her mouth, and hears Sabine's voice, so far away and just beside her ear, telling her to drink. Charlotte is too tired to move her lips, and yet, somehow she does, and then the liquid hits her lips, and it is something earthy, rotten, sweet. It slides across her tongue, and down her throat, and branches there, tendrils spreading through her chest, coiling around her heart, which now begins to beat again.

A single drum, then two, then three.

The pulse, so loud in Charlotte's chest, echoing like footsteps through an empty hall.

Alive, alive, alive, it says.

Before the rhythm fades, and the darkness folds over her again.

Erasing everything.

XI

Charlotte wakes the way the sun comes up: not all at once, but by degrees.

The world resolves around her, line by line and shape by shape, and at first she thinks the curtains must have been thrown back—but when she looks, she finds them drawn, the room still dark. And yet, she can see the stitching on the bedspread, the pattern on the papered walls.

A change, not in the room, but in her sight.

Then she remembers. The hand pressing her down into the bed, the teeth against her throat. She gasps and sits upright, twists round in search of Sabine, but she's not there, and suddenly the dark, weak as it is, and the stillness of the room strike her as ominous, unsettling.

Charlotte scrambles to her feet, and goes to the window, throws the curtains back—

And recoils.

It's dusk now, the sky above streaked pink, the sun vanishing behind the line of roofs, and yet, the light sends pain lancing through her head, along with a sudden wave of dizziness. She forces the curtains shut again, backs away until she meets the bed, her mind racing, and her heart—

Her heart.

It should be rioting against her ribs. Instead, it sits silently inside her, the stillness unnatural, and frightening. Because hearts beat. That's what they do. Sometimes soft and steady, sometimes loud as fists against a door. So long as they're alive, they beat.

A word forces up through her panicked thoughts, like a lighthouse in a storm.

Sabine.

She will know what's happening. She will explain.

Charlotte goes to the bedroom door and draws it slowly open, braced for more assaulting light. But the hall beyond is mercifully in shadow.

"Sabine?" she calls out as she searches the top floor.

"Sabine?" her voice echoes on the stairs.

But even as she looks, Charlotte *knows* she isn't there. Somehow, she can *feel* the absence in the house, as if her senses now extend beyond the borders of her body, her mind a wave, rolling outward, washing through each room, crashing up against wall, and furniture, and floor. And finding no one.

And yet, she cannot bear the thought of sitting idle, waiting to be found, so she searches, room by room, has just stepped into that secret study where they played cards, when she hears the front door open, the sound as loud as bookshelves falling, despite the many walls between.

Charlotte rushes to the foyer as Sabine comes striding in, sets a parasol aside, and if her heart were working, it would stop again, as her new senses take in the woman in the doorway, her hair now bright enough to burn the air, her eyes no longer candlelit but hazel flames.

Sabine looks up and smiles, and Charlotte feels a blanketing relief—there is no other word for it—the sudden certainty that she will be okay.

Until Sabine steps aside, and a second shape comes through the door.

George Preston.

Her stomach drops like a stone, but he is all relief.

"Oh, thank God," he says, rushing toward her. "We have been looking everywhere. If Mrs. Olivares hadn't found me—" Charlotte looks past him to Sabine, betrayal and confusion wicking through her. *Why?* she wants to ask, but George is already reaching out. "She told me to come at once. Said you were not well." He takes her hands and gasps. "My darling Charlotte, you're so cold."

When did she become his *darling Charlotte,* instead of just Miss Hastings?

Sabine nudges the front door closed, her face a mask of placid calm, while George's worry hangs in the air around him like a bad cologne—Charlotte swears that she can *smell* it—and when he reaches up to cup her face, she can hear the rushing of *his* pulse through the veins at his wrists, and the sound makes her dizzy. Her stomach twists, her mouth goes dry, begins to ache, and too late, she makes sense of what she's feeling.

Hunger.

Stranger, and stronger, than she's ever felt.

Sabine's smiles twitches in that private catlike way, and horror washes over Charlotte as she understands why he has been led here.

"No," she hisses, pushing George away, and even though he's taller, broader, he stumbles beneath her strength. He might have even fallen, if Sabine weren't there to steady him.

He looks between the two of them, confused, but Sabine simply shrugs and says, "I'll make it easy."

Charlotte doesn't see the barber's blade until the edge slides like a kiss along his collar. She gasps as George reels, his hand going to his throat, blood welling, ruby red, against his fingers.

The wound is deep. Not deep enough to kill, but he stumbles, pulls his hand away and seems surprised to find it slick with red. "What the devil . . ."

"Go on," says Sabine, sounding impatient now.

But Charlotte shakes her head. "Not him."

"Who better?" She wags the blade side to side. "They will think you have eloped."

George does not seem to hear them. He sways, frowns, blood dripping down his shirt front, flecking the marble floor, and Charlotte can smell it, she can *taste* it, the way she tasted sugar on the air when she was young, and snuck into the kitchen while the cook was making cakes. Like sugar, and not like sugar at all, thinks Charlotte as she clamps her hands over her mouth. She locks her jaw, only to feel two of her teeth prick her bottom lip. The taste of her own blood is nothing to the smell of his, and yet, she might have been able to fight the hunger off, if George hadn't staggered toward her, then.

If he hadn't come so close.

If he hadn't put his bloody hands on her arms, his bloody cheek by her face.

But he does. And then, she is pulling him against her, and her mouth is at his throat, and his blood is on her lips, and the foyer disappears, the whole world disappears, as Charlotte drinks.

She drinks, and that horrible stillness gives way as her own heart begins to beat again, George's pulse quickening inside her chest.

She drinks, and feels like she is falling, dropping, not into the dark this time, but into light. It blooms behind her eyes, unspools through every vein, a sun-glow warmth.

Charlotte tries to stop. She truly does.

When she feels him struggle. When he fights with all his strength. And when that strength goes out of him. When the pounding of the pulse becomes a ragged thing, weak, and fluttering. When the liquid gold slows inside her throat.

But by the time the world flickers back, and brings her with it, Charlotte finds she's on her knees on the marble foyer floor, George Preston laid out beneath her, and he isn't moving. The heartbeat begins to slow inside her chest, and she looks up to find Sabine looming overhead.

"There," she says. "Was that so hard?"

As if they had not just killed a man. And he *is* dead, that much she knows. His blue eyes are open, empty, the razor's cut glaring at his throat, but as she stares, the place where she bit down, bit *in*, vanishes without a trace. Her part in the violence brushed away, as if she was never even there. And for an instant, she thinks—hopes—he will come gasping back to life, as she did.

But then the instant passes, and George Preston is still dead. And until that moment, Charlotte didn't know if she believed in souls, but now she has no doubt—the body is a different thing, when life has fled. At once too heavy, and too light. A vessel *she* has emptied.

A horrible sound bubbles up inside her, half-laugh, half-sob, horror, guilt, and grief, not just for George, but for herself—what she has done. She doesn't realize she is crying until the first drops land on her hands. And stain them red. She reaches up, touches her cheek, and it comes away wet, not with tears, but *blood*. And the worst part is, she has to fight the urge to lick her fingers. Because the hunger is still there. She digs her nails into her skirts, into her skin, and feels—nothing.

Sabine kneels down beside her, and Charlotte opens her mouth to ask *What have you done to me?* or *What have I done?* But the question that comes out is only, "What am I?"

Sabine leans in, kisses her cheek, and says, "You are free."

Before Charlotte can say that this does not feel like freedom, Sabine draws her to her feet, and tells her to go upstairs and find another dress.

And it is absurd, of course, to worry about such a thing right now, but it is something to focus on, besides George Preston's body, and the blood, and the way her heart has stopped again, that horrid stillness returning in its wake, and so she goes. She turns her back on the gruesome scene and hurries up the stairs, and turns through Sabine's closet in search of something that will fit, focuses on the silk, the chiffon, tries not to hear the sound of a weight being dragged across a marble floor, tries not to hear the way it topples down the cellar stairs.

The dress she picks is winter green.

Charlotte sheds her own, and draws this new one on, wrestling with the clasps. When Sabine arrives, she is struggling to reach the last few buttons, while avoiding the mirror, frightened of what she'll see in the reflection.

"How do you feel?" asks Sabine.

Such a simple question, such a complicated answer. Horrified, of course. Fascinated, too. And confused. But the loudest one of all: "Guilty."

"Don't worry," she says. "It will fade."

The words are clearly meant to comfort, but the idea, that she could do a thing like that and feel nothing at all, is somehow worse. So instead, she tries to focus on Sabine.

Her hands, as they skim Charlotte's back, steady fingers doing up the last buttons of the dress. Her lips, as they kiss Charlotte's shoulder. Her arms, as they slide around Charlotte's waist. She lets herself lean back into the steadiness of the embrace, and for a moment, she feels safe.

At last, she braves the mirror, if only to meet the other woman's gaze. On the way, her eyes glance off her own face—how can she look so normal, so unchanged?—before escaping to Sabine.

"What do we do now?"

"Now," says the woman in the glass, "we leave."

It's dark by the time they step outside.

The sun is gone, the dizziness gone with it. In its wake, Charlotte feels alert, alive—and hungry, though she tries to force that last one from her thoughts, along with the knowledge that she is not simply leaving behind a handful of dresses, or a house, but an entire life.

She cannot wrap her mind around it, and so she doesn't try. Instead, she lets Sabine lead her to the waiting carriage.

They have no trunks, no change of clothes, her possessions back in the house on Merry Way, Sabine's left behind as well.

"Better," she says, "to travel light."

And yet, as Charlotte climbs into the carriage, she cannot help glancing back at the grand and empty house. "Won't you miss it?"

Sabine settles beside her on the velvet bench. "I miss the last cherries of the season. I miss chocolate melting on my tongue. I miss the way sun used to feel against my skin in spring. I don't miss walls and doors. Besides," she says, sliding her arm through Charlotte's, "others stay put, and wither in their boxes. We draw up our roots, and find new ground in which to grow."

"How many times have you done this?" asks Charlotte. "How many lives have you lived?"

"Enough, and not enough," she answers as the driver snaps his reins.

The carriage pulls away onto the road, and Charlotte looks back—or starts to—but Sabine catches her cheek, the gesture gentle yet firm, a silent command to let the past stay where it is, firmly in their wake.

XII

Charlotte was nine when she found the rabbit dead.

By the time she came across the poor creature, it was little more than fluff, and fur, and blood. A patch of horror on the lawn.

The sight of the rabbit lying there, so still, its body curled in against the outside world, was enough to break young Charlotte's heart. Which wasn't hard—it had always been a fragile thing. Just like the little bunny, its ruined body almost weightless as she took it home.

Somewhere along the way she began to cry, and could not seem to stop. She stood in her mother's workshop door and stroked the rabbit's cooling ear, unsure what to do to make things right.

In the end, they'd dug a little hole between the roses and buried the rabbit there, deep enough that nothing would dig it up. And to be sure, her mother made a sculpture of the rabbit, to set on top, and Charlotte would stop and crouch down to stroke its little ear every time she passed.

For weeks, James claimed that they were having rabbit stew for dinner, even when they weren't, and Charlotte would feel that sadness welling up again.

As if all her feelings lived right beneath the surface.

Just waiting to spill out.

Charlotte thinks about that rabbit now, as the carriage trundles on, wheels over cobblestones, then earth. She is wide awake despite the hour, her whole body humming strangely, every inch of her alert. Perhaps if she had a book— but she does not, and so her mind turns on itself, replaying those hours between the proposal and the carriage, the pieces of her life toppling one into the next.

Sabine stares out the window, a flatness to her gaze that says she's looking past the world, not at it. She seems so calm, composed, while Charlotte feels like she is spinning, her mind so full of questions.

What is she now? Is there a word? What does it mean to live and die and live again, as the monster did in *Frankenstein*? Was it death she felt back in Sabine's bed, or something else? A vital spark, extinguished, then rekindled, and if so, is it the same animating force, or a new one? And who made Sabine before Sabine made her? And why does the sunlight leave her dizzy? And how can she live and move and think without a heart beating in her chest? And why does she crave blood?

There was a moment, with George Preston, when the pulse had failed in him—but not in her—when Charlotte felt like she was holding his life as well as his heart.

And then the moment died, and so did he.

And she cannot help but wonder, what sets the two of them apart? What keeps her own life going while his stopped? Was it the blood? The heart? The soul?

She hasn't found the voice to ask these thoughts aloud, but apparently she needn't bother—Sabine sighs and blinks, returning to herself, and says, "Your mind is very loud."

Charlotte startles, amazed that Sabine can hear—or feel—what she is thinking but then, is it so strange? After all, *she* could feel George's panic, his worry, his fear, and wasn't it Sabine who said she could not keep her feelings to herself?

"What do we take from them?" she asks. "Is it only blood, or something more?"

"Does it matter?"

But it does. Of course it does. A soul is an entire thing. All or nothing, there or not. But blood. Blood exists in quantity and by degrees. "Well, yes," she says, her spirits lifting at the thought. "If it's only blood, then they do not need to die."

To her surprise, Sabine only shrugs.

"Perhaps," she says, her gaze returning to the window. "But I've found it's always better to finish what you start."

They kill the carriage driver outside Canterbury.

Well, *Sabine* kills him, while Charlotte looks away, hands clasped over her mouth.

At first, she watched with a kind of static horror, struck by the strange contrast of their bodies—the graceful line of Sabine's arms, one wrapped over the driver's mouth and the other around his chest, the sound of his bones cracking beneath the force, the rictus mask of shock as Sabine's teeth sank deeper still, through skin made fragile by her strength. Charlotte could hardly bear the violence of it, the horror—but that's not what made her turn away.

No, it was the way her mouth went dry, the way her teeth began to ache, hunger rising in revulsion's wake.

Now Charlotte stands with her back to the scene, her gaze trained on the town waiting in the distance—it's almost midnight, but she can see the outlines of the buildings, the halos made by gas lamps and lanterns—while she waits for it to end, is relieved when at last she hears the thud of dead weight hitting earth.

She turns, trying not to look down. To think, she has managed nearly nineteen years without encountering a human corpse, only to see two—the cause of one, the witness to another. The horror laps against her, threatening to overwhelm.

"We should bury him, at least," she says.

They are just off the road, and the ground is soft and damp. But Sabine says no, and fetches the lantern from the driver's perch, along with what looks like a bottle of spirits, hidden beneath the bench.

"Dead bodies make dead earth," she says, handing the lantern off to Charlotte. "And dead earth is dangerous."

She takes up the driver's body as if it is a sack of wheat and flings it into the carriage, then upends the bottle over it and tosses the empty glass inside, does it all with such an easy, practiced air.

"Dangerous?" asks Charlotte, as Sabine holds her hand out for the lantern. "How?"

"Few things can hurt you now," she says, letting it swing from her fingers. "Only the destruction of your heart will end your life. But sunlight will make you sick. And grave dirt will draw you down."

With that, Sabine tosses the lantern into the wooden carriage.

Instantly, the fire catches, spreads, so bright it burns her eyes. The heat rolls off, and Charlotte feels herself draw closer, mesmerized by the new dimensions in the flame.

Until Sabine catches her hand.

"Of all the ways to die," she warns, "fire is the worst."

With that she draws Charlotte away from the burning carriage, and down the road, toward town.

XIII

Margate, England
One week later

Growing up, Charlotte was always afraid of the dark.

Most children are. But unlike most, it never kept her from staring into shadows. Instead, she felt perversely compelled, her gaze always drifting to the places where the darkness gathered, thick as curtains. She couldn't seem to help herself. She'd look until her eyes grew tired and her mind played tricks on her, conjured monsters out of nothing.

But now, when Charlotte looks into the dark, she finds it full of details.

The night diffuse with moonlight, and the butter-gold of lanterns, the curls of light reaching far beyond their edges, the shadows thin as panes of glass, and her eyes sharp enough to pick out the tiles on the rooftops, the ripples in the wood. She sees the cathedral looming in the distance, hears the whisper of the breeze against its bells, makes out the scent of ale clinging to an empty cask, the rustle of Sabine's skirts several yards ahead.

It is late, and most of the shops are shuttered, but despite the hour, sections of the town still stir with life. It whispers from inside darkened houses. It calls from open windows, and spills from a tavern down the road—the scrape of chairs, the clink of glass, the rise and fall of voices.

A sign marks the structure as an inn, and Charlotte wonders if that is where they'll stay. Sabine seems to be considering it, too, until the door swings open, and a man stumbles out into the street. He turns up the road, humming tunelessly, and Sabine says nothing, but slips into his wake.

Charlotte follows.

Ahead, the man trips on a loose cobblestone, catches himself, swears, and carries on another block before coming to a stop before a weathered door. He slumps against it, fumbles with a key, and just as he gets the door open, Sabine calls out.

"Sir?" Her voice satin soft, and sweet as cream. "You've just dropped this."

The shilling catches on the lamplight.

He squints at it through the fog of liquor. "Thanks," he slurs, "'s very decent of you."

Sabine answers with a perfect smile. "Well," she says. "I do try to be decent." As she speaks, she steps into the light, the lantern glancing on her copper hair, and Charlotte swears she can *feel* the muddle of the man's thoughts foaming in the air. Curiosity, confusion, and something a shade more sinister.

"You shouldn't be out at this hour. Two young women such as yourselves." He licks his lips as he says it. Ah, thinks Charlotte. That's what it is. *Hunger.*

"We meant to ride through the night," explains Sabine. "But our driver fell ill."

She steps closer still, offering the coin, but when his hand closes over it, her gloved fingers come to rest on his. "But you're right, it's far too late for two young women to be out without a chaperone. You should invite us in."

Any suspicion gutters like a candle, blown out by her words, the odd vibration in her voice. Charlotte can't see Sabine's expression from this angle, but she sees the man's resistance melt away as his mouth breaks into a foolish grin.

"Come on, then," he says as he lights a lamp and leads them into a narrow sitting room. "Make yourselves at home," he adds, heading toward the hearth.

"Such hospitality," muses Sabine as he pokes a mound of embers, stirring them to life again. He goes to hoist the kettle, but loses his balance. Charlotte reaches out to steady him.

Beyond his shoulder Sabine flicks her fingers, giving her a pointed look, the meaning clear.

Drink.

As if it is that easy. And perhaps it is. After all, Charlotte's hand is still on his arm, and his eyes are glassy and his breath is hot. This close, she can see the stubble on his cheeks, smell the blood beneath his skin, that hollow hunger pooling like a pit.

And yet, hungry as she is, she hesitates.

Sabine's expression turns severe. "I won't keep cutting up your food."

She says it quietly—but not quietly enough. The man twists round. "What was that?" he starts to ask, before Charlotte pulls him back against her, and bites down.

It isn't hard.

The skin tears beneath her teeth, and blood rushes up, breaks over her tongue. That first mouthful is like a spill of golden light, washing through her cold, still limbs, warming her from the inside out. The man stiffens against her, trying and failing to break free—Charlotte's still surprised at her own strength. She feels the life slide down her throat, take root inside her chest. Coil around her heart, which, at last, begins to beat again.

Then Sabine is at her side, fingers dancing down her back, her lips lowered to her ear.

"My feral rose," she whispers, her voice tangled with the pulse, a melody of dizzy pleasure.

Charlotte closes her eyes again, and lets herself sink.

The room drops with her, falls away, as light blooms to every side. She is lying in the grass at Clement Hall, bathing in the summer sun, and this is perfect, this is peace. This moment, rose gold behind her eyes, beneath her skin.

Until the man says, *"Please."*

That one word, and the illusion crumbles. A desperate plea, gasped into a darkened room, and she is back, the air around her painted thick with fear, and her horror rushes up to meet it. Charlotte recoils, limbs and teeth retreating as she lets go.

The man stumbles, collapses, struggles to his feet again, and she doesn't *tell* him to run, but how relieved she is to hear the front door slam, to have his body gone, even as his heart still pounds inside her chest.

Charlotte's head is spinning, her legs unsteady and her cheeks hot, as if she's downed a glass or two of sherry. Sabine looks from Charlotte to the door and back again, dismayed.

"He said please," she murmurs, fighting to suppress a dizzy giggle. It is not funny, of course, and yet for some reason, she almost laughs.

Sabine does not.

Her jaw clicks shut, expression cold. She doesn't raise her voice—she never has—but she storms out, and Charlotte sinks onto a stool beside the hearth, waiting for the room to level.

The fire crackles, but otherwise the house is suddenly so quiet, so empty, that something turns inside her. A sudden, horrible sadness, stronger than she's felt in years. The stolen heartbeat slows behind her breast, and her eyes begin to sting, and she's relieved when Sabine reappears. Until she drops something small and bloody in her lap. It takes Charlotte a moment to realize what it is.

A human heart.

"The one who said please," says Sabine before tossing two more down on top, "and the two men he'd already told."

Charlotte stares down in horror at the three hearts, nested like bloody little bodies in the bowl of her skirts.

Sabine dusts off her palms. "You see?" she says, sinking onto the sofa. "This is why you should always finish what you start."

Charlotte's stomach turns as she gets to her feet and casts the hearts one by one into the fire. She stays there, kneeling by the stove, watching the hearts burn as Sabine spreads herself over the cushions, and closes her eyes, and seems perfectly at home.

Unbothered. Untouched. As if the horror doesn't so much as—

"Stop," says Sabine, her eyes still closed. "It does no good to dwell."

Charlotte frowns. "It doesn't bother you?"

"Why should it? What is more natural than death?"

"But *this* wasn't natural. It was you." She looks down at her ruined dress. "*Us.*" Her fingers trace the bloodstains on her skirts. "How do you live with it?"

She can *hear* the shrug in Sabine's voice. "It's easy."

"It shouldn't be," she hisses. "They were people."

"They were food." Sabine sighs, exasperated. "Honestly, Charlotte, did you mourn the eggs you used to have for breakfast? The chicken in your pie?"

Charlotte rounds on her. "It's not the same."

Sabine is sitting upright now, cleaning the crescents of her nails. "Isn't it?"

"How can you be so cavalier?" she snaps, expecting the other woman to lash back, to scold or raise her voice. Instead, she meets Charlotte's gaze and smiles, almost gently.

"People die," she says. "Every hour of every day. The vast majority will do so through accident, or sickness, age, or folly. And yes, a handful at our hands." She rises to her feet, approaching Charlotte. And even though Sabine is only slightly taller, she always seems to loom, larger than her height and wider than her frame. "Death comes, and sometimes it is kind, and often it is cruel, and very rarely it is welcome. But it comes, all the same." Sabine's hand comes to rest against her heart. "The difference is, we make something of that death. Their loss is our gain."

Charlotte looks up into those burning eyes and feels her anger flicker. Her guilt and grief retreat as Sabine lifts her other hand to cup her cheek.

"Charlotte." Even now, the sound of her name on Sabine's tongue, the way those fingers slide through her hair, curl against her neck, makes her thoughts fray and the room around them fade. A different kind of heat blooms beneath her skin, and she welcomes it.

"I appreciate your mind. Your thoughts. Your curiosity." Sabine's mouth grazes hers, teeth skating on her bottom lip. "But I think it's time," she purrs, "we find another use for it."

She leads Charlotte up the stairs, and Charlotte lets herself be led.

While down below, the hearts burn to nothing in the hearth.

She sleeps, and dreams of Clement Hall.

She is in the garden, and her mother is calling for her. Her father and brother, too. Their voices tangle in the hedges and bounce off the stone path. She tries to call out only to find she has no voice. She tries to go to them, but finds she has grown roots. No matter how she fights, she cannot seem to speak, or move. She is entombed inside herself.

They search and search, but never find her.

Charlotte wakes to find herself entangled, a pale limb draped over her waist, tendrils of red hair trailing like weeds across her throat. She marvels at how different Sabine looks, disarmed by sleep, how soft the bluish shadow of her eyelids, the fringe of copper lashes, the delicate bow of her lips, right before they twitch into a smile.

Sabine pulls Charlotte closer, and she forgets about the dream. Until later, when they are getting dressed again, and she sees a little table by the wall, an ink pot and parchment perched on top.

"I want to send a letter home."

Sabine stands at the open wardrobe, turning through the dresses there. Gowns that must have once belonged to a daughter, or a sister, or a wife. Her hand slows, lips pursed in disapproval, but she doesn't try to stop her.

Charlotte takes a seat and dips the quill, tries to find the words that will assure her family.

In the end, she writes that she is sorry for escaping as she did.

She writes that she wanted a different kind of life.

She glances at Sabine, who's twirling slowly, a white dress held against her front, as if dancing with a ghost, and writes that she is happy, ends by promising that she will come to see them soon.

She slips the letter in a post as they leave town, feels a sudden wave of sadness when it's gone, and then, a lightness. A wash of hope.

It is a lie, Sabine told her, *that you only get one story.*

And she's right.

This is how the first one ends, Charlotte tells herself as the letter disappears, taking young Miss Hastings with it.

This is how the next one starts.

ALICE

(D. 2019)

I

"Just *stop.*"

Alice's voice is a knife, slicing through the hotel room.

Lottie trails off and the silence that settles in her wake is somehow even worse. Three bodies, and no heartbeats, no movement, no sound save the constant, steady whisper of the shower through the wall.

Alice is sitting, knees drawn to her chest, on the hotel floor, and Ezra's slouching in a chair, and Lottie is in exactly the same place as when she started, perched at the foot of the bed, her mind and face unreadable, unlike Colin, or Hannah, or the man in the nice car, whose thoughts and wants spilled out into the air like steam, so thick she could see and smell and taste them. But whatever Lottie's feeling now, she's found a way to keep it to herself. Ezra too, his expression steady, his mind a quiet blank, and Alice knows that her own head is probably wide open, all her fear and anger and confusion clouding up the room like smoke, but she doesn't care.

Let them hear what she is thinking.

"Sabine seduced you," says Alice. "Is that it? You fell for her, and she stole you away. And somehow, that's enough of an excuse. Because she made you what you are? She hurt you. So you hurt me. And it's all just some cruel cycle?"

Hurt people hurt people, she's heard the words a hundred times. But Lottie is shaking her head, a slow, metronomic movement, side to side.

"No," she says, rubbing her eyes. "No, you aren't listening."

"Why should I?" snaps Alice, surprised by her own anger, not because it's there—it always is—but because it's spilling out. For years, she's held it like a coal inside her chest, a searing heat that she keeps swallowed so it only hurts herself. But she can't contain it anymore, she doesn't want to, shouldn't have to, what's the point?

"Why should I care about an old love story, Lottie? I want to know why *you* did what *you* did to *me*, not—"

But just then someone knocks.

Alice cuts off sharply, and they all look to the door, but it's Ezra who stands, who goes to answer it, and it's like a seal breaking. Alice comes unstuck, rising from the floor on legs that should be stiff, but aren't, and Lottie stands and slips into the bathroom. Alice catches a glimpse of the woman, still standing in a daze beneath the showerhead, her chin tipped back and her eyes shut, as if lost inside a private storm.

Alice watches, and marvels at how gently Lottie guides the woman from the shower, how tenderly she feeds her limbs into a plush white robe, how carefully she glides the wet hair out from beneath the collar and sits her on a padded stool, crouches down so they are eye to eye when she tells her she's wandered into the wrong room.

The woman blushes in embarrassment, and hurries to her feet, confusion streaked through the steam-filled air around her. How silly she feels as she rushes out, past Alice, and past Ezra.

And just like that, the woman's gone, she's free, she's *still alive,* and Alice fights back a petty rage.

(It isn't fair. It isn't fair. It isn't fair.)

Even though she knows deep down there's nothing fair about life, the give and take, the luck of the draw, knows that it isn't the woman's fault for getting out, away, when she herself did not.

Ezra's still standing in the open door, talking to someone in the hall. The barista, Alice thinks, the one from White Thorn Black Roast. He reaches out and takes a thermos from her outstretched hand.

And then the door is closed, and it is just the three of them again.

Alice sinks into a crouch, fingers clutching at her knees, and Lottie resumes her place on the corner of the bed, and Ezra unscrews the thermos top.

"Delivery," he says by way of explanation as he swipes three glasses from the bar. "Long night. And getting longer."

He pours, the contents viscous, red, and at some point, Alice knows, she'll stop being so startled by the sight of blood, but right now, it still hits her like a blow to the face. The shock, the recoil, and worst of all, the want, like the world is shrinking to a cup-sized point.

Ezra hands a glass to Alice, offers one to Lottie, too, but she declines, cheek twitching away, as if that's easy, as if everything inside her isn't yawning open at the sight, and Alice remembers what he said, on the walk to the

Taj, about hunger, and how to live with it, and she thinks maybe, maybe she can resist the urge to drink.

But then Ezra lifts his glass toward Alice in a small, imaginary toast, tips it back, and Alice loses that fight before it starts, and from the moment it touches her lips to the moment she swallows, she feels a little better, a little calmer, a little saner, tries to make the feeling last, but it's already gone, and all that's left is the echo on her tongue, and a hole that seems even wider in its wake, and she wishes she hadn't even tried to fill it, and she knows that if Ezra refilled the glass, she'd do it again, and she hates Lottie more than ever, for making her this way, and that thought must be ringing through the room, because Lottie clears her throat, and looks down at the fingers knotted in her lap.

"I know you're mad," she says. "I know you want me to skip ahead."

She swallows, and looks up at Alice, small red tears clinging to her lashes.

"But to understand what happened to you," she says, "you need to know what happened to me first."

CHARLOTTE

(D. 1827)

I

Charlotte has so much to learn, and Sabine is there to teach her.

How to kill, of course. But also, how to *live*.

How to travel, skipping like a stone, never landing in one place—or stop, and sink into the pattern of a life. How to draw out the hunt for weeks and savor the reward—or condense the game into a single night. And if Charlotte cannot bring herself to take much pleasure in the kill, at least Sabine never lets her wallow in the aftermath.

And since those first years are happy ones, they blur.

It does not matter where they go.

They are an island, alone together in the vast wide world.

And they are happy.

Perhaps that is what makes them monsters—the fact their love is marked by violence, and death, and yet.

And yet.

She would not change a thing.

By night, they are like children, set loose in a garden of delights, the darkest hours turned into a playground of the senses, a festival, a ball.

They dance. They drink. They dream.

And in the morning, Sabine pulls Charlotte down into the sheets and whispers poetry against her skin, lines about midnight soil and soft red petals and sharp white teeth.

And every time, Charlotte drifts off surrounded by the scent of her lover. Like damp earth and dry bark. And in the circle of her arms, she feels safe.

She feels home.

How easy it is now, to trace the fractured path, follow it back to the moment when the first crack formed. How easy it was *then*, to pretend that it was nothing.

They have stolen into an empty German castle, a hundred rooms left shuttered and unused, and there, Sabine teaches Charlotte how to lay claim to a space and make it hers.

How to draw a threshold using nothing but her will.

Later that night, when they are running barefoot through the halls, chasing each other in some made-up jest, Sabine fast on Charlotte's heels, she runs into an empty room and declares it *hers*.

Dances backward into the middle of the chamber, each step announcing *This is mine, this is mine*, the way Sabine just taught her.

Sabine, who tries to follow her into the room only to be rebuffed, as if the air has turned to stone.

They both freeze, surprised by how quickly she has learned, how well she keeps her lover out. Charlotte laughs, delighted, and Sabine smiles, flashing teeth.

"Well done," she says. "Now let me in."

And Charlotte, so proud of her new skill, says, "No."

Just like that, the balance tips.

Charlotte has seen Sabine annoyed, and bored, frustrated and impatient, but until that moment, she had never seen her *mad*. She is startled not only by the rage, but by how much it frightens her. The way Sabine's whole demeanor shifts, the smile dropping from her face as her amusement dies. Anger strikes like flint behind her eyes.

Charlotte abandons the game, and her hold on the chamber. She forces herself to smile as she says, "Of course, my love, come in."

The threshold dissolves, the room no longer hers alone, and just like that, Sabine's good humor flickers back, the offense seemingly forgotten as she lunges forward.

Charlotte lets herself be caught, laughing in relief as Sabine pins her down against the floor.

~

Charlotte loves Sabine.

How can she not?

This woman, who is a force of nature. Who bends the world instead of bending for it. Who looks at Charlotte with such open want, and touches her without an ounce of shame. Who never steals a kiss, but instead lays claim to it, as if it is already hers.

Sabine, who proves a master gardener.

And Charlotte, so eager to be tended.

So grateful she has found a hand that makes her bloom.

For years, they live in stolen houses.

Sleep in other people's beds, the heavy curtains drawn, the days spent buried in the dark. Most nights, Charlotte stays up long enough to watch the black give way to dawn, and wakes in time to watch the sun go down again, though even those pale filaments are hard to look at it.

If she had known she'd never be able to enjoy the light of day again, she would have lingered that last afternoon, savored each and every hue. Charlotte asked once if that was why Sabine wore shades of goldenrod, and burgundy, and Prussian blue—because she missed the vibrant colors of the day—but Sabine only chuckled and said she'd never been so sentimental. She merely liked the way they looked against her skin.

Sabine is not one to dwell.

But Charlotte cannot help it.

Just as she cannot seem to shed the grief, or guilt, the weight of things she'd felt in life, her new hunger expands as well, finds the curiosity she had before and makes it ravenous. She raids the libraries of every house they pass through, greedy for language, philosophy, novels, anything she can touch, and take, has to restrain herself to only one book from each place, and leaves the last she's finished in her wake.

Most nights she stays up reading long past dawn, then climbs into bed beside Sabine, who rouses only long enough to fold her in. Even then, tired as she is, Charlotte sometimes lies awake, her mind brimming with questions. About life. About time. About *them*. Until Sabine strokes her hair and bids her hush, as if the volume of Charlotte's mind is keeping her awake.

If Sabine herself has ever wondered about such things, she does not say.

There is so much she does not say.

Charlotte often wishes she could feel the contours of her lover's mind,

read the outlines of her ideas, her hopes, her dreams, but Sabine's thoughts
are always guarded, her head is always closed. A matter of age, Sabine says
when she asks, but Charlotte swears she is being kept out. More than once
she tries the door, prying at the mental locks, but every time she is rebuffed,
met by a warning look, and nothing more.

Rarely, Sabine will offer up a glancing mention of her past.

An absent comment dropped like a breadcrumb in her wake. Charlotte
hoards them hungrily. A boat docked in Seville. The Carnevale in Venice. A
church. A pair. A painter. A friend. But when she asks for more, Sabine
withdraws and says, "It does not matter now."

Once, early on, they pass through an empty villa in the hills of Spain,
and Charlotte finds Sabine standing on the balcony, looking over the night-
soaked grounds at an olive grove below.

"What is it?" she asks softly.

Sabine inclines her head. "An echo," she murmurs, and when Charlotte
tells her to go on, she shakes her head and claims she can't remember, and
Charlotte knows then that it must have been a place she lived *before*. Before
time stopped. Before she changed. Those are the only years she never talks
about.

One night, when they are strolling arm in arm down a Paris road, Sabine
notes the date, and casually reveals that she is twenty, only to add that she
has been that age three hundred years.

Three hundred years.

The mind boggles at the size of such a life, the scope, the scale. Charlotte
gasps, and Sabine crooks a brow. "What is it?"

"Think of all the books that you could have read!"

And Sabine laughs, a lovely, earnest sound that makes Charlotte feel like
she is falling in love all over again.

"We have to celebrate," says Charlotte, and Sabine steals a kiss, and assures
her that they will.

Charlotte is full of questions, but Sabine does not seem to mind.

It's true, she teases Charlotte when she thinks too loudly for too long, but
she always seems amused when she voices them aloud, as if charmed by her
persistent curiosity.

Until Charlotte asks if there are others.

They are walking arm in arm, the strangers around them reduced to shapes and shadows by a late-night fog, when she wonders casually, almost to herself, how many of their kind are out there.

Sabine goes stiff beside her.

"Am I not enough?" she asks, and there it is again, an anger so sudden and cold that Charlotte shivers, fights the urge to draw back as she says, "Of course. Of course you are. That is not the point."

But Sabine is staring at her now, the light behind her eyes gone out.

So Charlotte lets the matter go.

Sabine was right.

Everything gets easier with time.

Even killing.

And if the horror of it never truly disappears—every time Charlotte takes a life, the guilt is there to greet her—then at least it is mercifully brief, fading almost as quickly as the heartbeat in her chest.

She decides early on that she will only take the lives of men.

She even goes so far as to seek out the ones with meanness in their thoughts, violence in their air, tells herself it is a kind of virtue. As if one life is worth more than another.

Sabine teases her, says it is like choosing tonic over wine, that women taste far sweeter. But Charlotte insists, even though she knows deep down there is no difference in the end. Regardless of their sex, their innocence or guilt, the last thing these men will ever feel is fear. And it will be her doing.

Charlotte tells herself she takes no pleasure in the act, that it is a means and nothing more. But that is not wholly true. She craves that moment in the sun, the borrowed heart, the flush of heat, the power of the blood. But there is another piece—the way she feels when those men are in her arms.

When they are weak, and she is strong. When they are trapped.

And she is *free*.

II

Hampshire, England
1879

It is easy to lose track of time.

After all, the days look different, but the nights appear the same. The darkness bleeds like watercolor, and time runs with it. A month becomes a year. A decade. Three. Then four.

And suddenly it's almost Christmas, and Charlotte is stepping down from a carriage, her boots sinking a little in the English soil, and she knows, even with Sabine's fingers like a veil over her eyes, that she is back in Hampshire. She can hear the breeze through dry tall grass, can smell the hawthorn and the dogwood, the birch smoke rising from the hearth, half hopes, half fears that when Sabine takes her hands away, Charlotte will find herself staring up at Clement Hall.

Instead, when she's allowed to look, she is greeted by a stranger's stately house, the windows candlelit and traced in garlands. A ribbon of pale pebbles for a drive, a wreath of holly on the door, a rooftop laced with frost. It might as well be made of gingerbread, it is so beautiful.

"A gift," says Sabine, leaning to kiss the slope of skin just beneath her jaw. "I know it's not the same, but—"

Charlotte cuts her off, throws her arms around her neck.

"It's perfect," she says with every kiss.

All these years, and Sabine still manages to take her by surprise.

She cranes her head, studies the cobalt blue of early night, the winter sky she knows so well, and wonders how far they are from Clement Hall.

"A mile down the road," answers Sabine. "I thought you'd like a taste of home."

Charlotte nods. Sabine is always telling her to look forward, never back, but these last few years she has been longing for just that.

A taste of home.

It's a turn of phrase Charlotte doesn't fully grasp until they're walking up the drive. Until she's forced to face the fact that the house Sabine has chosen for them isn't empty.

Yet.

But Sabine only smiles, looking pleased as a cat, and Charlotte knows there is no turning back. They knock, claiming to be carolers. It is the season, after all, for charity, for kindness. How quickly they are let inside.

The wife offers them tea—Charlotte will always remember that—and the husband takes their coats, the air around them unsuspecting, filled with nothing but the scent of pine. Sabine follows the woman from the room. Charlotte stays, and takes the man.

He doesn't scream, or thrash, or plead.

She has learned how to make the killing fast, to bite down hard and deep, leaving them frightened but too stunned to fight. But she prefers to take her time. To bury the violence in something gentle, sweet, only the tips of her teeth breaking the skin. To take their life so slow they barely notice that they're hurt until it's far too late to fight.

So that's what Charlotte does. She is as kind as she can be, lets him sink against her as she lingers in the sunlight, in the heartbeat, in the warmth, as long as she is able, and then when there is nothing left, she lays him down.

She feels the tears slip down her cheeks, brushes them away as she goes to find Sabine.

Strange, she isn't in the kitchen.

The wife is there, propped in a chair, her head resting on her folded arms as if she's drifted off to sleep. Charlotte touches the woman's face, half ex-pecting her to wake, when she hears the scream.

It comes from overhead, spills down the stairs, and Charlotte rushes up, the stolen heart still beating in her chest as she reaches the bedroom at the end. And stops.

Across the room, Sabine holds a girl dressed in nothing but a nightgown against her front. A *child*, no older than thirteen. Her terror, thick as paint, is splashed on every wall, and blood is weeping from her cheek, her wrist, her throat.

"Sabine," says Charlotte, but she doesn't seem to hear.

In her arms, the girl twists and pleads, trying to get free. Sabine loosens her grip and the girl tears away.

"*Help!*" she cries out, scrambling one step, two, before Sabine catches her again, pulls her back, and clamps a hand over her mouth.

"Who are you calling for?" she purrs. "Everyone is dead."

Horror washes over Charlotte, brighter than she's felt in years.

"Sabine, *enough*," she snaps.

The girl sees her and thrashes like an animal, eyes wild and afraid, as Charlotte starts forward, determined to put a stop to this, to end her suffering. But when she gets close enough to try, Sabine pushes her away.

Sabine, who until that very moment has never laid a hand on her except in hunger, love, or want. Never left a mark unless it was a part of pleasure.

That Sabine now pushes Charlotte hard enough to send her staggering. She stumbles back into the bed frame, the wood behind her splintering from the force. Charlotte's vision flickers black and white, and she recovers just in time to see Sabine sink her teeth into the child's throat.

It is a shallow, brutal bite, not deep enough to kill, only to tear, to hurt.

The girl claws and scrambles, feral in her fear, but Sabine's grip is a cage, unbreakable, and soon her thrashing turns to feeble twists, her screams to whimpers. She pushes weakly at Sabine, a final, desperate pawing until at last she slumps, the fight and then the life snuffed out of her.

Charlotte stands there stunned and angry as Sabine finally lets go, the body dropping to the floor. A heap of limbs that now will never grow.

Charlotte stares at her love—

And stops.

She has known Sabine for more than twice her mortal life. Five decades spent in each other's company. Long enough to study every facet of Sabine, to learn the tones of voice that go with every mood, the way her limbs drift when she is tired, and drag when she is drunk, and dance when she is glad, but never stop unless she sleeps. The way she moves and speaks and loves and kills.

Long enough to know that this is *not* Sabine.

Her eyes are black and bottomless, so unlike the burning hazel ones that Charlotte knows and loves. There is a stranger looking out. A stranger tugging at her smile.

"What's wrong, my love?" she asks in a dreamy voice as she steps over the corpse.

"Why did you do that?" demands Charlotte. "You didn't need to—"

"Need to? No . . ."

"You *shouldn't* have," she snaps.

"Says who?" The black eyes narrow, cold and angry. "You?" She reaches Charlotte, who tries to step back, only to find the broken bedpost in her way.

"Stop," warns Charlotte, her voice unsteady.

Sabine reaches up to stroke her tearstained cheek. "My fragile-hearted little flower . . ." Her hand slides past, into Charlotte's hair. "You want to know why I did it," she whispers. "Why I let her scream and fight. Why I stoked her fear." She leans close, too close, and smiles, blood staining her teeth. "I like the way it *tastes*." Her fingers twist, a stranger's hold in a lover's hand, the curls drawn tight enough to hurt.

Charlotte flinches, but doesn't try to pull free, just looks into the stranger's eyes and says, "*Let go of me.*"

And whether it's the sharpness of the words, or the disgust and anger rolling off her, the stranger blinks, and disappears.

Sabine stares back at her.

The candles reignite behind her eyes.

Her body recoils slightly, as if burned.

Her grip loosens and lets go.

"Charlotte," says Sabine, and at least her voice is *hers* again, but Charlotte cannot bring herself to stand and listen to it. The moment she is free, she turns and leaves.

Walks out of the room, and then the house, and then keeps going, her dress wicking up the night-damp grass, clinging to her legs with a chill she registers, but doesn't feel. She walks because she cannot bear to stop, let alone turn back, but at some point the balance tips, and she's no longer fleeing one place, but being drawn forward toward another, the ground sloping beneath the weight of memory. Until she looks up, and there it is.

Clement Hall.

Not the long front drive and grand façade, but the sprawling gardens at its back.

The gardens, which she revisits every time she drinks. In her mind they are unchanged, unchanging, but even in the dark she sees the subtle work of time, her mother's wilderness pushed out, the edges tamed. The patches where frost has killed a plant or tree, the spots where new ones have been planted.

But the bulk of it is just as she remembered.

Her steps crunch softly on the pebbled path as she takes in the same rose-covered trellises and ivy arches, bare in winter. The same fountain at the garden's heart, the figure looming at its center, two fingers chipped from the time she played horseshoes with its lifted hand.

The same night sky stretches overhead, as wide as it has always been, though the scattered points now seem to her a tapestry of light. A star shoots by, and she is fourteen again, and James is with her in the dark, arranging the telescope he received that Christmas, calibrating it against Polaris and murmuring the winter constellations to himself.

"Orion . . . Taurus . . . Auriga . . . Carina . . ." he says, swiveling the lens on its brass stand.

It is a crisp, clear night, and her nose and lips are chapped with cold, but she can't bring herself to burrow down into her scarf, not when all the wonder comes from looking up, and any moment their father and mother will appear at the back door and call them in, out of the dark.

But then Charlotte blinks, and her brother and his telescope are gone, and she is alone again.

Her gaze goes to the house.

It is the middle of the night, and nearly all the shutters have been drawn, but ghosts of lamplight seep here and there between the slats, and she wonders, five decades on, what member of her family lives there now?

Her father is surely gone. Her mother, too.

But James? Could he be up there, in his bed?

Charlotte cannot help herself. She knows she shouldn't—Sabine has warned her a dozen times about leaving the past in its place. But it's the image of Sabine that drives her forward, up the path. Away from one life and toward another.

With each step, she tells herself she will turn back. With each, she tells herself she is only getting close enough to feel for signs of life, to make out the shape of minds within.

The sculptures her mother made peer out at her as she goes by, half-hidden by a rosebush or a hedge.

The fox. The crow. The cat.

And the rabbit.

Charlotte slows, and stops, and kneels. She runs a hand over the clay, feeling for the soft indents of her mother's fingers, the thumb pad pressed like a signature into the back. How far she is from the girl who found its ruined body. How close she feels.

She strokes its small stone ear thoughtfully, and her mother's parting words come rushing back.

Some people keep their heart tucked so deep, they hardly know it's there. But you have always worn it like a second skin. It will make your life harder. But it will also make it beautiful.

"Who's there?"

The voice scratches at the air.

Charlotte rises and spins round, scouring the dark until she spies the woman bundled in a lawn chair. She scolds herself—she should have heard the woman's heartbeat. Should have felt her mind staining the air. Now that she sees her, she can't imagine how she didn't.

The woman is old—far too old to be out here at this hour, in this cold. A shawl rests around her narrow shoulders, but her hands are thin and bare, knotted in her lap. Her hair, once black, is gray, and gathered at her neck. Her eyes, once jade, have faded to a paler shade of green.

But it is still Jocelyn.

Her Joss.

"I know you're there," she rasps, and though her voice is so much weaker now, it is the exact same tone she took when they were young, and playing hide-and-seek. When Joss was forced to be the seeker, and she was so convinced that Charlotte would leap out and frighten her—which she did, more than once, just so Jocelyn would shriek.

Charlotte doesn't leap out now.

She comes forward carefully, until she's close enough to make out Jocelyn's shallow pulse, the soft tangle of her thoughts. A murmur of sadness, shot through with calm, contrasting threads of grief and hope and dread.

Charlotte continues until she's near enough that the moonlight catches on her hair and cheeks, and Jocelyn looks up with those watered-down eyes, and sees her—Charlotte, who has not aged a day since eighteen—and the air around her narrow shoulders ripples, not with shock, or fear, but relief.

"Oh," she says with a soft sigh. "It's you." As if they've been apart for hours, days, instead of decades. Jocelyn shifts a little in her chair. "Come to haunt me again, I see."

Her slippered feet slide back and forth across the grass. An absent gesture, one she had when they were young.

Charlotte kneels before the chair, so they are eye to eye, face-to-face.

Jocelyn's breath forms thin clouds that rise around her cheeks, and out of habit, Charlotte begins to breathe as well—she has learned to make a bellows of her lungs in winter, to force the air in and out, even though she doesn't need it.

Charlotte stares into her first love's eyes. She has imagined this reunion a thousand times, but now she cannot find the words.

"Joss . . ." she says gently.

"I dream of you, you know," says Jocelyn. And then, "I dream of us."

The words claw at Charlotte's ribs. Wrap like hands around her throat. She wants to throw her arms around her friend, but doesn't trust herself, her strength.

"I dream of another life," Jocelyn goes on. "One where I wasn't so afraid." A sigh. "I was such a coward, Lottie," she murmurs, and that name cracks something deep inside her.

The tears Charlotte has been holding back since she was first sent away now come rolling down her cheeks. To her surprise, Jocelyn reaches up one frail hand to catch the bloodred drop. "Did you find someone brave enough to love you?"

Sabine flares behind her eyes. Not as she is that night, but as she's been, almost every night before, proud, and bold, and bright enough to burn.

"Yes," Charlotte whispers.

"Good," says Jocelyn. Her eyes go sharper then, mouth twitching with mischief, and she is eighteen again, racing away with the journal in her arms. Their hands knot together, one young and one old—and both cold. Jocelyn squeezes, but Charlotte doesn't dare squeeze back.

"How cruel," says Joss, the words little more than breath, "some nights you feel so real."

Just then a door swings open, light spilling like a backward shadow down the steps.

A young man calls out into the dark. "Nan?"

Then his steps are coming down the stairs and Charlotte forces herself to let go of Joss's hands, to pull away, retreat into the shadow of the nearest hedge. He goes right past her, his hair sleep-mussed and his voice bright with concern; she almost gasps.

God, he looks like James.

Her heart twists with sudden hope, then sinks as she remembers how many years have come between them. And sure enough, this boy does not look like James as he would now. He looks like James as he was that spring, when Charlotte left Clement Hall. Younger, even. Her brother as he was that Christmas Eve when they were studying the stars.

Charlotte watches as he heads straight for the chair, and the withered woman in it.

"Nan," he says, the air around him thick with worry. "It's the middle of the night. What are you doing out here?"

Jocelyn blinks, gazes round the garden, doesn't seem surprised to find it empty.

"Oh," she says, dragging her attention from the dark. "Talking to ghosts."

He frowns, and all the things he thinks but doesn't say cloud the air around his head. "Come," he says, "let's get you back to bed."

He helps her from the chair, scolding gently about the hour and the cold as he leads her up the stairs, and into the stream of lamplight, his shoulders strong, and hers hunched, her gray hair ignited silver. Charlotte watches until the door swings shut, snuffing out the light. Listens until she can hear nothing but the whisper of the garden, her turning thoughts, her too-still heart.

Then she sinks into the grass and draws her knees into her chest, her whole body shaking with the grief.

How easy to forget the way time wears on other people when she is with Sabine, the two of them preserved like insects inside amber. How easy, and then how hard, to see the proof of it, that life races on, relentless in its pace.

Sabine was right.

This is why the past is left behind. Why they can only move forward, like Eurydice and Orpheus, never glancing back, lest they be trapped among the dead.

Charlotte stays until the darkness ebbs.

Until the first wisps of light begin to seep around the edges of the sky and throw tendrils through the garden. Until the warning ache sets in beneath her skin, behind her eyes.

Then she stands, and walks away.

She plucks a single rose on her way out, cradles the red bloom against her chest as she retraces the path that carried her across the downs. By the time the stolen house comes into sight dawn has broken fully, molten daylight spilling over everything. Her head pounds, limbs shivering as she crosses the last stretch of lawn and stumbles through the door, into the safety of the darkened hall.

Charlotte braces herself against the wall, the sickness withdrawing like a tide. She steels herself and looks around. The corpses have been cleared away, the only evidence of last night's crimes a missing rug, a few stray flecks of blood against the wall.

The house is quiet, but not empty.

The knowledge fills Charlotte with a tired dread, and also grim relief. She does not want to be alone. Not now.

She climbs the stairs and finds Sabine where she always is, in the finest room, on the finest bed.

But despite the hour, she is not asleep.

Instead, Sabine sits perched at the foot of the bed, before the window. The curtains have been parted, so she sits facing the early-morning light, as if in penance. Charlotte flinches, crosses and pulls the curtains shut, plunging the room safely back into shadow.

Sabine slackens, just a little, in relief. Charlotte lies down, and Sabine lies with her, so they are face-to-face atop the sheets. Charlotte looks into her eyes. Eyes she knows so well, amber-brown and candlelit, no sign of the stranger from earlier that night.

Sabine doesn't ask her where she went, doesn't ask her anything, only reaches up to touch her cheek. Charlotte flinches back, and then, seeing the pain that crosses Sabine's face, takes her hand and brings it to rest against her soundless heart.

Sabine speaks into the sliver of space between their lips.

"Forgive me," she whispers. Fifty-two years, and it is the closest she has ever come to an apology. Her golden eyes find Charlotte's. "I don't know what happened. I don't know why. I only know it wasn't me." And for the first time, Sabine lets her graze the edges of her shuttered mind, lets her feel the aura of confusion, fear.

"Please believe me," she says, before the walls go up again.

And here is the awful thing about belief.

It is a current, like compulsion. Hard to forge when it goes against your will, but easy enough when it carries you the way you want to go.

In that moment, Charlotte wants so badly to believe Sabine.

And so she does.

"It's all right," she says, stroking her lover's cheek. "I'm here."

Sabine sags in relief, leaves a trail of kisses down her throat.

Fatigue rolls over Charlotte like a tide, and she turns away, Sabine's hand still clasped in hers. Sleep drags at her limbs, her mind, and she lets herself sink into it, is just slipping beneath the surface when Sabine whispers into her hair.

"Promise me something."

Charlotte makes a *hmming* sound, awake enough to listen, but too tired to form words. Sabine shifts closer in the bed, until their limbs are flush, their bodies molded to each other.

"Promise," she says, soft and low, "that you will never hurt me."

Charlotte frowns. It is not the promise she expected her lover to extract. *Promise you will always love me,* perhaps. *Promise not to leave again.* But this? It strikes her as an odd request. After all, *she* has never tried to hurt *Sabine.*

She cannot imagine that she ever will.

Charlotte does not wonder, then, why Sabine would ask for such a thing. She does not know the power of the words. The weight of them. And she is tired. So tired. She will tell Sabine what she wants to hear, if it will bring her peace. If it will let Charlotte rest.

"I promise," she murmurs.

Sabine sighs.

And Charlotte lets the dark fold over her.

They rise at dusk.

By night, they're gone.

Charlotte feeling rested, and Sabine seemingly restored, so much her old self that Charlotte is convinced that what she saw the night before was nothing but an awful dream. Some kind of fit, or perhaps even a possession. The stranger that replaced Sabine a foul spirit, bound up with the house.

And so, they rid themselves of both.

They set out arm in arm beneath the veil of night, Sabine awash in beauty, and Charlotte in relief. They escape that cursed property, the demons lurking in it, and she tells herself that all is well. Her lover is back. The danger has passed.

And for a while, at least, she is right.

III

Years pass, and for the most part, the two of them are happy.

Charlotte, who loves so hard it shakes her bones.

And Sabine, who answers her every whim, gifts Charlotte journals when she longs to write, and charcoals when she wants to draw, and canvas when she decides to paint. Sabine, who stands like a shadow at her back, watching as the brush brings light and color back into the world. Who's read Charlotte like a book so many times she has her memorized.

Sabine, who can charm strangers with a word, a look, a turning of her cheek, whose temper kindles quick, but whose laugh is rare as diamonds, and whose attention still feels like standing in a pool of light.

Sabine, who steals with her through moonlit gardens and museums, hides among the sculptures as if she could ever blend in. Who dances barefoot through every room to music only she can hear, and who makes every night feel new, which is no small feat after so many years.

Sabine, who often fondles one of the tokens she wears around her neck, staring past it as if reliving the hunt, the kill, and who begins to sleep so deep sometimes it frightens her, the way her cheeks look sunken, the way, without the reassuring rise and fall of breath, the rest resembles death and Charlotte, unsettled, twists and turns until she stirs.

Sabine, who still knows how to make Charlotte blush, and shiver, and delight. How to unravel her, kiss by kiss, until she comes apart. Who sometimes in the heat of passion bites too deep, drinks enough to leave her dizzy, weak.

And who once—and *only* once—held Charlotte down too hard in bed, and left bruises on her wrists. And even though they faded instantly, the next night the air around them prickled with guilt, and Sabine made amends by telling Charlotte a story from her life before their life, when she was called María, and Charlotte thought it was a gift, that name, and the next night called her by it, and the look on her lover's face was black enough to frighten her.

Enough to make her waver.

But Sabine, Sabine is there to steady Charlotte.

To kiss away the worries.

To vow that nothing bad will ever happen, so long as they're together.

Paris, France
1914

And then, the world goes to war.

It is not the first time, of course, and it will not be the last, but this time it is a horror on a scale that even in her violent century Charlotte has never seen or known or felt. And she *does* feel it, no matter where they go. The weight of thousands frightened, wounded, grieving, is too much, even for her tried and tested soul. A ceaseless suffering, without reprieve.

She has always had a fragile heart, but now it feels like it is splintering.

She wakes to find her pillowcase stained red, from crying in her sleep, while Sabine grows impatient and annoyed.

Charlotte leaves their borrowed rooms at dusk, and walks, and walks, desperate to feel a thread of hope, hidden like contraband among the dire mood.

She stops before a Parisian printer's shop, watches as a man with black-stained hands pulls a lever, a ream of paper flying past. The headlines printed heavy, black. A tally of the dead and damned. The horror coats her skin like ink, follows her back to the pied-à-terre they've taken, right along the Seine.

She finds her lover leaning elbows on the iron rail, taking the night air. Sabine, who somehow despite it all remains unbothered. As if the cloud of constant anguish does not touch her. As if she can simply block the sorrows out.

Charlotte wishes she could do something to help the cause, but when she tells Sabine, she is met with mocking laughter.

"Who do you think," she says, "has killed more Englishmen this year? You or Germany?"

"That isn't fair," snaps Charlotte.

"Tell me, do you keep a running tab?"

Charlotte turns away, as if to block her out.

Sabine takes her by the shoulders, bends to whisper in her ear, and Charlotte assumes it will be something soft and soothing. But when she speaks, her voice is harsh. "This guilt is growing tiresome."

Charlotte winces, shakes her off, arms wrapped tight around herself. "And yet, I thought you loved me for my feelings."

Frustration flashes across Sabine's face. She shakes her head. "Go ahead, become a medic. Join the nursing corps. I'm sure the many bleeding wounded will feel safe under your care."

"You are being cruel."

Sabine's eyes burn into hers. "I am being honest, Charlotte. You cling to the suffering, you make it yours, as if you think you must. As if you think that it will somehow keep you human, but it can't, because the human part of you is *dead*."

Charlotte flinches as if struck, the word ringing through the room, her head.

Silence stretches in the wake, and then Sabine sighs.

"Their pain does not hurt me, but yours does."

She draws Charlotte in, and Charlotte lets her. Buries her face in Sabine's shoulder, clings to the familiar scent as the long fingers stroke her hair.

"You are right," she murmurs. "I loved, and still love you for your heart. But I hate to see you suffer. Especially when it does no good."

"The world is so dark," whispers Charlotte. "So full of death. There must be something we can do."

Sabine brings her fingertips to Charlotte's chin, and lifts her face.

"Yes," she says, "we can live."

IV

1918

People spill into the street.

They laugh and cry and dance and drink, giddy with the news.

The war is over.

The world exhales, and Charlotte feels lighter than she has in years.

The air is awash in hope and joy and sheer relief. Charlotte wraps it round her like a cloak, lets the good mood sink into her bones.

She is naïve enough to think the worst is over now, and she marvels at the beauty that rises in the horror's wake. The defiant way the world recovers, grows back stronger than before.

Even Sabine is in a brighter mood, though it's hard to tell if it's because the Allies won, or simply because Charlotte is better company again.

There is something else.

Sabine has begun to go her own way at night sometimes, to wander off and hunt alone, but she always comes back bright-eyed and happy, humming with life, and always with a gift in hand—a single sunflower, a silver comb, a first edition of *Camilla*, because she knows it was the book that swept Charlotte off her feet.

That is the thing. Even after all these years, she *knows*.

Every inch of Charlotte's mind.

Every chamber of her heart.

It is easy, isn't it, in retrospect?

To spot the cracks. To see them spread.

But in the moment, there is only the urge to mend each one.

To smooth the lines.

And keep the surface whole.

V

London, England
1927

"Happy anniversary, my love."

Charlotte is standing on the terrace, watching the night settle over London, when Sabine comes up behind her and whispers the words in her ear.

They have been together now one hundred years.

A *century*.

On paper, the word looks so much smaller than its worth.

"We'll celebrate," purrs Sabine, "but first . . ." She turns Charlotte in her arms. "A gift."

It lies there in her open palm.

A small gold pendant on a matching chain. It is lovely, but the longer Charlotte studies it, the more certain she is that she's seen it before, though she can't remember where or when. Not until she sees that the small letter etched into its front, which at first she took for a C, is in fact a G, and that the pendant is in fact a cuff link, hammered flat.

A strange pit forms in her stomach, and she knows, even though it's been a hundred years, that it belonged to George Preston. Her first kill.

The young man with the water-blue eyes, and the floppy blond hair, and the body that made such an awful sound when it toppled down the cellar steps.

Charlotte stares at the pendant, torn between amazement that Sabine has kept it all this time, and horror at the fact, and the idea that Sabine, who knows her mind so well, would ever think she'd want it.

Charlotte has always found Sabine's collection morbid. The way she takes these tokens like trophies from her kills, while Charlotte rids herself of any evidence, wishes she could shed the memories as well, so they could never haunt her.

Charlotte wants to recoil from the trinket, to fling it off the balcony.

But it is their anniversary, and Sabine's mood is high, her eyes alight with happiness, and so Charlotte only smiles, grateful that she's spent the last few years learning to put up walls around her mind, to shield the thoughts that are not safe to share.

And so Sabine believes her when she calls the trinket lovely, when she turns and lifts her curls so she can put it on.

"To the next one hundred years," murmurs Sabine, and Charlotte shivers as the necklace settles, cold and heavy, at her throat.

Sabine wants to paint the town red, and so they do.

Four bodies dropped into the Thames before Big Ben strikes one, and then, giddy and blood-drunk, they end up at the Cavalcade, one of the few clubs that not only turns the other cheek to the nature of its clients, but seems to revel in its oddness. A place where some women wear suits, and some men wear makeup, and no one cares who you dance with, who you kiss.

The air is full of jazz, and want, and gin. Heartbeats to every side, their hunger beating like a drum, and they are dancing, and Charlotte is so glad she did not make a fuss about the gift, because they're *happy*.

Sabine is radiant in lace and emerald crepe, her charms and pendants looped like pearls, copper hair pinned up beneath a sequined band, while Charlotte is awash in cream, fringe flaring just above her knees with every turn.

They dance, and even though it's been a hundred years, they move within that fateful wind, and they are happy, just the two of them inside the storm.

Until Sabine's attention snags on something.

Charlotte turns to look, assuming she's found another mark, someone to slake that endless appetite, is surprised to find she's staring at a *man*.

He's handsome, with rich brown skin and raven hair, dressed in a crisp white shirt and red suspenders, elbows leaning on a burnished rail. And the longer Charlotte stares, the more she understands why Sabine was drawn. There is *something* about him—a stillness at odds with the raging club, a sense of being out of time or place.

And then, between one moment and the next, a woman appears at his side.

She is black and gold, her dress shining like light against her dark skin, and the strange feeling expands, surrounds the two of them—an uncanny quiet, a feline grace—and if Charlotte had a pulse, it would begin to race, because in that instant, she knows.

The strangers are like her.

Like *them*.

The woman locks eyes with Charlotte, and as she does, the club around them seems to peel apart, the floor to tip forward, Charlotte tipping with it. The entire moment lasts a lifetime, and a single trumpet roar, and then Sabine is there, drawing her back, a silent *no* in the flexing of her hand, and by the time she steals another glance, the railing is empty, the two figures gone.

Charlotte's spirit gutters.

A hundred years, apart, alone, with no one but Sabine.

A hundred years without another confidante, or friend.

A hundred years of waiting, wanting, and then at last, they were right there. She was so close. She could have caught the woman's hand. Could have heard the man's voice. Could have asked if there were others.

The loss is so sudden, so acute, but Charlotte knows better than to show it. To let her lover see, or feel, or hear. So she turns, puts her back to the empty rail, her focus on Sabine. She lets the music drown her, sinks beneath the beat until it stops. Until the club is closing, and they are ushered out into the late-night air.

And there they are.

The two strangers, idling beneath a streetlamp, a photograph amid the noise and bustle of the West End. Her—lounging in the front seat of a roadster, a pearl cigarette holder perched between her lips, and him—leaning back against the polished side, flicking a lighter absently against his slacks.

They are striking, yes, but more than that, they are *familiar*.

It's not just the light that shines behind their eyes, or the quiet absence of their hearts. They feel in tune, like the same song played on different instruments. Or perhaps the same instrument, playing different songs. Charlotte always thought that music, that resonance, came from Sabine alone. But now, she understands. It is the nature of them that brings that quiet harmony.

Charlotte feels her legs carrying her forward, her body tipping toward them once again, before Sabine takes a single, fluid step, putting herself in front of Charlotte, as if they pose a threat.

The woman cocks her head, and plucks the holder from between her lips, and grins, revealing the tips of pointed teeth.

"There they are," she says, an edge of laughter in her voice. "See, Jack? I told you it was worth sticking around. A city this big, ain't every night you meet a friend." Her accent knocks the last letters off of half the words.

"You say we've met." Sabine inclines her head, her face a placid mask. "I do not think we have."

The woman's smile doesn't falter. But it's her companion, Jack, who speaks.

"What a lapse on our part," he says in a crisp English voice. "Allow us to make amends."

He gestures at the roadster. Sabine doesn't move, and so, neither does Charlotte.

"Come on now," the woman adds in that strange drawl. "Surely you aren't planning on turning in just yet. Not when the night's so young. Hop in," she says. "I know a place that serves till dawn."

Charlotte bites her bottom lip, feels like she is full of bees, humming with the sheer force of curiosity and want. She wants to surge forward, into the waiting car, but she remembers how angry Sabine got when Charlotte had merely *asked* if there were others like them in the world, so she's prepared for the refusal, the rebuke.

Instead, Sabine rests her fingers at the base of Charlotte's back and says, "Well, what shall we do?"

Charlotte looks up at her, as if it is a trick, a trap, but Sabine's expression is a placid mask. "This is your night," she says, "so you decide."

Charlotte should have hesitated, she knows that now, feigned reluctance at the very least. But she can't contain her excitement anymore. She breaks into a happy smile. "Let's go with them," she says, buzzing with hope. "It will be fun."

Sabine smiles back, and kisses Charlotte's temple before nudging her ahead.

The woman slaps the side of the car with her open palm. "Come on, then. Jack, be a good sport and get the door."

⌒∿

The night air whistles and the engine roars.

The car tears through the London streets, the woman—Antonia— behind the wheel. When she said her name, her accent made it four beats instead of three—a melody of high and low.

By the time the roadster comes to a stop in Southwark, only Antonia's hair remains unscathed, the glossy black finger waves snug as a cap against her head. Jack combs his own hair back in order but Charlotte's curls have run wild in the open air, and filaments of copper have come loose from Sabine's sequined band. She tosses the ornament away, and her hair uncoils.

Antonia parks before a warehouse of sorts, one of the many structures throughout the city that at first glance looks like it's not just closed but boarded up. Abandoned.

But this is the twenties, and things are almost never what they seem.

Indeed, Charlotte can hear the music wafting up from down below like steam. Sabine's fingers twine with hers as Jack brings his hand to rest against the warehouse door, looks back at them, and winks.

Years later, Charlotte can remember the way that door fell open onto honey-colored light. But she still can't define the *feeling* of that place.

The dreaminess, the languid grace. The colors, like a sunrise just before it starts. The promise of a day. Imagine a cabaret, only the tempo has been slowed, the volume dropped by half, rendering the whole thing softer and more intimate.

Guests of all genders and complexions gather at small tables, heads together and voices low as, perched above them, women wearing little more than well-placed feathers contort themselves with feline ease. Servers, some dark and others fair, and all in fine suits and holding silver trays, weave between the tables, while on a round stage a man with silent-film good looks and a somber voice adds a thread of music to the room.

"Welcome to the Way Down," says Antonia, drifting through the center of the club as if she owns it. Which, it quickly becomes clear, she *does*. A handful of patrons raise their drinks in her direction. One goes so far as to brush his lips across the peaks of her gloved hand. A server takes her wrap and calls her *Miss Antonia*. Another leads them to the best seats in the house, a table raised on its own platform at the back.

"How marvelous," sighs Charlotte as they sink into their seats, her attention flicking from the gathering back to their hosts as Jack leans in to light the new cigarette that's waiting in Antonia's holder.

She takes a drag, fills her lungs just to blow it out.

"I know it does nothing," she says, smoke sliding through her teeth, "but I must admit, I like the affectation. And Jack here tells me I look sophisticated when I smoke."

"I do believe the word I used was *sexy*."

"Well, that, too. Go on, then, fetch us a drink?"

Jack rises and strolls off, reappears a minute later with a tray, laden with a bottle and four short glass cups, their patterned sides opaque. Charlotte assumes it is merely a formality, another farce—how many glasses of wine, or cups of tea have she and Sabine left undrunk at their tables—but then he pours, and the contents come out dark, and thick, and red.

The scent of blood reaches her immediately. Charlotte's skin tightens, and her throat goes dry, teeth aching as the hunger turns her hollow, even now, despite the night they've had, the bodies in their wake.

She takes up a glass. How strange blood looks, outside the body, how surreal without the struggle. Anger washes through her. If she had known this was an option—

If she had known there was a *choice*.

"To new friends," announces Antonia as they raise their glasses. All except Sabine. Antonia glances toward her. "It's bad luck, you know, not to toast."

Sabine's mouth twitches. "Alas," she says, spreading her hands. "I don't drink anything that's already been"—her gaze flicks down and up again—"*decanted.*"

Charlotte keeps her expression careful, though inwardly she winces. Sabine is being rude, *blatantly* so, throwing down a gauntlet, just to see how they'll react. And even though Charlotte cannot read their minds, she feels the air around them turn to glass.

Jack's gaze narrows, just a fraction.

But Antonia only smiles, showing teeth. "Yes," she drawls, "it does lose something, doesn't it?" She waves her fingers, and a server appears at her shoulder, a fair-skinned man with sun-gold hair.

"Miss Antonia?"

"Send Meredith to the office," she says, her attention still fixed on Sabine. "Tell her to wait there." The server nods, withdraws, and once he's gone, her gaze flicks to Jack. "Darling, show our guest the way?"

A clever parry. To force Sabine to choose between pettiness and thirst. She hesitates only a moment, then stands and follows Jack, but not before kissing Charlotte deeply, nipping at her bottom lip as she assures her that she'll be right back.

There is an instant, as she walks away, when Charlotte finds herself suddenly unmoored, as if the cord between them has drawn taut enough to break. Then it does, and Charlotte is still there, alone and in one piece.

"Where were we?" says Antonia. "Ah, that's right." She lifts her cup again. "To new friends." She knocks the glass against Charlotte's, and drinks.

Charlotte tips her own glass, frowning slightly when the blood passes her lips. The first thing she notices is the lack of pulse, the absence of a heartbeat. Still, she feels the blood seep through her as she swallows, warmth blooming in its wake.

The world doesn't fall away, and there is no moment in the sun, but at least her thirst retreats. A brief respite—and in the wake of iron and earth, she tastes a sweet residual. Gin.

Charlotte cannot help herself. She wonders aloud whose blood it is.

"Does it matter?" asks Antonia.

"Shouldn't it?" Charlotte looks down into the empty cup, the film of red. "For years, I would only take certain men. And even then I'd search their minds, trying to find one who deserved it."

Antonia inhales, eyes flaring with her cigarette tip. "That's a nice idea," she says. "But it don't work."

Charlotte looks up. "What do you mean?"

"Life is messy. People, too. And you can tie yourself in knots, trying to make yourself feel better, or you can face the truth."

"Which is?"

Antonia sighs out a plume of smoke. "No one should play God. Least of all us."

Charlotte feels sadness creeping through her like a chill, but Antonia doesn't seem bothered by the topic. She only crosses her legs and leans in, elbows resting on her stockinged knees. Up close, her eyes are dark and bright at once, candles behind tinted glass, her lashes painted gold.

"Now tell me, Charlotte," she says in that downy drawl, "where are you from?"

"Hampshire," she says. "And you?"

Antonia laughs. "Here I was thinking it was plain as day. I hail from those United States."

Charlotte brightens. For more than a decade, she's wanted to go, but Sabine recoiled at the thought of spending weeks aboard a ship. Insisted everything they could ever want or need was on this side of that vast stretch of water. Said fire might be a bad death, but drowning sounded worse. And then, as if to prove her point, the *Titanic* went and sank, and Sabine laughed, a brutal, mocking sound, and they never spoke of it again.

"America," says Charlotte now. "I've always wondered what it's like."

"That depends," says Antonia, flicking the ash off the cigarette, "on your complexion. I imagine you'd fare a yard better than I did. That said . . ." Her cool hand drifts up to Charlotte's chin. "I'd wager you've a bit of pigment in you. Not much, of course," she adds, hand falling away. She leans back, dips a fingertip into her cup, lets the blood bead and fall back into the glass. "But over there, they measure every drop."

Charlotte frowns, looking down at her own hands. She can still remember Aunt Amelia pursing her lips.

How tan you are. Your mother's side no doubt.

Come away from the window. You hardly need more sun.

In the end, she needn't have worried. Charlotte's skin, like the rest of her, is trapped in time, halfway to the bronze she would have been in summer, that patina of freckles now forever on her cheeks.

"Of course, times are changing," muses Antonia with a shrug. "And I'll be sticking round, to see they do. But in the meantime, I've made a fine life here in London. Me and Jack."

"How did you meet?" asks Charlotte, hungry for details. "Were you both already—or did you make—" Antonia arches a brow, and she falters, suddenly unsure. "Is it rude to ask these things? I'm sorry. It's just, I've never met any-one else who's been . . ."

She trails off, uncertain of the words to use.

"What?" says Antonia. "You mean buried in the midnight soil?"

Charlotte stiffens at the use of Sabine's words. Because of course, until that moment, she assumed they *were* Sabine's. Something she'd invented, a private poem, a bedroom invocation that belonged to them alone.

Her face goes hot, but Antonia breezes on. "Never met another? Where has that Sabine been hiding you?" Her voice is breezy, the question rhetori-cal, but Charlotte still tenses, a stiff smile rising to her lips.

"How long have you two been together, you and Jack?"

"Going on seventy years now. And no, I didn't make him, though I knew the man who did. We found each other, after." She looks past Charlotte and grins. "Speaking of makers and love . . ."

Coils of copper hair drape like arms around Charlotte's shoulders as Sabine and Jack return.

A look passes between Jack and Antonia, so subtle and so quick Charlotte catches it only because she's looking, as Sabine plants a kiss along her collar. The stolen pulse still echoes audibly behind her ribs, blood blooming in her cheeks.

"Did you miss me?" she whispers against her skin.

"Always," answers Charlotte as her lover takes her seat. So does Jack, and for a moment no one speaks; the whole scene hovers on a knife's edge between uncertainty and dread.

But then Sabine leans forward and refills the other cups, and it's like a hand, smoothing ruffled fabric. As the glasses empty, and fill, and empty again, the air unwinds around the table.

The hours slide by.

Jack and Antonia finish each other's stories, their easy banter like a warm bath.

Jack and Charlotte talk of growing up on English soil.

Sabine recounts her entry into London society, how she only learned about the Season thanks to a shop window and a pretty dress.

And the whole time, Sabine is at her very best, a house lit up from every room. That coy smile and that feline grace, and the same magnetic charm that first drew Charlotte all those years ago here again on full display. She is radiant, and every time she so much as glances Charlotte's way, she blushes from the sheer force of the attention.

The bottle is emptied and another one arrives, the glasses refilled, and Charlotte empties hers again, and again, until one of Antonia's stories leaves her giggling, a fit she can't seem to stop, and Sabine cheerfully informs the group that it might be time to put her love to bed.

There are no windows in the Way Down, but Jack produces a watch and declares that it's an hour until dawn. True to Antonia's word the bar is still serving but it's clearly slowing down, only a handful of tables still occupied as the four make their goodbyes, Jack kissing Charlotte on each cheek, and Antonia insisting that they simply must do this again.

She squeezes Charlotte's hand, kisses her cheek, and says that no matter the hour, or the night, or the year, she and Sabine are always welcome there.

And as they make their way home, in that quiet hour before dawn, the closest London ever comes to sleep, Charlotte leans her head on Sabine's shoulder and smiles, convinced it's been the kind of night that they will all remember.

A perfect anniversary.

"What a wonderful night that was," says Charlotte once they're back inside the flat.

Sabine says nothing, and that's when she notices how quiet the room has gone.

How cold the air has turned around them.

No, no, no, thinks Charlotte as she turns toward Sabine, and finds her gripping the bedpost so hard the wood beneath is splintering.

"Am I not enough?" she says, and even though her voice is quiet, it is as sharp and cold as broken ice.

Charlotte stiffens, the clinging softness of the gin suddenly gone. "Of course you are," she says, confusion mingling with fear. "Sabine, I only meant—"

"I saw how much you brightened," she snarls. "I felt how glad you were to go with them."

What shall we do? Sabine had said. *You decide.*

It was a trap. She should have known. And now—

"Are you so sick of me?"

Charlotte shakes her head, even though Sabine's back is to her. She grasps at calm, feels it slipping through her fingers. No, everything was good, everything was right. She saw the old Sabine, the one she fell in love with.

She is still in there, somewhere, inside. She only has to get her back.

Charlotte crosses the room, wraps her arms around her lover's waist. "You are all I want," she whispers between her shoulders. "All I need. Let's go to bed."

Sabine doesn't move, doesn't soften.

"Please," Charlotte says as she slips off the dress, lets it pool beneath her on the floor, a heap of beads and silk. "Please," she says as she circles Sabine, reaches up to cup her face, looks her in the eyes, the light in them flickering, on the verge of going out. "Take me to bed, Sabine."

For a horrible moment, nothing.

Then Sabine twists, pinning Charlotte up against the cracked bedpost. She kisses her, hard, teeth slicing Charlotte's bottom lip. She doesn't break away, not as blood—her blood—fills her mouth. Not as Sabine pushes her down onto the bed, one hand holding her wrists, and the other parting her legs. Not as she arches, offering the column of her throat, and Sabine bites deep, teeth sinking to the bone.

Why does Charlotte stay?

That is like asking—why stay inside a house on fire?

Easy to say when you are standing on the street, a safe distance from the flames.

Harder when you are still inside, convinced you can douse the blaze before it spreads, or rushing room to room, trying to save what you love before it burns.

VI

1943

Charlotte walks between the shuttered stalls, scouring the ground for flowers.

She searches what's left of the little makeshift market, and finds mostly leafless stems. Half-trampled buds. Heads crooked or bent or losing petals.

Before this new war broke out, she spent whole evenings wandering the empty aisles of Covent Garden's flower stalls, surrounded by the heady scent of peonies and roses. But Jubilee Hall was commandeered, like so much of London. Put to better use.

Everything is worse this time.

The wailing sirens, the shaking ground, the constant haze of fear.

Month after month the residents of London vanish—some to the safety of the countryside and others to the front, while death wafts back across the Channel, and clouds the air like smoke.

Charlotte hates it here, has tried a dozen times to talk of fleeing north, or south, or west, but Sabine insists they stay in London. It's easier to hunt, she says, when so many disappear.

Charlotte suspects it is a test.

To see if she will keep her word, or seek out Antonia again.

Her head turns, eyes drifting even now toward Southwark as she wonders if the Way Down is still there. She doesn't know.

She stops, foot hovering over an almost perfect rose.

A stunning find, given the dregs that litter the ground.

Charlotte kneels, adding the bloom to the other castoffs she's collected.

She drags in a breath, tasting the air, and immediately wishes she hadn't. That patina of grief and panic fills her chest, her mind, makes her feel like she's going mad. Sabine was wrong. There is no way to block it out. She's *tried*. Tried to clog her ears, cordon off her mind, but it is impossible. All she can do is hide how much it still disturbs her.

Sabine has no patience for Charlotte's *hysteria*, as she has named it, while

Charlotte, for her part, can hardly bear her poise. Nothing seems to disturb Sabine, whose chief complaint is that the rationing has made the blood taste bland.

Charlotte stared at her when she said it. Wanted to be aghast, and instead felt only sad. What happened to the woman who seduced her on the stairs? The one who taught her how to dance in hidden parlors, how to dream and want and take more than she was given? The one who ran barefoot with her through empty castle halls, and made her heart feel like it had never stopped beating?

Charlotte wonders where she is right now.

They were together earlier that night, strolling down a half-empty road, as strangers with hunched shoulders hurried by, and Charlotte suggested that they pick someone together. But Sabine was strange, distracted, too restless in her skin, and eventually she pulled away, and announced that she would take a walk alone, and meet Charlotte back at home.

Charlotte watched her go, and felt . . . relieved.

She is so tired of keeping up appearances, pretending that this lonely life isn't wearing her from stone to sand.

She crouches to rescue a trampled peony, and brings the makeshift bouquet to her nose. Closes her eyes as she inhales and imagines herself back at Clement Hall.

A memory of laughter. The tickle of fresh grass. Her mother's voice, and—

An air-raid siren whines to life, a wretched, haunting howl.

Charlotte sighs, presses the little bouquet to her chest. She looks up at the sky, searching for the edges of a plane, wonders what would happen if she held her ground, and something fell. Would her fragile heart be crushed, or would she crawl from the rubble?

She starts walking, ignoring the citizens who dart for cover, the older man who waves, trying to point her toward the nearest shelter.

Maybe it is the fresh coat of panic, but Charlotte quickens her pace, suddenly eager to get home, to Sabine.

Their current flat reminds her of the house on Merry Way, with Aunt Amelia and her charges—two stories tall, too large for just the two of them, claimed when the last inhabitants decamped to somewhere safer, greener, farther from the noise.

She arrives, the flowers in one hand and the keys in the other, and finds—

Blood.

Blood on the doorknob.

Blood on the stairs.

Blood, sliding like fingers down the wall.

The gruesome trail leads to their bedroom, where she finds Sabine standing in the center of the room, covered head to toe in red. It streaks her face, drips from her hands, pools beneath her bare feet on the floor.

Charlotte recoils at the sight, the wood creaking beneath her shoes. Sabine's head drifts up, her eyes black, the pupils wide. She smiles dreamily.

"There you are," she says in an airy voice, too kind to be the stranger's, too wrong to be her own.

"My love," says Charlotte, fighting to sound gentle, "what have you done?"

Sabine lets her head fall back. Her gaze trails across the ceiling. "They came apart like Christmas paper." Her arms drift at her sides, as if through water. "Ribbons, everywhere."

Charlotte shivers.

There is no violence in her voice, but what's left is somehow worse. This languid monster in her lover's flesh.

She wants to turn and run.

To flee this room, this flat, this life.

Instead, Charlotte forces herself forward. "Come," she says, taking Sabine's hand. "Let's get cleaned up."

She runs a bath, and for once, Sabine makes no effort to reclaim control. She lets herself be led into the tub, lounges as the water to every side turns pink, then red. Purrs in pleasure as Charlotte washes her hair, scrubs the gore from beneath her nails, cleans and tends the body that she has loved so long and knows so well. Remains pliant as Charlotte dries her, limb by limb, and then takes her to bed. Settles her there among the pillows.

"I can't hear your thoughts," Sabine murmurs sleepily. "They are so quiet." The faintest crease forms between her brows. "Are you keeping secrets from me?"

Charlotte shakes her head. "No," she whispers, her mind locked tight. "I am just tired." She smooths the furrow with her thumb. "Aren't you tired?"

"Yes," says Sabine, sinking back among the pillows.

Charlotte curls in against her side, and strokes her hair, waiting for the light to come back on behind those eyes. But it never does. And so instead, she whispers the poem, the one Sabine kissed into her skin night after night over the years.

"Bury my bones in the midnight soil.
Plant them shallow and water them deep.
And in my place will grow a feral rose . . ."

Until she's sure Sabine is asleep.

Then slowly, slowly, Charlotte frees herself. Sabine used to reach for her every time Charlotte so much as moved, but she sleeps so deeply now, so rarely stirs once she is down. As if she is buried beneath dirt instead of blankets.

Lost to herself, her love, the world.

Charlotte slips from the bed and pads silently across the room. There is a blade in the top drawer of the nearby desk. A blunted edge, more like a letter opener than a weapon, but it will do.

She climbs back onto the bed, and kneels over Sabine.

Sabine, who even now looks like a painting, tendrils of wet hair spread across the pillow, tokens dripping like roots between her breasts. She lies so still, she looks already lifeless.

Charlotte swallows as she lifts the blade and drives the metal point down toward Sabine's chest.

It slices through the air.

And stops.

The tip hovers there, an inch over her heart, as if it's met a wall. Charlotte stares in shock, grits her teeth, tries to force the blade down, knuckles white around the hilt. Realizes that it's not the knife, or the air, holding back the blade. It's *her*. Her own limbs restrained, her body held in place by ropes she cannot see. Her mind races, reels, and with a dawning horror, she understands.

Not ropes.

Words.

Ones said more than fifty years ago, when Charlotte left her home behind a final time. *Promise that you will never hurt me.*

How strange the words had struck her, even then, as they lay curled together in the bed of that cursed house, after that darkness had taken her the first time.

Promise that you will never hurt me.

Of all the things Sabine could ask for. All the oaths she could extract.

How simple this one seemed to Charlotte then.

How easy to say yes.

But those words cinch around her now, her hands trembling as she tries to force the knife those last few inches. *Can't.* Her eyes burn in frustration, grief. A crimson tear runs down her chin. Drips onto Sabine's cheek.

Perhaps it is the scent of blood that wakes her.

Perhaps it is the way Charlotte's walls are crumbling, her panic spilling out into the air.

Sabine's eyes flutter, and drift open. Still black, still bottomless.

They take in the blade, still frozen over her chest, and Charlotte, just beyond it. And the look that sweeps across her face isn't shock, or rage. Instead, her mouth twitches in amusement. As if this is another game, and Charlotte has just tipped her hand.

Charlotte drops the knife and scrambles backward off the bed, as Sabine sits up.

"Silly Charlotte," she says, reaching for the blade as she backs away across the room. She balances it thoughtfully, the weight tipping side to side, before her cold black eyes flick up again. "Why don't you come back to bed?"

But there is no going back, not now, and so Charlotte turns, and runs.

She expects to make it one stride, two, before Sabine's arms close over her, and she drives the blade into her heart. But she makes it to the end of the room, and then, to the end of the hall, and then, to the bottom of the stairs, and then, out into the street, and there is no rending in her chest, no death or darkness rushing up, only the night air, and the ghostly echo of the sirens, and she forces her body forward, on, away.

Charlotte is Orpheus, Sabine, Eurydice.

And she does not look back.

VII

Charlotte walks barefoot through the London streets, arms wrapped around herself as she crosses Southwark Bridge in nothing but a nightgown, the sky lightening with every step.

She reaches the warehouse just after dawn, shivering from sickness now as well as fear, and leans against the door, only to find it locked.

She knocks, but no one answers. No sound of steps within.

Charlotte lets her forehead fall against the wood as her fingers wrap around the handle. The lock crunches beneath her grip, the door gives way—

And still she cannot enter.

Her limbs snag on the threshold, the invitation she was given, all those years ago, either expired or revoked.

Charlotte sways, and sinks to her knees on the stone curb, head pounding and bones sore. She is trying to gather the strength and will to stand again when she hears the clip of shoes, and Jack finally appears, hair slicked back and shirtsleeves rolled, suspenders hanging from his waist. Jack, who helps Charlotte to her feet, murmurs *Oh dear,* and *Darling,* and *Come in.*

Like them, the Way Down is still there.

The walls have been painted a different shade, the tables rearranged, and it's empty at this hour, but Charlotte feels that same sleepy and pervading warmth, that welcome air, as Jack leads her to a booth. Antonia appears at the top of the stairs, plucking pins from her hair, and what Charlotte remembers most is not the gentle way they handle her, but the total absence of surprise. Sixteen years, and yet it's clear, they've been expecting her.

Antonia brings her a shawl, more for comfort than for cold, or perhaps simply for modesty, and Jack sets down a glass, but as Charlotte reaches for it she's met by a ghoulish reflection in the polished surface of the table—her curls wild, cheeks streaked with bloody tears. How lucky that she met no one on the road.

Jack and Antonia sit across from her, waiting for the tale, and so she tells it.

Charlotte is amazed by the calmness in her voice. The way it doesn't break.

"I was out getting flowers . . ."

The flowers. She can't remember where she left them. Was it at the front door, when she first saw the blood? Or was it in the bedroom? She knows it hardly matters now, but as she hears herself recount the story—of coming home, of finding Sabine, of the bath, and the bed, and the blade that stopped—the rest of her is searching frantically for the bouquet.

She forces her mind back to the booth. Jack and Antonia are sharing a look as if engaged in silent conversation, and Charlotte cannot help but wonder bitterly, do they let each other in? Are their minds houses the other gets to walk through, exploring every room, while she is forced to stand outside the door and guess?

If Sabine had let her in, would it have made a difference?

Would she have been strong enough to stay?

Or would she simply have fled sooner?

"I'm sorry for coming here," she says aloud. "I didn't know where else to go. But if I've put you in danger—"

"Don't you worry about that," says Antonia, waving her hand. "This is *our* house. No one's getting through that door without permission."

Charlotte's gaze flicks down the short hall, and as she does, one of the shadows seems to peel away, incline its head, and grow a sleepy smile.

Silly Charlotte, why don't you come back to bed?

She shivers, blinks. Her tired mind is playing tricks on her.

"Drink that," says Jack, nudging the glass forward. "It will help."

Charlotte nods, and takes it, tastes something sweet behind the iron as she swallows. Warmth spreads through her, a softness in its wake.

"Jack, darling, you go on up. I'll be there soon."

He nods, withdraws, and Antonia slips onto the cushioned bench beside her, coaxes Charlotte to lie down, let her head rest in the other woman's lap.

"Go on," drawls Antonia, stroking her curls, "try to get some rest."

Charlotte wants to refuse, convinced she'll never sleep again, but as those graceful fingers pet her hair, and the daylight presses down from up above, a horrible fatigue steals over her.

"Why are you being so kind?" she asks, even as she begins to sink.

Antonia's voice follows her down. "We grow together in this garden."
And then, somehow, she sleeps.

Mercifully, she doesn't dream.

She wakes at nightfall—no windows in the club, and yet she knows, time ringing like a bell against her bones—sits up to find a set of fresh clothes folded and waiting on the table. A cotton dress. A cashmere sweater. A pair of shoes.

She ducks into the bathroom and dresses, scrubs her cheeks, pins up her hair, adjusts her face until the reflection looking back is less the haunted girl in last night's table, and more the one she's known these last one hundred years. By the time Charlotte steps out into the club again, a handful of servers have arrived, the Way Down going about its business, of course, because the world has not stopped for anyone but her.

Antonia reappears, descending the stairs in a pearl dress, hair coiffed in perfect waves, lips painted ruby red. Jack strolls down behind her, hands in his pockets, and Charlotte knows she has to go, is still gathering the strength to rise and leave, to face the city—the black-eyed version of her lover surely out there, searching for her in the dark—when Antonia produces a train ticket for the northern line.

It is such a kindness, and yet, there is a grim truth about that ticket, one Jack and Antonia are not saying.

It is not safe to stay in London.

How ironic, after all the times she begged Sabine to leave.

"Jack will walk you to the station," says Antonia. "He would drive you, but there's hardly any petrol . . ."

Charlotte shakes her head. "No, you've done too much already. And if Sabine . . ."

They came apart like Christmas paper.

Antonia drapes an arm around Jack's shoulders. "Don't you worry about our Jack," she says, kissing his cheek. "He can hold his own well enough, isn't that so?"

Jack smiles, tips an imaginary hat. "It'll be my pleasure to see you get there safe."

Antonia meets Charlotte's eye, seems about to speak, but then the door swings open. Charlotte stiffens, certain it will be Sabine, but it's only the first patrons of the night arriving, and with that, Antonia turns her charm on them as Jack escorts her out and up into the waiting dark.

~~~

They walk together, side by side, Jack with his hands in his pockets, and Charlotte holding his elbow tight. Her nerves are tense, her senses scrambling for purchase, her imagination transforming every shape they pass into a woman, and every woman into Sabine.

Sabine, dressed in the violet gown she wore the night they met, one gloved hand raised to hail a cab.

Sabine, leaning against a shuttered shop door, covered head to toe in blood.

Charlotte squeezes her eyes shut until the darkness blooms with stars.

"You know," says Jack. "We think ourselves immortal, but we're not."

Charlotte blinks, forcing her attention back to him.

"Live long enough, and things begin to rot." He draws a hand from his pocket, taps a fingertip against his chest. "Compassion, affection, humility, care." One strike with every word. "They drop away like petals, till all that's left is stem and thorn. Hunger, and the urge to hunt."

Charlotte frowns, even as her mind begins to race. Could that be it? What's happening . . . her Sabine was never *gentle*, never *kind*—or if she was, those things were gone by the time they met—but there had always been a ferocious kind of light, a biting humor, passion, and wit. When did they first begin to disappear?

Was it the house in Hampshire?

Or the German castle?

"In a way, I suppose it's all rather poetic," muses Jack, "the grudging mortality of all those things that made us human."

Anger rises like bile in Charlotte's throat. "Forgive me," she growls, "if I don't find the poetry a worthy price."

He nods, says nothing for a block, then two, and then the words come spilling out. "Antonia has told you, I believe, that she was not my maker. His name was William. A common name for an uncommon gentleman. When I was still young, he made me promise." He pauses, sparing her a glance. "As you now know, promises among our kind are binding."

Charlotte swallows, nods.

"Well," continues Jack, "William made me promise that when he ceased to be himself, I would kill him. And since he could not be trusted to tell me when that moment was, I would have to choose it for myself. I would have to measure, have to weigh, have to decide how much a person—*my* person—can lose before they are lost."

She stares, stunned, waiting for him to go on.

When he doesn't, she cannot help but ask. "What happened?"

To that, Jack offers only a wan smile, but she can see the pain in his eyes, fast as a camera flash before he buries it, and clears his throat. "The fact is, whether death takes you all at once, or steals pieces over time, in the end there is no such thing as immortality. Some of us just die slower than the rest."

Jack offers a kind smile as he says it, as if the words are meant to make her feel better. But as they near St. Pancras, Charlotte feels a new dread creeping in.

If that is true, and all of them are bound to wither, rot, what will it look like when her own humanity begins to ebb? What will it feel like? How will she tell? What if it steals over her so slowly she doesn't notice? What if it sweeps in so fast she never sees it coming?

If Jack hears these questions, they go unanswered.

They walk, arm in arm, into St. Pancras, that vaulting tunnel of glass and steel, damaged, bombed, yet somehow standing.

He leads her to the platform, her train already there. Strangers mill about, reading papers or sipping from flasks, some in groups and some alone, and Charlotte searching every one for that long face, that copper hair.

Certain, even now, that Sabine will hunt her down.

If she's not already there.

Jack hands her the ticket and wishes her good luck, laying a cool-lipped kiss on each cheek. "Courage," he says, "you've a long way to go," and she doesn't know if he's talking about her journey or her soul.

Jack starts to go, then stops, turns back. "Oh, almost forgot." He pats a pocket, drawing out a card. "On behalf of dear Antonia," he says. "If you ever find your way to America, she wanted you to have a friend."

Charlotte takes the card. On the front, the image of a black rose with white thorns. On the back, the word *Boston*. And just beneath, added in slanted cursive that must be hers, a name: *Ezra*.

With that, they part, though Jack vows to stay on the platform until the train has pulled away. Charlotte boards. For the first time in so long, alone.

It is a lie, she tells herself as the train rumbles to life, *that you only get one story.*

And yet, as she stands in the train car, facing the windows and the platform sliding away, empty save for Jack, she swears that she can feel Sabine, like a weight at the end of a rope. The cord between them drawing tight enough to snap as the train leaves the station, picking up speed. She waits to feel the moment of relief, when the cord breaks, and she is free.

It doesn't come.

But neither does Sabine.

Charlotte sinks at last into her seat.

And sobs.

ALICE

(D. 2019)

I

Lottie's voice trails off.

She's standing at the window, looking out with her back to the room, and in the reflection on the glass Alice can see the crimson tears rolling down her face, waits for her to go on, to explain, but she's stopped, and Alice doesn't know if she plans to start again or if that's it, and Alice looks from Lottie to Ezra, who's just sitting there, arms crossed, as if he's heard it before.

By now, it's either very late or very early, Alice doesn't know the place a night cuts off, stops being one and starts being the other, all she knows is that she's been listening to Lottie talk for hours, long after the hotel has put itself to bed, and she still hasn't told her *why*.

She shakes her head, shoving to her feet. "All that, just to say you got away?"

"No." Lottie blinks, shaking free of her own memories as she turns from the window. "I'm trying to tell you that I *didn't*."

"You want me to feel sorry for you? Because you had a toxic ex?" Lottie lets out a small sound, half-sob, half-laugh, but Alice just throws up her hands. "I'm sorry she hurt you," she says. "But it doesn't make up for what you did—"

"The story isn't over yet," she says.

"Get to the part that *matters*, then," snaps Alice.

"It *all matters*," she snaps back. "Stories matter, Alice. When you live long enough, they're all you have."

"I had a story, too," she seethes. "Before you ended it. I had a life. I had a—a chance to—" Her voice cracks. "I had a future. And now—"

Lottie looks up. "You still do."

"Oh, *fuck off!*"

Alice doesn't realize she's lunging toward Lottie as she says it, not until Ezra appears between them, one hand gently but firmly holding Alice back, as if she's the danger here—because of course, he's not her friend, he's Lottie's.

Lottie's guard has fallen down, and her guilt and grief are poisoning the air, seeping into the room, into Alice, making her feel things she doesn't want to, cannot bear to anymore, and for what? For what? No, fuck this.

She's had enough.

Alice turns and storms toward the door, half expecting one of them to try and stop her, but they don't. She wrenches the door open, so hard the hinges squeal, and plunges out into the hall, and she doesn't stop, not when she reaches the stairs, or the marble lobby at the bottom, or the glass front doors, or the sidewalk, or the street, or the entrance to the darkened Commons.

Doesn't stop until her feet find grass and even then, she can't shake the feeling that she's drowning. Her brain insists that she needs air but her lungs know that she doesn't, and the stillness inside of her is suffocating, and—

"Breathe."

She didn't hear Ezra coming after her, but he's there. "Just breathe," he says. She glances back and glowers at him, but he only shrugs. "Trust me, it will help."

And Alice doesn't trust him, wants to, might have, before he held her back, but she has to do *something* to stop this crushing pressure on her ribs, so she closes her eyes, drags in a deep breath, counts to four, then blows it out again, the way she learned to years ago. In, then out, then in again, making a bellows of her lungs until her nerves stop jangling, and her mind begins to quiet, and her body wrings out all the awful feelings that soaked from Lottie into her.

She breathes until she feels the night steady, the ground beneath her and the sky above. She breathes until she begins to feel more like herself again.

"Better?" he asks. She nods, afraid that if she stops to talk, the brittle calm will shatter. "Bodies hold on to certain things," says Ezra. "Old habits, and all that. For years, I smoked a pipe."

Alice stares at him, trying to picture it, and the image is so incongruous she almost smiles.

"Don't laugh," he says, "it was more common back when I was . . ."

She notices he doesn't like to say the word for what he was before, the same way she can't bear to say the one for what she is now.

"The point is, the tobacco didn't do anything, but there was just something about the familiarity of the act of packing the pipe and lighting it.

A sense memory of sorts. The wooden bit between my teeth. The way it calmed me."

Alice breathes in and out, clinging to the safety of the motion, how normal it makes her feel, even as the night-soaked Commons reminds her that she's not. It whispers to her, from the rustling trees, to the flapping of birds, to the three bodies wandering the paths, three sets of steps, three beating hearts. She blows out another breath, and when she trusts herself to speak again she asks, "When did you give it up?"

"Back in the seventies. Didn't really fit in anymore."

"I don't know," she says, eyeing him. "I hear it's making a comeback, with the hipsters."

Ezra grimaces. "No thank you." His eyes track over the Commons. "I had a friend who loved the smell of fresh-baked sourdough. He couldn't eat it, of course, but the scent alone was enough to pretend that if he really wanted to, he could."

"Great," mutters Alice. "You guys get pipe smoke and fresh bread, and I get anxiety. Doesn't seem fair."

Ezra's mouth quirks. "The point is, we find ways to hold on to who we were. In hopes it will keep us from becoming someone else."

She swallows. "Does it work?"

"No. But sometimes it softens the blow."

Alice closes her hands into fists, clenches them until she feels the crescents of her nails slice into her palms, but the pain is nothing but a ghost.

"I wanted to be someone else," she says. "That's why I came to Boston. Back home, I was . . ." *Catty's little sister,* Alice almost says.

Always in her shadow, always in her wake.

Instead, Alice shakes her head. "I wanted to be someone new. That's what this was supposed to be, a starting point. But now—"

"It's not a death sentence, Alice."

She glares at him. "Tell that to my pulse."

"Fine, if you want to be pedantic. But it's not. Lottie meant what she said. You can live a life. Yes, it will look a little different than the one you thought. But it can still be a life." He looks back over his shoulder at the hotel. "You should let her finish."

Alice feels the anger rise again, constrict around her heart. Anger at Ezra, for protecting Lottie. Anger at Lottie, for smiling at her in the dark, for running with her through the rain, for making her believe that that night could really be the start of everything. Alice folds her arms, but it makes her feel like a petulant child, so she uncrosses them again. "It won't change what happened. It won't change what I am. What she did."

Ezra nods, as if he understands. "You're right, there's no going back. But it might help you go forward. Take it from someone who has a few centuries behind them. You learn how heavy some feelings weigh, how much they'll drag you down. Anger and resentment are the worst. They're like rocks in your pockets. Too many, and you'll drown."

Alice turns, and looks across the street at the hotel, the windows staring back like glassy eyes, all of them dark, save one. Lottie is nothing but a silhouette, a girl-shaped shadow, one hand against the glass.

It wasn't me, she said when Alice first walked in. *It wasn't me.*

Now she takes a deep breath one last time, and then forces herself back toward the hotel.

To find out how the story ends.

CHARLOTTE

(D. 1827)

I

Rome, Italy
1953

It's true what they say, that cities rarely sleep, but there is an hour when they *doze*.

A perfect stretch of time, after the bars and clubs have shuttered, and before the bakers have risen. When the piazzas are empty, the avenues deserted, the wanderers so few that she can hear their heartbeats.

In that hour, Rome belongs to Charlotte.

She wanders through the streets, pretends that the city is a museum and she's the only patron. She walks, and marvels at the scale of the buildings, the newer ones delicate, colorful, ornate, the older ones imposing blocks of stone.

But the fountains are her favorite.

She visits them each night, as if they're friends. Knows the Latin carved into their backdrops and their bases, has memorized the many figures, twisted in battle, or lunging up from the depths, or bowing beneath the weight above.

Charlotte reaches the Piazza Navona and stops, as she always does, before her favorite of the three. Takes in Neptune, locked in battle with a creature from the depths. A horse and nymph, frantically trying to escape. All of them trapped, frozen forever in this desperate moment, this precipice between victory and defeat.

Around her, the night is quiet.

The oil lamps are long gone now, their butter-yellow glow replaced by streetlights that turn the cobblestones blue-white. The only sounds are the humming power grid and the burble of the fountain. But as Charlotte leans down to run her fingers through the water, she hears the unmistakable padding of bare feet.

And her world shudders to a stop.

Silly Charlotte.

She was so careful at first, the way a child is after burning their fingers.

Every night, for months, she stretched her senses to their limit, every nerve alert. The first time she saw a glint of red hair, her entire body went cold, before she realized it was only a round-faced girl with a ginger bob.

The next time, it was a mannequin in a shop window.

The third, light glancing off a post.

But as the weeks turned to months, and the months to years, her mind stopped playing tricks. The shadows settled, the shapes resolved, and though Sabine still haunted Charlotte in her dreams, that was the only place she ever found her.

Until now.

Ten years—so long, so short, how could she think that she was free?—and she knows, when she turns, what she will see, so she doesn't, not at first. Instead, she sits perfectly still on the edge of the fountain, keeps her gaze locked squarely on the water's surface, her panicked face rippling as the steps slink closer.

Silly Charlotte.

And then, at last, the most welcome sound in the world.

A heartbeat.

Soft but steady and unmistakably human.

The world stutters back into motion, and when Charlotte allows herself to look, she sees a young woman ambling toward the fountain, sandals hanging from one hand, cigarette from the other. Her limbs, tan and coltish, in a summer dress short enough to graze her thighs. Honey-blond hair cut into a bob, eyes a stunning shade of blue—though Charlotte will later marvel at the way they range from teal to stormy gray, depending on her mood.

Everything in Charlotte loosens, and she finds herself laughing softly in relief as the young woman sits and swings her legs over the fountain's edge, bare feet sinking with a splash into the water. The stranger slips the cigarette between her lips and lets her head fall back, exposing the column of her neck as she sighs smoke up into the night.

Hunger blooms in Charlotte's stomach, tightens in her throat.

"Lunga giornata o lunga notte?" asks the stranger lightly.

Charlotte hesitates. She has only been in Rome a month now, is still learning the singsong shape of Italian. "Mi dispiace," she says slowly. "Non parlo . . ."

At which point the young woman chuckles, and plucks the cigarette from her mouth.

"I only ask," she says in English, "if this is the end of a long night, or the start of a long day." She has the kind of voice that carries its own brightness, a smile in the sound, as if she's on the verge of laughing. A voice that makes Charlotte feel light-headed.

"End of a long night."

"Stesso," says the young woman. "Same."

She holds out the cigarette, and Charlotte takes it, rests her lips where the other woman's were. She inhales, and the smoke doesn't burn, doesn't *do* anything—it is, after all, an imitation of breath—but she savors the excuse to share space with someone else.

Ten years Charlotte has been alone. A stranger among strangers. A ghost brushing against the mortal world. There have been passing glances here and there, but the closest she's come to touch is in the bodies she claims, the lives she's forced to take, and what they feel for her is hardly love.

Ten years, and as glad as she was to finally be free, somewhere along the way the freedom soured, turned to loneliness. She misses the warmth of company, the lightness of a life shared with someone else.

The young woman reaches to reclaim the cigarette, their fingers grazing as she does.

"Giada," she says, and Charlotte waits for her to repeat the word in English. But she only laughs, and taps her chest. "My name."

Charlotte blushes. "Oh. Sorry. Charlotte."

"Ah," says Giada, "Carlotta."

And that small change, from English to Italian, makes her feel rechristened, new. Charlotte is forever scarred, but *Carlotta* hasn't spent the last decade running from Sabine. *Carlotta* never belonged to her at all.

"It isn't safe, you know," says Giada.

Charlotte stiffens at the warning, as if she's read her mind. "How so?"

She crosses her legs and flicks her toes through the water. "To be out here, in the dark, alone."

Charlotte relaxes, then. "I could say the same to you."

"Ah," says Giada, cheerfully patting her purse. "That is why I carry rocks."

"Rocks are heavy," says Charlotte. "Your shoulder must get tired."

"It does. But the longer I carry them, the stronger I feel."

Charlotte stares at Giada—this strange and stunning girl—as she stubs out her cigarette. As she swings her legs out of the water. As she slips her sandals on and stands, and studies Charlotte. "I can see you don't have any rocks," she says, "so I will walk you home."

And it is ridiculous, absurd, but Charlotte hears herself say yes. Even as her teeth prick against her bottom lip. Even as the hunger aches inside her jaw. Even as she listens to the steady beat of Giada's human heart behind her fragile ribs and wants it for her own, Charlotte knows she will gladly starve if it means letting Giada walk her home.

It turns out they live on the same street.

What are the odds? Charlotte on one end, and Giada on the other. They laugh—*she* laughs, the sound so sudden and bright, it feels like something coming loose inside her, some great unraveling. By now, the darkness is dissolving, the dawn soon on its way, and Giada squints up at the sky as if gauging the time and says she knows a place they can get coffee.

"At this hour?" Charlotte asks, and she's met with a smile, a shrug.

"They like me there."

Of course they do, she wants to say. *Who wouldn't?*

If Charlotte were an ordinary girl, she would be left to wonder if Giada is just being friendly, but she can taste her interest on the air, like spice.

If Charlotte were an ordinary girl, she would say yes.

But she's not.

"I can't," she says, even though that isn't strictly true. After all, the sun won't *kill* her. She could stomach the early-morning light, suffer through the sickness as the day swept in, but it would be a weight around her neck, a stain seeping through the memory she wants to make.

So she says no, and Giada—who cannot see or taste Charlotte's hunger on the air, who cannot feel her desire, her loneliness, her want—wilts a little, her brightness dimming, until Charlotte offers dinner instead.

"Tonight," she says. "My treat."

And just like that, Giada is glowing again. Her smile, bold as brass. "You should know," she says with a wink, "I eat a lot."

With that she spins and strolls away, down the narrow block.

"Pick me up at eight!" she calls over her shoulder, and Charlotte cannot help but smile as she watches Giada's honey-blond bob bounce and sway and vanish through a matching door.

Hope flares in her chest, and she thinks, *This, this, this* is where her story starts.

How clearly Charlotte can see it, even now.

Giada skipping down the steps at dusk in white sandals and a pink sundress. A giddy glee as she announces that she's planned a tour. Not of the Roman monuments, or ruins, but of her favorite foods.

She leads Charlotte through piazzas, over bridges, and down winding roads, explaining that they simply cannot eat at just one place, since each has its own specialty, and so, as the night settles over Rome she leads Charlotte on a pilgrimage, from coffee beneath white canopies in Regola to arancini passed through a window in Trastevere.

Charlotte is well-versed in the art of blending in, has spent long enough pretending to be human that she can manage in mixed company. It is, of course, an illusion that works better at a distance, and stumbles under scrutiny. But thankfully, when Giada eats, or drinks, the experience devours her in turn, and by the time she finally looks up to see what Charlotte thinks, the cup has been tipped out, the food disturbed.

Giada, meanwhile, holds no allegiance to the order of savory and sweet, and so they take gelato in Campitelli (the dessert melts swiftly in the late-spring warmth, seeming to eat itself) before settling at last beneath the red umbrellas of a bistro in the corner of a piazza in Monti.

There, over a plate of carbonara, Charlotte twirling noodles round her fork, she learns that Giada is a model. Not the kind that poses for magazines, or strolls down runways in the latest fashion. No, she is a life model, surrounded not by flashbulbs but the scratch of pencils.

She poses for artists, sometimes in loose clothes, so they can capture the light and shadow of the fabric's folds. More often in nothing, she says, grinning between mouthfuls of pasta. "I'm very popular."

"Of course you are," says Charlotte. "I mean, you're gorgeous." The words spill out, and yet, *she* is the only one who ends up blushing. Giada simply smirks and shakes her head.

"Beauty matters more for photos," she explains. "In art, it's better to be *interesting*. But no." She sets her fork aside. "They like me because once I strike a pose, I can hold it. I will not move. Watch."

It is hard to imagine Giada stationary. In the brief time they've spent together, she's been an object constantly in motion. Feet sliding through fountain pools. Hands hooking round light posts. Even her honey bob seems caught in a constant sway.

And yet, as Charlotte watches, she goes still. She doesn't *slow*, limbs dragging to a stop. It is a sudden, overwhelming stillness, like flesh being turned to stone. The fingers of one hand raised off the table mid-gesture. Her mouth parting slightly, as if about to speak. Her eyes trained on some distant sight over Charlotte's shoulder. The overall effect is at once impressive and uncanny.

Charlotte applauds, waits for Giada to dissolve back into motion.

But she doesn't so much as blink.

Charlotte dips her hand in the glass of water, flicks the drops half-heartedly at Giada's face, expecting her to recoil, laugh, or wipe her cheek.

Nothing.

Charlotte bites her lip in thought, then reaches out and runs her fingertips along the back of Giada's hand, tracing, skimming her wrist. She can feel the heartbeat quickening beneath the skin, can see the color spreading through Giada's cheeks, and yet those are the only parts that answer. Just when Charlotte thinks nothing in this world will cause Giada to break, their waiter arrives, depositing a plate, and she springs back to life, hands clapping in delight.

"Seada! My favorite," she says, before dissolving into a flurry of Italian with the waiter. Charlotte watches, mesmerized as all that briefly pent-up energy comes spilling out. The waiter eventually withdraws, and Giada explains that it's a gift from the owner.

"They're dumplings, dipped in honey," she says, before popping one into her mouth and moaning in pleasure. A sound that seeps right into Charlotte, warms her from the inside out.

"Go on," urges Giada, nudging the plate toward her, "you have to try."

Charlotte takes one, the honey sticking to her fingers. She tries not to think about how much she misses food. Now and then, when she drinks, she catches ghosts of old familiar flavors in the blood, but it's not the same.

She misses the earthy sweetness of sun-warmed tomatoes, the vivid tang of blackberries, the sugar dusted over biscuits. Though in truth, it's been so long she struggles to remember, doesn't recall the taste as much as how it made her feel, the way a perfect bite could make her heart go fizzy and her whole mood lift.

The same way Giada looks now as she licks the honey from her thumb. Her eyes close briefly as she savors each and every flavor, and in that instant, Charlotte palms the seada, lets it drop beneath the chair, where a pigeon quickly rushes in to claim the prize.

When Giada returns to herself, Charlotte asks her how she manages to stay so still.

"I go somewhere else, in my head." She takes another seada. "Sometimes, memories." Then, eyes dancing, "Sometimes, fantasies." She winks and pops the dumpling in her mouth, and sighs, limbs loosening like syrup. Warring urges rise in Charlotte, but she allows only one to surface.

"I'd love to draw you."

"Ah!" Giada breaks into a grin. "So Carlotta is an artist, too." Charlotte blushes at the nickname, the glee in Giada's eyes, the sunlight in her voice when she bobs her head. "All right," she says. "Your place or mine?"

II

Charlotte leads Giada up the stairs.

There are still echoes of the last owner—in the furniture, the pots and pans—but she's done what she can to make the place her own. Books line almost every shelf, volumes in Latin, French, and English, collected piecemeal on her evening walks, from market crates and outside shops. Fresh flowers crowd a vase on the narrow kitchen table, and in the little sitting room she's painted the walls her favorite shade of green. A summer shade, a garden hue, like the lawn of Clement Hall—sometimes Charlotte stays up, sits in a corner chair and leaves the curtains open, watches the sunlight dance across the green, pretends the grass is moving in the breeze.

It's a nice enough apartment, more lived-in than lavish, but then, Sabine was the one who sought out luxury. Charlotte would rather feel at home.

Sabine—creeping in like a shadow even now.

She shakes her head, does her best to banish the ghost as the bathroom door creaks open, and Giada emerges in nothing but a borrowed silk robe, cinched around her waist.

"Where do you want me?" Her lips twitch as she says it, as if daring Charlotte to say *Here, with me*. Instead, she gestures to the velvet chair she's dragged into the middle of the room, the fabric midnight blue.

Giada nods and takes her place beside the chair, then slips the robe's knot and shrugs off the silk, letting it pool on the floor, exposing her curves, her bare skin, as smooth and gold as honey.

Charlotte clenches her jaw.

She hasn't fed, not since she crossed paths with Giada at the fountain. Before that, in fact. Two nights, then. Three?

She knows, from the drawn-out games *they* used to play, that she is capable of going weeks without a meal. She knows, but knowing doesn't make it easier. Her mind believes, but her body doesn't understand. Her teeth ache and her stomach twists, her throat dry and her still heart desperate to beat. Every moment is an act of will when the hunger goes so deep. A ringing bell inside her head. A tuning fork against her skeleton.

Charlotte pushes the thoughts away as Giada lowers herself into the chair, limbs bright against the dark blue velvet.

"You tell me when to stop," she says, offering Charlotte a variety of poses as she shifts her weight, treating the chair as if it is a picture frame, the new bounds of her world, the light rolling over her, the dimples in her thighs, the hills and valleys of her hips. If Sabine was the stone at the center of the fruit, Giada is the peach itself. Soft and supple and—

"Stop."

Just like that, she does.

That uncanny stillness sweeps over her again. But there is something else, something Charlotte missed before. That pent-up energy is still there, humming just beneath the surface, like water perched at the rim of a full cup, giving the impression that any moment it could spill.

It isn't the stillness that makes Giada such a perfect model. It is this.

"Can you stay like that?" she asks.

Only Giada's lips move as she answers quietly, "Of course."

Charlotte's pencil begins to race across the pad of paper, convinced that any moment the spell will break, and Giada will come to life again before she has a chance to finish.

But Giada doesn't move an inch.

Charlotte draws with a sure hand, ghosting out the guiding lines, gaze flicking from the paper to the chair and back again, every time expecting to catch some minute adjustment, and finding none. The only movement, the slow blinking of her lashes. The faint rise and fall of her chest.

She has always enjoyed drawing. When she was young, she'd practice rendering her mother's sculptures. And later, she would sketch a little of every place they went together, she and Sabine. Before cameras became commonplace, it was a way for her to capture pieces of her life. Moments pressed into paper. Filling sketchbook after sketchbook. She didn't keep them all, only the latest.

And even that she'd left behind in London.

She drew Sabine as well, of course. At least, she tried. Sabine had the kind of face, those angles, that light, that seemed designed to haunt an artist. But Charlotte could never seem to get it right.

But Giada comes to life beneath her pencil.

She is stretched like a bolt of fabric across the chair, her bare legs thrown over one arm, her neck cradled by the other so that her head tips back, throat exposed, the sharp end of her bob skimming the air like a paintbrush. Her face caught mid-turn toward Charlotte as she draws.

Ten minutes go by in this way. Thirty. An hour.

"You can't be comfortable."

A shrug, or at least, the *air* of a shrug, since Giada's shoulders never bob. The ghost of a smile, not even a ripple at the corner of her mouth. "You could distract me."

Charlotte's pencil whispers. "How?"

Giada hums in thought and says, "Tell me a story."

A brief and fleeting memory, light as moth wings: Jocelyn's head in her lap, one eye closed as she holds an oak leaf to the sun to see the veins shot through with light. *Tell me a story, Lottie.*

"A story," she echoes thoughtfully.

Charlotte knows a thousand stories. Fairy tales and novels, epic poems and children's verses. She could recite any one of them from memory, or she could make a new one up from scratch. For some reason, she does neither.

Tell me a story.

Why does she decide to tell the truth?

Perhaps it is the safe angle of Giada's face, the fact she would have to turn her head to meet her gaze. Or perhaps it is the fact these last ten years have somehow been the longest of her life. Perhaps it is the loneliness, the longing to be known by someone else, to be *real* for someone else, besides Sabine.

"Once there was a girl afraid of growing up," she says, her pencil still scratching at the page. "When she was a child, she was a giant, free and large and boundless. But growing up, she knew, meant becoming small, small enough to fit in a man's open hand. No longer a person at all, but a trophy, a trinket."

As Charlotte speaks, she draws, and as she draws, the shapes come together on the parchment, the lines joining, the limbs and torso rising to the surface.

"She wanted to stay young forever. But her body didn't listen, and then, neither did her heart, and soon—too soon—she was sent to London, to watch and learn and be made worthy of those men. So that one might choose her for himself."

Giada makes a derisive sound. "I knew the English were prudish, but I didn't know you were still so backwards, too."

"It was a long time ago," says Charlotte, smudging a line with the ball of her thumb as she presses on. "Now, some of the men she met there were handsome enough. Some were even kind. But looking at them all, she knew they were *heavy*. She knew she would be crushed beneath their weight."

Charlotte's pencil changes from a whisper to a rasping hiss as the lines grow sharper, more deliberate. She traces the body on paper, shades the fold at the waist, the crook of the elbow, the slope of the cheek until the woman on the page is no longer a stranger.

"Then, one day, she met a woman."

Giada hums in static pleasure. "A welcome twist. What was *she* like?"

The pencil stalls. The room flickers, and for a moment Charlotte is eighteen and standing on the stairs at that first ball, a voice like a secret in her ear.

"She was—"

Eyes like lanterns, hair like heated steel.

"—undeniable."

A hand drawing her away from the crowd.

"Perilous."

Fingers knotted in hair. Teeth trailing skin.

"Alluring."

"Sounds like a good time," teases Giada.

Charlotte swallows. She can almost feel Sabine peering like a ghost over her shoulder, fingers grazing the nape of her neck as she draws.

"It *was* a good time, at first," she says, setting in on Giada's hair, her lines as smooth as a brush sliding through. "The woman took so little and gave so much. She offered the girl friendship, offered her pleasure, offered her everything she ever wanted. And in the end, all she asked for was her soul."

At that, Giada *almost* moves.

A small spasm of surprise, a ripple on the surface, quickly stilled. Charlotte glances up, expects to see the other woman staring back at her, but her face hasn't turned, her gaze still trained on the corner of the room.

"A devil, then."

Charlotte nods. "But what good is a soul, really?" she muses, as if it's the first time she's stopped to wonder. As if it's not the question that plagued her that first night, that still plagues her after all these years. "It lives in the mind. A piece you cannot see or touch. A prize you are told to shield for a time you cannot know. Easy enough to part with something so abstract when the alternative is freedom. When the promise is love."

Charlotte's pencil skates back and forth, for a moment the only sound in the room, as if *both* of them are holding their breath. "She didn't know it then, but it turns out a soul is what makes the sun feel warm against your skin, what gives food taste, what makes you feel full.

"Still, the girl told herself it was worth it. After all, she had the woman's love, and that was enough. That would always be enough."

The drawing is almost done now, as much as a drawing can be. It is by nature an unfinished thing, the edges bleeding into empty space. But Charlotte knows there is a moment when a piece can be overworked, when the artist goes a stroke too far.

Charlotte knows that she should stop, before she ruins it.

But she cannot bring herself to put the pencil down.

"And then," she says, "the woman got sick, and her love sickened with her. It withered. And died. And then the girl had nothing."

The air around Giada churns with interest. Her mind, so open, so unguarded, teeters on belief. And Charlotte knows there is still time to change direction, to convince her it is nothing but a fairy tale.

That is, until the tear hits the paper.

A single, vivid bloom of red that rolls down Charlotte's cheek and lands on the shading at the base of Giada's throat.

It slides down the page, and just like that, everything is ruined.

She hears Giada's sudden indrawn breath, loud as breaking glass. Charlotte closes her eyes and waits for the shock and fear she knows will cloud the air, waits for Giada to lurch up out of the chair and flee. Waits, and tells herself she will not stop her when she tries to leave, and wonders if it's true. She keeps her eyes shut hard as she hears the soft groan of the chair, the cautious pad of Giada's feet, realizes they're not heading toward the door.

But toward her.

Charlotte blinks, and finds Giada kneeling, naked, in front of her, the air thick with caution, but also curiosity. Giada, reaching out to wipe the bloody tear from Charlotte's cheek, and the touch is enough to break the spell. Charlotte pulls back sharply, the drawing pad and pencils falling to the floor. "You should go."

Giada frowns. "Is that what you want?" she asks.

"No. But—" Charlotte falters. "—it isn't safe for you to stay."

"Why?" asks Giada.

Because I like you, she almost says. *Because I want you. Because there are too many kinds of hunger, and I can't pick them apart. Because I'm afraid. Because—*

"Because I'm hungry."

Charlotte grimaces as she says it, and for the first time, Giada must be able to see the twin points of her teeth, the way they prick her bottom lip.

"I took you to so many places," she says, sounding almost amused. "None of them were to your taste."

So she noticed after all.

"I'm sorry. I just . . ." Charlotte swallows. "I wanted to be with you. I wanted to pretend . . ."

Giada tips her head. "When the girl gave up her soul," she asks gently, "when the sun lost its heat, and the food lost its taste, how did she live? What did she eat?"

Charlotte's gaze rolls over Giada, following the veins that thread her wrists, her breasts, her neck. She doesn't want to say it, but what is the point of lying now?

"Blood."

The word falls like an anvil, yet Giada doesn't buckle, or recoil, or retreat. She only nods, as if reaching some private decision, and then, to Charlotte's shock and horror, she tucks her hair out of the way, offering the smooth slope of her throat.

"Go ahead."

"No." Charlotte clenches her teeth. "I can't."

Giada pouts, as if Charlotte is a fussy child. "Why not?"

"Because," she hisses, fighting to ignore the heartbeat drumming through her skin. "I don't want to hurt you."

Giada meets her gaze. "Then don't," she says, as if it is that simple.

But it isn't.

Is it?

Behind her eyes, she sees herself kneeling on a floor in Margate, three men dead, three hearts dropped into her lap. A warning to always finish what you start. But that was Sabine's rule, not hers. And if there is a world where she can drink but not kill, then Charlotte wants to find it.

Cautiously, she brings one hand to Giada's waist, drawing her closer until her mouth comes to rest at the base of Giada's throat. Giada shivers then, her pulse fluttering beneath her skin, and Charlotte feels like she's standing at the edge of a cliff, resisting the urge to lean forward, to fall. Resisting, until Giada brings a hand to the back of Charlotte's head, fingers sliding through her curls as she whispers, "It's okay. I won't move."

Charlotte closes her eyes and bites down, as gently as she can.

The soft skin tears like fruit, the blood sun-warm and honey-sweet. Giada tenses, and Charlotte thinks she will cry out, pull back, rip free. But she doesn't. Instead she softens, rests the weight of herself in Charlotte's arms as she begins to drink.

Sunlight flares behind her eyes, warmth spreading through her as her own heart begins to beat, slow at first, then faster, harder, and it is so bright, so strong, so wonderful she nearly vanishes.

But then she feels Giada's head droop against her shoulder, hears her heart begin to slow, and Charlotte does the one thing she never has before, after so many years, so many lives, so many bodies gone slack in her embrace, and scourged from memory, the one thing Sabine told her not to do.

She *stops*.

Her jaw loosens, and her teeth slide free. A narrow red ribbon pools in Giada's collar, the skin already knitting in the bite mark's wake. The heart races in Charlotte's chest as Giada sighs against her. When her head drifts up, her pupils are wide and glassy.

"See?" she says in a sleepy voice.

Charlotte cups her face, worried she drank too deeply, took too much. "Are you all right?" she asks, searching the air for any sign of pain, or panic, or regret. But Giada just rolls her head on her neck, and smiles.

"Magnifica."

She stands, too quick, swaying on her feet. But Charlotte is there to steady her. Giada leans against her, hums softly, as if thinking.

"Tell me what you need," says Charlotte.

"Bed," she answers sleepily, and Charlotte leads her into the adjacent room, lowers her onto the bed. She turns to go, to let her rest, but Giada's hand catches hers.

"Come back," she says, pulling Charlotte down on top of her. Unbuttoning her dress with expert fingers, grazing skin warmed by her own heart, her own pulse echoing behind Charlotte's ribs as the air around Giada fogs with want.

Giada, spread beneath her, blond bob like a crumpled halo on the pillow, their mouths finding each other in the dark. Giada's laughter, soft and sighing, cut off as Charlotte kisses her.

Charlotte is so aware of Giada's softness, how easily she'd bruise, that she keeps one hand braced against the bed while the other traces Giada's curves the way her pencil did—conducting an artist's study until the girl beneath her squirms, impatient, and guides her fingers lower, an invitation on her lips.

Charlotte hesitates, not because she doesn't want this—she *does*—simply because it is new. Sabine—she doesn't want to think about Sabine, not now, not *ever*, but she can't help it—Sabine always led and never followed. She saw pleasure as a thing to control, to give, not take, so Charlotte learned only to receive.

Now, with Giada spread beneath her hands, she isn't quite sure what to do.

But she has always been an eager student, and Giada shows her what she wants, and how, guides her with her rising breath, her arching back, her pleasure curling thick as smoke as she tightens around Charlotte's hand, her own teeth raking Charlotte's shoulder as she comes.

Afterward, Giada rolls toward her in the dark, tucking Charlotte's curls behind her ears. Kissing the tip of her nose before her eyes float shut. And even though the pulse has trailed off in Charlotte's chest, for the first time in her life she can still hear it, because it is still there, beside her in the bed.

III

"It's too cold for gelato," declares Charlotte.

"Nonsense," says Giada, dragging her toward the shop, open despite the winter chill. She orders a scoop of lemon, spoons it in her mouth and shivers, half in cold and half delight, closes her eyes and holds the sugar on her tongue until it melts.

Charlotte shakes her head.

Falling for Giada is the easiest thing she has ever done.

It shouldn't be, and yet it is.

In hours, they are tangled. In weeks, they are bound. Their days and nights take on a rhythm. The first half of the day belongs to Giada and her modeling. The last half of the night to Charlotte and her needs. The rest of the time, they are together.

And for the first time in years—so *many* years—Charlotte knows what it feels like to be happy.

For the first time, she doesn't even dream about Sabine.

Giada takes another bite and moans in pleasure, and then as if on cue, a frigid breeze whips down the road and she yelps and turns up the collar of her coat. Charlotte laughs, even as she pulls her close, wishing she had some warmth to give. Instead, she peels off her own scarf, a prop, since the cold never really bothers her, and knots it around Giada's neck. Loops an arm through hers, if only to shield her body from the wind.

They walk like that, hooked at the elbows and heads bent together, Giada stealing lemon mouthfuls with the little wooden spoon, and for once Charlotte doesn't feel self-conscious—it's not such a strange sight, two young women walking arm in arm, in a culture full of so much passion.

"What do you think?" muses Giada as she brings the last bite to her lips. "Will it make me taste even sweeter?"

Charlotte grins, nudging her beneath an awning. "Let's find out."

Giada laughs, that bright, full-throated sound, as Charlotte presses her into the wall, lips trailing down her throat.

Just then, someone hisses.

A horrible, phlegmatic sound.

Nearby, an old man has stopped to glare at them. He snarls something under his breath, and Charlotte doesn't need to know the words to feel their weight. To see the way they land like an open hand on Giada's golden cheek. The way she reels back, face contorting into anger, before she launches into a fury of Italian. The way she pushes off the wall, lunging toward him, and Charlotte has to sling an arm around her waist to hold her back.

"Leave it," she warns as he backs away, shaking his fist.

"Why?" demands Giada as he shuffles off, still muttering under his breath. She twists in Charlotte's arms, her face burning hot with rage, a sight at once foreign, and beautiful, and frightening. "Why should I? Why should *you*? Why should he get away with it?"

Because they always have, thinks Charlotte. *Because they always do. Because that is the way of the world.*

But the world is supposed to be changing. Some years, it seems it does, in leaps and bounds. Others, the progress is so scant it hardly registers. And in that moment, Charlotte realizes that she is as tired as Giada is mad. And unlike Giada, there is something she can do about it.

"Go home," she says. "I'll be there soon."

Giada shakes her head, a gleam of violence in her eyes. "I want to stay. I want to watch."

But Charlotte refuses. Giada sulks a little, but in the end, she goes.

Charlotte watches her coat bob away, waits until it's gone.

Then turns and makes her way back across the square.

"What was it like?" Giada asks that night, when Charlotte sinks onto the bed.

She runs her fingers over Giada's skin, and doesn't say that he was just a dying man with a dying mind, that his blood tasted like cheap wine, that he never even begged her for his life, that his heart didn't even linger in her chest, that when it was done, all she felt was tired, sad.

A sadness that reminds her of another life, the last years in London, the

V. E. SCHWAB

ones that made her wake with tearstained pillows, made her heart feel like it was wrapped in lead.

And she never wants to feel that way again.

Instead, Charlotte climbs beneath the covers and pulls Giada close, wondering if she would still taste of lemon and sugar or if the flavors have already melted, when Giada says, "I want to be like you."

Charlotte closes her eyes. The words don't take her by surprise. The last few days the air around Giada has been laced with questions, wonder, want.

"No," she says. "You don't."

"I do," presses Giada.

"Is this because of that man?"

A rare gravity sweeps over Giada's face. Her eyes have gone from blue to gray. "No. And yes. It is because of this world, and how it treats us. It is because of how we're expected to let it. So maybe yes—maybe I want to know what it's like, to not be afraid."

And Charlotte cannot blame her—not when she's spent her life carrying a purse full of rocks—but she doesn't understand that what's she asking for is heavier.

Charlotte shakes her head.

"Mia Carlotta—" protests Giada.

"*Don't*," she pleads, rolling over.

"Why not?" asks Giada.

Because, thinks Charlotte, *there's no such thing as immortality. Because I love you as you are, and I cannot bear to change you. Because I saw the venom in your eyes tonight. I felt the violence in your limbs, the way your passion became rage, and I know that it would bloom like rot inside your heart.*

Because of Sabine.

"Because it is a curse," she says instead. "And I would not wish it on you."

"Curse," scoffs Giada. "A word used by those burdened with something others want. You call it a curse. I call it a *gift*. To stay young, and beautiful, and strong. To live forever."

"Bound to the night."

She shrugs. "The sun is overrated."

"And hunger."

"I am hungry." She nips Charlotte's shoulder. "I am ravenous."

"Giada—"

"And I love you," she says into her skin. "I love you, Carlotta, and I don't want it to end."

Grief and guilt wind like thorny limbs through Charlotte's ribs, and she curses this day, that man, herself. But she knows what she must do. She sits up and turns toward Giada, reaches up to cup her face.

"I love you, too," she says, looking into her eyes, past the light, to the shadows behind. "I love you," she says, when what she thinks is, *Let it go.*

It is an easy thing to bend a mind the way it wants to lean. Far harder to push it the other way. Sabine was always better at coercing. But Charlotte does her best.

Let it go, let it go, let it go, she wills.

And by some miracle, Giada does. She flings herself onto her back among the sheets.

"Fine," she says dramatically. "But just you wait. I will get old, and ugly, and you won't want me anymore."

Charlotte wilts in sheer relief.

"Never," she swears, sweeping over Giada like a blanket.

"I will always want you," she says.

Always, always, always, Charlotte thinks as she kisses the questions away.

IV

1959

The windows are open, the night is warm, and Charlotte is making dinner.

She stands at the counter in the kitchen of the one-room apartment they have shared for more than six years now. Charlotte wears Giada's apron cinched around her waist, her hands moving in a well-learned piece of choreography.

She brings a ripe tomato to her nose, smells the soil and the sun, the earthy acid of the leaves, and for a moment—only a moment—Charlotte is convinced that if she bit down she would taste those things, instead of ash and rot. But she doesn't, sets the ripe fruit down, preferring to live in the promise instead of the grim truth.

Besides, the meal is not for her.

The onions hit the pan with a gasp, begin to sizzle as she peels the skin from the tomatoes, squeezes just hard enough to make the seeds spill out. She chops the tomatoes, adds the sausage to the pan and stirs, no temptation to the smell of burning meat. She adds the saffron and the wine before turning the tomatoes in, just as she's watched Giada do a dozen times, with Charlotte's arms hooked around her waist, chin resting on her shoulder as she pronounced the dish, rolled it over her tongue.

Malloreddus alla campidanese.

It sounded like a song on Giada's lips.

A hundred and fifty years on this earth, and Charlotte's mouth still breeds consonants, teeth clipping words into sharp relief. Time should have worn the edges down by now, softened her accent into something smooth, ambiguous, but it seems pressed in amber with her skin, her curls, the other details of her life before.

She has learned to read and speak Italian, but the musicality of the accent still evades her, while Giada's dances, sways, full of gentle swells, a paper boat bobbing in a bath.

Malloreddus alla campidanese.

"What does it taste like?" Charlotte asked the first time Giada made the dish.

She took a bite, closed her eyes, and answered in a sigh. "It tastes like home."

Now Charlotte covers the pan and lets it cook, tries to focus on the dish instead of her own appetite. She confides nearly everything in Giada. Everything except for this—that she is always hungry.

"Have you had enough?" Giada will ask after offering Charlotte her wrist, her throat, and she will say *yes,* when the truth is that there is no such thing, that the hunger ebbs and flows, but never dies—that she could drink and drink and drink from now until the end of days and never know the meaning of the word *full.* She is a colander, not a goblet, a vessel full of holes. So she says *yes,* and goes for walks while Giada sleeps, cleans up the mess wherever it is left, and pretends that she is sated.

Laughter echoes up the stairs. Giada usually sings when she comes home, knowing Charlotte will be able to hear through the intervening walls and floors, but as she crosses the flat and the sounds grow brighter, more solid, Charlotte can tell this isn't music. Giada's talking to someone, one of the downstairs neighbors, no doubt, carrying on in jaunty Italian before they say good night and peel away to their own rooms.

Charlotte opens the door, strikes a pose in her borrowed apron, imagining the laughter, the delight in Giada's eyes as she reaches the top floor, tugging the pins from her hair, kicking off her shoes.

But Giada isn't alone.

Charlotte has never felt vertigo, or the sickness that comes over bodies at sea, but staring at the woman on Giada's arm she feels something like it, the sudden loss of balance, the nauseous rocking of a world unmoored.

Sabine.

Sabine, whose hair hangs loose and long and bright enough to burn the air.

Sabine, whose hand is hooked through Giada's elbow, fingers dimpling soft skin.

Sabine, who smiles patiently, like a parent who's caught a child in the act of stealing, and is about to punish them for their own sake.

"Speak of the devil!" says Giada, seeing Charlotte there. "I ran into your friend down on the street. She said—mi dispiace, I've forgotten your name."

"Sabine." The word tumbles out of Charlotte's mouth.

In the hall, its owner smiles.

She's dressed in black leather pants, tight as poured paint, and a coat the color of a fresh bruise, the sleeves flaring wide, the fabric studded all over with shining beads, as if someone shattered a mirror and then stitched it back together, each piece too small to reflect anything but light. Necklaces tangle like weeds around her throat.

"That's right!" continues Giada, oblivious to the way the air has turned to ice, to the fear in Charlotte's face, the crook of Sabine's mouth as the light flickers on and off behind her eyes.

"Giada," Charlotte murmurs softly, but her lover doesn't hear. She's rambling, energy spilling over the way it always does after a job, all that movement bottled up by the hours of posing, while Sabine stands still as a statue, eyes boring straight ahead, as if Giada isn't even there.

"She said she was passing through Rome, and hoped to see you, couldn't remember if you lived at nine or nineteen . . ."

Panic rings through Charlotte like a bell, and she knows Sabine can hear it. It's been so long, she's let her walls come down. There was no reason for them anymore, she thought.

She thought that chapter of her life was over.

What a fool.

The room flickers, and Charlotte remembers a winter in Vienna. A lavish flat. A marble chessboard, one of the many relics left behind. A curtain of white beyond the windows, a pretty but miserable month, and so Sabine taught her how to play. And no matter how good Charlotte got, Sabine was always better. Her favorite thing to do was chase Charlotte's king into a corner. But once there, she would allow her to escape, forcing her to flee around the board.

Check, check, check, she'd say until she got bored enough to end the game.

Charlotte stares at Sabine now, across the narrow threshold.

It is hard to look away—it has always been hard to look away—but right now, she keeps her focus on Sabine because she is afraid to glance at Giada. Afraid to remind Sabine that she is there. If Charlotte had a heartbeat of her own, it would be racing. Instead, there is only a horrible leaden weight, a static like the night before a storm.

And in that moment, that suspended breath, all she wants to do is go back, unpick the the last six years, unravel it all to the moment her blood dripped onto the drawing, the moment Giada broke her pose, and rose, and crossed the room to touch her cheek, just so she can catch Giada's fingers, keep them there, look into her lovely face and tell her how the story ended. To name the one that took her soul.

But she didn't, and now she can't, and Sabine is just standing there as if to say, *Your move, my love.*

"What are the odds?" asks Giada cheerfully.

Sabine's smile splits open like a seam.

"Indeed," she says, and there is that voice again, that whetstone scrape, that feral purr that once made Charlotte come undone. Sabine runs a hand over Giada's fair hair as if stroking a child. Or a pet. "Who knows how long I might have wandered?"

Giada finally notices the apron cinched around Charlotte's waist. "Is that mine?" she asks, and then, "Something smells delicious!" She turns toward Sabine, drawing breath, and Charlotte can tell that she's going to invite her in.

"NO," snaps Charlotte, and maybe it's the harshness in her voice, or maybe it's the fear in her eyes, but Giada finally grasps that something is wrong. Her good mood falters, and her smile falls.

"Giada," says Charlotte softly, her hand twitching forward in a silent plea, *Come to me, come quick,* and Giada understands, starts forward toward the open door, toward her, toward home, but Sabine's hand is still resting on her hair, and as she pulls away, it vises, and the woman's head snaps back, her balance thrown. She yelps, in shock, in pain, as Sabine's arms fold around her, hold her close, like dancers, cheek to cheek.

Charlotte lunges forward, one step, two, catches herself just before the open door. She has had the sense to claim this flat, to pace the floor and touch the walls and call it hers. And now the doorframe is the only thing standing between her and Giada, between her and Sabine, between her and the death waiting in the hall.

This is check, not mate, and they both know it.

Sabine's mouth twitches. "Do you see?" she coos to the woman in her arms. "She does not love you."

"That isn't true," gasps Charlotte. "Giada, look at me."

She does, fear shining in her eyes. "Carlotta—" she whispers.

"If she did, she would come out." Sabine's gaze hangs on her but the words are pressed, knifelike, into Giada's cheek. "If she did, she would have kept you safe. Would have made you like her. Like me."

"*Sabine*," snarls Charlotte. "*Let her go.*"

"But here you are, so soft, so fragile." Sabine's hand must have tightened in Giada's hair, because she whimpers, her head pulled back, her throat exposed. "Nothing but a plaything. A distraction." Sabine's teeth come to rest in the curve of her neck. Giada trembles, and Charlotte's nails dig into the doorframe.

"Don't."

"There is still time," says Sabine. "She can still save you. All she has to do is step across that threshold. All she has to do is come out, or let us in."

Hatred rolls through Charlotte. Her fingers carve divots in the wood. She is a coward, but not a fool. She knows Sabine better than anyone, knows there is no saving the girl beyond the door. That if she moves, she will only damn them both.

"What do you think, Giada?" teases Sabine. "Will she do it, if you beg?"

Her grip loosens, just enough for Giada to look Charlotte in the eyes again.

"Mia Carlotta," she pleads softly, "will you—"

Sabine snaps her neck.

The crack echoes in the stairwell.

"Too late."

Charlotte clenches her teeth against the scream, but a ragged sob still escapes as Giada slumps, lifeless, to the floor. Something deep inside her tears, pain and fury sharp as sunlight, and Charlotte wants to lunge through the door, to rip the heart from Sabine's chest.

But she can't. She *can't*.

Charlotte knows her hands will stop before they can break skin, frozen by the words she spoke, all her anger rendered impotent by a promise made eighty years ago.

Sabine looks down at Giada's broken body. The blond hair trailing across the wood. Her limbs so perfectly still, as if she's simply holding a new pose.

"You should have come back to bed."

Charlotte drags her gaze from the dead to death itself. "How did you find me?"

"How could I lose you?" Sabine steps over Giada. "You are my heartbeat. My feral rose. I laid you down in the midnight soil. I watered you until you bloomed. It is my job to tend our plot, and prune any weeds that try to grow."

As she speaks, Sabine closes the distance until only the doorway stands between them. Charlotte holds her ground, silently reminding the floor and the walls that this is *her* house, that she has paced the length of every board, in every room, and whispered her name into the walls, and declared the space her own.

Just as Sabine taught her all those years ago.

And still, she doesn't know if it will hold, not until Sabine stops at the threshold. The hem of wood, a boundary as thin as glass.

"I've missed you, Charlotte." She leans in, as if to fog the pane. "Why don't you let me in?" This close, she can see the way Sabine's eyes flicker, hazel to black and back again, like faulty wiring, can smell the coils of her hair, earthy and sweet, can glimpse her old lover dancing like light beneath the surface of a deep, dark well.

It would be easy to let her eyes unfocus, to believe the woman standing at her threshold is *her* Sabine. The one who made her feel safe. Feel loved. Feel free.

But she isn't that person anymore. Hasn't been for ages now.

"You are not welcome," growls Charlotte. "You can't come in."

Sabine smiles, and the illusion breaks, the woman she once loved melting away like wax, revealing the dead-eyed stranger, who cocks her head and says, "Something is burning."

Charlotte stiffens, then smells it too.

She turns and rushes down the hall, into the kitchen. Smoke rises from the stove, along with a rancid odor, singed meat and burned sauce. She turns off the burners, stares down into the charred remains of the dinner she was making. For Giada, whose laughter always walked a step ahead. For Giada, who could never sit still, except when she was working. For Giada, who—

She sweeps the pots and pans from the stove, metal ringing as it clatters to the floor, contents splattering the cabinets, and at last her anger overtakes her fear, and she thinks No, *fuck this, fuck her*, storms out of the kitchen and down the hall, back to the front door, which still hangs open.

Sabine is gone.

But Giada isn't.

Her body lies in a heap on the hall floor, an awkward jumble of limbs, head bent at an angle even she could never hold. Charlotte steps over the threshold, knows that Sabine won't spring out of the shadows now, because it would be no fun, because that's all it is to her.

Check.

Not mate.

Charlotte sinks to her knees beside Giada.

She lifts her, as gently as she can, and carries her inside. Somewhere between the doorway and their bedroom, Charlotte splinters, begins to cry. Heaving sobs that rack her body, bloody tears spilling down her cheeks. She cannot stop, and so they both end up stained, Charlotte trailing red like a mortal wound as she takes Giada to bed, lays her body in the nest of sheets they always seem to leave behind.

Charlotte lies down beside Giada, feels the warmth slipping away second by second as her body cools. Giada's cheek is turned away. She could be sleeping, but she's not, and Charlotte turns her stained face into the pillow, and screams. Screams until her lungs give way. Until her heart shatters in her chest. Until there's nothing left.

She wants to stay, to cry herself to sleep, but she can't.

"I'm sorry," she whispers hoarsely into Giada's hair.

Then she gets to her feet.

She doesn't pack. There is no point.

The only thing worth saving is already dead.

She leaves the front door open, so someone will come.

And then, once again, Charlotte runs.

V

She knows now that she is being hunted.

She cannot stop. She cannot rest.

For months she wanders in a daze, hollowed out by death, and yet, propelled to live. And so, she lives in constant motion, never stopping long enough to learn the layout of a place, let alone put down any roots, beyond the nightly wards that keep her safe. And yet no matter where she goes—Oslo, Prague, Berlin—she is certain she can feel Sabine trailing in her wake.

Silly Charlotte. Let me in.

There are nights when she wonders what would happen if she did. Whether Sabine would kill her quickly or take her time, though she suspects she knows which one it is. She has never longed for death, but what Charlotte fears more is that Sabine doesn't mean to kill her. After all, there are worse things. She can still remember their anniversary in London, the way Sabine's teeth sank down to bone. The aching pain of being emptied. Over and over again.

Still, it is not the pain that scares her most of all.

It is the fact she can't fight back.

That violence is a one-way road, thanks to her promise. If Sabine gets her hands on Charlotte, she can peel her like a piece of fruit. And Charlotte cannot even lift a hand to stop her.

So she drifts.

For months. For *years*.

She moves, and moves, and moves, Sabine's promise hanging like a guillotine over her head.

It is enough to drive her mad.

Perhaps it does.

She feels like she is cracked inside, broken edges scraping at her heart, her lungs, all her brittle feelings leaking into one another. The sight of happy couples makes the splinters spread.

Charlotte watches the fifties end, a new decade ushered in, and cannot take it anymore.

She has never been so lonely.

So alone.

She longs for company, for *comfort,* for the simple warmth of being held, of being seen, and known. She thinks of going back to London, but does not dare return to Antonia and Jack, much as she could use a friend, lest she carry Sabine to them like a sickness.

And so, at the top of 1961, Charlotte Hastings boards a ship and sails for Boston.

She stares at the retreating line of English coast and reminds herself how much Sabine hated the idea of crossing oceans. How often she declared that she would never leave, that all she could ever want or need was there in Europe.

How eager Charlotte is to see it go.

Still, it is not an easy journey. A week on the water, hunger digging its teeth into her bones, the subtle wrongness of the sea to every side. The days spent locked inside her cabin, the sun beating against the boat. The nights spent drifting round the ship, counting the heartbeats, and clinging to the memory of Sabine's reluctance, her disdain. The promise of a place where she is not already waiting.

Charlotte clutches the small black business card Jack gave her, rubs the emblem with her thumb until it starts to fade. Memorizes each printed letter of the city name, and tells herself it will be the place her story starts.

And then, at last, the sight of land ahead.

The ship dragging slowly into the port.

Charlotte nearly flings herself ashore, makes it a few uncertain steps before she crumples to her knees, palms flat against the dock of this new country, this new life.

"Miss, are you all right?" a stranger asks.

Another, "Miss, are you unwell?"

But it is dusk, and she is shaking not with fear or illness, but relief, and hope.

And *cold.*

Charlotte thought she knew winter well enough, but here it is so brutal even she can feel the frigid burn. The streets are covered in a mess of ice and slush, the parks clad in snow.

Her papers declare her Mrs. Charlotte Hastings. A *widow*, a word that seems to free her from a multitude of inquiries when she takes a room in a shared house. They do ask what brings her all the way to Boston, why she would cross an ocean all alone, if she has any family here. And she tells them she does not, but she has a *friend*.

Ezra.

She runs her fingers over the letters, follows the lines of Antonia's neat but sloping script, wishing the card had more than a name, a city, a symbol. It takes her nearly a month of asking pedestrians and waiters and hotel concierges before one directs her to a bar with an emblem matching the one on the card.

A narrow brick front, a set of steps leading down to a sublevel door, a small bronze placard to one side declaring it the White Thorn Club.

Charlotte shudders in relief and goes inside.

It is not what she expected—she imagined something like the Way Down, with its dreamy atmosphere, its ageless grace—but this club is small, made smaller by the curtains hung around, stifling the light from the candles on each table. And yet, there is an energy she recognizes, an air that puts her anxious heart at ease.

A handsome human in a tailored suit greets her by the door.

"Ezra?" she ventures, to which the man guffaws. Charlotte frowns, confused, but he just shakes his head and gestures to a corner table.

"You take a seat," he says. "I'll find the man in charge."

She sits and waits, smooths her skirt and studies the coaster on the table, runs her fingers over the hollow curves of the rose, the two pale spikes on the stem.

Soft red petals hiding sharp white teeth.

A man clears his throat, and she looks up.

Charlotte doesn't know what she expected from Ezra—someone with Antonia's elegance, perhaps, or Jack's charm, but this man has neither. He's vaguely disheveled, his sleeves shoved up to his elbows and his collar open, hair a mop of brown that looks in desperate need of a cut. He doesn't even greet her, just drags up a chair, spins it round, and flops down, arms crossed against the back.

Charlotte would honestly suspect she'd found the wrong man, if not for the perfect quiet of the air around him and the faint glow behind his eyes.

"Can I help you?" he asks, a phrase Americans seem to hand out as casually as *Hello,* but he sounds like he means it.

And Charlotte, who has spent a fortnight thinking of what to say, finds her mind gone blank. Her eyes begin to burn. The stranger sits there, waiting for her to speak, amusement tugging at his mouth when the seconds pass in silence until finally she finds her voice and says, "Antonia."

His brows go up in obvious surprise.

"She sent me," explains Charlotte. "That is, she told me I should find you, if I ever found myself in Boston, and in need of a friend."

Friend—why does the word lodge in her throat? Why does it ache behind her ribs? Perhaps she doesn't know how true it is, how badly she needs it, until it's said.

Ezra leans forward, resting his chin on top of his arms. "That does sound like her. How is our dear Antonia?" he adds, slipping into a Southern accent as he says it, and Charlotte is forced to admit she doesn't know, that it's been nearly twenty years since she gave her the card with Ezra's name.

"I didn't know," she says, "if you would still be here."

"Oh, you needn't have worried about that." He rakes his fingers through his hair, only for it to fall again across his forehead, somehow messier than before. "Boston and I go hand in hand. I've been here since the Revolution. And I know what you're going to say," he adds, holding up a hand to stop her. "I *do* look good for my age."

When Charlotte fails to laugh, Ezra sighs dramatically. "You know, I'm always amazed when vampires take themselves so seriously."

Vampire. It's an odd word, one Sabine disdained, even before Bela Lugosi with his widow's peak and overly affected speech.

As if Ezra senses her distaste, he says, "Let me guess, you prefer the metaphor of gardens, and roses."

She glances pointedly at the coaster, printed with the bar's emblem, and Ezra holds up his hands. "Guilty. But you have to admit, calling it Bloodthirst might render me too niche."

Charlotte *almost* smiles, then. It feels like stone splitting. Like her body has forgotten how.

A waiter appears and puts two cups and a porcelain pot of coffee on the table. He leaves without pouring, which she thinks odd, until Ezra takes the liberty, and though the liquid is thin, and dark, the aroma of roasted beans doesn't quite cover the unmistakable scent of iron.

She takes a cup, curls her fingers around it as if for warmth.

"So, Charlotte," he says—which is when she realizes she never told him her name. "Ah, I tipped my hand. The world is smaller than it used to be. Antonia did call me," he says, nodding at a phone on the bar. "To say you might be coming round."

Charlotte sets the cup down. "Did she tell you why?" she asks, unsure which is worse, if he already knows about Sabine, or if she'll have to tell him.

He shakes his head. "Not her story," he says.

And Charlotte knows he's giving her a choice. To tell or not to tell. To share the burden or keep it to herself.

But she is so tired of carrying the weight alone.

And what is a friend, if not someone willing to share it.

It's hard at first, every word takes something with it, but then it is like running downhill—she cannot seem to stop. Ezra's expression darkens only once—when Charlotte recounts the night she tried and failed to kill Sabine—though she doesn't know if it's the act that upsets him, or the fact she couldn't do it. He never says.

By the time she's done, the other tables in the place are empty, the waiters gone, the doors to the White Thorn Club closed for the night.

Ezra sits in thoughtful silence for some time, and then he asks.

"Why didn't you turn her?"

The question hangs on the air, the way it has hung on Charlotte since that night. Sabine, pinning Giada to her. So fragile. So human.

"You could have made her like you. But you didn't."

Charlotte bites her lip, stares down into her empty cup. She could say that she wanted to surround herself with life, not death. Or that she couldn't bear the thought of someone loving her the way she loved Sabine and being forced to watch her wither.

Both of them are true, but in the end she just shakes her head and says, "I loved her as she was. Besides," she adds, "it wouldn't have saved her from Sabine."

"Probably not," says Ezra, rising to his feet. "But it might have given her a fighting chance."

Charlotte frowns, remembering her ex-lover on the threshold. That smile, like a cat toying with its food. "No," she says, pushing herself up. "It wouldn't have."

Ezra nods thoughtfully. And then he does a stunning thing. He hugs her. Folds his arms loosely around her shoulders, the simple, solid weight of him more welcome than a heart, a pulse.

"I'm sorry, Lottie," he says, and the nickname, the easy way he says it, makes her smile. A piece of her old self, perhaps the only one that survived Sabine.

He leads her to the door. Unlocks it for her, letting in the winter wind.

Charlotte pauses there, staring into the dark. "What if the ocean wasn't enough?" she whispers, as if saying it too loud will make it real. "What if she follows me?"

Ezra leans in the doorway. "She probably won't," he says, taking a card and pen from his pocket, and scrawling something on the back. "But I'll keep my ears and eyes open."

He hands her the new card, the club's number printed in his messy hand.

"If you're worried, just call," he says. "But I'm sure you'll be fine."

She takes the card, and steps out into the dark, hoping that he's right.

VI

1961–69

Sixty minutes to an hour.

Twenty-four hours to a day.

These are mortal measurements, for mortal lives.

But when you live forever, time is something far less constant.

When you are happy, a decade rushes by.

When you are sad, a minute crawls.

When you are lonely and afraid, time seems to lose all meaning.

Blink, and a year is gone.

Blink, and it has only been a night.

Only, it is not a life at all.

It is a prison sentence.

Charlotte watches, waits, senses tuned and hackles raised, every time someone looks her way. Every time a stranger comes knocking at her door, or a neighbor says her name, she braces for catastrophe. And every time she so much as glimpses someone with Sabine's looks—her hair, her gait, her coloring—every time she wakes from a too-vivid dream, she phones Ezra. Ezra, her only way of marking time, by what she hears in the background of the call.

"Anything?" she asks over The Beatles, The Byrds, The Supremes.

But his answer is always the same.

No sign of her.

No word.

Still nothing.

And every passing month, every patient *No* from Ezra chips at her enduring vigilance.

Sabine is a ghost, haunting only Charlotte.

And ghosts, like memories, have a way of losing strength.

It's not that she forgets. She never will.

But time wears the edges off all things. Including vigilance.

And by the end of that wretched, lonely decade, Charlotte finally begins to think, to hope, that Sabine has lost interest in their game.

That she has run far enough.

That she is *free*.

VII

1971–79

Charlotte buys herself a yellow Beetle.

She is tired of holding herself captive, bound to Boston, as if by keeping the water in her sight, she will know if danger comes across it. And so, she packs up, and points the car west, and drives.

Some people look up at the night sky and they feel small in a way that scares them.

But the sheer size of that wide-open sky, so full of stars, makes Charlotte feel small enough to disappear.

And that makes her feel safe.

She drives with the windows down, and fills her lungs, pushes the gas pedal to the floor and screams into the white noise of the rushing night. And for the first time in years, she doesn't feel like she is running. She keeps her focus firmly on the road ahead.

Mile by mile, Charlotte feels herself come back to life.

It is the solitude that gets her in the end.

The need to feel something more than fear, fatigue.

Perhaps if she could rot a different way.

Become a cold and calculating hunter, like Sabine.

But Charlotte wasn't made for it. Her heart is too hungry.

She doesn't go in search of company, for what it's worth. The girls find her. They're the ones who come knocking at the door.

She simply lets them in.

In Nashville, there's Grace, who spills out of a diner with a flock of friends after a midnight gig, and ends up taking Charlotte home instead.

In St. Louis, Renée catches her eye across a bar one night, sends over a drink.

In Chicago, Luce, who comes right up to her, bold as brass, and wants to dance, who leans her elbows on the Clark Street Bridge and announces that she's not afraid to die. That the real curse would be to live forever.

A string of girls who hook their fingers in the loops of Charlotte's jeans to draw her closer. Who welcome her into their homes, their hearts, their beds.

And for the first time in so many years, Charlotte spends her nights surrounded by the energy of youth, the cheerful zeal, warm bodies against hers. She smiles, and laughs, and begins to thaw with hope, and wonders how she survived all those years alone. Realizes what a fool she's been, to waste the decades hiding instead of living.

How obvious it is, in retrospect.

Sabine did not need to follow her across the ocean. She only had to convince her that she *could*, so that she would feel hunted—haunted—by the specter of impending doom.

Sabine is not the one who has been haunting Charlotte these past years.

Charlotte has done all the haunting for her.

Now, at last, she decides that she is done.

And then, the girls begin to disappear.

The first time, she tells herself it's nothing.

That Grace's band picked up and went back on the road, and that is why she cannot get ahold of her, why no one answers when she calls. She was a free spirit, after all.

But then the second, Hannah, invites her on a date, and fails to show. No word before or after, no note or call.

And then the third one—Luce, fearless Luce, who stood beside her on the bridge and spoke of life as brief and beautiful—is pulled out of the river.

Charlotte sees the caution tape.

She finds the friends and family holding vigil.

And she knows.

She calls Ezra from a pay phone outside Union Station, voice shaking as she says, "It's her."

"Are you sure?" he asks over the sound of an acoustic guitar. "Cities are big places, Lottie. We're not the only monsters out there. Sometimes bad things happen."

She wants Ezra to be right, she really does.

But she goes back to the bridge that night. A makeshift memorial has grown around a pole, flowers and candles and notes, but she goes past it, onto the bridge itself, halfway across, to the spot where she and Luce had stood.

And that is where she sees it.

A single red rose, tied to the metal post.

Check.

Charlotte abandons the yellow bug.

She takes a flight out west—her first. She braves the glaring sun a moment, despite how sick it makes her feel, just to look out the curving window, watch the vast wide world slide past so far below. How quickly the plane moves, its giant stride carrying her away.

Never again, she tells herself as the plane lands in San Francisco.

Never again, she tells herself for weeks, then months, then years.

As the darkness folds over her again.

A life without a life.

Her lonely heart.

One night in Seattle, she walks past a rack of greeting cards.

Flimsy paper things, printed with trite little sayings. One catches her eye, in the section marked *Condolences*: a picture of a clock wrapping its arms gingerly around a girl, beneath the words *Time Heals*.

And Charlotte thinks, they've gotten it wrong.

Time doesn't *heal*.

It just wears you down.

Tricks you into thinking, as the present slips into the past, that it will stay there.

Safely buried in your wake.

VIII

New York, New York
1994

And then, she meets Penny.

Charlotte doesn't *want* to fall for her—for anyone again—but she won't deny how nice it is to be the object of affection, how lonely she has been. And perhaps, if she is being honest, some part of her thinks that she deserves it, after all those years of vigilance.

Deserves to be seen, and wanted, and held.

Besides, there is something special about Penny.

Penny, who works nights at a bodega, and devours books as fast as she can buy them from the secondhand shop around the corner, books that fill every shelf of her tiny apartment in Queens because she can't bear to sell them back.

Penny, who takes her breath away, with her black hair, her green eyes (like Joss, and not like Joss at all), and her infectious laugh, and her insatiable mind.

Penny, who calls her Char, and starfishes in her sleep, and tastes like curiosity, and hope, and the energy drinks she mainlines to stay awake.

Penny, who doesn't disappear.

Not after a month, or two, or three.

Charlotte marks the passing weeks with such relief, and then, on their four-month anniversary, Penny asks her to move in. She gives her a key with a pendant shaped like a cartoon drop of blood, from when she donated that spring, and it's so silly, but the sight makes Charlotte smile every time she pulls it from her pocket.

Every time she slips the key into the lock.

Until one night she comes home and finds Penny propped upright in their bed, head drooping as if she was waiting up for Charlotte and simply drifted off. Except the front of the tattered Eagles shirt she wears to sleep is stained with rivulets of rusted red.

Charlotte stands pinned in the bedroom doorway, as if unable to cross the threshold. She stares at the scene, denial racing to catch up with what she sees, because this can't be happening.

Not again.

Not again.

Not again.

Except, it is.

It is, and Charlotte forces herself forward, step-by-step, until she's almost to the bed, and that's when Penny shudders and wakes up.

Charlotte's legs go weak beneath her with relief, and she sinks onto the bed. Because Penny's all right, isn't she, it must be paint, not blood, and she's okay, and everything is still okay.

Until the moment Penny looks right at her, those green eyes now lit strangely from behind, and smiles, revealing pointed teeth.

"Hey, Char," she says, and she doesn't seem frightened, or confused, not even when she sees the shock on Charlotte's face.

"Hey, hey, it's okay," says Penny, reaching for her hand. "I'm okay." But she's not, she's not, her fingers are already cold, and Charlotte cannot hear her heart. "It's all right," murmurs Penny, the way she does after one of Charlotte's nightmares. "It's all right. Sabine told me what would happen."

The sound of that name, in Penny's mouth, turns the still air to ice inside her lungs.

"What?" she wheezes. "I don't—"

Penny grips her hand, so tight, too tight, she doesn't know her strength. "She told me you were scared to do it, so she had to. Because she didn't want you to be lonely. And now you won't be. So you see, it was a gift. From both of us. To you."

The room tips.

The cracks in Charlotte deepen, and she fights the urge to scream. Because Sabine knows—she *has* to know—why Charlotte hasn't turned a single lover all these years. Because she cannot bear the thought of being *their* Sabine. Of them staying with her as the parts they love begin to rot away, until all that's left is a stranger, or a monster, or both.

Sabine knows, and that is exactly why she's done it.

And Charlotte is fighting to hide the horror, must not be doing a good job, because Penny's face drops.

"You don't seem happy," she says, green eyes flickering with worry.

Charlotte shakes her head, even as she forces out a smile, and says of course, of course she is happy. She's *so* happy Penny is all right. She folds her arms around the girl, tries not to hear the silence where her pulse should be, Sabine's scent still clinging to her.

Penny laughs against her in relief, pulls back and says they should go out.

"To celebrate!" she announces, lunging up from the bed with sudden, manic glee. "And I'm hungry. Like, really hungry." She goes to the rack against her bedroom wall, begins turning through the outfits there.

"Don't worry about that," says Charlotte, rising from the bed. "I'll show you how." She passes the dresser, fingers curling around a silver long-handled brush. "I'll teach you everything."

Penny takes a sequined sweater from the rack. "Oh!" she says, the small gems winking as she lifts it. "Think of all the bo—"

But the word dies on her lips.

The sweater falls.

There is no cry, no sob, no drawn-out death. Penny simply stiffens as the silver handle drives through her back, her ribs, her heart. And then the life goes out of her. She sags backward against Charlotte, so light, and yet so heavy that Charlotte feels her knees give way beneath the weight, sliding with her to the floor, where she strokes Penny's hair and wonders if she is beginning to wither, too. If something *is* dying in her after all, the part that knows better. The part that should have learned.

How else could she have let this happen?

Something kindles inside Charlotte, then, burning through the guilt and grief.

Rage. She rises, makes her way back through the apartment, snatches the blood drop keychain from the kitchen table, and goes up onto the roof.

Three in the morning, and no one up there, nothing save for a string of burned-out Christmas lights and half a dozen empty bottles and Manhattan winking in the distance.

"Enough," she hisses to the empty roof, the Queens night. The word goes nowhere—the darkness seems to snuff it out—and so she says it louder, and louder, and louder, until it is a chant, a shout, a shriek.

"DO YOU HEAR ME, SABINE?" she screams into the dark. "I SAID ENOUGH."

A light goes on nearby. A window opens. A neighbor yells at her to *Knock it off*.

Charlotte doubles over, lets out a final, guttural scream.

It echoes. And dies.

And no one comes.

IX

Charlotte sits on the roof till almost dawn.

Till the anger has burned out, left a hollow in its wake.

She stands and forces herself to go downstairs, exhaustion dragging at her edges as the sun comes up, but she doesn't rest. Instead, Charlotte cleans the flat, washes the dishes, puts everything back in its proper place. The books. The clothes. The silver brush (she wipes her fingerprints off the handle—she's heard they use those now, in solving crimes).

She fixes everything but Penny, who still lies curled like a child on the bedroom floor, the skin drawn taut over her bones.

Charlotte collapses on the sofa until dusk.

Then sits up and reaches for the phone.

It rings, and rings, and rings, but finally, he answers. "White Thorn Black Roast."

"What happened to the White Thorn Club?" she asks.

Ezra's voice loosens, just a little. "Got a facelift. Haven't you heard? Grunge is out. Caffeine is in." The heady beat no longer hangs behind him. In its place, she can just make out the rise and fall of Debussy. Charlotte tries to laugh, but can't. She coughs, and feels the tears well up instead.

"What's wrong, Lottie?"

She closes her eyes, imagines he's right there, sitting across from her, leaning back in his chair, arms crossed, one knee bouncing restlessly beneath the table. She talks, and Ezra listens—he always listens—but when she's done, he doesn't tell her it will be okay. He doesn't tell her anything. In her mind, his mouth is pinched, his brows drawn.

"Did I do the wrong thing?" she asks, knowing Ezra will not coddle her.

And he doesn't.

"By killing her or loving her?" he counters.

Charlotte flinches. "You told me I was being paranoid."

"Yes, well, I guess we've both been proven wrong."

Someone calls for Ezra. She hears a chair scrape back, a muffled *Be right there.*

Charlotte folds forward, presses her forehead to her knees. "What am I supposed to do?"

"Be alone," he says, and the thought is enough to break her.

"It's too hard," she whispers. "I try, and try, but—"

"For fuck's sake, Lottie," snaps Ezra. "Either these girls' lives matter more than your need for love, or they don't."

And there it is, the brutal truth, hanging on the line, accompanied by the soft bars of "Clair de lune." He's right. She knows he's right. It is her heart. That is what Sabine laid claim to.

"Is that how you get by?" she asks. "Alone?"

"Well, *I* don't have a homicidal ex," he says. "But yes. Humans live short and fragile lives. That is why we either take the ones we love and make them like us, or enjoy their company and let them go. Take them into your bed, if you like, but not your heart, and *maybe* they'll get out alive."

She swallows. "Isn't it lonely?"

"It doesn't have to be. After all, loneliness is just like us," says Ezra. "It has to be invited in."

X

So that's what Charlotte does.

She learns the difference between lonely and alone.

She falls for no one.

Indulges only in the briefest of encounters, trysts that end as quickly as they start, a chance to warm her hands and feed her heart, one-night stands recorded in the blank last pages of a paperback she took from Penny's place.

The Secret History, it's called. How fitting.

She keeps the entries simple, brief.

Maddie. The bluest eyes I've ever seen.

Jess. Freckles like stars across her cheeks.

Chloe. Rings on every knuckle.

Names, notes, fragments of memory, each entry like one of Sabine's tokens, and yet, the opposite, because she is not keeping track of the lives she's taken, but of the ones she has saved, protected by her diligence. Her ability to take and leave instead of stay.

For years, in fact, Charlotte doubles back, to make sure each and every one is *safe.*

For years, she drifts in her own wake, and every time she is rewarded for her sacrifice, because every time, these girls whose lives she's only grazed, they are alive. They are okay. And that is what matters, isn't it?

Not her comfort. Not her longing. Not her need for love.

What matters is that they are okay.

For years they are, and so, somewhere along the line, Charlotte stops doubling back, stops checking each and every name. Because it's hard, and it hurts, and because there is no need.

Sabine has clearly tired of the hunt.

Gone on to find another game.
She didn't know—how could she know?
So please, believe her when she says—
"I'm sorry, Alice. I really thought you would be safe."

ALICE

(D. 2019)

I

The words echo through the room.

And for a moment, no one moves.

At some point Ezra shifted to the window, where he stands, his back to the night, while Lottie is still sitting on the edge of the bed, arms wrapped around her ribs, and Alice is on the floor between a sofa and a marble coffee table, gripping the stone edge until her fingers hurt as a scream tries to claw its way up her throat.

Because the thing is, there are good ways to die.

Old age is up there, of course, but there's also sacrifice, saving someone else, for instance, a loved one, or a stranger. There are deaths that have value, have meaning, or at least have *purpose*. There are tragic accidents and suicides, there are acts of violence and revenge, and if you trace them back along the timeline of events, there is a reason, a cause to the effect.

But Alice is sitting there, trying to process the fact that her death wasn't part of some big picture, some elaborate design. It wasn't even an act of careless hunger on Lottie's part. It wasn't about need, or even want, and the question that's been beating like a drum in Alice's head—*Why me? Why me? Why me?*—doesn't have an answer, other than *Why not?*

Because it wasn't about her at all.

It was a shot fired by a jealous ex. She was just collateral in someone else's war, and Sabine killed her because she was there, because Lottie couldn't keep her hands to herself, she did it to prove a point, to play a game, and that means it was meaningless, her death was *meaningless*, and she doesn't realize how hard she's been gripping the marble surface of the table until finally it breaks. A vicious crack, a fissure running through the stone and back, echoing through her with a pain she barely even feels.

"Alice," says Ezra gently, as if she's a skittish pet, as if the soft cadence of his voice is going to make it any better, will smooth the shattered ruins of her life.

"I died for nothing," she whispers, because she's afraid that if she starts shouting, she'll never stop, and then she thinks, *Fuck that,* and raises her voice and says, "I died for NOTHING."

"Alice, I'm—" starts Lottie, but Alice is already on her feet, already shoving Lottie so hard she stumbles back into the wall.

"Don't you dare say you're fucking sorry."

"I did everything I could."

"Obviously not," says Alice. "You could have stayed the hell away from me."

She pushes again, but this time Lottie catches her wrists and pulls her in, arms folding around Alice's back, and Alice is sobbing now, her vision red, and Lottie says, "It's all right, it will be all right," as if the words are a spell, as if they can fix any part of this, but there's no fixing it, because there's no going back.

Alice wrenches free, stumbling away.

(And it turns out you *can* in fact have a panic attack without a beating heart, or a working pair of lungs, because the room is spinning and Ezra has her by the shoulders, eyes locked on hers as he tells her to *breathe,* or at least she thinks that's what his mouth is saying, but she can't hear the word, not over the white noise climbing in her head.)

Alice tries to inhale but the air isn't going in this time, her lungs won't inflate because they're dead (*she's* dead) and she just wants to go back, back to the weekend and the party and the wall, wants to unravel her life moment by moment and stitch it together differently but she *can't,* and it's not fair (it's not fair, it's not fair, it's not fair) and Alice thinks that maybe she can't breathe in because she's screaming, and then Ezra is there again, bringing a cup to her lips, and his mouth is saying *Drink this,* and it smells different, tainted, wrong, but Alice doesn't care, not anymore (she is so tired and so angry and somehow even through the fog of panic the hunger is still there, the only sharp thing in the blurring room), so Alice drinks and knows the moment the blood hits her tongue that she was right, and it is wrong, but she doesn't care, if it will make the pain stop.

So she drinks, and by the time the glass is empty her head is spinning, or the room is spinning, and then it's like someone snipped the strings holding her up, because her legs go out, and Ezra catches her, eases her down to the floor, and she curls up there, the way she wanted to back in the little cemetery by the church.

Only this time she doesn't fight her way up again—

She lets the ground reach up, and pull her down—

Down—

Down—

Into the dark.

II

Alice is in the kitchen when she hears the crash.

El's at the shop getting streamers and she's working on Catty's birthday cake, wee Finn sitting on the counter as she measures, mixes, pours, and Alice loves this part—cooking is too wild, too much left to chance, but baking is like maths and chemistry, which are her best subjects this year in school—and she's just letting Finn add the milk when the sound rings through the house, and Alice has the sense to put her little brother safely on the floor before she rushes toward the sitting room.

And finds Catty.

Catty, who's moved on from Derrick to a guy named Malcolm, who's nineteen and not from Hoxburn, just passing through, because he has the kind of job that takes him places.

Catty, who's barely passing sixth year, and seems hell-bent on mystifying the counselor assigned to help her find a path because they don't get that all she wants is to be discovered, to be *seen*.

Catty, who found one of Mum's photos in a box instead of on the shelf, and took a bat to the wedding portrait on the mantel.

(All that practice in the gravel lot behind the pub.)

And that's bad enough, but there's glass on the floor and wee Finn toddles in before Alice can get it swept up and cuts his heel. Nothing a couple plasters don't fix, but feet bleed just as much as heads and hands, and then El returns, and tells Catty to *grow up or get out.*

The next day, Catty blows out the candles on her seventeenth birthday cake.

And the next day, she is gone.

She doesn't leave a note, doesn't turn on her phone, and she's too old to be considered a runaway, so there's nothing to do but wait and hope.

El blames herself (even though Dad says that Catty's been gathering sticks for years, armfuls of kindling, waiting for an excuse to strike the match), and Dad's face is lined with worry, and Finn is too young to understand, so he goes around peering behind doors and under tables as if Catty's just playing some drawn-out game of hide-and-seek, and for the first time in her life Alice fails a test because she can't sleep, lies awake every night listening for the sound of her sister sneaking back in.

For a week, the walls of the house feel too thick, the air too tight, like the world is holding its breath.

And then, Catty calls.

"Hey, Bones," she says like it's any other day.

Alice is home alone, and she wants to scream, to sob, to throw her arms around her sister but she can't because she isn't *there*, so she just says, "Where the hell are you, Catty?"

And her sister *laughs*.

She laughs like nothing's wrong.

"Right now? York."

It knocks the wind out of Alice. So far away, so soon. Catty told her once that there was a rope running between them—"Heart to heart," she said, poking Alice right between the ribs—and every time one moved, the other would know, so Alice tried, told Catty to run and hide, and said she would use the rope to find her.

But it didn't work.

Alice couldn't feel it, couldn't find her, and finally Catty showed up on her own, and shrugged, like the world hadn't just caved in, and said, "I guess it's easier for big sisters."

"York?" Alice asks again, pulling up a map. The number of miles, the route the train would take, the path like a red cord stretching south.

"Yep. And guess what? It's just as haunted as Mum said it was. All those little alleys full of ghosts and—"

"Please come home," says Alice, but she can practically hear Catty shaking her head.

"Why would I do that?" she asks, a tight laugh catching in her voice.

Because I'm here, Alice wants to say. *Because you promised me we'd go together.*

"Look, one day you'll understand," says Catty. "The world is big and full of chances. Hoxburn isn't."

Alice's eyes begin to burn. Tears spill down her cheeks. "You should have waited for me."

("Slow down.")

("Catch up.")

"I couldn't."

Catty doesn't say she's sorry (never has), but Alice can hear the pang of sadness in her voice before it picks back up. "But you finish school, get those good grades, and go to one of those big fancy universities, and I'll be there. By then, I'll be all set, have enough saved up. And it will just be the two of us."

"What about Malcolm?" mutters Alice.

"Oh, he's gone. He was just a ride. A way out."

Alice's stomach twists, relief giving way to worry. "You're alone?"

Only she's not, because now Alice can hear another voice somewhere behind her, and then Catty's saying, "Hey, I gotta go. Hang in there, Alice."

"Catty, wait," she says.

"Catty, please," she says.

"Catty, just tell me—" she says.

But it's too late. Her sister's gone.

"Daft girl," says Dad when he finds out, and he sounds furious, but that night he tries to call the number back a hundred times.

Of course, by then, the phone is off.

Alice lies there, pressing the pendant against her chest until she can feel her pulse beating through the metal, pretends it's the other end of their shared rope, that it won't break, no matter how far Catty goes.

Heart to heart, she whispers into the dark, as her pulse slows—

And slows—

And—

Alice wakes at dusk.

Not slowly but all at once, lurching back, one hand still clutching the necklace through her shirt. For a moment, she doesn't know where she is, or rather, she *thinks* she knows, back in her single bed in her shared room in her dorm suite, and she must have climbed beneath the blankets, taken a nap after class, and that's what she's always done when she's sick.

But then she swallows, and tastes the dregs of copper in her throat. She isn't sick, because sick is a problem that can be fixed, and when she rolls over she sees she's not in her bed, but on a sofa, a blanket she doesn't need draped over her shoulders.

And she remembers.

I really thought you would be safe.

Alice sits up, and sees blood staining the cushion under her cheek, feels a second's lurching panic before she feels the crust of tears beneath her eyes. Her gaze drifts to the marble coffee table with its deep crack, a glaring reminder of a rage she tries to summon now, and can't.

She checks her phone and sees a series of increasingly worried texts in the suite thread—asking where she is, if she's okay, please, just let them know, say something, don't make them call campus police. Alice doesn't know how to answer that so she lies and says *Sorry*, says *Yes*, says she's *Staying at a friend's*, even though they all know she doesn't have anything close to friends outside the suite, barely knows anyone from class.

Alice pockets the phone and looks around.

No sign of Ezra, or Lottie.

The room is empty, the curtains drawn, twilight spilling through a narrow gap, and maybe it's Lottie's story, or maybe it's the dream she had, the memory, but she finds herself hooking the gold chain with her fingers and drawing the pendant from beneath her hoodie.

The pendant, which isn't a pendant but a locket, a vial.

Her little piece of home.

A *bit of glaur*, Catty called it—dirt, but not just *any* dirt.

Her mother's, taken from the grave, a gift from Eloise on that blue-tinted wedding day.

She unscrews the hidden lid and tips the smallest bit into her palm, and the moment it touches her bare skin she is back in the cemetery plot, and all the strength is rushing out of her, the life leeching backward, her limbs shriveling and her heart drying up and—

Alice recoils, wrenching her hand back so fast the flecks of grave dirt rain down onto the splintered marble.

"No, no, no," she whispers, dropping to her knees beside the table, trying to salvage the dirt, even though it's little more than a capful, a coin, and every time it touches her skin that sickness surges up to meet it.

At last she gives up, and screws the tiny gold cap back onto the vial, and what's left of the dirt inside, shoving the pendant back beneath her shirt. She leans forward, fills her lungs, and blows, scattering the thin dusting on the marble, is about to retreat beneath the blanket, try to disappear again when she sees a bag that must be Lottie's, tucked between the table's feet. Only, it's not the bag that holds her gaze.

It's the book that's sticking out.

A battered paperback, but she's read it twice, and she would know the cover anywhere. The marble face turned half-away on the black ground, the serifed type declaring it *The Secret History*.

Penny's book.

Alice plucks it from the bag and opens it, flipping to the blank back pages where Lottie kept her litany of conquests, her list of names, no better than the tokens Sabine wore around her neck. Alice doesn't read them all, except to note how many there are, the names filling not one page, but two, before her eyes go straight to the most recent line. Brief as a tombstone in damning purple ink.

Alice. Scottish. Gentle. Tastes like grief.

She reads it twice, three times, till the lines become words and the words become letters and the letters break apart and still she can't understand how her entire life has been reduced to six words in this small and sloping script.

And ah—there it is, the anger Alice couldn't find when she woke up.

There it is, striking up again, as quick as flint.

The page crumples beneath her hands, and she's about to tear it, when the lock on the hotel door chirps and the door glides open, and Lottie comes in, dressed in fresh clothes and holding a store bag—the fancy kind with tissue sticking out the top—hooked on her elbow, as if she's been *shopping*.

Lottie sees Alice, book clenched in her hands, and Alice *wants* her to lunge forward, to say *No*, to say *Don't*. To try to pry her precious list away, so Alice can take something from her, too.

But Lottie just stands there, watching, waiting, and suddenly the words are just words, a stupid postscript in the back of a battered book, and Alice flings the paperback aside and climbs back onto the couch, drawing up her knees as Lottie steps over the book, and sets the bag aside, and says, "I'm glad you're awake."

Alice glares, and she adds, "Sorry for drugging you. It was Ezra's idea. He has more experience with things like this."

"Things like this," echoes Alice darkly.

"In the beginning, we're . . ." she searches for the word, "volatile. Every feeling, every need, is dialed up, the good and the bad. He thought you might hurt yourself. Or at the very least, destroy the room."

This last said with a shred of lightness, too like a joke.

Alice clenches her teeth as Lottie lowers herself into a nearby chair, sinks her fingers into her curls, and sighs, the air around her tinged with tension. Alice asks the question that's bothering her most.

"Why didn't you kill me?"

Of course, until the early hours of last night, Alice was convinced she *had*—that this strange girl had walked into her life and stolen it from under her. Now she knows that Lottie's not to blame for *that* part—at least, she's not the one who stopped her heart, even if she's still the reason why it happened.

"I liked you," answers Lottie limply. "We had fun and then—"

"Not that night," says Alice. "After. When you found out what I was. What *she* made me." Alice swallows. "Sabine." The name, like a bitter cordial on her tongue. "When I showed up here. Changed. Like Penny."

Lottie's expression darkens. "I didn't want to."

"So you *wanted* to kill Penny?"

She winces at the name. "No. It broke my heart."

"But you did it."

A whispered, "Yes."

And it occurs to Alice then, that just because Lottie hasn't killed her yet doesn't mean she won't still try, that maybe the only reason she waited was because Ezra might disapprove. Alice looks toward the door, wondering if and when he'll—

"I sent him home," says Lottie. "This isn't Ezra's problem. It's mine."

And Alice doesn't appreciate being called a problem, but her thoughts skip past that to the fact Lottie knew exactly where her mind was going.

"How did you—"

"Your head's too loud. You might as well be shouting."

Alice frowns. "How do I think quieter?"

Lottie comes and sits across from her, perching on the edge of the cracked table, close enough that their knees touch, close enough that Alice can see the faintest threads of gold, like filaments of light, in her brown eyes. And even now, despite everything, Alice finds it hard to look away. She feels an echo of the longing that circled her that night, the force that drew her forward, and wonders what could have been, if things were different, if she had woken the next morning and hadn't been alone in bed.

Lottie's heart-shaped face burrowing into her shoulder, her violet curls tickling her chin, her cool arms wrapped around her waist, her lips against her ear as she whispered about breakfast.

But then Alice thinks of the list in the back of the book, and knows that's all she was to Charlotte Hastings, all she would ever be. *Alice. Scottish. Gentle. Tastes like grief.*

Lottie's hand settles on her knee, forcing her attention back, and the look on her face says she knows. There's pity in her eyes, and Alice doesn't want it.

"Show me how it works," she says.

"It takes practice, to put up walls. To keep your thoughts safely to yourself. But in the meantime, you can try and cover it by thinking pointedly. Focus on one thing you *want* me to hear, instead of all the things you don't. It's not words, really, so don't try thinking of a number or anything like that. It's feelings. Emotions, desires, that kind of thing."

Alice looks Lottie in the eye, and focuses, as loudly as she can, on her *distrust.*

Lottie nods. "That's fair," she says. "I haven't earned it yet."

Alice can't believe it worked, almost smiles before she remembers that it's Lottie's fault, and that thought must have come through loud and clear, or at least the blaming part, because she looks exhausted, drawn. And yet, the walls around her mind have gone back up, and no matter how hard Alice strains, she can't glean the faintest hint of *Lottie's* thoughts.

"You want to know why I didn't kill you?" she says, looking down at her hands. "I wish I could tell you it was kindness, or that I knew you'd been through enough. But it's not. It's because I'm tired, Alice." Her gaze flicks up. "I'm tired of running. Tired of living in fear. Tired of playing cat and mouse, of knowing it's only a matter of time before Sabine catches up again. I didn't kill you because *someone* has to stop her, and I can't. But maybe you can."

Alice almost scoffs

She wants Sabine to pay for what she did, wants to hold her down and drive a stake right through her heart, watch the life go out of her eyes and her body turn to dust.

She wants Sabine to look at her before she dies, to understand that it's her fault.

That she created her own killer.

She *wants* it, of course she does, but Alice is no fool. She may be new to all this, but she suspects that there's a power differential, that someone—something—as old as Sabine is much, *much* stronger than she is, and she's about to point this out, that what Lottie is proposing might as well be suicide, when she says, "You'd get your life back."

Alice's mind shudders to a stop so fast she can almost hear the gears. "What?"

Lottie chews her lip, and nods. "Sabine made you. She took your life. But you can take it back."

"What are you talking about?" asks Alice.

"I didn't know that, back when I found Penny. I wish I had. And it wouldn't work if it had been a year, a month, even a week, but you're *newly made*," says Lottie, eyes alight. "Which means you're still connected to her. Your blood. Your life. It's like a rope that runs between you."

Alice's hand drifts to her collar, the pendant cold against her skin.

"If you kill Sabine, you'll sever it. And you'll go back to being what you were before."

Alice cocks her head, uncertain. "What I was?"

"Alive," says Lottie.

The word flares like a torch in Alice's chest. *Alive. Alive. Alive?*

Doubt rushes up to meet it, because that isn't how it works in all the stories, the good books and bad TV, there's never any going back, but then again, this isn't any story, this is *hers*. Alice versus common lore, and if Lottie's right, if there's a way to fix this, if there's even a sliver of a chance that it could work—

What does she have left to lose?

She looks down at the paperback and thinks of that single line, those six, sad words—*Alice. Scottish. Gentle. Tastes like grief.*—and decides, right then and there, that they won't be the last record of her life. The sum total of her story.

Alice looks up at Lottie, searches her face, but all she sees is hope, and it's like a mirror, catching the sun, reflecting the light. Alice feels herself begin to warm.

"All right," she says, "what do I have to do?"

III

The clothes spill from the shopping bag as Lottie empties it onto the bed.

A pile of shimmery fabric that turns out to be short dresses—all of them in autumn colors, emerald and goldenrod and violet—along with some makeup and a pair of heeled boots in Alice's size, as if she knew she would say yes.

"Get dressed," she says. "We're going out."

Alice runs her hand over the clothes, frowns at the fabric, or really, at the lack of it, remembering what Ezra said about the cold, and blending in. "To *where?*"

Lottie doesn't answer, just grabs her hand and pulls her toward the bathroom. The grieving girl Alice met last night is gone, replaced by someone happy, effervescent. She guides Alice to a stool before the bathroom mirror and begins running a brush through her hair, untangling the snarls of blonde until the teeth slide smooth.

"We won't have to go looking for Sabine," she says. "She'll come to us." She tosses the brush aside and begins looping locks of hair around her fingers, pinning it up into a messy bun. "In fact, she's probably been following you this whole time."

"Why?" asks Alice, meeting Lottie's gaze in the mirror. Her brown eyes are lit with that strange light, but when she looks at herself, she sees it, too, a kind of backlit glow. That one small piece of them, unnatural, alike, and with it, the understanding settles over her.

"Because you didn't kill me."

Lottie purses her lips, gives a tight nod. "To her, it's always been a game. *Her* game, which means her rules. Stay and die, or run, and live, and lose." Her expression darkens. "Sabine knew what she was doing when she planted Penny in the midnight soil. She knew I would rather kill a girl I loved than let her walk this road with me, knowing where it goes. She knew, and made me prove it."

For the first time, Alice wonders if there were others, between Penny and herself. Other girls Sabine caught, and turned, and killed. The list of names in the back of *The Secret History* was long, longer than she thought it would be. Did they all survive their one-night stands, their brief encounters?

Lottie spins the stool toward her, and the mirror is gone, and they are face-to-face as she kneels. "But now, with you, I've stopped playing by her rules. And she'll want to know why. Hold still," she adds, and Alice's mouth twitches, because that's one command she can obey. Lottie leans close, close enough that her breath would tickle Alice's face if she were breathing, and draws two expert lines of black along the outer corners of her lids, one cold and steady hand guiding her chin.

"How do I kill her?" asks Alice as Lottie dabs a plum tint on her bottom lip. A shadow crosses her face, and Alice wonders if it's the memory of her failed attempt or the idea of Alice's success that troubles her. If, no matter how badly Lottie hates Sabine, some part still loves her, too.

But then the shadow's gone. And maybe it was just a trick of the harsh bathroom light, because Lottie takes up a mascara, and wields it like a stake, resting the tip between Alice's bottom ribs.

"You have to kill the heart," she says. "Sunlight makes us weak, and grave dirt makes us ill. But only our hearts stay mortal."

The imaginary weapon drops away, but Alice brings her fingers to the place it was, touching the soft dip of skin between the bones, and that's when the absurdity of the task rolls over her. What was she thinking? Sabine is five hundred years old, and she is eighteen, there's no way she'll get close enough to try, and even if she does—

Lottie raps her gently on the forehead with the wand.

"Too loud," she warns. "You can't let her hear you think like that, or you'll never pull it off."

"Then I'll never pull it off," snaps Alice, panic building now. "This is insane. I don't know how you expect me to do this, let alone do it without tipping my hand—or head. She's going to feel how scared I am."

She wishes Ezra were still there, his presence like a steady hand, but he's not, and Lottie's the one who reaches out and cups her face.

"You can be afraid of Sabine—she's always had a taste for fear, and it would be strange, given what you know, if you weren't awash in it. Just remember what I told you. If you can't stop your mind from latching onto something, make sure it's something else. And when in doubt," she adds, "think about *me*."

Alice lets herself look up, into Lottie's eyes, wishes she could see behind them, feel the shape of her mind, but the air is quiet, steady, and maybe it's the madness of what she's about to do, or maybe it's just the way Lottie's leaning over her, but the question slips out.

"Why me?"

Lottie blinks, a furrow forming between her brows. "Hm?"

"I know what you wrote about me after," Alice says. "But that night, why did you pick me? Is it just that I was there? And you thought I'd be an easy mark? Some sad, lonely girl hugging the wall, waiting—"

"No." Lottie's voice is low, but stern. "I chose you because you were special."

Alice lets out a soft, mocking sound, but Lottie presses on.

"Do you remember what I told you, about Sabine, and what she said drew her to me on the stairs that night? That I was loud and full of longing. That whatever I felt, I couldn't keep it in. It took up space, even when I didn't. That hunger to be seen." Lottie's thumb brushes Alice's cheek. "That's why I chose you, too. Because I looked at you, and I saw *me*. Who I was." Tears shimmer, crimson, at the corners of her eyes. "And for all that happened after, for everything she did to me, I still remember what it felt like, to be noticed, to be wanted, to be seen. I wanted you to feel that, too." She pulls away, wiping her eyes. "But on top of all that," she adds cheerfully, "I thought you were hot."

Alice laughs, a small, sad sound that tears free from her chest. She shakes her head as Lottie turns away.

"I'll let you get dressed," she says, closing the bathroom door behind her.

In the end, Alice chooses the green dress. A rich emerald, like moss after rain, that makes her skin look even paler, the veins at her wrist and throat thin and blue and still. She studies herself in the mirror.

New Alice, she thinks. *Just for one night.*

But it's not Alice staring back.

The girl in the mirror is someone else, the hem ending at her thigh, her legs made longer by the heeled boots, and with her blond hair pinned up, the dark color at her lips, she expects to look like a stranger, but she doesn't.

She looks like *Catty*.

Alice swallows, and flicks off the light.

She steps out of the bathroom. "I look like bait," she says, and she meant it as a joke, but Lottie doesn't laugh.

She only smiles and says, "I'd fall for you again."

Alice's heart, silent as it is, seems to give a little lurch. The way it did when she first passed her in the dark. When she pulled her off the wall. When they fell into her bed.

Lottie smiles, flashing that dimple in her cheek. "Like that," she says, reading the shape of her thoughts. And Alice is glad that Lottie doesn't ask her if she's ready, just takes her hand and says, "Let's go."

Lottie's laugh rolls down the street.

The night yawns wide around them, full of movement, light, and life, and they walk together, arm in arm, Alice tucked against her side. Right before they left the safety of the Taj, Lottie drew her close and whispered in her ear, "Once we leave, you have to *want* to be with me. You have to make her think that you are *mine*."

Alice stiffened when she said it. Most of her wanted to rebel, to pull away, but some small part wanted to lean in and that's the one she listened to as they stepped into the street.

"Where are we going?" asks Alice now, but Lottie only grins.

"Don't you worry about that." Her voice is low, heady with pleasure, every inch of her radiating the same confidence that drew Alice toward her at the party, like a moth to a light, and she will never forgive Lottie for the part she played in leading Sabine to her, but there is no use dwelling on it now, not when there's so much at stake.

She rests her head on Lottie's shoulder every time they stop and stand, waiting for a light. Doesn't resist when Lottie's lips graze hers, when she tells Alice that she tastes like winter.

"Not grief?" Alice whispers back, and Lottie silences the question with a kiss.

"No, not grief at all," she says, the words trapped between them.

It's a two-person performance for an audience of one.

Sabine, who could be out there somewhere, watching them.

But every time her thoughts veer toward the word, the name, the woman it conjures—where she is, where she might be—Lottie gives her arm a warning squeeze, and Alice fights to quiet her mind, or at least, to turn her thoughts somewhere else.

Think about me, Lottie said, and Alice tries, she really does, tries to focus on the way her curls bounce with every step, the warm tan of her skin, the fact she seems so full of life, but then she tries to imagine the girl she was, before, standing on the ballroom stairs, the girl she could have been, and it's a slippery slope from there to Sabine, and as soon as she even thinks the name it's like quicksand, her mind struggling against the thought of what she has to do, of the layers of armor that surround a heart, and she has to drag herself free and think of something else.

Something else, which could be anything, but it's not. Because her mind only goes one place when left alone, and already she can feel the past dragging its feet, looking back over its shoulder, and here's the thing, it might surprise you, but Alice doesn't *want* to think of Catty.

She doesn't want to, but she can't help it—

It's the rope that keeps her from escaping—

The rope that hauls her back again.

Catty calls from Sheffield, Leicester, Cambridge.

Every time she is a little farther south.

And every time, Alice reminds her that she can come home.

And every time, Catty says, "Now why would I do that?"

Days turn into weeks, and in some ways, life stops, and in others, it goes on, and the worst part isn't the missing, but the fact that it gets easier. She is still worried, of course, so worried, but the fear dissolves into something worse:

Relief.

Because those weeks are, in their awful way, the easiest in memory, without the eggshells, and the broken glass, the poison words and the land mines of her sister's temper.

Alice is making popcorn when her cell phone hums inside her pocket.

(She's learned to keep the ringer off, so Dad won't try to snatch it from her.)

He and El are in front of the TV, searching for a film, and Finn is going round the house, getting pillows for a fort, and the house smells of butter and feels as soft, as warm, as Alice answers.

"Hey, Bones." Catty's voice frays in her ear. "Guess where I am?"

"Hold on," she says, tugging the bag of popcorn from the microwave, hissing as the steam burns her fingertips. She leaves the bag on the counter and slips out the side door, into the dark.

Catty hasn't stopped talking.

"Made it all the way to London. Can you believe it? I'm sitting on the steps of that big fountain in Trafalgar Square, just like Mum was in that one photo."

("Do you remember?")

Sometimes Catty sounds groggy, and other times she talks so fast, Alice can barely keep up. Tonight her voice is dreamy, far away. But there's something off about it. Far away, as if the distance has gathered up like wool between them.

Alice frowns. "Are you okay?"

It's freezing out, and she wishes she'd put on a coat, even as she forces herself forward, across the damp ground, away from the house, so they won't hear her on the phone.

"Me? I'm grand," says Catty. "Just wish you were here to see it, too."

Why couldn't you wait? Alice wants to snap. But what she says is, "We can go back. You can show me everything."

"It's so big," drawls Catty. "The world is so big."

Just then, the door swings open. Butter-yellow light spills out, and Finn is there, in his footy pajamas, his favorite pillow to his chest.

"Alice?" he calls, searching for her in the dark. And for the first time in her life, she feels the rope Catty always talked about, pulling her back toward him.

"Hey Catty—" she starts, but her sister gets there first.

"Gotta go. Phone's almost out of minutes. Miss you, Bones." And then she's gone.

"Alice?" Finn calls out, sounding worried now.

"Coming!" she calls back, shivering a little as she hurries—

Back toward the house—

Eager to get out of the cold.

By the time they get where they're going, Alice has almost forgotten that Lottie's warmth, her charm, is just a ruse. She is so good at playing her part, but then, she's had so long to play it.

As for where they've ended up, it seems to be a club.

Not the kind of place she found herself last night (which feels at once like a lifetime ago and the measure of a single blink). There's a line out front, a red velvet rope, two dozen young, pretty people waiting to get in, and dressed in less than Alice is, despite the cold, but they don't join the queue.

Instead, Lottie locks a hand round hers, pulls her toward the door, and the woman with the clipboard there, and if compulsion is the work of confidence, she has it in spades. The bouncer doesn't even hesitate when Lottie meets her gaze and says, "You've been waiting for us, haven't you?"

And just like that, they're through, into the heaving space beyond, which must have either been a warehouse or a church in its past life, and is now a hollow cavern, lights playing on the vaulted ceiling, people tangled up beneath, dancing on the concrete floor.

The air is filled with bright, electric pop. Steel stairs run up to railings overhead, and a DJ on a balcony, his edges traced with neon light, and it's loud, too loud, not just the thumping music but the heavy beat of two hundred hearts, two hundred minds, two hundred bodies, taking up space, so overwhelming that Alice wants to put her hands over her ears, wants to escape back out into the open night, but Lottie is there, dragging her into the throng.

And Alice thinks that there's no way Sabine will find them here, surrounded by so many people, starts to scan the massive crowd, but Lottie's hand tightens and she pulls Alice hard enough to spin her round, into the circle of her arms.

"Don't worry about her," she says, "just dance with me."

Alice wants to say that she can't think, can't breathe, it's too hard, too much, but Lottie grabs her waist and pulls her close, and Alice looks into her eyes, which say, *With me, with me,* and somehow, the club noise begins to fade as Lottie smiles and pulls their bodies flush, a tiny pool of silence in the pounding beat.

They move together, hip to hip, and limbs entwined, and soon the world feels like it's reversing, time rewinds, and it is Saturday night and Alice Moore is leaning up against the green wall in the Co-op, and Lottie is there, asking her to dance, and they are tangled, growing together in the center of the room, and the smoke alarm never goes off, and the party never spills out into the street, and Alice is never standing in the rain and they are never running hand in hand back to the dorms, never tripping up the stairs in storm-wet clothes, never stripping in the dark, and crashing down into her bed, and Lottie never leaves, and Sabine never comes.

They are just two girls, dancing.

And they have their whole lives ahead.

IV

If they could just stay, pressed in the amber of that moment, maybe every-thing would be okay. The club pulsing around them, Lottie's hands against her hips.

But then the music dips, and Lottie tugs Alice close enough to kiss and whispers, "I'm going to get a drink. You should, too."

And then she pulls away.

One moment she's an anchor in the storm, and the next her hands are sliding free, and Alice says, "Wait—"

Alice says, "No—"

Alice says, "Don't—" because they didn't talk about this part, and Alice feels her fingers tighten on Lottie's hand, willing her not to go, not to leave her there, unprotected and alone.

Because she's afraid.

She's terrified, and Lottie should be able to tell, to feel her mind spinning out, but there are so many people creating so much noise that maybe she can't, because she just twirls Alice like it's all part of the game, tucks a lock of blond hair back behind her ear, such a tender gesture, and then she pulls free and drifts back, until she's swallowed by the crowd.

And Alice wants to go after her, to grab her arm and haul her back, but before she can the gap is gone, the bodies already filling in. She feels suddenly adrift, at sea, surrounded by two hundred strangers, living breathing people, and the reality of that comes crashing in, and her throat goes dry and her jaw begins to ache and she backs away, or tries, but her shoulders instantly collide with another person, and she says, "Sorry" (the word made strange by the sudden sharpness of her teeth, the space they take up in her mouth).

Alice turns, searching for a break in the crowd, but she can't find one, so she forces her way through, the bodies knocking against hers, the pulses hard as hammers through their skin, her head going light from hunger, until at last, at last, she's on the other side, and there's space to move (not much, but just enough), a gap between the people and the wall.

She follows a sign for the bathroom, tells herself she just needs a second to collect her thoughts, tamp down the panic, but she ends up in a narrow alcove, a makeshift hallway studded with doors, thinks she might have gotten lost along the way until she finds the right door, but just as she's about to go in, a girl comes stumbling out and runs right into her.

Alice steadies the girl, who is all apology, cheeks flushed bright from dancing or from drinking, or a mix of both, and she's still holding on to Alice, who can smell her sweat and hairspray and beer and under that, the bright, metallic tang that now makes her vision flicker and her head go light.

("I'm going to get a drink," said Lottie. "You should, too.")

Alice feels the pulse through the girl's palm, sees it flutter at her throat, and then the girl squints, leans close, her pupils wide as saucers, a thin blue ring around their edges.

"*You*," she says, and for a second Alice is afraid she knows her, from school, but the girl just stares and says, "you look like you are made of stars."

And it's dumb, she's clearly drunk, or high, but it's the kind of line that makes Alice blush inside, even as she laughs.

"I'm sorry," says the girl, shaking her head, "I've had a bad night."

"Me too," says Alice, because she's shit at flirting, always has been, but maybe there's something to the truth, or maybe there is starlight behind her eyes, a shimmer of the strange and magic to her now, because the girl bites her bottom lip, blood rushing to the surface of her skin, the air around her painted with want as she says, "Can we make it better?"

Old Alice would have blushed, and stammered.

New Alice only cocks her head and says, "Well, we can try."

And the next thing she knows, the girl is leaning back into the wall, dragging Alice with her, and then her mouth is on her mouth, and Old Alice would have stopped right there, let the kiss be just a kiss.

But New Alice is so hungry.

Her mouth moves south, to the girl's jaw, her neck, and she could still stop, if she really wanted to, but what she *wants* is to feel something besides that hollow panic, that ringing fear, so she sinks her teeth, as gently as she can, into the girl's throat, decides, even as the blood spills across her tongue, and down her throat, that she will stop in time, that she will be like Lottie, not Sabine, that she will learn to take only what she needs, and never what she wants.

So even though the heartbeat has just started in her chest, even though the pulse beneath her hands has not even begun to falter, Alice lets her teeth slide free. She pulls back, and lifts the girl's chin, glad to see that she looks glassy-eyed, a little dazed, but otherwise unhurt.

Alice smiles at this triumph, opens her mouth to tell her she'll be fine, but someone else speaks first.

"Now, Alice," says a voice, right there in her ear, "didn't Charlotte teach you?"

Up until that moment, Alice didn't know that she'd heard the voice before (the memory of that night so neatly expunged, a fallow plot in place of memory). But now the sound rattles something loose in her.

A hand, pressing her down into the sheets.

The same hand that reaches past her now and closes around the girl's throat.

"You should always finish what you start."

The swift clean snap of bone, and the girl crumples, like dead weight, onto the darkened floor, and Alice turns and finds herself face-to-face with a nightmare. With a dream.

The heartbeat dies inside her chest as she says the name.

"Sabine."

A girl watches a widow step down from a horse, and wonders who she is. "Call me Sabine," she will say, the name glinting like a prize.

A wife slaughters the husband in her bed, and sheds her old life like a coat. "Call me Sabine," she will say as he falls.

A girl at her first ball is rescued by a stranger.

"Call me Sabine," she will say, as if they are already friends.

Alice stands pinned to the spot, a dead girl at her feet, and in front of her, Sabine.

As she listened to Lottie's story, she built a mental image of the monster at its heart. She imagined her by turns a goddess, a devil, a force of nature.

And the real Sabine *is* all those things.

But somehow, she is a woman, too. Flesh and bone, at once less lovely and more striking. Six feet tall in a violet dress made of layered lace, with ropes of molten hair, and eyes that might once have burned like matches but now are lightless. Black.

And when she speaks, the voice slides like fingers through her hair. Coaxing. Calming.

"Hello, Alice."

Lottie warned her about the strength of Sabine's will, the way it could bend minds, but she should have warned Alice about the power of her *voice*, the downward pull of it, the quiet danger resting just behind the sounds in a way that makes Alice think of freezing to death—how supposedly the cold sneaks up on you, and before you know it, you've given up, walked right into your own grave.

Alice shakes free of Sabine's voice, but it turns out that's even worse, the veil of calm replaced by panic, because even though the girl's heartbeat has died inside her chest, she can feel terror kicking like a rabbit in its place.

She's always had a taste for fear.

Alice doesn't know how to hide it so she doesn't even try, lets it spill out to every side, and Sabine must be able to taste it because she smiles a perfect, horrible smile, at once wolfish and feline, the sharpened white-tooth grin of predators, and what was Alice thinking—in what world could she ever—*No, no, no,* she fights the thoughts down, buries each traitorous one beneath the same word. *Lottie. Lottie. Lottie.* And as she does, she tries to twist away, to look down the darkened hall, past Sabine and back toward the club and the crowd, hoping to catch sight—

But Sabine's cold fingers come up beneath her chin. The same fingers that just broke a human girl's neck, easy as snapping. She turns Alice's face so there's nowhere else to look but up into those haunted eyes, five hundred years of hunger staring back.

"We'll find Charlotte later," she says, and the words sound like a promise as much as a threat. "Right now, you and I have things to talk about."

And before Alice can say *No*, before she can cobble together some version of resistance, Sabine says, *"Come with me,"* and this time the voice isn't just a voice, it's an order, rolling over Alice, and the sounds and the lights of the club cut out, as if someone pulled the plug—no, as if someone pulled *every* plug in *every* outlet, in *every* building—and after that, the club might as well have opened up beneath her feet, because she can't see or hear or feel a single thing.

Alice's whole world goes black.

V

When Alice lurches back into her body, she's standing in an elevator.

The darkened hallway of the club is gone, replaced by walls and doors of hammered copper, a hundred bits of warped reflection staring back. Alice's vision is stained red, as if she got blood in her eyes, but no matter how many times she blinks the color is still there, until she finally realizes that someone has changed out the overhead light, replaced the normal white with *red*, tinting the world inside the elevator crimson.

She's not alone. Sabine leans against the other wall, humming softly to herself as the elevator rises up, and up, and up.

Panic floods Alice's mouth like bile, because there's a void where time should be, and she doesn't remember leaving the club, doesn't remember walking through the streets of Boston—she must have, because she can smell the night air on her skin—doesn't remember getting here, but here she is, Sabine humming beside her as if nothing is wrong.

Alice shrinks back into the wall and tries to smother her racing mind, her frantic thoughts, tells herself—quietly, quietly—that this is what she wanted, or at least, what she needs.

The elevator dings as it reaches the top, and then the doors are sliding open, onto a penthouse, exposed brick with floor-to-ceiling views of Boston, the floor a stretch of black concrete, polished to a shine, and Alice remembers what Lottie said about Sabine's love of luxury, her insistence on fine things.

Sabine strolls into the penthouse foyer as if it's hers—which it might be now, but it was clearly someone else's first. There are picture frames face down on all the shelves, marks on the floor where the low furniture has been dragged into a new shape. The scent on the air is leather, cologne, musk.

Sabine glances back at Alice pressed into the elevator walls, clearly waiting for her to follow. Alice pushes herself off the copper, starts forward, but something happens at the elevator doors. A sudden force, heavy as stone, holding her back, and she thinks it must be her own body trying to protect her, until Sabine chuckles.

"Of course. Apologies. *Come in.*"

And just like that, the air loosens, the boundary dissolves, and Alice steps into the penthouse. The elevator doors slide shut behind her with grim finality as she forces herself forward.

Sabine sinks onto the edge of a low suede sofa, and leans down to slip off her shoes, and while her head is bowed Alice steals a look around the massive room for anything that might serve as a makeshift weapon, but apparently the businessman Sabine has stolen this place from cared more about fine art and books than weaponry.

"Relax," says Sabine without looking up. "If I wanted to kill you, you'd be dead."

Alice tenses, tries to rein her thoughts back in, even as she says, "I am."

Sabine tuts. "Death is rot and ruin. Death is bones and dirt. You are a rose that grew out of it." Her gaze drifts up, and Alice sees that the light in her eyes isn't entirely gone. It flickers, somehow dark and bright at once, like coals. "You should be grateful."

Alice clenches her teeth against the words she'd like to say to that. But one still hisses out. "*Grateful?*"

Sabine's mouth twitches, and she rises, bare feet padding across the concrete floor as she approaches, and Alice, to her credit, doesn't retreat, even though it takes every modicum of strength to let the distance close between them.

Sabine is almost to her when she says, "Sit."

The word lands like a hand on Alice's shoulder, and her knees fold before her mind can register, a chair catching her before she hits the floor. And she doesn't know how she's going to do this, do anything, when her own body listens to Sabine instead of her.

Why didn't Lottie warn her this would happen?

Why did she let her think she had a chance?

Sabine drifts behind Alice, and she listens to the soft padding of her steps as she looks around for something, anything she might be able to use.

But if there was clutter, Sabine has done away with almost all of it.

On the table in front of her there is a single photography book, the cover showing the Scottish Highlands of all places.

On the kitchen island, the knife block has been emptied, but beside it there's a vase of flowers just beginning to wilt.

On a bar cart against the wall, she spots something that clearly didn't come with the house: a glass carafe atop a warming plate, the contents thick and crimson.

Alice's throat tightens at the sight, and then she notices the steps have stopped, a heady silence pooling behind her back right before a cold hand slides along her collarbone. Sabine drapes her arms around Alice's shoulders, a coil of red hair snaking down her front.

"Tell me, Alice," she whispers in that voice like sand and silk, "why are you here?"

Alice frowns, forces one truth from her head in favor of another. "You made me follow you."

She feels Sabine's mouth twitch against her cheek. "Did I?"

Alice blinks, and she's back in the club, the world dropping into darkness. "You compelled me."

Sabine hums in thought. "When you nudge a body, do you know which way it always falls?" The arms withdraw, and Sabine rounds the chair to face her. "It falls the way it's leaning. Compulsion is a lie you tell yourself. The truth is, you're here because some part of you wanted to come with me."

Alice could deny it. But the thing is that she's right.

On some level, if she's being honest with herself, she wanted this, she *needed* it, not just for the plan to work, and not just because of what Sabine did, what Lottie did, what Alice has to find a way to do.

No, ever since she first woke up the day after the party, the world tipped off its axis, the ground gone out beneath her feet, Alice has felt like she is falling. She thought finding Lottie would make the feeling stop, but it didn't, because Lottie wasn't the one standing at the bottom.

Sabine is.

She's the ground at the end of the long, long drop.

And now that Alice is here, the falling has stopped.

Sabine tips her head to one side. "Exactly. Now," she says, "what are we going to do about our Charlotte?"

Our Charlotte.

Alice tries to conjure the warmth she felt when they were walking down the street, when Lottie turned and kissed her at the corner, but instead her mind goes to the club, the moment Lottie let go of her and slipped away.

Leaving her alone.

To be caught.

"She killed you," says Sabine, and the words force her back.

"*You* killed me," says Alice, unable to stop the anger that rises up, can almost feel it wicking off of her. But Sabine only shakes her head.

"No," she says, lowering herself onto the sofa. She stretches her arms along the top, her hair cascading down the back. A dozen pendants hang on brittle chains around her neck, tokens from her latest kills, and Alice searches, wondering if there is something of hers there, stolen with the rest, or if she doesn't count.

"Charlotte *knew* what would happen if she took you to bed," says Sabine, "and she did it anyway. Just like she did to all those other girls." She lets her head fall back, her throat exposed as her gaze drifts over the ceiling high above. "Even Penny." The name hangs there before her chin tips down, her strange eyes finding Alice. "Did you hear about poor Penny?"

She nods, and Sabine sits forward, hands and hair trailing down the sofa in her wake.

"So tell me, dear Alice," she says, those eyes searching her as if she's a puzzle to be solved, "why our Charlotte didn't do the same to you."

Alice blinks and in that fraction of a second, she is back in the hotel, Lottie meeting her gaze in the mirror and mouthing the words before Alice says them.

"She told me I was special."

At that, Sabine laughs. And it's a horrible sound, not because of the tone—bright and high as bells—but because it's just as hollow.

Indignation rises inside Alice, and it feels better than fear, so she doesn't try to hold it back. "Maybe you're just mad that she's finally moved on," she mutters. "Maybe you can't stand that she's found someone else."

Sabine's laughter dies. Her smile doesn't, but it's gone as cold and stiff as ice.

"Alice, sweet Alice," she purrs, "Charlotte doesn't *care* about you. She hates you. Hates what you are. What *we* are. She looks at you and all she feels is guilt."

Alice winces.

"You're just another broken toy discarded in her wake. But don't worry. *I* won't let you go to waste."

Alice doesn't know what Sabine's planning to do, but she knows she's running out of time, and she forces herself to breathe, in and then out, trying to think and unthink at the same time, trying to find a way out of this, or through. The scent of blood wafts toward her from the cart against the wall, fills her nose and throat. And it gives her an idea.

She swallows, glances up.

"I'm thirsty."

Sabine cocks her head, amused. "Of course you are." She flicks her fingers toward the bar cart. "Help yourself."

Alice feels her body come unstuck from the chair, has to force her legs not to betray her by surging up too fast. She stands, and tries to imagine the air is made of syrup. She wades slowly toward the cart, fingers shaking as she reaches for the carafe with one hand, and her necklace with the other.

She doesn't dare look back over her shoulder but she listens, as closely as she can, for any sign Sabine has moved. Even without a heartbeat, without the steady in and out of breath, bodies make sound. The suede sofa groans beneath the slightest motion. Her hair will whisper if she rises, the lace will shift against her skin, and even as Alice thinks these things, she tries not to, instead fills her head with Lottie.

Think about her.

(And how she kissed you.)

Think about her.

(And how she promised you.)

Think about her.

(And how she left you *again*.)

Fear and panic begin to bubble up, but instead of shoving them back down, Alice lets them boil over, spill into the air around her as she tips the last of her mother's grave dirt into one of the glasses, and pours the blood over the top. Every passing fraction of a second, she expects to turn and see Sabine right there, knows that face will be the last thing she sees before the world snaps off like a light.

But the moment passes, and Sabine doesn't come, and the vial is closed, the necklace back beneath Alice's dress, and the glasses are in her hands, and she is turning, and Sabine is still there on the sofa, her head tipped back but her eyes locked fast on Alice, like a cat considering a mouse.

Alice nearly falters, but carries the glasses to the coffee table, sets one before Sabine, and then, instead of returning to the chair, she sits on the sofa beside her, just out of arm's reach. If Sabine cares about the closeness, it doesn't show.

Alice lifts her own glass to her lips and drinks, feels the well open inside her, the blood dropping down, down, and out of reach without even touching the sides. She empties the glass and sets it down.

Languidly, Sabine sits forward. "You and I," she says, "are going to help each other."

Alice tenses as she watches Sabine's hand drift toward her glass. "How?"

"You're going to help me catch Charlotte."

Alice almost laughs, despite herself, at the absurdity of it, of this, of the fact that somehow after everything these two have put her through, she is still just a pawn to them, a piece, to be used, or thrown away.

"Is that so?" she says through gritted teeth, fighting her anger down again as she forces her attention to the glass before Sabine, watches as her fingers graze the rim of the glass. Only to nudge it back toward Alice. "Go ahead."

Alice tenses. "You aren't thirsty?" she asks, trying to keep her voice—her mind—from showing anything.

Sabine's mouth twitches. "Always. But I don't drink anything that's already been decanted." She flicks her fingers toward the bar cart. "That was all for you."

Disappointment washes over Alice, but she fights it back, knows she can't let it get too loud. Instead, she thinks about the hunger, looks from her empty glass to Sabine's full one, and thinks about how hard it is, how horrible, that even knowing that it's tainted, she has to fight the urge to reach for it, to drink, the hunger inside her somehow disconnected from her sense of reason, and no wonder it's the thing that makes them reckless, like Ezra said, the hunger that undoes them, when the rest has rotted.

Sabine settles back, and this time the light catches on something beneath her dress. At first, Alice thinks it is a bit of jewelry, like the pendants hanging round her neck, but then she sees the silver glint of the mesh and realizes with rising horror.

That Sabine is wearing fucking chain mail.

Alice feels the last of her hope gutter, right then and there, because how the fuck is she supposed to—*no*.

She forces her panic to change course, her attention going back to the sofa, back to Sabine, remembers something Lottie said, that all she had left was the hunt.

The need to stalk, to catch, to kill.

Alice shifts a little closer on the couch and asks, "What happens when we find her?"

Sabine's lips press into a thin grim line. "I think it's time for this game of ours to end."

A game, even now. A fucking game. Alice lets annoyance stain the air. She doesn't care. "I never asked to play."

Sabine inclines her head, reaches out a cool hand to Alice's cheek. "I know," she says.

Alice doesn't recoil, even though she wants to. Because there's only one way out of this, and if she had a human heart it might give her away, but she doesn't. Not anymore. So she reaches up, and lays her fingers over Sabine's, and says, "I'll help you. If it means *she* pays."

Sabine looks at her again, only this time not like she's a problem or a puzzle, but a pet. Her hand slides through Alice's hair, cups the back of her neck.

"Maybe there is something special to you after all."

Alice smiles, feels herself go warm as Sabine's mouth hovers over hers, because Lottie was right, there is a power to her, a heat to her attention, like all the lights switched on inside the house. Like the sun coming out from behind the clouds.

But when Sabine leans in to kiss her, Alice pulls back.

Sabine's eyes narrow in annoyance, but she only ducks her head. "Sorry," she says with a light chuckle. "It's been a long few nights." Her gaze flicks back up. "Would you mind if I had a shower first?"

First, that word like a promise in the air.

Sabine's hand unwinds itself from Alice's hair, slides like a tear down her cheek, drops away.

"By all means," she says, the benevolent host, nodding to the open doorway on the right. Slowly, Alice rises from the sofa, and ambles toward the room as if she has all the time in the world.

She glances back once, to make sure Sabine is watching, then steps through into a master bedroom, and then a master bath, leaving each door ajar in her wake. Alice turns on the shower as hot as it will go, and peels out of her clothes, fills her mind with a song she knows by heart.

When I was a child / I got lost in the woods.
The trees parted for me / made such a clear trail
Then closed up behind me / now I'm turned around
Been trying so long now / to find a way out.

And by the time she's done with the first verse, steam has filled the tiled room, so thick it fogs the mirror, too, but when Alice pauses at the slate sink, she doesn't search for her reflection. Instead, she sings aloud, soft but high and sweet, as her hands press flat against the stone counter.

"*I live in these woods now / the trees hold me close.*"

Her voice just loud enough to cover the sound as it cracks.

Alice pushes off the sink and steps into the shower, singing the last line, the one Catty never listened long enough to hear.

"*No longer lost now / I found my way home.*"

Catty leaves a voice note on a Monday.

(Not a call, if it had been a call, she would have answered, day or night, which Catty must have known.)

"Hey, Bones," it starts, as all their conversations do, and when Alice listens to it later, the first thing she'll always notice is that her sister sounds exhausted, her voice foxed at the edges, the way it used to be when they shared a bed, and stayed up talking under their covers until their thoughts went slow, dragged down with sleep.

"You ever think about how mad it is, that we only get one life?"

The sound of a lighter flicking. A long inhale.

"There are all these things I want to do. People I want to be. And sometimes it breaks my heart, that I'm stuck with just this one."

A pause, the kind she loves to take, and Alice can see her, can't she? Striking a pose.

Waiting to be noticed.

"Wouldn't it be better if it were a game? If we could play until we lose, and then just start again? New Alice. New Catty. Maybe that's what death is, and we just don't know it. A chance to play again."

A laugh that's not a laugh. A sound lodged in her throat.

"Sorry, I'm tired . . . What did Mum used to say?" A sigh. "I know, you don't remember . . . something about tired minds being good soil for bad thoughts. How the best thing you can do is go to bed. Bet I'll wake up, and feel brand new."

Catty leaves that message on a Monday.

And on Tuesday, Alice's whole world just—stops.

Her cell phone rings (her number, it turns out, is the only one saved in Catty's phone) and even though she doesn't recognize the caller, she picks up, and she knows.

She knows in the silence before the man starts talking, in the breath he sucks in.

She knows, before he asks to speak to a parent, a guardian, to *anyone* but her.

She knows, before she hands the phone to her father, before she watches his face collapse, and then his knees—

She knows that her sister is dead.

Brilliant, terrifying, angry, tired Catty, hit by a car in Glasgow, which is how Alice learns she never got away, never made it to London. Maddening, gorgeous, miserable, proud Catty, who didn't call from Trafalgar Square, didn't journey south at all, who was in fact an hour north of Hoxburn, with nothing on her but a crumpled tenner in the pocket of her jeans, and a cheap pay-as-you-go phone in the pocket of her coat, which somehow survived the accident.

Catty, who, according to the driver, stepped right out in front of him.

The driver, who stayed with her until the ambulance came, even though it was too late. There was nothing they could do.

And Alice can't fathom how she didn't *feel* it happen.

The moment the metal connected with Catty's side, the moment she folded like a house of cards beneath the wheel, the kind of violence that's supposed to vibrate down the line, the kind of absence that yawns like an open pit, a sinkhole.

She should have felt it right at the moment Catty stopped, not an hour later, when the phone rang and she was doing dishes, elbows sloshing in the soapy water so it took her an extra few seconds to dry her hands, dig out her cell. Seconds that meant nothing because by that point, Catty was already dead.

It was fast, the man on the phone assures her father, and all Alice can see is Catty sprinting down the road ahead of her.

Slow down.

Come back.

VI

In Scotland, there are different kinds of rain.

Gentle drizzles and steady storms, and driech days where the air is wet though the water never seems to fall.

But the day they bury Catty, the rain comes raging down. It pummels the earth and plasters the grass, turns the cemetery rows to mud, and beats its fists against Alice's umbrella as she stands at the foot of the fresh grave that sits beside her mum's.

CATHERINE ABIGAIL MOORE.

The name on the tombstone looks wrong. A name she didn't even like, now carved in stone. Her life, stopped at seventeen.

"Daft girl," whispers their father as Granddad grips his shoulder and Dad grips hers, and El has one hand on Alice and the other on Finn, all of them holding on to someone as if without the holding they might fall, all of them but Alice, whose hands are knuckles-white around the wooden grip of the umbrella. Whose boots are sinking into the muddy earth, as if trying to grow roots.

Afterward, the town huddles like sodden crows around the tables of Granddad's pub talking gently, as if the world is made of glass, and Alice can't stand the soft looks, the kind remarks, the way the whole brittle room makes her want to take a bat to all of it, and Alice is afraid that if she stays inside a moment longer she'll start to scream, so instead she gets up and walks out into the rain.

And at first, the shock of the cold makes her gasp, the way it did that spring they plunged into White Loch, but then the shock wears off, and for the first time since she heard about Catty's death Alice feels like she can breathe again.

She closes her eyes and spreads her arms and waits, as the rain soaks
through shirt and skin and down to bone—
Waits, as it batters her open hands—
And she can pretend—
To feel her sister's fingers closing around hers.

Now Alice stands beneath the water, waiting.

Waiting, until she hears the whisper of a lace dress being shed. The clink
of chain mail slipping to the tiled floor.

Waiting, until Sabine's bare feet cross the bathroom, the steam so thick
she doesn't see the place the counter of the sink is cracked, the jagged line
where a slice of slate the length of a hand has been shaved off. Broken free.

And then Sabine is there, behind Alice, in the shower.

Her arms fold around Alice, the necklaces tickling the skin between her
naked shoulder blades, and in that moment, she remembers.

She remembers being on the edge of sleep.

Remembers the cold weight of Sabine's body holding her down against
the bed.

Remembers the way the hair wound like weeds around her throat.

Remembers the scent, like iron and wet earth and dead flowers.

Remembers the sound her heart made when it failed inside her chest.

She remembers, and then she turns in Sabine's arms, and looks up into
her eyes, and drives the jagged piece of slate between her ribs.

Into her heart.

Sabine doesn't scream.

She doesn't fight, she just looks down at Alice and frowns, bemused, opens
her mouth to say something that never comes out because she's already crumbling, collapsing into ash and rot and whatever's left after five hundred years.

One moment Sabine is wrapped around Alice, and the next she is gone.

The piece of slate clatters to the shower floor, ash swirling round it to the
drain.

Alice stands and watches until there's nothing left of Sabine but a dozen
tokens on weathered chains, pooling on the tile floor. Her fingers shake a
little as she finds the knob and turns the shower off. A low tremor of fear
leaving her body as she takes a towel from the wall, and dries herself, and gets
dressed again, boots hanging from her fingers as she pads barefoot back into

the main room, the damp heat of her steps leaving ghosts on the concrete floor.

Alice reaches the sofa, and her knees go out.

She sinks onto the suede, breathes in, then out, a single, shuddering breath as she lets her head fall back, and closes her eyes and waits and waits and waits to feel alive again, water dripping from her hair with the steady rhythm of a heart.

VII

There were three years between Alice and Catty Moore.

Three years that become two and then one and then somehow, Alice is seventeen and a half, older than Catty ever was. She spent those three years being exactly the daughter that she's supposed to be, the kind that doesn't fight, or scream, or run, and now she's at the top of her class, best grades in the whole school, small as it is, and her whole life ahead.

(That's how the counselor puts it, when he sits her down, lays the future out across his desk as if it were a path.)

She could get into Glasgow or Edinburgh, sure, but he thinks she'd make the cut at Oxbridge, too, so she applies to those, and then, on a whim that's not *really* a whim so much as an apology, or maybe an offering, she applies to one more school. Doesn't tell her parents because she knows she won't get in, but getting in isn't the point, and besides, it's not for them. Not even for her, really.

She clutches the golden pendant around her neck—

(She went back to the graveyard, when the rain had stopped and the ground had dried, scooped a tiny bit from Catty's plot to add to the vial.)

—and looks at the photo of their mum tacked above her desk, the one with her beneath that turning maple tree in Boston, and hits Send. And when the letters come a few months later, her parents laugh, and cry, and hug her tight, and say they are so very proud.

"It's your choice, of course," says El.

"But Harvard?" her father adds. "It's so far from home."

Alice knows, wants to say that is the point, that the world is so very big, and Hoxburn isn't. That Catty never made it, but *she* will. That she loves her family, she really, really does, but there's a photo, on the mantel, taken a year ago, Dad and El and her and Finn, the four of them huddled on the banks of White Loch, grinning like fools after an early April swim, looking like a happy family.

(And they are, they are. And yet.)

Alice will never be able to shake the feeling that it's three plus one.

That they have everything they need right here, and she does not.

That her whole life is out there—

Waiting to be lived.

Alice waits, and waits, and waits.

She doesn't know how long she sits there, in the empty penthouse, eyes closed and head tipped back against the sofa, her wet hair ruining the suede. Only knows that at some point she hears the elevator grind to life, its bulk rising through the floors. She hears the doors chime and then slide open, the soft click of heeled boots crossing the flat, passing through the bedroom, into the bathroom, before returning and coming to a stop beside the sofa, the soft thud of a bag being dropped on the concrete, and then, a weight sinking onto the seat beside her.

Alice opens her eyes, but she doesn't look at Lottie.

Instead, she looks up, the way Sabine did—at the ceiling high above, noticing for the first time that the beams up there aren't steel, but wood, knots like eyes staring back.

"You told me if I killed her, I'd come back to life," says Alice.

"I know," says Lottie softly.

"It didn't work."

"I know," she echoes.

Alice looks at Lottie, then, resentment flaring through her, but Lottie just stares back, with those backlit brown eyes, and a look that says it's her fault for believing, a look that says she should have known better.

And maybe Alice did. Maybe she always knew, deep down, it was a lie. That some roads will always be one-way.

But Lottie *lied*.

They sit in silence for a minute, maybe two, and then Lottie bends forward, sinking her fingers into her mess of curls, shoulders shaking, as if she's about to cry. "I thought I would feel something when she died. A lightness. Or a weight. Some sign that it was over. But I didn't. I didn't feel anything."

Alice stares at Lottie, unable to believe that even now, she's only grieving for herself.

"You lied to me," says Alice, and this time Lottie sighs.

"I didn't really. I said you'd get your life back. Now you will."

"This isn't my life," she mutters.

"It's *a* life," counters Lottie. As if they're bickering over semantics.

As if a life is a life is a life—

"You won't be alone," Lottie's saying. "I'll help you. I promise."

"You promise," Alice echoes dryly.

"Both of us are free now. Thanks to you."

"Thanks to me . . ."

Alice can't look at her, so she looks down instead, her gaze dropping to the bag Lottie set on the floor, the one she first noticed in the hotel room. In it, she sees the battered paperback, and something else. The metal glint of something thin and silver. A letter opener, or a knife, or a long-handled brush.

Did you hear about poor Penny?

"Everything will be okay," Lottie's saying, half to herself. "The worst is over now."

And it's funny, she's shaping the words, and Alice hears them, but at the same time, she hears Sabine's low voice, rolling through like rain.

Tell me, dear Alice, why our Charlotte didn't do the same to you.

She hears herself asking that question in the hotel room.

Why didn't you kill me?

I looked at you, and I saw me.

She looks at you and all she feels is guilt.

The voices are tangling inside her head, until she doesn't know which ones to listen to. But she knows one thing for sure, and that's that Lottie *lied.*

Perhaps that's why Alice doesn't stop Lottie when she reaches for the glass of blood, the one that's still sitting on the coffee table.

Why she simply sits and watches as Lottie brings the poison to her lips, and tips it back, and drinks, her throat bobbing as she swallows. Watches as she tastes the wrongness in the dregs and tries to spit them out.

Of course, by then, it's far too late.

Lottie begins to gasp, and choke, her face taking on that awful gray tinge that climbed up Alice's own arms back in the cemetery, that pallor like a fresh-made corpse, and then she's slipping off the sofa, she's on her hands and knees, clawing at her throat, mouth opening and closing as she gasps out "What" and "Please" and "Help."

Alice rises to her feet.

She wants to be angry—it would be so much easier if she were angry—but the truth is, the anger's all used up, leaving something weary, hollow in its wake.

Lottie rolls onto her back, chokes out, "Why?" as Alice pulls the weapon from the bag, and it's a silver hairbrush after all. And at the sight of it, Charlotte's eyes go wide with panic.

She coughs, trying to explain, but her lungs are shriveling inside her chest, the grave dirt dragging her down with it, turning the veins black beneath her skin, blood pooling in her eyes.

But Alice remembers what she said.

How grave dirt would sicken, but not kill.

How only the heart could die.

So Alice sinks to her knees on top of Lottie.

"Everything will be okay," she says, parroting the words. "The worst is over now."

She wedges the silver handle of the brush between her bottom ribs, and in that moment, Lottie *changes*. All her pretenses—of confusion, of kindness, of compassion—die away, and so does the image of the beautiful girl perched on the bed in the dark, curls stained violet.

In its place, Alice sees the one who danced with Sabine through stolen halls.

Who butchered families in their homes.

Who let girls die because she couldn't bear to sleep alone.

Lottie starts to fight, then, thrashing like a feral cat, manages to throw Alice off, even scrambles back across the polished floor, but this isn't a cemetery plot, a piece of poisoned land she can escape, the ruin is inside her. Even still, she is full of life, or fight, rolls onto her stomach, nails chipping against the concrete as she crawls away, but Alice catches her, forces her onto her back again, pins her to the floor.

Alice, no longer soft, and gentle, and full of grief, as she drives the makeshift weapon in, and up, between flesh and ribs, hitting Lottie's heart.

The light flickers on and off behind her eyes.

And then at last, goes out.

Lottie's body stiffens once beneath her, then gives way, crumbling to rot beneath Alice's weight, a girl-shaped pile of debris, slivers of bone and dampened ash.

Alice sags and rocks back onto her heels. She wipes her hands on her green dress, and stares at the place where Lottie was, and maybe it's because she hadn't been dead as long as Sabine—or simply that she hadn't rotted to the core just yet—but there is *more* of her. The pile like a heap of wet earth, the silver brush sticking out like a petrified bloom.

"Bury my bones," Alice whispers to herself, a horrible sound like a laugh rising in her throat. She presses her palms against her eyes until her vision goes black, then white.

Get up, get up, she thinks, counts to ten, then blinks and rises to her feet, skirts Lottie's ashes as she heads for the elevator door, forcing herself forward sstep-by-step.

Because if she's learned anything it's this:

There is no going back.

VIII

Alice steps out of the elevator.

She crosses a lobby she wasn't there to see, and pushes open a pair of doors she doesn't remember walking through, and exits onto a Boston street.

It takes her a moment to get her bearings, to point herself in the right direction.

She starts walking, scuffing her boots a little with each step. It is so quiet inside her now, without a pulse, but even at this hour the city around her is full of sound. The thud of the bass in a passing car. The whisper of the television in a nearby flat. The bartenders announcing last call. The dishwashers cleaning up kitchens. The people out late now heading home to sleep.

Her hand drifts to the pendant, now empty, around her neck.

Catty is gone.

Their mum is gone.

But Alice is still here.

She digs her phone out of her pocket, taps over to Catty's voice note as she walks, holding on to her sister's voice as if it is a rope.

Hey, Bones.

You ever think about how mad it is, that we only get one life?

(It is a lie, Sabine told Lottie and Lottie told her, that you only get one story.)

Maybe that's what death is, and we just don't know it. A chance to play again.

It must be cold, thinks Alice, watching a group of people spill out of a closing bar and turn up their collars. She remembers that she's wearing nothing but a thin green dress, and folds her arms a little tighter across her chest, blows out a breath she doesn't need until they pass.

Until she's alone again with Catty's voice.

What did Mum used to say? I know, you don't remember . . . something about tired minds being good soil for bad thoughts. How the best thing you can do is go to bed. Bet I'll wake up, and feel brand—

Alice doesn't let the message finish.

She taps the screen, is about to start it over again, when the phone buzzes with a call.

Home.

Alice hesitates, then answers, and her dad's voice greets her, bright, the way it always is first thing in the morning. He's always been the type to get up early.

"Hey, Al. Oh shit, just seeing the time. Did I wake you?"

A tired laugh escapes. "No, Dad."

"I forget how late you stay up, studying. All the times I'd come in and find you head down on the books." A car goes by, and she can almost hear him frowning. "Are you out? On your own?"

"I was at the library," she lies. "I'm just walking back to campus."

A disapproving grunt, and then, "I'll keep you company until you get there."

And Alice doesn't tell him how far away she is, doesn't say it isn't worth it, or that she'll text him when she's back so he knows she got there safe.

She just says, "Okay, thanks," and spends the next half hour walking, and listening to him talk about Finn starting school, and the painting classes El's begun to take, and some drama at the pub concerning brands of gin. She listens to him talk about everything and nothing, about life going on, the way it does, until she's back across the bridge and the familiar buildings around campus are coming into sight.

"Hey, Al," he says.

"Yeah, Dad?"

"I know uni can be hard. Everything feels new. But you've got this, you know that, right?"

Alice looks up at the sky, the stars, brighter than she's ever seen them. "I know."

She tells him that she's made it safe, and he tells her loves her, always has and always will, and she says it back, and then he's gone.

Her building sits, waiting, at the edge of the Yard, but Alice isn't ready to go in just yet. Instead, she turns and starts to walk again. It's early, after all, and the night stretches out ahead of her. A road with no end.

(How frightening. How freeing.)

As for the stillness—the unnerving silence behind her ribs, a reminder of what she is, and what she isn't—what does it matter?

Alice will be okay. She'll find her way through the dark.

She tips her head back as she strolls, forcing air she doesn't need into her lungs, again, and again, until it feels like breathing.

Until the sound of her steps beats like a drum inside her chest, reminding her she is alive.

Alive.

Alive.

And she is hungry.

ACKNOWLEDGMENTS

A confession: I forget.

It is a long-running joke among my friends, family, and team that when it comes to my own creative process, I am, in fact, an unreliable narrator. But it's true.

I am so daunted by the scope of the task that once I've survived the excavation of a book, the transference from brain to page, I begin to mentally erase. I revise my memory of the experience, smoothing over the tracks. It's really quite inconvenient. I'm sure my mind does it so that I'll start again. Unfortunately, it also means that every time I trick myself into believing it's the first and only time I've struggled, and that once I've finished work on a novel, the experience is largely lost to me.

I may forget large swaths of my creative struggle, but thankfully I don't forget the helpers. The people without whom I know this novel would not make it here, to you.

My editor, Miriam, who has helped me carve not only this story, but so many, from the stone.

My agent, Holly, who has been there, year after year and book after book, to gently remind me that I am right on track, whatever I'm feeling.

My parents, who laugh and pat my head when I exclaim that it's never been this hard, because they too know *it always has*.

My publicist, Kristin, who has now born witness to this madness enough times that she knows to keep receipts.

My sister-in-spirit, Jenna, who makes the world feel steady, even when I feel like I'm a sea.

My friends-turned-family, Cat and Caro, who always know what I need, even when I don't.

My *entire* team at Tor, who trust my mind from first ideas to final words, and champion my work with so much love it leaves me breathless.

My readers, with whom I have always tried to be honest. Every time I have confessed my fears, my doubts, my insecurities, you have been there to hold a mirror to my best parts, not my worst.

I also owe a debt.

To my copyeditors, my proofreaders, and my Harvard tour guide, Halima, for helping me get the details right. If there are mistakes, they are my own.

To the booksellers and librarians, who take the story from my hands once it is ready, and help make sure it reaches yours.

And to you, whether you are first-time reader or a longtime fan, your support has let my embark on this journey, book after book, year after year, as strange and winding as it is.

Now, let's do it all again.

ABOUT THE AUTHOR

Jenna Maurice

VICTORIA "V. E." SCHWAB is the #1 *New York Times* bestselling author of more than twenty books. Schwab's series and standalone titles for readers of all ages have made her a major literary figure whose notable works include the Villains series, the Shades of Magic universe, and *The Invisible Life of Addie LaRue*. When not haunting Paris streets or writing in the corner of her favorite coffee shop, she lives in Edinburgh, Scotland.